THE WALLS OF ROME

◆— THE HISTORIES OF SPHAX SERIES —◆

ROBERT M. KIDD

The Histories of Sphax series

For Charmian

Allobroges

River Rhodanus

River Droma

Col de la Traversette

Insubres

Insubres

River Padus

The Island

Genua

Boii

Casali

Volcae

Pisae

Nages

Arretium

Massilia

Perusia

Sphax's Journey

Rome

– PART ONE –

THE
CREATURES
OF ARTEMIS

ONE

Sphax sank the knife deep between rat-face's scrawny shoulder blades. When it met the resistance of bone and sinew, blind rage drove him to twist it viciously, searching out the black heart that had blighted the last ten years of his life. The bastard didn't even cry out as he slumped to the ground. Sphax felt not a flicker of remorse for ridding the world of such a creature. But he did have one regret; that it was only Marcellus' body lying twitching at his feet in a bloody pool, not his father's.

Gaius Lucilus would have to wait his turn. His time would come. He'd sworn it before sleep every night, sworn it after every whipping and vicious beating, sworn it solemnly for the last ten years of his life as a miserable slave. That sacred oath was burnt into his soul just as painfully as the fugitivus had been branded into the flesh of his forearm after the last time he'd run away. He would have his revenge, and if the rumours of invasion were true, he might have the opportunity to take revenge on the entire stinking cesspit that was Rome.

How was it his fault that Marcellus' grey stallion had picked up a stone? He rode the poor creature like a donkey! What's a man to do when his master lashes him across the cheek, hands him a knife, points to his horse's hoof then turns his scrawny back on him? What clearer sign could the gods provide?

Sphax flipped the body over with his foot. Marcellus was still wearing that stupid sneering expression he'd worn when he'd lashed out; an expression that said, 'you, slave, are not even worthy of eating my shit.' But this time it was mixed with something new, written on the corners of rat-face's gaping mouth. It was surprise. Yes! That's exactly what it was.

He'd been staring at the corpse for a long time before his burning hatred started to lift a little, then the barking call of a raven circling above snapped him out of his stupor. He realised he was shaking uncontrollably. Looking around anxiously he scanned the road. Thank the gods it was deserted. It wouldn't be for long though. They'd overtaken a column of legionaries six miles back and he could just make out the cloud of dust their hob-nails were kicking up. Ahead, on the hilltop, he could see the walls and clay-tiled roofs of Perusia shimmering in the mid-day heat, and above all, crowning the summit, the marble columns of the great temple of Juno.

He had to act fast. His life now depended on it. First he had to dump rat-face's body as far from the road as possible. Somewhere wild and overgrown where it would never be discovered, unless wolves or bears did him a kindness and finished the job for him. There must be no evidence. Rat-face had to disappear from the face of the earth. For such a scrawny bastard, Marcellus proved to be surprisingly heavy, and it took all his strength to lift and drape his body over Dido. Poor Dido! His mare was already weighed down by a heavy wooden chest and two leather saddle bags his master — he swore never to use that hated word again — had insisted they take with them. As he mounted Arion and whistled for Dido to follow he was already casting around for a track that led off the road. After half a mile he found exactly what he was looking for. A shallow stream crossed the Via Amerina and trickled towards a steepening valley flanked by cypresses and stands of wild olive. He crossed the road and followed the course of the stream as it meandered into the shade of the trees. The valley sides steepened, buttressed by rocky outcrops topped by juniper and rowan, and soon he lost sight of the Amerina. As the stream quickened he kept to its bed and allowed Arion to pick his own path through the pebbles and shallow pools at the water's edge. After a further mile the trees and rocky outcrops retreated and the stream slowed to a sluggish trickle as it entered a wide barren plain. Then he saw it.

The fates were indeed smiling on him today. Ahead of him, stretching as far as the eye could see, was a lake of golden reeds swaying gently in the sultry heat.

Nudging Arion to a halt he dismounted and with mud oozing to his calves, led Dido deep into the reeds.

He stripped Marcellus of his bloody tunic and red patrician sandals. The silver shell ornament on the back was worth at least fifty asses. He couldn't bear to strip off his loincloth. Last night they'd stayed at a popina that was no better than a brothel. Whilst rat-face had spent the night whoring, he'd endured a sleepless night in a flea-ridden stable. He slid Marcellus' body into the mud, then screwed up his tunic and threw it deeper into the reeds.

Once back in the shade of the trees beside the stream he carefully emptied the wooden chest and bags. There were two spare saffron-dyed tunics, a beautiful toga of Egyptian linen, a blue woollen riding cloak, ivory combs, razors and a silvered hand-mirror. But there was also something strange about that chest. It had been packed to the brim, yet a glance at its contents told him they should only occupy half the chest's capacity. Feeling around the leather base he suddenly heard a metallic click and the bottom of the chest flipped open to reveal a secret compartment covered by a woollen cloth. He couldn't believe his eyes when he removed the cloth. It was stuffed with bronze and silver coins, a treasure trove! He ploughed his palm through the dozens of silver didrachm stamped with a picture of a she-wolf guarding Romulus and Remus. He was rich.

He also found letters and documents to Crassus, the manager of Lucilus' Myrteta estate, three miles north of Perusia. Glancing through these reminded him that time was pressing. They were due to arrive at the estate before nightfall today. Marcellus had sent the rest of his servants ahead yesterday to prepare for his visit. They were expected. He was certain that if they didn't turn up by noon tomorrow the alarm would be raised. First there would be a local search, and after finding nothing the hue and cry would begin in earnest, the dreaded *fugitivari* would be unleashed and there would be a manhunt. For three days in his fourteenth year he'd tasted freedom before being caught and dragged back to Rome in chains.

This time it was different. He would be hunted down as a suspected murderer. He had to disappear without leaving a shred of evidence behind him. Only that way might he avoid the barbaric Silanianum, where all members of Lucilus' household would be questioned under torture and put to death if it was found they had any knowledge of rat-face's murder. He couldn't bear it if anything happened to Elpis and Airla! Sphax reckoned he had a day's start. One day. That was all.

Sphax did have a plan, or at least he thought he had a plan. But now, dejectedly, he realised it was nothing more than wishful thinking, a fool's dream. His plan had been to escape and join Hannibal's army marching on Rome.

Hannibal and the war with Carthage were the talk of Rome. Gaius Lucilus and his senator cronies talked of little else at the Circus or exercising on the Campus. He'd listened eagerly, desperate for news and information. On one eavesdropped occasion, Numidian horsemen were

He'd feigned an expression of foolish ignorance, then pleaded 'I know that I was taken into slavery near the island of Corcyra, that my father was a Numidian and my mother a noblewoman from Carthage, but to my eternal shame I know nothing of these places or their whereabouts. What sort of man is it who can't point to his birthplace and say, there lies my homeland?'

Elpis had still looked sceptical, but nevertheless started clearing away the parchments. 'Very well,' and he began wandering around the room collecting what had seemed to Sphax like a random series of items before resuming his chair at the table. He'd begun by arranging a brown tunic plucked off a peg by the door into a long series of folds and tresses that stretched almost the length of the table. After nudging the cloth backwards or forwards it had eventually taken on the appearance of a gaping mouth. With an orator's flourish he'd swept his hand over the tunic, declaring, 'the Mediterranean Sea.' Next he'd placed two large wooden chopping boards next to each other, but offset at an angle he'd kept adjusting. Taking a long string of sausages, Elpis had joined one end to the inner board and arranged the rest in a straight line that abruptly curved back on itself. Sphax hadn't wanted to appear disrespectful, but he couldn't help grinning at the image. It had looked like a meaty dangling penis. By now Airla was standing beside him, arms folded beneath her considerable bosom, smiling incredulously at her husband's bizarre creation. From a fruit bowl Elpis had picked apples, pears and grapes. He grabbed a few more wooden plates and then returned to the table. Plates were placed to the right of the sausages until they curved around to join up with the tunic to Sphax's right. Finally, Elpis dotted apples and pears around the gaping mouth. 'First things first,' and plucking another grape he'd placed it carefully in the middle of the string of sausages. 'Rome. Where we presently reside.'

Sphax had always suspected that Rome was no better than a festering boil on the side of a prick. Elpis had just confirmed it for him. He'd sensed Airla's irritation with her husband as he began plucking yet more grapes from the bunch. He'd placed a grape on the edge of a small plate to the right of the sausages and beamed at Airla, 'Corinth. My birthplace. Where Airla and I will return one day.' Placing a grape under Sphax's nose he'd announced, 'Carthage. Your birthplace!'

'My mother told me the story of my birth many times. I was born in my father's city, in Numidia, not in Carthage, and when I was delivered they thought me stillborn. It was only when my nurse carried me to the balcony and raised me to the sun rising above the great desert that I was able to take my first breath and begin life.'

Elpis had stared at him. 'Then it is true. Our ancient geographers were correct after all. Beyond the mountains lies a great desert. Then, my dear Sphax, you are seated in your birthplace.' Suddenly animated by Sphax's revelation he'd risen to his feet and swept his hand along the brown cloth to the edge of the table. 'This is the African coast, Numidian lands which stretch to the Outer Sea, a sea which can only be reached through the Pillars of Hercules,' pointing to where the cloth met the outer board. Sweeping his hand to Sphax's right he'd continued, 'To the east of Carthage lies Libya, and beyond, Egypt.'

This was all very well, Sphax had thought, but the information he desperately needed was the whereabouts of Hannibal's army, and how he could reach it. So far his 'birthplace' plan had worked *too* well! He could see Elpis looking thoughtful and preparing new questions about the Great Desert. 'But where is this town Saguntha, Sir, the one that Hannibal sacked?'

'Saguntum,' Elpis had corrected, returning from his reverie and placing a grape midway down the outer board then circling it with his finger. 'This is Iberia, where Carthage holds sway.'

'So by now Hannibal could be …' and in his excitement Sphax had leapt from his chair, creating convulsions in Sicily, Sardinia and Corsica before jabbing his finger on the middle board as it crept towards the sausage prick. 'Here!' he'd cried, 'or even here,' pointing to a spot just north of Rome.

Elpis had laughed, then put the Mediterranean islands back in their rightful places. 'He has many obstacles in his path, even before he reaches Gaul,' he'd said, circling the middle board with his finger. 'You might say that the whole of nature is against him. Here,' waving his hand over the junction between the two square boards, 'is a great mountain range, the Pyrenees, here lies the Rhodanus, a river that is swift and wide, and beyond this his greatest obstacle of all, the unsurmountable Alps. Wild and locked in snow and ice for most of the year, these mountains are impossible for wild goats, let alone an army of men. All the while he will be journeying through the lands of the barbarian. Gauls are murderous savages! No, Sphax, it is impossible, it cannot be done. You can sleep easy in your bed. There will be no invasion, at least not by Hannibal.'

As Elpis had spoken Sphax's heart had begun to sink. It seemed that all the excitement he'd felt over these last few weeks, along with the flicker of hope it had kindled, had been dashed by cold reason and common sense. He was just an ignorant boy who knew nothing of the world. Then a thought occurred.

'But surely, Sir, if Hannibal has to surmount all these obstacles on his path to Rome, then Rome's legions will have to overcome the very same obstacles if they wish to meet his challenge?'

'No, Sphax, Rome commands the sea, so it will be easy to transport its legions westwards. They would land at Massilia, then either cross the Rhodanus and meet Hannibal west of the river, or defend its crossing points, which are few in number. Massilia is a Greek city, but that counts for little in Rome's eyes.' Sphax had caught the bitterness in his voice.

'Where is Massilia?' excitement and hope suddenly revived.

'Here,' Elpis had said, placing a grape at the edge of Gaul's board. It had looked tantalisingly close to Rome's sausage prick, Sphax had thought.

'Do many of Rome's ships sail there?' he'd asked, as casually as he could manage.

'All Rome's harbours on the Ligurian Sea trade with Massilia. There is great commerce in everything from wine to slaves. But why do you ask, Sphax?'

It had been time for him to keep his mouth firmly shut and make excuses to leave before he'd give the game away. Luckily, Airla had put a stop to any further questions by collecting the grapes and fruit from around the table. 'That's enough geography for today … and put my tunic back on its peg, husband,' she'd said irritably, leaving Sphax free to make his getaway.

* * *

Recalling Elpis's geography lesson reminded him of his plan. He had to reach the sea, then take ship to Massilia. He knew the sea was somewhere to the west, but how far. Days? Weeks? Idly, he picked up the mirror and saw the face reflected in its polished silver. Despite his predicament he burst out laughing. His face was filthy! There were still bits of straw lodged in his raven-black curls from his sleepless night in the stable. Shepherds sheared their sheep more carefully than his hair had been cut. He looked exactly what he was; a filthy ex-slave. But this gave him a glimmer of an idea.

He could never pass for a Roman. His mother's Carthaginian blood coursed through his veins and he had her green eyes and something of her fair complexion, but to a Roman he would always look like a swarthy African, a barbarian. Dressed up as a patrician, riding such a fine stallion with Dido in tow, fingers would point, 'Thief!' would be shouted and a magistrate summoned. Soon he would be stopped, questioned and shackled. Just like the last time he'd tried it. There had to be another way.

It came to him as he was watching Arion drinking contentedly from the stream. He remembered the morning Gaius Lucilus had bought the stallion from an estate south of Rome. Gaius had stayed on as a guest for the evening, leaving him and a servant to lead Arion back to the city. Riding Dido with Arion in tow he'd ridden for miles down the Via Latina, past noble carriages, merchants on horseback and sweating legionaries, through crowded town squares and villages without a single eyebrow or accusing finger being raised in his direction. It was a commonplace sight, a servant returning his master's horse. He could easily pass as the servant of a merchant or rich trader. It might work. Could he keep up the ruse for the days or even weeks it might take to reach a harbour and a ship? Yes, he could do it! He would become a well-to-do servant, and grinned at the prospect that he was already moving up in the world.

Sphax looked afresh at the items laid out on the grass. He would have to wear one of the tunics.

Saffron-dyed tunics were expensive, but he couldn't wear the rags he was standing in, they were those of the slave class and would give him away. That wooden chest didn't look right either; the leather straps and iron braces riveted in bronze had been exquisitely crafted. Secret compartment or not, it still looked like a chest of silver. What servant would be entrusted with such a possession? It would have to go.

He began his new life by lying naked in a shallow pool of the stream, washing away the filth and mud from his hair and body. The water was cold and refreshing. When he emerged from the stream and slipped the fine linen tunic over his head, he felt reborn, a new man.

Distributing the contents of the chest amongst the leather bags was easy. He was careful to divide and secrete the silver coin, keeping most of them in rat-face's purse on a belt beneath his tunic. He reminded himself to buy sandals; only slaves and the poor went barefoot. A servant would never ride his master's horse, so he would have to buy a lead-rope for Arion. In the end he couldn't bear to part with the sandals or the beautiful toga of Egyptian linen, so found room for them.

The pressing problem was what to do with Arion's saddle, bit and reins? His first thought was to toss them away, along with the chest and his own clothing. But after considering this for a while he'd realized this would be foolish and might even give him away. Romans were incapable of riding a horse without the aid of a saddle, and Sphax couldn't bring himself to inflict a bit and reins on his mare, he saw them as instruments of torture. But a rider on a saddleless horse would draw far too much attention to himself, so he'd made up his mind. For the first time in her life, poor Dido would have to be burdened with a saddle. Sphax despised saddles. There was an old Numidian saying: saddle a wife but never a horse! He'd been taught to ride without one from the age of four. By the time he was six he could dismount slithering backwards from his pony's croup. At seven he showed off by kneeling upright on its back, or at the gallop, reaching down to pick pebbles from the ground. All Numidians love horses.

As for Marcellus's fancy equestrian sword, sheathed and buckled to the saddle, that was an easy decision. He would need it where he was going.

* * *

Everything went better than he'd dared hope. To begin with his stomach tightened in dread at the approach of every traveller he met along the road, but with each unremarkable passing he started to relax. Soon he was smiling and greeting his fellow travellers, who were after all, perfect strangers. By mid-afternoon he passed through the southern gate into Perusia.

It was something Elpis had said that decided him on Perusia. He recalled that the Greek had mentioned there was a great trade in slaves from Massilia. Sphax had travelled to Perusia almost every year in the company of

Gaius Lucilus and a retinue of servants. It lay a short distance from his Myrteta estate. He remembered there was a thriving slave market in the city. It seemed like a good place to ask if they bought slaves from Massilia, and from which seaport they were shipped.

Loitering around the viewing platform in the market he'd struck up a conversation with a talkative lad about the same age as himself, a servant to one of the slave masters. He'd told Sphax they were expecting a shipload from Massilia next week. 'Where do they come in from?' he'd asked innocently. 'Usually Pisae, then on to Arretium. They get the pickings, we the dregs, that's if they haven't already been assigned to Rome.' There wasn't an auction that afternoon, but looking around Sphax could see the misery written on the faces of the men, women and children shackled to posts, their copper history plaques draped around their necks. He shuddered. He'd always loathed such places, they made his flesh creep. At that moment the slave master cast a stern eye in their direction and the lad hurriedly slunk off. But it had been enough. His road was now clear; it led through Arretium to the sea at Pisae and a ship bound for Massilia. Fate had indeed smiled on him today, but for one grey cloud. He remembered visiting Arretium two years ago and recalled the journey had taken at least three days. And where was Pisae?

The prospect of three day's extra travel were liberally compensated for by the joys of owning a purse. A purse stuffed with coin was akin to being invited to feast with the gods. Sphax knew nothing of money. He'd been careful to hide all the silver coins, nevertheless his purse still contained more money than a labourer could hope to earn in a year. That afternoon in the market he'd eagerly filled a sack with a flask of fine wine, olives, fruit and cheeses. He'd bought virgin oil and four baked loaves of good wheaten bread, not the cheap barley bread he was used to. Back in Rome all this would have cost a month's wages, but here in the provinces it was as cheap as piss. He'd sampled and bought a variety of cooked meats he'd never tasted before such as smoked ham and cured pork. It was a delight he hoped he would grow accustomed to in this new life.

Acquiring a coil of hemp rope he cut a length and tied it off in a neat loop around Arion's neck; the rest of the rope he stored, thinking it might come in useful. On the way to buy sandals he passed a street barber waiting patiently for trade outside a taberna. After hesitating a moment he decided to take the plunge. Later, finding himself in a quiet backstreet he retrieved the mirror and couldn't believe the reflection that met his eyes. Gone were the twisted masses of shaggy curls. He thought that even Airla would not have recognised the face in the mirror.

There was still light left in the day and he was keen to put a few miles between himself and Perusia before the search for him began. Time was pressing. In the market place he'd listened carefully as a leather trader described the road and direction he must take, and as he rode through the northern gate he was anxiously listing his purchases, checking that he'd not forgotten something important.

The road and country north-west of the city was very different from the Via Amerina he'd ridden from the south. In places the roadway was badly rutted and in poor repair. Soon he entered a wild and desolate heathland with few signs of habitation. In Rome there is a common saying that to travel alone on the roads is to court certain death from robbers and bandits. Sphax wasn't worried. The robber who could outride him on horseback was yet to be born, and Arion was the fleetest stallion in Rome. Travellers were few on these roads. Except for a couple of rumbling ox-carts grinding their way through the ruts, the only sounds he heard were those of songbirds or the distant bells of goatherds high in the heathland. As the light began to fade he could see that the road ahead followed the curve of a broad lake with hills rising steeply from its shoreline. If he could reach the lake before nightfall he would have fresh water for the horses.

Setting up camp beside the lake, his first thought was to make a fire. Its warmth and comfort would have been welcome on his first night alone in the wilderness, but he thought better of it: it would have been visible for miles around and might attract unwelcome attention. Pouring some of the wine into a wooden bowl he'd bought in Perusia, he broke off chunks of bread and dipped them into the bowl and sampled some of the cheeses. He couldn't remember having eaten anything so delicious and satisfying. The moon was rising above the ridge of mountains in the east and the air was growing colder. Freeing Dido from the burden of her saddle he used it for a pillow and wrapped the toga around him. Gazing up at the stars emerging in the night sky he thought to himself that life wasn't so bad after all; his belly was full, he owned two fine horses and a purse worthy of a patrician. Best of all, ahead of him lay the open road. At last he was a free man. But the last thing he did before tiredness and sleep overtook him was to unsheathe the sword and place it within easy reach.

Sphax suddenly jolted awake in the half-light before dawn. Arion was pawing the ground with his hoof and snorting violently. It was this that had woken him. Blinking, his eyes still heavy with sleep, he realised that Dido was also standing her ground above him, pawing and facing some unseen enemy. He reached for the sword and got to his feet.

Less than a stone's throw ahead of him was a huge boar, ears erect, tusks levelled, its massive bulk poised and balanced, ready to charge. For a few heart-stopping moments, human and wild beast stared at one another. Sphax felt every nerve in his body trembling, and the hand gripping the sword was shaking wildly. Then, in the blink of an eye, the beast suddenly turned and trotted off into a thicket beside the lake. If the beast had charged, his sword would have been about as much use as a wooden spoon. Was it a sign, a warning? Artemis had once sent a great boar to warn Oeneus of Calydon. 'Gods are not people like you and me, Sphax,' Elpis had been fond of telling him, 'but mysterious powers and forces. We have to look for their signs.' Was this a sign?

For several miles the road followed the gentle curve of the lake until it reached a rocky promontory where the lake turned abruptly to the south. At this point the road parted company with the lake and turned to the northwest to climb a ridge. The country was much the same as it had been yesterday; wild heathland with scrubby clumps of trees and rocky outcrops.

It started raining heavily in the afternoon. Even with rat-face's blue cloak draped firmly around him he was soon soaked to the skin. Even the birds refused to sing that afternoon. As darkness began to gather he left the road on a track that led into a forest. He was hoping it might lead to a woodsman's hut or shelter. But he was out of luck. As the track emerged from the trees it petered out in a clearing scattered with rocks and large boulders. Choosing an overhanging boulder that would at least provide some shelter he made camp. He was soaking wet, chilled to the bone and felt thoroughly miserable, but he would have to make the best of it. At least the toga and spare tunic would be dry inside the saddle bags, he thought. Draping the cloak over the overhanging rock above his head he weighted it down with stones, then cut branches and attached them to the hem of the cape to make a crude shelter. It dripped incessantly, but it was better than nothing.

Sphax first heard the cry as he was carrying the saddle back to his shelter. His blood ran cold at the sound. It wasn't really a cry, it was a howl, and it was soon answered by another to his left, then another directly ahead of him. Soon the forest all around him was echoing to the infernal sound of howling wolves. His only thought was fire. It was almost dark by now but scrambling around in the undergrowth at the forest's edge he collected anything dry enough to burn. Desperately searching through one of the bags he found what he was looking for. Gripping the fire striker in his left hand he placed the kindling wool beside his wood pile and started striking the flint towards it. He soon had a glow, then a flame, and after blowing vigorously for some time the wood caught and at last he had a fire. As he went in search of more dry wood the howling continued intermittently, always at some distance, but nevertheless, too close for comfort.

Sphax had heard chilling tales of wolves. Their cunning and savagery were legend. He knew they rarely attacked people, but it was not unknown. Building the fire as best he could he fed it regularly with the driest wood and prayed to the gods to stop the rain so its flames would cease smoking and sizzling. Moments later the gods answered him by sending a bolt of lightning that illuminated the clearing as if it was mid-day. The crash of thunder that followed on its heels terrified the horses. Nothing frightens horses more than thunder. Desperate now, he scrabbled around in the bag to find the extra length of rope and as calmly as possible approached the poor creatures, talking all the while to calm and reassure them. He gathered in Arion's lead and was about to tie the rope around Dido's neck when there was another flash and almighty crash. At that both horses squealed and bolted in panic, charging into the forest and the darkness. It was pointless chasing them, they would be half a mile away before he'd even reached the edge of the forest. He knew that Dido would always stay close to the stallion, but would the pair of them be a match for a wolf pack? Would he be able to find them in the morning? He would never make it alone on foot. His life depended on those horses.

It was the longest night of his life. Fretting and anxious for the safety of the horses, sleep was out of the question as the wind rose and the rain lashed down on his shelter. He almost lost the cloak to a sudden gust. As the storm raged, flashes lit up the forest for miles around and during one particularly vivid bolt, he was certain he saw a pair of wolves silhouetted against the trees at the edge of the clearing.

Sometime late into the night he must have fallen asleep, yet Artemis had spared him, and he woke to the light. If you could call it light. An eerie mist shrouded the whole valley, swirling amongst the trees and giving everything a ghostly appearance. The fire had gone out and there was no sign of the horses. He couldn't carry the bags and the saddle far, so strapping the sword around his waist he went in search of them, stopping every now and then to whistle and call out their names. When he reached the roadway he looked anxiously in both directions, but there was no sign of them. He whistled and then yelled out their names at the top of his voice. Finally, to his intense relief, he could hear hooves beating towards him and out of the mist they both appeared, nickering happily and tossing their heads in welcome. Thank the gods they were safe, he thought.

Within a short time they were packed and trotting down the road with Sphax breakfasting on bread and cheese from the saddle. Most of the time he couldn't see more than a stone's throw of the road ahead, but occasionally the mist swirled aside like a curtain to reveal a valley that was growing steadily shallower and less wooded. When he guessed it was about mid-day – he hadn't seen the sun all morning and was relying on his stomach for timekeeping – he led the horses to the river they'd been following and let them feed and rest. He gave them the last two apples from his sack, and then sat on the riverbank chewing cold meat and swigging the last of the wine.

Later that afternoon the heavens opened and rain again fell in torrents. He was soaked to the skin within a quarter of a mile. It could only have been the middle of the afternoon, yet the light seemed to have gone from the day as he rode on in a gloomy twilight, rain bouncing off the stones and running in rivers beside the roadway. He feared another thunderstorm and attached Arion's lead rope to his saddle as securely as possible, but he knew it would never hold the stallion if he panicked and bolted.

The leather trader in Perusia had told him that he would eventually meet the Via Cassian coming up from the south, and that just down the road was a village and stables. 'Just down the road' proved to be a ten mile weary ordeal. It wasn't much of a village either, just a single street with a few houses and barns, but to his immense relief he caught sight of the ramped entrance to a stabulae, which meant his horses would be fed and stabled. His spirits revived at the sight of glowing light behind shutters and smoke rising from rooftops. Leading the horses through the archway into a walled courtyard he could see the stables to his left, well lit by lamps.

A man appeared at the open doorway holding a lamp above his head to get a better view of the approaching stranger. 'Have you come far?'

'Too far on a day like this,' Sphax replied guardedly, water dripping from every fold of his cloak. 'I'm returning my master's horse to Arretium, but that will have to wait until tomorrow. I can go no further tonight.'

Sphax handed over the lead ropes and followed him into the stables, amazed by their size and how well appointed each stall was. 'Fine stallion,' the man said, running his hand down Arion's mane. 'I'm Antonio by the way. I'll go and get my brother Marcus and tell mistress Clodia to prepare a room for a guest. Marcus always deals with the customers, I just get in the way really ... but I do my best' he said, babbling and grinning like a child.

He was removing the saddle and bags from Dido when Antonio returned with his brother. Marcus was a great bull of a man, with a shaven head, jackal eyes, and a deep scar cleaving the left side of his face. Sphax had seen the like before, ex-legionaries, given land for years of service or a pension to set them up in a bar or some brothel in Rome. Unlike his brother, Marcus spoke rarely, and communicated mostly by grunt.

Giving nothing away, Sphax explained that he would be setting off for Arretium at first light to return a horse his master had bought in Perusia. He nodded towards the stallion, but Marcus didn't appear to have listened to a word he'd said; his eyes just shifted restlessly between the leather bags and Arion. 'Five asses,' he growled, eventually.

This was an outrageous price! Sphax shot him an offended glance which only seemed to make his brother Antonio uncomfortable. Without meeting Sphax's eye, Marcus repeated 'Five asses ... in advance.'

What choice did he have? Slinging the bags over his shoulder and ignoring his brother, he placed the coins in Antonio's palm. He was almost at the door when something made him go back and retrieve the sword buckled to Dido's saddle. He took his time strapping it to his waist and made sure to cast a glance at Marcus on his way out. That was the only occasion he ever saw Marcus smile.

Mistress Clodia had a pinched, worried expression, as if she'd spent most of her life looking over her shoulder. She led him up narrow stairs and a corridor to a tiny room above the inn. From what he could see by the meagre light from her oil lamp, the room had been swept. A bedroll had been spread on the wooden floor and beside it stood a washing bowl and jug, pisspot and candle. He left his saddle bags beside the shutters, picked up the candle and followed the mistress back down to the inn.

Besides himself, the only customers that evening seemed to be a couple of old men playing knucklebones in the corner, and a drunk slumped over a table, snoring his head off. He sat at the marble counter as a young girl in a hooded tunic served him a bowl of puls with chopped pork, bread and wine.

'Antonio tells me you're taking your master's horse back to the city.' He hadn't noticed Clodia entering from the kitchen. Against the evening chill she'd put on a respectable but shabby brown stola, fixed with an iron brooch at the shoulder. He nodded and dipped the last of the bread into his wine. 'He must be rich to own a horse like that.'

'He is, mistress,' thinking this had better be convincing, 'he's a leather merchant who deals in fine saddles. He trades mostly with Massilia. I'm his stable master. Is Antonio your husband?' he added quickly, changing the subject.

'Husband!' she laughed, 'he's slow in the head, that one. No, he's Marcus's kid brother.' He needed to end this conversation now, before he gave anything away.

'Where's the privy, mistress? It's been a long day's ride and I need sleep.' The privy was outside in the courtyard, beyond a woodpile and huge storage jars filled, judging from the overpowering scent in the air, with oil and pine resin. At last the rain had stopped. He glimpsed the stars and the air felt fresh and renewed. On his way back through the courtyard he noticed a faint light coming from the stables. Peering in at the entrance he saw it was Marcus holding an oil lamp aloft in Arion's stall, muttering and grunting to the creature. It should have been the most comfortable night's sleep he'd enjoyed in days, but he tossed and turned all night, sleeping fitfully.

He awoke at first light, walked over to the window and flung open the shutters. It was as if the world had no memory of thunder, tempests or torrents of rain. There wasn't a cloud in the sky and the air smelt sweet and dry. He would travel far today, well beyond Arretium, though he would enquire there of the roads to Pisae. But his first urgent call was the privy. Then he noticed someone had scribbled on the stucco beside the shutter, and he chuckled. It appeared that Antonio would suck his cock, if he asked him nicely.

He hadn't noticed last night how grand the courtyard had once been. Surrounded by a high wall, the centrepiece was an old mulberry tree in a circular walled bed. There were still signs of herb and flower beds, all now neglected and decaying. Under the shade of the mulberry it must have been pleasant to sit on the now broken seat during the hottest part of the day and gaze out at the green hills and woods beyond the courtyard walls. Now everything was gone to rack and ruin, littered with broken things, discarded amongst the clay storage jars and barrels. The ugly wood pile was stacked against the wall of the inn, almost reaching up to the open shutters of his room.

He brought his two saddle bags down from his room and sat at the table the drunk had occupied last night. Marcus and Clodia seemed to be arguing, her worried expression more marked than ever. Marcus glanced in his direction then yelled out, 'Where's that good for nothing slut? If she's still in bed I'll brand her again.' Moments later the servant girl arrived with a bowl and bread, flustered and red-faced from a weal on her cheek. Breakfast was more puls, but this time without the chopped pork. He ate what he could, found his purse and took it to the counter where the mistress was standing. Out of the corner of his eye he could see that Marcus was watching him closely.

'Twenty asses,' she muttered, avoiding his eyes. Sphax's jaw dropped. He stared at her. This was more than a week's wages in Rome.

'You're trying to cheat me, mistress,' he said finally. 'I'll pay you ten, but even ten is robbery.' A fist suddenly slammed down on the marble and Marcus leaned over the counter and thrust his face a nose's length from Sphax's.

'You'll pay the woman, arsehole ... in full!' In a flush of anger, Sphax felt an irresistible urge to draw his sword and ram it down the foul smelling mouth that was offending his nose. But he knew if he tried it would end badly. He'd never used a sword in his life. Besides, a brawl would draw a crowd. He was a stranger. The last thing he needed was to draw attention to himself. It wasn't his money, after all. What did it matter? All he wanted at that moment was to get as far away from this place as his horses could carry him. He placed ten bronze coins in front of Clodia, hoisted the bags to his shoulder and made for the stables.

Antonio was clearing straw from Dido's stall when he entered. He took one look at Sphax's thunderous expression and left. He'd already saddled Dido and secured the leather saddle bags when a voice from behind him growled 'You can take the nag, but the stallion stays. He's mine now.' It was Marcus, barring the entrance to the stables. It took him a moment to take in the significance of these words, but then an uncontrollable rage surged through him and Sphax strode towards him. This time he wasn't going to back down. 'If it wasn't so puny,' he yelled, 'I'd tell you to stuff your prick up your own arse. My master will return with fifty men and flay you alive …' His hand had found the hilt and he was about to draw the sword when he felt a sharp prick of iron against his ribs. Marcus had a sword pointed at his chest. It was a short ugly legionary's weapon, and the nicks and notches attested to the fact it had been well used. 'What's in those leather bags, boy? Bring 'em over to me.'

'If that's what you want.' Sphax's mind was already racing. Stepping back a pace from the sword and turning towards Dido's stall, he realised there was only one thing he could do now. Sheathing his sword he slowly retreated towards her open stall, raised two fingers to his mouth and whistled a shrill pitch, then yelled 'Fly, Dido! Fly!' Snorting in panic with her ears pinned back in terror, Dido charged out of the stall towards him. Transferring all his weight to his left leg he bent it slightly, flexed, and calculated the leap he would have to make. His left ankle caught a little on the saddle horns as he sprung, but he had both arms firmly locked around her neck as they both emerged into the sunlight of the courtyard. Behind him he heard the sound of a sword clanging to the paving and realised that Marcus had been thrown backwards by Dido's unexpected charge.

'Yoo, Dido… yoo, yoo' he repeated gently to bring her to a halt, managing this after a couple of circuits of the mulberry tree in the middle of the courtyard. He could see Marcus staggering to his feet and recovering his sword. Sphax drew his own sword, pointed it at Marcus and yelled 'I'm going to kill you!

You're a thieving bastard and you're going to die!' With that he nudged Dido and rode up the ramp to the road outside.

He brought Dido to a halt in the middle of a deserted Cassian. Tears of rage and humiliation were streaming down his cheeks. He had no recollection of how far he'd ridden or how long it had taken. Nor could he remember a single sight he'd passed along the way. His only recollection was of the waves of emotion that had raged through him, feelings that ranged from shame and humiliation to searing anger and frustration. He was not a coward. Yet he'd fled, run away. At that moment he felt nothing but shame and guilt.

If he was ever to live with himself, he would have to turn around and face his fears, or be forever diminished by them. Few of us are aware of those moments in our destiny that decide our fate for good or ill, but somehow, Sphax knew that this was such a moment. He *had* to go back. Touching the precious pouch he always kept at his breast, he nudged Dido around and trotted back down the road.

TWO

Arion had always been Gaius Lucilus' horse. Only he or his rat-faced son had been allowed to ride the stallion. Nevertheless, for the last three years Sphax had trained him, nurtured him, groomed and nursed him through sickness, taken a beating for him whenever Gaius had lost a race – always due to the man's stupidity – and celebrated the stallion's famous victories. Arion would never be able to replace Dido in his affections, but he still loved the stallion, and wasn't about to abandon him to the mercies of that thieving bastard, Marcus. He would rescue the stallion and take revenge on the thief.

As soon as he caught sight of the village he turned eastwards off the road, making for the lightly wooded hills that rose beyond the village. Once he'd entered the safety of the trees he knew he couldn't be seen; nevertheless, he kept to where the trees were thickest. He caught occasional glimpses of the roofs and walls of buildings which helped him find his bearings. When he judged he'd reached a point roughly opposite the inn's courtyard he dismounted and tied Dido's lead firmly to a tree.

Checking the position of the sun he guessed it would soon be mid-morning. It was already hot and he was getting hungry and thirsty. At some point he would have to water Dido, but his own hunger and thirst would have to wait: there were more pressing things on his mind right now. Staying low, he crept downhill to the edge of the treeline. By good luck he'd judged it perfectly. Lying on his belly beside a thorn bush, he could look down directly into the courtyard of the inn. He noted every single coming and going; Clodia to her storage jars, the servant girl to the wood pile or Antonio's visits to the privy. He didn't see much of Marcus. A couple of times he crossed the courtyard to the inn, but on each occasion he soon returned to the stables. Sphax would somehow have to lure him out of the stables. But how? A diversion perhaps? His worst fear had always been that Marcus might try to sell the stallion as soon as possible, but no strangers or guests arrived whilst he'd been watching. Arion was still in his stall, he was certain of it.

It was late in the afternoon when he retraced his steps up the hill to where he'd tethered Dido. Searching through the bags he found what was left of the cooked meat and stale bread. It was hardly a feast but he felt better for it. Thirst was his pressing problem. Carrying his stoppered jug he searched the nearby woods for a stream or watercourse, looking for the tell-tale signs of moss or dark green foliage. Despite the torrential rain that had fallen over the last two days, in these hills everything appeared dry and parched. Eventually he found a shallow spring and with some patience, managed to fill his jug. Guiding Dido to the spring he left her to drink her fill whilst he went through the plan he'd devised. He'd already gone over it a dozen times, but it wouldn't hurt to go through it again.

Searching the ground beneath the trees he selected five thick pieces of deadwood about a forearm's length. Taking his spare rope he cut lengths, then tightly wound them around the top of each piece of wood. Finding the fire starter, flint and wool kindling, he held the horseshoe shaped metal in his left hand and tried out the flint using some dry leaves as kindling. In moments he had a flame. He placed all the items carefully in an empty food sack, then checked the rope binding on the wood to make sure it wouldn't come loose. When he was satisfied he sat back against a trunk and took a swig from the jug. All he needed now was darkness.

In the twilight Sphax took up a position by the thorn bush and waited for the darkness to deepen. Finally, with a silent prayer to Artemis he set off cautiously down the hill with the sword strapped at his side. He felt nothing but rage coursing through him now. These Romans cheated, robbed, murdered and enslaved. This wasn't just about Arion. For the first time he felt the thrill of going to war. Rome would answer for his slavery and the murder of his parents. He would be avenged. Why wait for Hannibal and his Carthaginians? His own war on Rome was about to begin.

At the courtyard wall he followed it until reaching a section that would be directly opposite the entrance to the stables. The wall was only a head taller than he was, making it easy to jump up and support himself long enough to take a good look inside the stables. Marcus was in there all right, he could see him brooding on a stool by one of the stalls. The stables were well lit by several oil lamps. Marcus wasn't taking any chances. No one was going to steal up on him in the darkness that night.

Sphax lowered himself back down to the ground and collecting the deadwood brands and his sack, followed the course of the courtyard to the point where it joined the back wall of the inn. Soon he was over and crouching amongst the barrels and clay storage jars. The gods were with him that evening, for not only had they banished the moon, they seemed to have sharpened his senses. He could already smell what his nose had been searching out, what he'd remembered from last night's trip to the privy: the pungent aroma of pine resin. Removing the ill-fitting wooden seal on one of the jars he plunged each brand into the thick sticky liquid, twisting vigorously so that the rope he'd wound around them gained a good coating of resin.

He was half way up the woodpile when he heard a door bang and someone staggered into the courtyard. He froze. 'The maiden said stay a while ...' It was

Antonio, roaring drunk and singing at the top of his voice on his way to the privy. Once the privy door shut, Sphax continued up the woodpile, taking great care not to displace logs. Progress was slow, encumbered as he was by his sword, the sack and the wooden brands, but he eventually gained a height where he could reach up to the shutters of the room he'd slept in last night. This was the moment he'd been dreading. The one possible flaw in his carefully laid plans; had Clodia or the servant girl bolted the shutters from the inside? He'd worked out contingencies of course, but everything would be so much simpler if they'd forgotten to bolt them. He was in luck. He swung the shutters open and hoisted himself into the pitch black of the room. Closing them behind him he felt in his sack for the fire striker and flint, then placed one of the brands on the floor in front of him. The rope wick, smeared as it was in pine resin, burst into flame at the first strike, illuminating the little room as if it had been lit by a dozen candles. Resting the unlit brands in the pisspot he walked towards the door, listening intently. Beyond the door lay a corridor that opened on to more guest rooms. Gingerly he raised the latch and opened the door. As he stepped out into the corridor he received a terrible shock.

Standing an arm's length away was the young servant girl, staring wild-eyed at him, rooted to the spot. He was sure she was about to scream so he grabbed her by the shoulder, dragged her back into the room and dropped his brand so he could hold her tightly with a hand over her mouth. 'I'm not going to hurt you,' he whispered frantically. 'I swear it! I've come to take back my stallion. That's all. Then I'll leave. If you swear not to cry out, I'll release my hand.' She bobbed her head up and down vigorously. Sphax knew he was taking a huge risk, but released his hand and held his breath.

In between gasps for air she whispered 'I want to run away … escape.' He knew the feeling all too well. 'Will you take me with you? I have to get away.' This was not part of his plan, but if he delayed any more there wouldn't *be* a plan. Outside in the courtyard he heard Antonio's voice in full song as he returned from the privy. 'Yes,' he said without thinking, 'but first I'm going to burn this place to the ground – that's the only way I'll get Marcus out of the stables.'

She simply giggled nervously then grinned at him. That wasn't the reaction he'd expected. 'I'll help,' she said, retrieving the flaming brand he'd dropped. 'All the rooms are empty tonight. Set fire to the bedrolls, they're full of dry straw. Light some more torches for me and I'll fire the other rooms.' He still didn't trust her, so followed closely on her heels as they placed flaming torches in four other rooms. When they returned he took the last torch from the pisspot and placed it by the bedroll.

'Not there!' she hissed, and placed the torch and bedroll by the door, so the flames would lick up its wooden panels. He got the feeling she was enjoying this. 'What now?'

'We get out of here.' He opened the shutters a little to check there was no one in the courtyard, then lowered himself to the woodpile and helped her climb down. He could already smell smoke. They were soon over the courtyard wall and he was describing where Dido was tethered in the woods. 'Wait there until dawn,' he whispered. 'I can't risk riding the stallion through those woods in the dark. I'll have to wait until daybreak. Stay close to my mare.'

Before scurrying off into the darkness, she suddenly turned and pleaded, 'If you get the chance, kill Marcus for me. Kill the bastard!'

Checking constantly for signs of smoke or fire in the upper storey of the inn, he took up his position again behind the section of wall that looked directly into the stables. It seemed to take an age, but sometime later he heard several voices shouting and yelling at one another in the courtyard. 'Come Marcus! Quickly! The inn is on fire.' It was Clodia's voice, rising in panic, desperate. 'Quickly husband, you must come now!'

'What is it, woman?' he heard Marcus growl at her. In that instant there was a thunderous crash as the shutters in the room above the woodpile burst open, followed by a tongue of searing flame that lit up the courtyard as if at mid-day. Sphax could even feel the wave of heat as it hit his forehead. Looking up he saw the entire roof of the inn was now engulfed in flame. Clodia screamed, and then all he heard was the sound of running feet. It was now or never.

Leaping at the wall he soon scrambled over and ran across the courtyard to the stables. Arion had been stalled at the back, well away from prying eyes. He gathered in the stallion's lead and walked him quickly out to the courtyard. In the flickering light of the flames his eyes met a scene from Hades. There were now perhaps half a dozen people yelling and screaming at one another, charging around wildly amidst the showers of sparks, or trying to move barrels and jars away from the gathering inferno. Flames lit up the entire courtyard, making it impossible to hide, so despite the chaos all around him, Marcus spotted Arion immediately and strode menacingly towards them drawing that ugly sword from his belt.

'You!' he snarled. 'This is your work … isn't it?' he raged, gesturing at the flames with the sword. Sphax dropped Arion's lead rope and quickly drew his own sword as Marcus charged at him, thrusting the blade at his belly. Sidestepping, he slashed out at the blade and felt the shock jar down the length of his arm as iron struck iron. Backing away, he put a few sword lengths between himself and Marcus. Arion was snorting wildly now and pawing the ground as Marcus charged again, this time trying a slashing blow aimed at his neck. Again, Sphax stepped aside, easily avoiding the blow and slashing out himself. He must have pierced flesh for Marcus cried out and the tip of his own sword was smeared red.

Sphax realised he was faster and more agile than his opponent. Marcus was breathing hard and out of control with rage. Sphax moved away from Arion who was getting increasingly agitated. He didn't want the stallion to get hurt. Marcus had caught his breath and was coming at him again, slashing the blade through the air like a scythe. At that moment Arion let out a sound Sphax had never heard before, a cry so terrible he hoped he would never hear the like again. It was like a piercing scream of rage. Arion reared up on his hind legs and brought his hooves crashing down on Marcus's shoulders. Marcus staggered backwards, falling heavily on his back as the sword slipped from his grasp. He never got up again. Now in a state of wild frenzy, the stallion reared again and again, each time bringing his hooves down on the head and chest of the limp body on the ground.

Sphax talked to the stallion, calming, soothing words that would coax him back from his frenzied madness. Eventually he became calm enough to approach, and Sphax led him gently away from the unrecognizable bloody pulp that lay beneath his hooves. He'd been so intent upon staying alive that he hadn't noticed anything beyond the tip of Marcus's sword during the fight. Now he looked around, taking in the flames still leaping from what was left of the inn and the crowd that had gathered beside the mulberry tree in the middle of the courtyard. There were perhaps six of them now, all dumbstruck, staring in horror. He recognised Clodia and Antonio, but none of them was looking at him. Their eyes were fixed on the stallion, and he could see terror written on every face.

Standing beside the stallion, he shouted above the roaring flames so all would hear. 'Walk, Arion. Kill anyone in your path! Kill them all!' With Arion's first step the crowd fled in terror through the archway and out into the street, melting away into the night. That is how he was able to walk slowly and calmly through the arched ramp that led to the road beyond, mount in safety, and then ride slowly north.

* * *

She was fast asleep on the grass when he returned at first light. Untying Dido he quietly led both horses to the spring he'd found yesterday and let them drink their fill. If she was still asleep when he returned he'd made up his mind to saddle Dido, pack the bags and continue his journey alone. No one would ever suspect the servant girl of starting the fire, so if she couldn't be found, they would assume she'd perished in the flames. He couldn't imagine Clodia weeping over a servant girl or sending out search parties to look for her. He'd convinced himself that if she came with him she would be more trouble than she was worth. He had a good story to account for his journey and the horses. Why tempt fate?

Unfortunately for Sphax it didn't quite turn out like that. When he returned he saw she was wide awake. Catching sight of him she leapt to her feet, desperate for news. 'Is he dead? Did you kill him? Tell me … tell me!'

'Yes, Marcus is dead,' he said in a matter-of-fact tone.

'You killed him,' unable to keep the surprise and disbelief out of her voice.

'I wouldn't have returned with Arion if I hadn't. Yes, I killed him,' he lied. She sank to the ground and leaning back against a trunk, started weeping. Without once meeting his eyes, she spoke between sobs. 'Thank the gods the bastard is dead. Whenever Clodia turned her back he used me as his whore. He hurt me ... flogged and beat me. When I tried to run away he used the branding iron on me ...' she stopped abruptly to tear back the tunic from her right forearm, revealing a word seared into her flesh that he recognised only too well. 'I hated him more than anyone living in this world, and now he's dead.' Her tears had dried when she finally looked up at him. 'I'm free of him,' she said quietly. 'Free!' He hadn't noticed her pale sapphire eyes before, they were the blue of a winter's sky.

'I'm Sphax,' relieved that he was able to grin at her at last. 'What's your name?'

'They call me Fionn, but I don't know the name my parents gave me. I was taken into slavery as a small child and have no memory of my mother or father.'

'How old are you?'

'I'm not sure,' she frowned, 'sixteen, I think.' She had long fair curls and the palest skin he'd ever seen, almost pure white.

'Well, you were certainly not born in these parts.'

She shot him a quizzical look. 'Neither were you, judging from your looks. I was told I was born in the far north, beyond even Gaul. Now that I'm free I will go north, and find my people.'

'You'll never make it,' he told her bitterly.

'Yes I will!'

'Sooner or later someone will stop you, start asking awkward questions, pointing fingers. They will always sniff out a slave. I tried it once when I was fourteen.' He too rolled back his right sleeve to reveal the *fugitivus* sign.

'You're a slave!' she cried, jumping to her feet, shocked. Sphax smiled.

'Not any more. I'm going to join my countrymen and Hannibal's army. We're going to invade Rome and teach the bastards a lesson they'll never forget. First I'll kill Gaius Lucilus, then Caius Flaminius. He ordered the murder of my mother and father. There are a few more. I've written down all their names on a list. Anyway, they're all going to die, the lot of them. After that I might have a rest and not kill anyone else for a while.'

'You *are* going to be busy.' Sphax was too engrossed in his glorious vision to catch the irony. 'Who is Hannibal?'

'Don't you know anything? He's a famous general in charge of all the armies of Carthage marching on Rome.'

'What makes you think he'd want a little runt like you in his army?'

'I'm a Numidian. A Numidian noble, related to Carthage. We're the best horsemen in the world. Of course he'll want me in his army! He'll probably put me in charge of his cavalry.'

Fionn burst out laughing. 'I'm sorry,' she said quickly, trying to keep a straight face. 'I don't mean to be disrespectful. I'm just teasing. I'm sure you're a good horseman.'

'Believe me, he'll welcome me.'

'How will you find this general?'

'His army will be near a great river, somewhere north of Massilia. But first I must reach Pisae, and then take ship to Massilia.'

'Massilia lies across the sea then,' her bright eyes widening. 'Where is it?'

'In Gaul.'

'Then I will come with you,' she said excitedly, 'if I'm to find my people I need to travel north through Gaul.'

'You can't,' he blurted out in alarm, struggling to find a good reason why she shouldn't. 'I have to move fast and you can't ride.'

'If you're such a famous horseman you can teach me. Surely it can't be that difficult.'

'Oh but it is,' he said, desperately racking his brain for a more convincing argument. 'And how do I explain that I'm travelling with a runaway slave? We'll both be caught.' Exasperated, she paced around him with her hands on her hips.

'Then I could be your servant ... or sister— '

'Do we look like brother and sister?' he said sourly. He could see she was still deep in thought, almost oblivious to his presence.

'Wife! That's it. I can pretend to be your wife.'

'No!' he said firmly. Her lips pursed and she gave him a sulky, reproachful look with those winter-blue eyes beginning to moisten. 'You don't want me to come with you, do you?' He sighed deeply, avoiding those eyes.

'It's not that,' he said as gently as could, 'it's just that … you look like I did a few days ago. You look like a slave.' He paused for effect. 'We would never get away with it. We would both be caught.'

For a few moments there was silence between the two of them, but he could see that she was still deep in thought and hadn't given up trying to persuade him. Finally she sat on the ground and looked up at him coyly. 'If I had a better tunic and a stola with a pretty brooch, sandals, perhaps even a shawl, I would make a very pretty and respectable wife for you. What could be more natural than a merchant on his fine stallion, returning to Massilia with his pretty young wife riding respectfully behind him on her little black mare?'

'Except you can't ride,' he said, adding in perfect innocence 'and where will you get such clothes?'

'You could buy them for me. In Arretium,' she said slowly. His jaw dropped and he stared blankly at her. She gave him a knowing, almost sly look. 'Clodia thought you had a purse of silver. I heard her arguing with Marcus about it.'

Sphax was shocked. 'Did she search through my saddle bags?' he demanded.

'I think she tried, but you disturbed her. She said something about sandals with a lovely silver shell.' He recalled stuffing the red sandals carelessly into one of the bags, so it all made sense.

'Marcus wanted your horse. But Clodia wanted those bags. She wasn't interested in the horse. That's what they were arguing about yesterday morning.' Sphax recalled the argument between them.

'Why didn't you warn me?' he said angrily. She leapt from the ground and confronted him face to face. This girl had a temper that matched his own.

'What could I have said? Me, a slave girl, their servant! You would never have believed me. You would have got me into more trouble. I got this for my pains yesterday morning,' pointing to the ugly red weal on her cheekbone. 'Marcus thought I'd been listening.' Her temper was beginning to cool. 'You don't know what it was like living with those two thieving bastards, they were two wolves from the same litter.'

'I'm sorry,' he admitted, 'you're right, there was nothing you could have done.'

'At least you got the chance to kill Marcus. Give me a knife and I would gladly slit Mistress Clodia's throat.' He knew she meant every word of it.

'Look, we have to get moving, time is pressing— '

'You mean I can come? What do you think of my plan? Nobody would question us if we travelled as man and wife, and you wouldn't have to make up that stupid story about the stallion. Marcus never believed you. He knew you were lying.' Sphax knew she was speaking the truth. She was right. And it was, after all, a good plan. He made up his mind.

'Let's go,' he said, strapping the last bag behind Dido's saddle.

* * *

For the rest of the morning Sphax had more entertainment than he could ever remember. At times his sides ached with pain from his great belly-aching guffaws. If he could have staged such a comedy at the theatre, he would have become the richest man in Rome. The source of all this comedy was Fionn's unparalleled ability to fall off a horse in the most comic and surprising ways. At first she contented herself with the time-honoured tumbles of the novice; slithering to the ground either side of Dido's neck, disappearing backwards from her croup or down either flank. She even managed it when he walked in front holding Dido's rope. But having exhausted these possibilities, she began inventing new and innovative ways of dismounting which became ever more spectacular and astonishing. He had to rescue her from an overhanging branch that had lifted her clean out of the saddle, but it remained a mystery how she'd managed to get turned upside down with her tunic draped over her head. He'd enjoyed lifting the largely naked body down from the branch whilst Fionn, buried under a tangle of tunic, screamed curses at every four legged beast that had ever walked the earth.

When she wasn't falling from the saddle, she was charging off in all directions. Dido had been trained to respond to the subtlest of touches of his thighs, so when gripped in a wrestler's strangle lock, naturally the creature took to her heels in panic. Poor Dido, every time Fionn fell to the ground she would walk over and lick the girl's cheeks tenderly. Dido was braver than him. He stayed well clear of the cursing, red-faced figure beating her fists on the ground like some demented harpie.

The plain fact was that Fionn was the most foul-mouthed, argumentative, stubborn and headstrong person he'd ever met. He might have been talking to the trees for all she listened to his advice. When at last Arretium's red-bricked walls came into sight Fionn seemed almost disappointed when he made her dismount; she'd managed to stay in the saddle for the last two miles.

The city was seething with crowds that morning gathered to celebrate the Cerealia, the festival of Ceres. Sphax was relieved. No one would ever spot them amongst this multitude. Along with their raucous audiences, every square and public space was crammed with acrobats, jugglers, fire eaters or rope walkers. A vast stage had been erected in the centre of the city where dancers and the renowned Etruscan flautists were performing before appreciative crowds. Every street was crammed with parading mothers and daughters garlanded in leaves and spring flowers, carrying bowls of grain before them. He could see from Fionn's wide-eyes that she was entranced by all of this. Every time a fire-eater was about to breathe out a sheet of flame, Fionn would cover her face with her hands in astonishment, or gasp in amazement as a rope walker balanced delicately high above their heads. For Sphax it was a different story. In Rome this evening they would be preparing the burning torches that would be tied to the tails of wild foxes to be released in the Circus. This marked the Cerealia, three days of chariot racing in the Circus, and if Lucilus' team lost, it became for him a festival of beatings and thrashings. He'd never liked the goddess Ceres much.

Neither of them had eaten since yesterday, so eventually their bellies got the better of them and they jostled their way through the crowds to quieter streets in search of a stable. Crowds were no place for horses and made progress painfully slow. By law, merchants and shopkeepers were supposed to honour the goddess and shutter up their premises, but few could resist turning a pretty profit when the streets were so thronged with visitors. As a consequence, nearly every bar and shop in Arretium was open and doing a brisk trade. They soon found stables and hidden in Dido's stall, Sphax removed all the coin from the saddlebags. Seated in a dark corner of a nearby bar they both wolfed down plates of pork and bread he'd ordered. Pouring each of them half a cup of wine he tried to get Fionn to think about the journey ahead. Since they'd sat down her chatter had been full of Thracian tumblers or Nubians breathing out tongues of flame. Such sights were commonplace in Rome, but for Fionn, this was a colourful new world.

'We must get you out of those rags,' he said, 'you're beginning to attract unwelcome attention.'

'Who says it's unwelcome? Anyway, it's not the rags they're ogling,' she added wickedly.

Back on the streets they soon came across a row of shops painted with gaudy designs advertising everything from clothes to jewellery. An elderly matron ushered them inside, keen for their custom and already babbling away about the merits of Apulian wool or hemp from Picenum. Sphax gazed through the open shutters at the folk passing by on the street, shifted his position on the stool he'd been given and began to examine his fingernails. After that he examined his sandals, the roof timbers, the construction of the door frame and finally the mosaic design on the badly pitted tiles. After what seemed an eternity of boredom he was asked to find his purse.

Fionn hurried him out of the shop with a bright blue stola over her arm. Now in a fever of excitement she linked her free arm through his and dragged him down the street to the next doorway. 'I need shoes, some pretty jewellery ... perhaps a palla? No, a cape would be more sensible for riding. With a hood? What do you think?'

He could only think of the prospect of interminable boredom. Reaching into his purse he dug out six silver didrachm, enough to buy up the entire stock on the shelves of the shop they'd just left. Pointing to a wide square down the road he said, 'Meet me there when you've finished. I need to buy a saddle for Arion, food for our journey and some means of cooking. We still have a long way to go, or have you forgotten? Be careful and don't get drawn into conversations.' As he strode off she was still staring dumbstruck at the coins in her palm.

Shadows were beginning to lengthen as Sphax returned to the square. He was burdened with a saddle slung over his shoulder, hemp bags containing everything they would need for the journey and a head full of directions to Pisae. The streets were still thronged with drunken revellers. Anxiously looking around, he didn't recognise her at first. Then he finally noticed the stunningly beautiful young woman in the blue stola with a rose pink cape draped around her shoulders. Fionn was sitting on a bench outside a shop-front and her transformation was nothing short of miraculous. She had even found someone to braid her hair, which she wore plaited in blue cloth around her forehead, fastened with a brass pin and pheasant's feather. Wisps of golden curls had been allowed to escape, drifting on to her shoulders and the nape of her neck. Her cloak was held at the throat by an oval fibula clasp set with blood-red carnelian stones. Sphax just stood in front of her and gaped. She was well aware of the effect she was having on him, and after enjoying the moment for as long as she could tease it out, stuck a tongue out at him and burst out laughing. 'I said I would make you a pretty wife.' But that wasn't enough to break the spell she had just cast on him.

* * *

For the next three days they travelled north along the Cassian through the gently rolling countryside of Etruria with its rich farmland and estates. The road was busy with carriages, merchants and strings of packhorses, but everyone greeted them politely, without the slightest hint of suspicion. Each day was much the same as the last. Awakened by fluting orioles singing from their high perches in the trees, they would set off in the early light, stop whenever hunger or thirst demanded, and make camp before dusk, well out of sight of the great road. On their first night he'd insisted they not make a fire, but the following evening he relented and they were both glad of the hot stew she cooked. Just like him a few days ago, Fionn had never before tasted such rich and varied meats and cheeses. Every evening she would lick her lips in sheer delight and talk of nothing but food until the wine made them both drowsy.

Everything had somehow changed between them; he now felt almost shy and awkward around her. When she caught him silently gazing at her she would lower her eyes or gently smile before turning her head away from him. He wanted to look into those winter-blue eyes for ever, but was at a loss how to tell her or what words to use, so he ached and burned in silence.

On the fourth day they skirted Florentia and followed the broad valley of the Arnus river. They could almost taste the salt on the wind and knew Pisae and the sea were drawing close. Days of experiencing the steady rhythm of hooves on stone had improved Fionn's riding beyond measure. She now sat confidently astride the saddle and had learned to rest her hands on Dido's shoulder and trust to her sure-footed motion. For some reason she now listened intently to Sphax's advice and had mastered bringing the mare to a halt by leaning backwards, or, by shifting her weight forward in the saddle and applying gentle pressure with her knees, raise the pace. On stretches where the ground was flat and the going soft, he led the horses off the Cassian and they practised cantering. He wouldn't risk her falling on the hard surface of the road. Judging from the flushed excitement on her cheeks, he thought she really enjoyed these chases.

As they continued down the broad valley, always with the glittering ribbon of the Arnus to their north, the country grew steadily wilder as woods became forests and rolling hills gave way to rocky outcrops and barren ridges. Occasionally they caught the iridescent flash of blue and orange as parties of bee-eaters flew between the trees. As dusk was gathering they followed a track off the road for a couple of miles and found a sheltered grassy hollow beside a stream. He had lost count of the milestones that day and they were both tired and saddle-sore.

After they'd eaten their fill they sat by the fire drinking wine. Fionn had asked him to describe his mother and father, and tell her something of his life before he was taken as a slave. He spoke of his earliest memories, of the city beyond the mountains that looked out over the sands of the great desert, of the courtyard in their house with its pretty flower beds, pools and running water. He described the excitement everyone felt when a caravan arrived from across the desert, displaying the wealth of ivory and gold in the market place. In the silences he watched her in the flickering firelight, lying on her back with her eyes closed, hands folded over her breasts. He told her of elephants and lions, of the splendour of Carthage, but when it came to his voyage to Corcyra he began to falter and eventually fell silent.

He looked over to her. Somehow she must have sensed his eyes were upon her, for she opened hers and gazed softly up at him, 'I'm so sorry, Sphax, is that where … they were murdered?' He nodded briefly, not trusting himself to speak.

He was almost asleep when he heard the first howling cries. Beside him Fionn tore away her cloak and sat bolt upright, tense, listening. More howls, but they were some way in the distance. 'Sphax! What's that? I'm frightened.' He checked the fire was still blazing away.

'They're only wolves, and they won't come anywhere near our fire,' recalling his own alarm almost a week ago in the forest clearing. 'Don't worry, you're safe with me.' Fionn threw her cape over them both and nestled beside him underneath the toga he always used as a blanket. He could feel the warmth of her body and the touch of her skin. Soon their lips met for the first time as his hands searched beneath her tunic for her breasts, then her thighs and what lay between. Artemis had finally answered his prayers and driven her into his arms.

The sun was already high when they eventually re-joined the great road. After discovering the joys of lovemaking he was in no hurry that morning, so it was late in the afternoon when they caught their first glimpse of Pisae. Beyond its walls, spread out in a vast blue arc lay the glittering sea. Gazing out at that distant blue horizon, lost in the afternoon haze, reminded him that Pisae was not the end of his journey, just the beginning of a new journey, a journey that would be equally fraught with danger. Far more so, he thought, for he was going to war. Fionn was also staring out to sea, lost in thought. He wondered if she had ever seen the sea before. 'My home lies somewhere over that sea,' she said wistfully; 'I will never return to this accursed land.'

THREE

'It's hopeless,' Sphax said angrily. 'Poseidon's becalmed us in this shit-hole and now mocks us with excuses.'

'You're talking in riddles again, my love. I'm just an ignorant barbarian, remember. Speak plain.' Fionn lowered the silver mirror she'd requisitioned from his saddlebag and rose from her seat in the sunlight beside the open shutters.

'Poseidon's our god of the sea,' he said by way of explanation, waving his hand dismissively, 'but that's of no consequence. We could have passage to Corsica or Sardinia, even Rome, but not to where we are going. They're all filthy liars. They are making excuses because they hope to be paid in Roman silver for transporting the consul's legions to Massilia. But I found out this morning that the legions are sailing from Genua, miles away up the coast. Until they realise this, we're stuck here, I'm afraid.'

It was now their third day in Pisae. They had arrived at dusk, found stables and then a room at a grand old hospitia by the Lucca Gate. Early next morning Sphax had found his way down to the quay where the river Auser meets the broader Arnus. He counted eight merchant ships moored alongside; all of them looked high in the water as if awaiting cargoes, so he was hopeful. He tried each captain in turn and every one of them came up with the same set of excuses why they could not sail for Massilia. They could sail, indeed they might well be sailing for that port, but not just yet, not today, not with this wind, without a cargo, ballast, or more silver, always they asked for more silver.

The following morning the excuses had varied a little but the message was exactly the same. That morning a deep-bellied grain ship had tied up. He'd tried his luck with its grizzled old captain with hardly a tooth left to his name and skin the colour of ink-splattered parchment. In speech no better than hissing sibilants, Sphax had made out Corsica and Sardinia, but not Massilia. It was never Massilia.

He'd found a crowded bar behind the warehouses down by the quay and struck up a conversation with a young lad who unloaded cargoes for merchants in the city. For the price of a carafe or two of wine he'd discovered the game the captains were playing. They were hoping to transport grain or hobnails, anything a legion needs on campaign but couldn't carry on their triremes. Rome paid well. But the laugh was on them, he'd told him. 'Yesterday a great fleet of sixty ships was sighted, every warship Rome possesses, and where do you think they were heading?' Sphax had shaken his head. 'Genua!' the lad had spluttered into his cup, finding this a great joke. 'If the captains thought they were sailing from Pisae then the Romans have played them for cocksuckers. As if they would ever use the scum tied up at this quay!'

'And after Genua?' Sphax had asked anxiously. 'Where will they sail for?' The lad had shrugged, indifferently.

'The captains say Massilia. But what do those bastards know!' So, the legions were marching to Genua, then by sea to Massilia. Elpis had been right! It thrilled him to think that Hannibal must be approaching the great river the Greek had mentioned. But it also sent him into paroxysms of frustration.

He'd discovered another infuriating detail that morning; just one of his silver coins was more than generous for passage to Massilia, but if a traveller was dull-witted enough to pay one silver coin, dangled long enough he might be persuaded to part with two. That was the game these thieving captains were playing.

He paced around the room kicking things, taking out his frustration on their sleeping couch and saddlebags. 'That won't help,' Fionn said irritably, 'what good will it do to break a toe? What's a fair price for passage to Massilia?' He told her what the lad had said.

'So, if I offered them three of your silver coins they would agree?'

'No! The cheating bastards would just demand four –'

'You're far too honourable, my love,' she said, raising an eyebrow, 'that's how people trade. Give me three of your coins and I will find us passage.'

He stared at her incredulously. 'If you hand over that much wealth you will never see it again.'

'Who said I was going to hand anything over? They simply have to see the silver in my hand, that's all,' she said coyly. 'Two can play their game.'

He sighed, washing his hands of the whole business. Reaching for his purse he handed over the coins. 'I'll come with you.'

'No!' she said emphatically. 'They've already seen you coming. I'll go alone.'

By the middle of the afternoon she was back.

'We sail tomorrow morning on the tide. The old rogue thinks I'm going to pay him three silver pieces and be his whore for the voyage, all for the passage of two horses and my slave. Won't he have a shock when the slave turns out to be my husband?' She handed him back the silver. 'Arrive late. Just before the tide turns, and make sure you have that sword strapped at your side.'

For a while he just stood there in the middle of the room, speechless in admiration, then he began questioning her about the ship and the arrangements she'd made. It was the captain of the old grain ship she'd struck a bargain with, the one who looked like the backside of a goat with only two teeth to his name. Fionn giggled when she told him the worse that could happen was that she might be sucked to death by the old goat. She had left them loading jars of wine to trade in Massilia. The crew consisted of just four slave boys, too young to make any trouble. With a fair wind they would be there in three days.

As she'd continued talking, Sphax slowly began to remove her garments; starting with her stola then slipping her tunic over her head, next he began untying her breast cloth before finally kneeling before her, kissing her feet and removing her shoes. At no point did she object. He was running his fingernails gently down the lovely curve of her spine when he suddenly had an idea and got up to search through one of the saddlebags. He found what he was looking for and made her stand naked before him, then strapped the dagger, still in its black leather sheath, around her waist. It had done for rat-face, it would easily see off an old goat. He gazed into those winter-blue eyes; 'just in case I'm not there to defend your honour.' She looked like an Amazon, the most brazen and sensuous sight he'd ever beheld, and it inflamed him.

* * *

For someone whose earliest memories were of the endless horizons of the desert, the sea should have held no terrors for him. But it did. It was a question of motion; he was used to the heartbeat motion of feet or hooves on solid ground, not the endless shifting swell of sea-waves. He could never fathom their rhythm or unpredictable motion. He felt helpless as they seemed to grind and churn their way through his bowels. As soon as the ship left the calm of the Arnus and its bowsprit breached the first swell on the open sea he began to turn pale and retch. Moments later he was below deck, kneeling on the straw beneath his horses, spewing up his guts and wishing he'd never been born. And that's where he stayed for the next two days, sharing the straw with his horses and the rats. He was hoping it would ease after a day or so, but it never did. Throughout this trial he barely managed a few mouthfuls of water; the very thought of solid food made him retch.

If he felt like death, Fionn had found her true element. The sea had spoken to something deep within her being. She had become a Nereid, a sea nymph, spending hours standing at the prow beneath the billowing supparum, rejoicing in the salt spray as waves crashed over the bow. On her visits below deck to comfort him she talked of nothing but great fish leaping above the waves or of glittering shoals of mackerel. On the morning of their third day at sea she rushed below deck to his sickbed on the straw. 'Sphax, you must come at once. You must see this for yourself.'

Three days ago when he'd boarded the ship in Pisae, the captain had recognized him and hissed 'So it is you!' Fionn had laughed, and flourishing a hand towards him announced, 'Captain Tarbo, may I present my husband, the renowned horseman, Sphax!' Filling the air around him with spittle, the old goat had yelled 'I've been tricked. I'm not sailing with him.' Sphax had flourished his sword and raised it above the mooring rope. 'Shall I cast off for you, captain, or cut off your ugly head instead? The rope or your neck? Which is it to be?'

But on this third morning of their voyage, as he'd struggled up the steps to reach the upper deck with Fionn's arm around him, he hardly cut a dashing figure, and was in no state to play the hero or defend anyone's honour, let alone his own. Tarbo and his crew knew it, and gave him the sneering looks of disdain they reserved for the most pathetic of landlubbers.

Then he saw for himself the sight Fionn wanted him to witness. Stretching the length of the horizon was a vast fleet of ships, countless, beyond number. On board one of those vessels was a consul of Rome, surrounded by his tribunes and centurions. This irresistible force had sailed for one purpose only: to destroy the armies of Carthage. He must reach Hannibal and warn him. And soon!

Seeing that vast armada brought him to his senses. This was no time to be skulking below deck. He had to stop this bellyaching and get a grip of himself. Those red-sailed ships on the horizon were now his enemy. At that moment the grain ship plunged into a deep sea-trough with the white swan's neck at its stern rearing into the air as the deck yawed and careered first one way, then the other. Despite gut-wrenching tugs deep inside his belly he managed to stay on his feet and stagger down the deck to where Tarbo was standing between the steering oars.

Drawing his sword he pointed it at the horizon and yelled 'Where are they making for? Massilia?' Captain Tarbo spat, ignoring him completely, eyes fixed upon the next set of waves the old hulk would have to negotiate.

'Shorten sail,' he screamed at one of his boys already scampering towards a rope attached to a flapping sail. For the next few moments Sphax was content just to stay on his feet as the ship wrestled with a rising south-easterly that was spewing foam-crested waves over her bow. In the time it took to saddle and bridle a horse the squall gathered in violence. As they breasted each successive wave he caught fleeting glimpses of a green headland in the distance. With a supreme effort he forced himself to scan the western horizon before the ship plunged into the next trough. The fleet was still there, but disappearing rapidly. He was clinging for dear life to the deck cabin below the steering platform when Fionn joined him.

'I can see land ahead. Not far now,' she yelled above the cacophony. They were flying before the wind, masts and yards creaking and groaning, straining with each successive blast from the rising tempest. Around him the sea had turned white. Blue had been banished from this watery world. Wherever he looked there was only foam-flecked white or brooding grey clouds.

Even an ignorant landlubber like himself could see that if the ship suddenly yawed sideways and met a wave amidships she would be instantly deluged and sink like a stone. Then the heavens opened, the rain lashing their faces. Before he and Fionn took refuge deep inside the deck cabin he caught sight of the hooded Tarbo standing resolutely on the platform above, eyes fixed on some unseen horizon, outstretched hands gripping the steering oars as the wind and rain lashed down on him.

With his back jammed tight against one corner of the cabin, Sphax closed his eyes and began praying silently to every god Elpis had ever mentioned. Starting with Artemis, he'd got as far as Hera when they suddenly reached calmer waters where the vessel was no longer at the mercy of the tempest. He followed Fionn onto the deck and saw they'd rounded a headland that was sheltering them from the worst of the south-easterly. It was still raining heavily, but no longer lashing their faces. Scampering around, the crew were adjusting the yards and ropes of the great square sail.

Fionn was shouting and pointing at something in the distance. Her sight was much sharper than his, but in a few moments he too was able to make out the shapes of houses and buildings rising above the shoreline. It must be Massilia, he thought. Crossing the deck he peered out at the sea to the south-west. They had entered a vast bay, but there was no sign of the Roman fleet. It seemed to have vanished, or been swallowed up in the maelstrom.

Tarbo was as ill-tempered as ever, yelling a stream of instructions to his crew laced with curses and threats. He seemed to be setting a new course which followed the shoreline and required constant adjustment to sails and rigging. The rain and wind was easing. Sphax joined him on the steering platform and asked him about the Roman fleet. Tarbo ignored him. Sphax repeated his question but was again ignored. Losing patience he turned on him; 'If you want to get paid, old man, you will answer me.'

Tarbo shot him a furious look, hawked and spat on the deck. 'They'll be in the sheltered waters of the Rhodanus by now, out of harm's way. What's it to you anyway?' It was Sphax's turn to ignore a question. But at least he'd discovered something important; the Roman fleet was not heading for Massilia after all, but sailing directly into the great river itself. Sphax prayed that the armies of Carthage had already crossed the river and the Romans would arrived too late to intervene. He climbed down from the platform and joined Fionn at the bow, gazing at the city where they were about to berth.

He did pay Tarbo, but only because he recalled the sight of him standing four-square against the tempest on his steering platform and decided he owed him something more than fair passage. As he led the horses up a makeshift wooden ramp to the stone quay above he tossed the old goat two silver coins for his trouble. It was not enough, of course. He and Fionn grinned at one another as they heard him spraying blood-curdling curses at them as they led their horses down the quayside.

* * *

Visitors were not permitted to bear arms in Massilia, so he had to hand over his sword at the gate before they were allowed to enter. It was of no consequence, he had such little skill with the thing. So far its only purpose had been to frighten old men. Besides, by that time he would have surrendered far more than a sword for the relief of walking on ground that didn't sway and shift under his feet. Fionn still carried his dagger hidden under her tunic, so it went unnoticed. Within a few moments he'd heard the tongues of half a dozen languages, though Greek predominated. Like Rome, it seemed all the world came to trade with Massilia. Thanks to Airla and Elpis, Greek was almost his second tongue.

The city itself was built on a rocky tongue of land that rose steeply from the harbour so that it was surrounded on three sides by the sea. There was something familiar about its tiered terraces rising from the waves. It was only later he recalled the summer he'd spent in a house at the top of the great stone staircase in Carthage, overlooking its harbours. The hills above Massilia rose to a ridge crowned by the temples of Apollo and Artemis. On their first evening in the city he'd left their room in the stabulae and walked in the moonlight to the top of the ridge. He knew he was forbidden to enter the sanctuary of the goddess, but beyond the colonnaded facade he found an open door and there was no sign of priests or servants. Inside, candles and burning oil lamps cast a soft mysterious light on the columns and friezes, throwing flickering shadows on the walls and ceiling. He felt uneasy, unsure. Then he saw her.

At the far end of the temple, between two huge marble columns linked to create a sculptured archway, stood an ebony statue of Artemis beside a stag. It was enormous, at least three times his own height, and the most lifelike figure he'd ever seen. It was as if the goddess was about to take the arrow from the quiver slung over her shoulder and let go the stag's antlers she held in her left hand. The goddess seemed to be smiling down at him beneficently, or was this just his imagination? Standing beneath that gaze he seemed so small and insignificant; a miserable flea that could be crushed between her fingers. He evoked a silent prayer before placing the dagger he'd taken from Fionn, reverently at the feet of the goddess. He left the temple silently and unseen.

The night air was chilly and Fionn's warm, naked body was calling to him, so he walked briskly down the hill in the darkness. He knew what Elpis would have said to him: 'The goddess is not a person like you or me, Sphax, but a mysterious force which acts upon the world. To understand the gods we need to study these forces, not offer them wine or foolish sacrifice. To my knowledge the gods don't eat!' But ever since he'd awoken to find himself staring down the throat of that wild boar, a doubt had arisen in his mind, nagging away at him. Boars were the creatures of Artemis, she hunted them, slew them. But she also commanded them. Had she sent a sign to him that morning, a warning? Was she displeased with him for killing Marcellus? He couldn't be sure. He would never be sure. But he wasn't taking any chances. Best to hedge his bets. That's why he'd laid the dagger that had slain Marcellus Lucilus at the feet of Artemis, as an offering, an appeasement. Just in case Elpis was wrong.

Even before they had eaten breakfast the next morning Sphax had gathered all the information he needed. The arrival of Hannibal's army north of Avenio and Consul Publius Cornelius Scipio's two Roman legions anchored in the Rhodanus was common knowledge and the talk of the city. Foolishly, Massiliots were convinced that Hannibal had come to lay siege to their city.

Even with two Roman legions camped down the road, the city was still in a state of near panic. Soldiers were everywhere and there was talk of a long siege. He'd seen for himself that Massilia's walls and defences were formidable, and its harbour, sheltered as it was by a natural amphitheatre of rock, could have supplied a garrison for years. And yet the fear in the streets was palpable. Hannibal was coming! Such was the reputation of the Carthaginian after the brutal sacking of Saguntum.

By mid-morning crowds were gathering at the western gate to welcome a Roman Consul into the city for the first time in years. Fionn pointed out a deputation of toga-clad senators hurrying down the street to join the throng at the gate. They decided it was time to leave. Whilst Fionn bought enough food to keep them on the road for three days, he returned to the gate by the harbour to recover his sword, deciding he might need it after all. By midday they were riding through Massilia's northern gate as the brothers Scipio were being carried through the western gate on their magisterial chairs, preceded by files of lictors.

Whilst the consul would be greeted by adoring crowds, Fionn worried about their reception when they eventually met up with Hannibal's fearsome army. 'How can you be so certain we'll be welcomed, Sphax? We're both dressed as respectable citizens of Rome. Surely they'll think we're spies, and kill us.'

'I speak their language and they will have heard of my mother and father. Trust me, we will be welcomed as honoured guests,' he replied confidently.

'There's something you're not telling me. Isn't there?' She was studying his face carefully.

'You'll have to wait and see, won't you,' he laughed. They were riding side by side on a good track, not up to the standards of a paved Roman road, but surfaced with crushed stone and ditched on either side. He was keeping half an eye on the position of the sun. After leaving the city behind, the road had bent towards the northwest, so unless it changed direction again he was content to follow it. A few miles further on the road did turn abruptly northeast, so they left it and followed little-used paths that led them into a wilderness of heaths and woods of stunted juniper. For two days they journeyed through a land the like of which Sphax had never encountered before. It was parched and desert-dry of watercourses, a land of wild ravines and craggy limestone escarpments bleached white by the summer's sun. Eagles and vultures soared on the up-draughts and lynx stalked amongst the groves of wild almonds and cypresses.

Water became a problem. Whenever they came upon a farm or a cluster of houses Sphax begged water and they filled every vessel they possessed. But these white-stoned farms and hamlets were far and few between in this barren landscape where only gnarled olives and almonds thrived. Back in Massilia he'd been told that this was also the territory of the Volcae, whose folk made a living trading and fishing by the great river, but so far they hadn't seen any signs of them or their settlements.

On the third morning in the wilderness they caught their first sight of the great river to the west. They had camped beneath a rocky crag whose bleached white rock had been weathered and sculptured into fantastical shapes and contours. Climbing to the top gave them a panoramic view of the country. Fionn, whose eyes were much keener than his, pointed to something glinting in the northwest. 'That must be Avenio. What do you think?' she added, 'a day's ride?'

At that moment he was more interested in the cloud of dust that was being kicked up by something in the plain far to the south. Squinting, he asked 'What do you make of that?' Fionn followed his gaze. 'Horses ... lots of them.'

'Are you sure?' he said, suddenly alarmed.

'Certain! Hundreds of them, riding north.'

'They can't be from Hannibal's army, they're at least a day's ride north of us, on the other side of the river. Dog's twat!' he cursed, 'they must be Roman. What can you see? Look closely, girl!'

'Sphax! They're miles away. I've good eyes, but ...' Shading her eyes from the sun she stared unblinking into the distance. 'I can see something red ... cloaks? Helmets? Definitely shields and spears.'

'Roman cavalry,' he said, now certain, 'scouting ahead, looking for Hannibal. We must leave now. We haven't a moment to lose.'

They rode north, keeping to the heathland high above the water meadows that bordered the great river. Over such broken ground their progress was not as swift as it would have been if they'd descended to the plain, but it meant they could keep the Roman cavalry in their sights at all times. He felt so proud of Fionn. With flushed cheeks and a look of grim determination she bent and swayed in the saddle, matching Dido's gait and rarely trailing more than a few steps behind the fast pace he was setting on Arion. For half the morning they managed to stay well ahead of the Roman cavalry. Before them lay a hill topped by another white escarpment of rock. He urged the stallion to a canter and sped for the top. At the summit he quickly dismounted and, shielding his eyes from the sun, watched the progress of the cavalrymen. They had now split up into three parallel columns, but there seemed to be no urgency about their riding. Neither could he see scouts riding ahead.

When Fionn arrived with Dido he helped her from the saddle and led her to a shaded place in the lee of a huge rock. 'Rest for a while. We're well ahead of them now.' He found a flask of water, bread, and the last of the cheese. Sitting with her back against the rock she smiled her appreciation. It was hot that morning. After a few miles her woollen stola had disappeared into the saddlebag and she was now stripped down to her linen tunic. Even so, she looked hot and flushed as beads of sweat gathered on her forehead. In a natural trough that had been weathered in the rock he poured out the last of their flasks of water so the horses could drink. That left them with Fionn's flask, but there was nothing he could do. The horses' needs came first.

Fionn soon joined him, much recovered, and together they watched the steady approach of cavalry from the south. 'Can you see anything to the north?' he asked. Scrambling over rocks and boulders she made her way to the other side of the escarpment. Moments later she was yelling 'Come, Sphax. Quickly! You must see this.' Vaulting the boulders he rushed to her side. Barring their path to the north lay another broad river whose waters branched into a myriad channels before entering the great river. It was not the sight of the river that had caused her excitement, but what was crossing it. To Sphax they looked like specks of dust, but they were moving. 'What can you see?'

'Groups of horsemen splashing across the river. Hundreds of them.'

'Describe them?'

'Well, they haven't got helmets like the Romans.' Fionn was aware she was rapidly using up her military vocabulary. 'They have little spears though, and round shields.' She suddenly smiled at him, astonished. 'They're dark like you, Sphax!'

'Can you see saddles?' now barely able to contain his excitement.

'That's strange,' she puzzled, 'they're riding without them.'

His heart leapt with joy! 'That's because they are Numidians. Like me!' A wave of ecstatic euphoria surged through him. He had found Hannibal. His journey was over. He was back amongst his own people. He had that joyous feeling of coming home. At last he felt truly free.

Like swarms of bees leaving a hive, the horsemen crossed the river and then in small knots surged forwards, not waiting for the others. There must be a limited number of fords, he realised, for more than three-quarters of their number remained on the far bank, waiting to cross. With a sickening jolt he remembered the Roman cavalry, recalled their disciplined columns. Rank upon rank of them. Racing to the other side of the escarpment he saw they were still some way off to the south, but they'd quickened their pace and he could now see scouts riding well ahead of the columns. There was going to be a battle!

Yelling for Fionn to join him he started to tear away at the straps and buckles that secured the saddle and bags to Dido. He strapped everything on to Arion's solid rump before removing the sword and buckling it around his waist. 'What are you doing?' she asked in alarm.

'What do you think I'm doing? Those are my people down there! There's a column of Roman cavalry heading their way. I have to warn them.'

'Please don't go' she begged, 'you may get hurt …' Nodding in the direction of the Numidians, 'You're not a soldier like them.'

'Don't worry, I'm just going to warn them,' he lied. Battle was certain. He knew it. He would have to fight. By the gods he wanted to fight! These were *his* people. 'Arion isn't trained to my touch yet so I'll ride Dido. Lead Arion to the bottom of this cliff. Don't try to ride him. Stay out of sight, hidden. Wait for me there.' He could see the tears beginning to well. He gripped her shoulders and looked fiercely into those winter-blue eyes. 'I swear to you by everything I hold sacred, I will return and find you. Dearest Fionn, I swear this.' With that he leapt on to the mare's unencumbered back and rode off at speed.

His worst fear was that small groups of Numidians would just blunder into the organised ranks of Roman cavalry and be swallowed up and overwhelmed. Sphax guessed that by the time he reached them, large numbers would still be waiting to cross the river. He hadn't even reached the grassland at the foot of the hill before events began unfolding exactly as he'd feared. It was now too late to warn them! Roman columns were manoeuvring into three separate lines whilst the Numidians charged furiously. What Fionn had described as little spears turned out to be wooden javelins, and now they were launching them at their enemies before nimbly turning their horses and riding away. Roman saddles were being emptied, but the attacks were being delivered by no more than three or four horsemen at a time, pinpricks that did little to disrupt the iron discipline shown in the Roman ranks. Sphax knew that when the Romans delivered their charge it would be like an irresistible wave that would sweep everything before it.

At last he reached the flat of the grassland. Urging Dido forward he rode like the wind, but he was still half a mile from the fight. At that moment the humid air echoed with the chilling sound of blaring trumpets as the entire mass of Roman cavalry surged forward into the charge, and the ground shook and trembled.

Like a great wave beating on a shoreline, the momentum of that charge swept aside the knots of Numidians. Its tide surged ever onwards, isolating and surrounding each new pocket of resistance whilst the reserve lines added their weight to the press or flowed on to the flanks of the now desperate Numidians.

Without thinking he drew his sword and charged the nearest Romans encircling a group of Numidians clustered around their crescent standard. Dido carved a path for him between two red-cloaked cavalrymen and Sphax slashed out at an arm, then a helmet. Bursting through the circle of Romans he halted and swivelled Dido around. The terrified young boy holding the standard was being assailed by three Romans hacking away at him. Sphax picked up Dido's pace and charged, but instead of slashing, this time thrust the blade into the exposed space below a Roman shield. There was a cry of agony and the man slid from his saddle.

Sphax joined another sword-wielding Numidian, but it was too late to save the boy holding the standard. A vicious slash from a blade almost severed his neck, spewing blood over Dido as he careered backwards from his mare. Now screaming with a rage that Sphax had never before experienced, he scythed his sword at the man who'd killed the boy, but the Roman parried skilfully with his shield. As Sphax recovered his balance he saw the man's sword was raised and about to split open his skull. Thrusting himself backwards on to Dido's croup the mare instantly responded, stepping backwards so the sword met empty air. A javelin whistled past him, striking the man in the jaw so powerfully that the iron tip emerged from his neck.

Sphax felt a sudden agonizing pain in his right thigh that made him cry out. Dido had instinctively began turning to face this new assailant and her movement had undoubtedly saved his life, for the spear point had been aimed at his belly. But now the Roman was unbalanced, his shield the wrong side of his body and spear-arm extended. Sphax slashed down on the arm that was holding the spear and almost severed it.

The Numidian beside him yelled, 'Keep your horse moving, lad. To stand still is to die!' It seemed like good advice. Blood was trickling down his thigh and the pain burned. More javelins sailed past, many finding flesh and bone. Someone had dismounted and seized the standard from the dead boy's hand. Another Numidian armed with a sword joined them. 'When I shout, we turn and ride as if we've got a lightning bolt up our arse. Got that, lad?' Sphax nodded and guessed the Numidian who'd been fighting alongside him was an officer. The Romans had backed off, out of javelin range, but it would be a fleeting respite: he could see they were lining up for a second charge, this time with even greater numbers.

'NOW!' The three of them turned their horses and fled. Taking this to be a general signal, the eight men who'd been hurling javelins over their shoulders turned and followed, carrying the standard with them. After galloping for half a mile they stopped in front of a fresh body of horsemen arriving on the field. Someone tossed him a javelin which he failed to catch, causing much hilarity. How could they laugh at a time like this, he marvelled?

'Mago. Malchus. Take your eshrins to the left and harry from the flanks. And line up, you arseholes! No more pisspot attacks in twos and threes. Do *not* close with them. Do you hear me?' It was the officer again, barking orders, riding amongst his men, patting backs and ruffling hair. He could see why they would follow him. From his voice to his noble bearing and powerful physique he exuded confidence and authority. Sphax guessed he was old, at least forty, and there was something wild and feral in that expression, yet those piercing grey eyes spoke also of compassion and wisdom. He wore his braided hair gathered tightly in a knot above his head and the hem and sleeves of his tunic were tasselled in gold thread. Sphax was amazed how quickly he seemed to restore order and confidence. The officer rode over to him. 'Who are you? I've never seen you before,' he said.

'I'm Sphax. I've ridden for weeks to join you.'

'Well you've chosen the wrong day for it,' he said drily, and everyone around him started laughing. 'You better stay close to me, lad.'

Forty riders had already ridden off at high speed. He guessed these were the eshrins of Mago and

Malchus. Whatever an eshrin was! Perhaps forty men remained. Someone handed him a shield and a couple of javelins. Bound in hide, the circular shield was quite light for its size, but along with the javelins, he'd never felt so encumbered on the back of a horse.

Horsemen were joining them all the time. Some, like his group, had managed to break out of encirclements and flee, whilst others had finally managed to cross the river to join them. 'Adherbal,' the officer shouted at a man leading horsemen back from the fight, many wounded and covered in blood. 'Take your men back across the fords and prepare an ambush. Collect any you meet along the way and stop the rest from crossing. We'll lead the Romans onto your javelins.'

'It will be my pleasure, Sir,' answered Adherbal. The survivors were now being roughly marshalled into three ragged lines, one behind the other. Numidians didn't seem to care much about dressed ranks. There must have been over eighty horsemen by now. The officer rode to their front. 'We're not going to behave like virgins in a whorehouse today, are we?' This must have been a familiar jibe for everyone started chuckling. 'Today we are going to be disciplined. You have already heard my plan. We lead them on to Adherbal's javelins on the other side of the river. Let's go and kill Romans!' Everyone started cheering and drumming their javelins against shields. The officer rode over to Sphax and asked if he'd ever used a javelin. Ashamed to speak, Sphax lowered his eyes and shook his head.

'Then you better use your prick, lad, because you're like a woman with that sword.' The men around him started laughing again, slapping him on the back as if he'd received a generous compliment. How pleasant it felt to be back amongst his own people! And then he realised he'd heard and spoken the first words of his mother tongue since the murder of his parents ten years ago. Sphax asked the man beside him who the officer was. The Numidian looked astounded by the question. 'Why, that's Maharbal,' he said.

The Romans were drawing close. But they'd lost all semblance of cohesion by now and were trotting forward as a chaotic mass of horses, urged on by officers in fancy plumed helmets, bronze cuirasses and leopard-skin saddle cloths. On their flank, Mago's and Malchus's horsemen were already snapping away at their heels, delivering volleys of javelins and then riding smartly away.

Sphax was in the third rank. He watched anxiously as the front rank surged forward in line, quickly gaining speed before hurling their javelins into the mass of Romans then turning and cantering back to the rear through the gaps in the lines. In this way the first rank became the third rank, giving horses time to recover before the next charge. After the next rank delivered their volley and retreated to the rear he could see the devastating effect these tactics were having on the enemy. Javelins hurled with force from a galloping horse were a dreadful weapon; be it iron, bronze or mail, they could pierce any metal forged by a blacksmith. In the hands of skilled horsemen who had trained their mounts to change direction within six strides, his people had been forged into a formidable weapon.

By now the enemy had ground to a halt. Each charge had delivered a fresh harvest of death. He guessed that Roman legions had rarely faced such tactics. They looked unsure and at a loss. His line had now become the front rank, about to charge. Sphax mopped the blood from his throbbing thigh with his tunic and tried to ignore the sickening lump of fear in his gut. With his heart pounding he prepared Dido to charge. At that moment a restraining hand gripped his shoulder. 'Not you lad, it would just be a waste of a javelin. You stay with me.' Sphax felt a flush of shame, but could see the sense in this as he watched his rank charge forward and deliver another devastating volley. In the space of three charges they'd emptied at least forty Roman saddles. 'What do you think they'll do now?' Maharbal mused.

'Oh, they'll charge. Believe me, Sir, they'll charge. They're such arrogant bastards! They won't be able to bear the humiliation we're inflicting on them.' Until that moment, Sphax hadn't realised the depth of hatred he felt for all Romans.

And that was exactly what happened next. Out-fought by these tactics, the Romans did what they always did; use the sheer weight of numbers to crush their enemies. As the next wave of Numidians charged, they met it head on with a charge of their own, swamping the horsemen and giving them little time to release their javelins. But it didn't stop there. The Roman horde thundered on, spreading out onto the flanks. Sphax knew they were outnumbered at least ten to one.

Maharbal was screaming at the last two ranks to turn and flee, whilst at the same time waving his javelin in the air to signal Mago and Malchus to do the same. But it was too late.

Sphax almost fell from Dido with the force of a spear that suddenly tore into his shield. Then the Roman ranks were on top of them. Drawing his sword he wildly slashed out at arms, necks or any flesh that came within reach of his blade, but he rarely drew blood. Everywhere became a seething, almost senseless mass of men and horses, a life and death struggle fought amidst the noise of war, the cacophony of screams, curses and wounded horses driven into frenzies of pain. They were so densely packed together that it became almost impossible to swing a sword. Men fell bleeding or dying from their mounts only to be crushed underfoot in the press. He'd once heard Arion scream, but that morning he heard that blood-chilling sound countless times. There was a reek to it all. It filled his nostrils. Not just the stench of blood and gore, but of bowels, pierced or slashed open, the stink of urine, shit and horseflesh. For that thin line of Numidians, wearing light tunics and armed only with shields and javelins, a close quarter fight with an enemy protected by armour and wielding swords and spears meant certain death. They were soon surrounded. Then the Romans began butchering at leisure.

Sphax had been urging Dido backwards, but now there was nowhere to go. There could be no escape. Sword and spear thrusts were coming from all directions. Thrashing his sword in a wild frenzy he knew the end was near. Maharbal seemed to be in the grip of a wild madness, ferociously slaying any Roman that dared approach him. Maharbal was keeping them both alive. For now. But death was still certain, only moments away. Then, in the next breath, there were Numidians to his left and behind him. A gap had suddenly been torn open through that circle of death and they seized it, fleeing for their lives. Only Sphax, Maharbal and perhaps a score of horsemen managed to escape the butchery.

They had been saved by Mago. Instead of fleeing as he'd been ordered, he and Malchus had seen what was about to happen and led their forty men in a succession of desperate charges to break through to Maharbal. Sphax would discover in time that the Numidians loved their general and would risk their lives to save him. In one of those charges brave Malchus had been gutted by a Roman spear.

They halted about a mile beyond the Romans. Most of their horses were blown, and at best would only be able to manage a trot in retreat. A rider had already been sent back to the fords to check that Adherbal had set the ambush and to access the numbers he'd gathered. Maharbal and Mago were silently watching the Romans whilst the rest of them slumped exhausted on their mares. Sphax was still shaking uncontrollably with fear and his thigh throbbed with pain. To try and calm his nerves he started counting. There were twenty-seven of them left.

It took the Romans some time to organise a pursuit. Their men and horses looked as exhausted as the Numidians, and their ranks were in chaos after that last charge. But Sphax knew the Romans. They would smell blood. They would want to return to the camp of Consul Publius Cornelius Scipio in triumph with a trophy or two, having annihilated the Numidians.

Adherbal himself rode back to them with ten of his horsemen. All the men around him nudged their horses closer so they could hear what he had to say. Adherbal was staring at their sombre faces, saddened and shocked. Addressing Maharbal he said, 'So few ... so few of you have survived.' For a moment he was unable to speak. 'I'm sorry, general,' he continued, then gazed back to where the Romans were forming up. 'I've left many good men back there.' Returning his gaze to the general a grim smile slowly gathered at the corners of his mouth. 'The trap is set,' he said firmly, 'I have three hundred and sixty men awaiting Rome's pleasure. It's perfect country. I could hide an army back there. Once they've crossed it, none of those cocksukers will get back across that river.' He glanced in the direction of the Romans, 'Not before we turn it red with their blood.'

Astride his grey Egyptian mare, Maharbal had listened in grim silence. Now he looked up at them, casting an eye over all the men gathered around him. Finally he spoke.

'We have all lost friends and comrades,' he said quietly. 'Good friends. Dear friends. Numidians!' His eyes suddenly flashed and his tone became hard. 'We must avenge them. It is our sacred duty. Praise ba 'al hamūn, we owe them that. Will you follow me once more?'

Sphax could see that this was not a time to thump shields, but all around him heads were nodding in solemn agreement. They set off at a walk. Some of the horses couldn't manage much more than that. Adherbal led the way with Maharbal and Mago in the rear, keeping an eye on the Romans. None of the officers tried to organize them into any kind of order. Sphax guessed Maharbal wanted to give the Romans the impression they were just beaten survivors retreating back to camp. Which was close to the truth ... for now. He couldn't resist looking back occasionally to check on the progress of the enemy, but none of the men around him bothered.

The Romans had taken the bait. They were following, and gaining on them.

As they approached the river he could see that the country beyond was studded with scrubby thickets and dense stands of willow. Guides had been posted at the fording points and led them over in three small groups. The river wasn't particularly deep, but in places the current was treacherously swift. Gaining the far bank Sphax swivelled around to see how close the Romans were. He had to admire the Numidians' coolness and nerve. The enemy were already gathering in large numbers on the far bank waiting to cross, yet none of the men around him seemed in the least concerned, or suggested quickening the pace.

It was only after they'd left the river behind that he started to notice them. It came as a shock, for they were so well hidden amongst clumps of willow, thickets and folds in the ground. Almost all of the horses were lying flat on the ground, their riders crouched beside them clutching shields and javelins. A shiver of excitement began to run through him. It must have been evident to the man riding beside him for he grinned and said quietly, 'Remember we're being watched, lad. Don't look around. Just keep going.' But it was difficult to hide his excitement. So far his count had reached sixty horsemen waiting to strike back, and those were the ones he could see! 'When will the order come?' he said to the man riding beside him. 'We must be at least half a mile beyond the river by now.'

'Easy, lad. All in good time. We want them shitting themselves trying to get back across that river. That's where we'll do the real killing.' Sphax was beginning to understand.

No signal was ever given. Not even a single battle cry was uttered by a Numidian. The ambush was sprung in deadly silence.

Now all was drowned out by the drumming of hundreds of hooves. The men around him also heard the sound and without a word, halted, turned their horses, and as a single body began trotting back to the river. Not knowing what to do, Sphax followed them. Within a few strides they started to pass riderless horses. Roman stallions with saddles, bridles and reins. A little further on they came upon the first of the dead and wounded strewn across the track. Wounded Romans were finished off with a javelin. No mercy was shown that day. As for the dead, they were instantly stripped of anything of value. By the time they caught sight of the river, most of the men around him were sporting the most splendid and expensive paraphernalia of war that Roman craftsmen could manufacture. One horseman was even wearing the white-tasselled helmet of a tribune.

As he approached the river bank, he let Dido delicately pick her own way through the carpet of Roman dead. Numidians also lay there, but mercifully few. The swift channels of the river itself had become the killing ground, where the slaughter had taken place. Littered all around him was the wreckage of war: splintered shields, discarded swords, spears and javelins, helmets pierced or crushed or simply cast aside in the stampede to escape. Then there were the bodies, human and animal. As Adherbal had sworn, in places the water did indeed run red with Roman blood.

On the grassland plain beyond the river, scattered bodies lay javelin-skewered on the grass, marking the course of the enemies' headlong flight as clearly as milestones on a Roman road. Half a mile further on Sphax caught sight of the Numidians returning triumphantly from their pursuit of the Romans. Maharbal, alongside his officers, was in the lead. Behind him he had over two hundred horsemen flushed and exalted from the chase. Maharbal halted his Egyptian mare beside Dido. 'Well, master Sphax. I'm pleased to see you're still alive.'

'Thanks to you, Sir. If I hadn't stayed beside you I would be dead by now.'

'Nonsense! You have courage and spirit, all you need now is a little skill. Are you going to join my people?'

'If you think I'm worthy, Sir?'

'Then welcome, lad. I'd be pleased to have you. Fall in with my men.'

'I must first ride back and find my woman.' Sphax pointed to the limestone escarpment far to the south. Maharbal was grinning at him.

'I hope she's better with a javelin than you?'

'I don't think so, Sir. She's a Gaul. But I also have a gift for Hannibal back there.' Suddenly curious, Maharbal raised his eyebrows. 'Arion,' Sphax said proudly, 'the finest warhorse in Rome. I trained him myself.'

'Manissa, Arobel,' Maharbal shouted at two of his men. 'When he's found his lady, escort this lad across the river and back to our camp. Bring him to my pavilion.' With that Maharbal signalled his men forward.

Manissa and Arobel were not pleased to be nursemaiding a young lad ten years their junior. Their minds were set on filling their bellies and getting drunk back at camp, but they made the best of it and were soon questioning him about his journey and the life he'd led in Rome. Both of them were curious about the city, especially its wealth. Retracing the path he'd taken early that morning took much longer than he remembered. In his anxiety to warn the Numidians he hadn't realised the miles he'd covered.

It was late in the afternoon when he caught sight of her. She hadn't stayed at the foot of the white cliff as he'd asked her to, but had led Arion down on to the plain where the battle had taken place. He saw Arion first. Fionn was kneeling over the Numidian dead sprawled on the grass, examining each body in turn as if searching for something. In a world of her own, she hadn't heard them approaching. He leapt from Dido and ran towards her. At last Fionn saw him and got to her feet. She looked wild, distraught, and he could see she had been weeping. Neither of them spoke, he reached out and they clung to one another.

* * *

Darkness had fallen when they eventually reached the Carthaginian camp. He'd ridden Arion, sitting Fionn in front of him. Dido was spent and could barely keep up, let alone bear a rider. After Fionn had bound his wounded thigh they hardly exchanged a word on the journey. It was enough for Fionn to feel the strength of his arms around her and the warmth of his breath on her neck.

Crossing the Rhodanus had been an ordeal for the Numidians. Arobel told them there were Volcae warriors defending the river bank opposite their camp. They had evaded them by riding far to the south at first light, then crossed the river by a fleet of boats, swimming their mares behind them. Arobel prayed fervently to the gods that the Numidians had left boats behind for them to re-cross the great river. In the twilight amongst the reeds and swampy ditches beside the river it was difficult to find anything, let alone a boat. Then Manissa, scouting ahead, shouted for them to join him. Arobel's prayers had been answered. Not only was there a boat, but Maharbal had also left them friendly Gauls to row them across to the safety of the opposite bank. Arion and the Numidians' horses were strong enough to swim the river, but Sphax was unwilling to risk Dido. Luckily their ferry was a large trading vessel that could easily accommodate the exhausted mare. After transferring their saddlebags and sacks to the boat, Sphax and the Numidians held the guide ropes over the side and let the horses swim whilst the Gauls rowed steadily. Once across the river they could see the welcome sight of campfires a few miles to the north.

Maharbal's pavilion was well lit and spacious, but sparsely and simply furnished with a sleeping divan, smaller couches for guests and a low table that had been lavishly spread with wine, bread and cold delicacies.

Other than shields and weapons, the only other item of furniture was a large cedar chest, the size of a man's coffin, elaborately carved with emblems of griffons and chimeras. A Seleucid carpet, rich in cochineal dyes, kept out the rising evening chill. Except for a *lebbade* peaked Phoenician cap in red and gold, Maharbal was wearing the same clothes he'd fought in all day. Sphax remembered his father wearing such a cap on visits to Carthage. Greeting them warmly, the general beckoned them to a couch.

'This is Fionn, Sir. A Gaul from the northern lands.' Fionn threw back the rose pink hood of her cape and the lamplight caught the wisps of golden hair as they fell on her neck and shoulders. Fionn wondered if she should bow, but in the end just smiled a shy greeting in the general's direction.

'Now I understand why this young pup was so eager to go back and find you this afternoon.' Fionn started to flush and lowered her eyes. 'Please take a seat, my dear, you must be weary after the trials of a day such as this.' A pretty servant girl brought cups for wine and offered bowls of olives and almonds. 'Tell me something of your history, young man, and of your journey to join us.'

As briefly as the painful account would allow, Sphax described the life he'd led as a slave in Rome, training Gaius Lucilus's horses for racing in the Campus and the Circus. Maharbal listened intently, occasionally questioning a detail or asking for elaboration. As Sphax begun describing the Roman fleet they had sighted before the storm, the general got to his feet. 'I think it certain they are anchored in the mouth of the Rhodanus,' Sphax told him. 'Also,' he continued, 'it was the talk of Massilia that consul Publius Cornelius Scipio had arrived with two legions. He and his brother were being welcomed into the city as Fionn and I left.'

With a grim smile Maharbal said 'You, boy, have found out what I and my Numidians failed to do. We must go at once to Hannibal and report this. He will question you. Be ready with answers.' To the servant girl he said 'Escort this young lady to the tent we prepared,' and glancing at Fionn apologetically added, 'I'm sorry my dear, but this matter cannot wait.' As they were leaving the tent Maharbal asked 'Who were your parents, lad? Do you know?'

'My father was Navaras, a Numidian prince; my mother, Similce, daughter of Hamilcar Barca.'

Maharbal stopped dead in his tracks and stared at him. 'No! That cannot be.'

PART TWO

THE RISING
OF THE
CAVARI

FOUR

'Uncle!'

There was a look of total astonishment in Hannibal's milky grey eyes. 'It is I, Sphax, the son of your sister Similce. Navaras was my father. I am your nephew.'

The circle of faces reflected in the golden light of the oil lamps froze to a man, transfixed, gaping at him in stunned silence. It took Hannibal some time to reply, and when he did eventually speak his voice was cold and distant, as if recalling a memory so painful it had long since been banished from his mind. 'Then I am looking upon a shade. My dearest sister, along with her son and husband, were murdered by Illyrians off Corcyra some eleven years ago. Her husband, Prince Navaras, my father truly loved as a son.' Hannibal paused menacingly, but still fixed his incredulous eyes on Sphax. 'Has this spectre, this vile impostor, anything more to say before I have him crucified?'

Sphax felt insulted beyond all sufferance! Blood flushed his cheeks and he lashed out an accusing finger at the man staring at him. 'Yes! I have much to say. You lie! Your mind has become addled. It is ten years, not eleven, since I witnessed my parent's murder aboard the ship that carried us on the fool's errand that led to their deaths and condemned me to slavery! And their murder had nothing to do with Illyrians! It was Barcid meddling that signed their death warrants and Roman treachery on the orders of Flaminius Nepo that carried out the butchery.' Now beside himself with rage, Sphax violently swept wine cups and the remains of a meal from a nearby table, scattering the contents to the four corners of the pavilion. His enraged voice had attracted the attention of guards. Sphax pushed them aside as he turned on his heels and stormed out of the pavilion.

He hadn't felt such rage since he'd sunk the blade into rat-face's flesh. These were his most sacred and harrowing memories. No one who walked this earth would twist or trifle with these memories! Sphax had taken no more than ten strides before a voice from behind him commanded, '*Wait!*' He stopped beside a blazing campfire, but did not dignify the command by turning around.

Hannibal strode past and faced him across the firelight, his face a dark brooding mask. 'You were taken into slavery by Rome?' Sphax didn't trust himself to speak. He simply swept the sleeve of his tunic back to his shoulder, revealing the *fugitivus* scar burned into his flesh.

'No one has ever called me a liar and lived.' Hannibal's voice was unnervingly calm, almost disembodied. 'And before they died I had their tongues ripped out.' His Libyan guards twitched nervously behind him, spears raised. 'Do you hear me, boy?'

In answer, Sphax shifted his gaze from the flames to look defiantly into his uncle's eyes, but still he said nothing.

'Only the son of Navaras would have the brazen impudence to speak as you have. You will serve under Maharbal and do his bidding. Now get out of my sight.' Without a word, Sphax strode off, leaving his uncle staring into the firelight.

* * *

He was awakened roughly by a Numidian shaking his shoulder. 'Maharbal wants you. Report to his pavilion.' As Sphax raised himself onto an elbow and rubbed what little sleep he'd had from his eyes, he thought it must still be the middle of the night. Fionn slept on, undisturbed by the messenger. He dressed quickly and, still half asleep, stumbled out of the tent. He could see a faint light beginning to gather in the east across the great river, but its waters still glinted with moonlight. Despite the early hour he could hear a great deal of activity going on at the riverbank.

Maharbal was alone, seated on his sleeping couch with a purple cape draped around him against the pre-dawn chill. 'You came closer to death last night in Hannibal's presence than at any time during the day when you were facing Roman spears. You're lucky to see this day.'

Sphax listened in respectful silence, then spoke quietly and calmly. 'It was the Romans who seized us, not the Illyrians. When they discovered that my father had been sent by Carthage as embassy to Queen Teuta, it sealed our fate. Rome was at war with Illyria and the Queen. For the Barcids, this was just another opportunity to gain a new ally in their fight against Rome. But for Rome it was a gift! Almost too good to be true. By blaming it on the Illyrians, Rome stopped Carthage meddling in the war and lost the Queen valuable allies by blackening her name and spreading the lie. The Romans left a crew on board to do the butchery. I didn't see them murder my father. I was only seven years old. I was held by two Roman soldiers and forced to watch as my mother ... was raped.' He could hardly bring himself to utter the words. 'They each took turns, and afterwards, slit her throat. I was spared for slavery. They took me on board their galley and then burned our ship.' Sphax's voice hardened. 'This is the truth, and I will kill any man who dares to question my memory of it. Whoever they are!'

Shocked and suddenly pale, Maharbal let out a deep sigh and closed his eyes for a moment. 'I'm sorry,' he said in a voice as hushed as Sphax's, 'no son should see his own mother die like that. Least of all a boy of seven. I too loved your father, Navaras, and all of Carthage adored you dear mother.' For a while there was silence between them before Maharbal added, 'Never tell your uncle how his sister died. Never! You must swear it. Madness is a fine line Hannibal has walked since birth. He already has enough hatred in his heart. I fear this would push him over the abyss. You must swear this to me by all the gods we hold sacred. Then we will never speak of this matter again. Will you swear this before me?'

'Yes. I swear it. I have never spoken of this before to a living soul. It means enough to me that you, at least, know the truth.'

Maharbal rose from his couch and placed an arm around Sphax's shoulders. 'Go and bring that magnificent stallion. We'll present it to your uncle. Perhaps that will sweeten his temper this morning.'

Dawn was breaking as he left Maharbal's pavilion, spreading its gold and blood-red cloak over the eastern horizon. Men had told him last night there would be a battle today. They would either cross the great river and scatter the Volcae warriors, or if defeated, march back to Iberia with their tails between their legs. And all the while a Roman army of two legions was closing in on them from the south. Sphax wondered if the day would be crowned in gold or stained blood-red. It was not in his nature to brood about what fate had in store for him, so he'd soon dismissed all such thoughts and was looking forward to greeting Arion and Dido.

Last night Sphax had been astonished at the size and complexity of the Carthaginian camp. It was a city of thoroughfares, stables, bakeries, armouries, even whorehouses, everything a teeming city required to mend, feed and service its thousands of warrior citizens. Women with young children, slaves, harlots, dancers and musicians walked its earthen streets or sat around gossiping beside blazing campfires. This was also a restless city that shunned the permanence of stone and clay, a city whose canvas and hemp walls could be packed and shipped at a moment's notice, only to be reassembled and begin its life anew at the whim of its general.

He greeted his horses warmly, blowing on their faces and fondly caressing their necks and manes. The mare had fully recovered from her ordeal of yesterday and Arion had been groomed and brushed as Sphax had requested. Amongst the thousands of horses tethered across the fields, his magnificent stallion shone out as exceptional. At least two hands taller than anything around him, Arion radiated strength and nobility. He was a horse of kings, with a lineage that stretched back to the earth goddess Gaea. Giving Arion to another man would be as painful as handing a cherished daughter to a husband, but there was nothing to be done. Best get it over with, he thought.

Maharbal walked with him to Hannibal's pavilion, then disappeared inside to confer with his general on the dispositions for the day. Sphax fidgeted outside, holding Arion's reins and muttering his final farewells to the creature he loved. Eventually Hannibal emerged, trailing a group of officers. 'Good morning, nephew. Maharbal tells me you have a great gift for me.' Sphax couldn't believe that the smiling and gracious expression greeting him this morning belonged to the same man who'd threatened to crucify him last night.

'It would please me if you thought so, Sir. This is Arion, the finest stallion in Rome. Amongst charioteers, he is held to be a champion amongst champions. A gift from Rome,' and smiling self-consciously added, 'one of many from that city, I hope.' His uncle walked admiringly around the beast, patting and stroking.

'Well spoken, young man. This is indeed a fine animal. And what became of his former owner?'

Hardly able to keep a straight face, Sphax said 'He lost the ability to ride, Sir ...'

'Well, I also have a gift for you, Sphax,' Hannibal said equally mischievously, and turning towards a much younger version of himself said, 'This is yet another uncle of yours. May I present my brother Mago? So, just when you thought one uncle was bad enough, now you have two to deal with. What do you think of that, young man?' The likeness between the brothers was uncanny. Perhaps Hannibal, the elder of the two was a little taller and thicker set, and Mago's eyes were slightly darker, but they shared that same iron-grey colour, just as they shared the same darkly brooding expression, square jaw and high forehead. Both men favoured trimmed beards and close cropped hair. They could have been twins.

'Indeed, I see that I'm blessed!' bowing low to Mago.

At that moment there was a commotion amongst the officers, with some of them pointing excitedly towards the northeast, across the Rhodanus. A chorus of voices spoke at once. 'It's smoke, Sir. It's the signal. It must be! Hanno is in place!' Hannibal silenced them instantly with a gesture of his hand. 'Gisgo will be my eyes this morning. What do you see, my friend?' A giant of a Libyan, dripping from head to foot in polished bronze and iron, shielded his eyes from the sun and stared across the river. 'Definitely a smoke signal, Sir. Too much smoke to be a single campfire. Two, maybe three miles northeast of the Volcae camp across the river. It's Hanno alright.'

'So be it,' Hannibal said decisively. 'You know my plan. We have prepared carefully. Hanno is now in place threatening their rear. We cannot fail! Today we'll cross this river and drive our enemies before us.' Looking from face to face for a brief yet compelling moment, Hannibal held the gaze of every officer gathered around him. There was something odd about those eyes. 'Gentlemen, our moment has arrived, let us seize it! Look to your men.' Gesturing to his servants to lead the stallion away he lavishing a broad smile on Sphax then proclaimed so all would hear, 'Today I will ride Arion, this gift from my nephew. Saddle and array him. Today this stallion will take his first steps on his journey back to Rome. Do you not see it?' Hannibal implored, raising his arms to the heavens. 'This is the surest sign from Melqart. We march on Rome. It is our destiny!'

On their way back to Maharbal's pavilion Sphax was still struggling to understand his uncle's baffling change of heart since their confrontation last night. Could it be the same man? It was as if Maharbal had read his thoughts. 'Your uncle has many faces. You would be well advised to recognise them and act accordingly. There are days on end when it would be unwise to enter his pavilion, yet others when all the hours that day provides would never be enough to satisfy his projects and ambitions. You must learn to navigate these seas, for all our sakes.' Slapping Sphax fondly on the back he added, 'But at least you have been acknowledged. Now you have uncles and a family at last.'

Trumpets were now blaring all around the camp and there was a sudden thrill and excitement in the air as men and officers fetched weapons and armour, or began mustering on the open ground beside the tents to be counted and marshalled. Once again he was struck by the sheer variety of race and colour in the army that Hannibal had assembled. Libyans, some as dark as night, camped side by side with fair skinned Iberians and Gauls, there were half-naked Mallorcan slingers who could fell a wolf at fifty paces, Cretan archers and even elephant mahouts who'd learned their skills in the distant lands of Parthia. This was a mongrel army, bound together by two things: a desire for plunder and a sworn hatred of Rome. Hardly lofty sentiments, but when spiced with Carthaginian silver, more than enough to draw contingents from every nation around the Mediterranean for this, their great march on Rome.

* * *

In Maharbal's pavilion many of his captains had already assembled. Sphax recognised Adherbal from yesterday. 'Gossip spreads swifter than a fart sours a tent, so I'm sure you all know by now that we're to nursemaid this one,' said Maharbal, nodding at Sphax. 'He turns out to be nothing less than Hannibal's long-lost nephew. I like this useless runt, so let's try and keep him alive, at least for today, then we can decide if he's worth the trouble.' A little relieved, Sphax saw that everyone was grinning benevolently at him.

'It's taken that lazy bastard Hanno three days to march north and cross the river. But at least he's in place now to the rear of the Volcae camp. There's no place for my Iberian stallions this morning – too heavy and slow. So we ride our ladies, crossing the river in anything that will float. Mago's moored all the heavier vessels up-stream, thinking this will impede the current. That's as likely as a Sicilian whore giving you back your money. We know from yesterday that the current is as swift as a jennet. You may end up anywhere downstream when you get across. Your first duty is to join up your eshrins. I will *not* have you charging in pisspot groups as you did yesterday. I will castrate any arsehole who tries this! That's exactly what those savages want, to pick us off one by one as we land. Hasdrubal and Astegal will cross upstream in the larger craft, the rest of us will row across swimming our horses as we did yesterday.' Maharbal grinned at them all for a moment but when nobody moved, yelled 'Dog's twat! What are you waiting for? Dancing girls? A game of tabula? Out of my sight!'

Sphax started to leave with the other officers but a voice bellowed behind him, 'Not you, slackhead! You stay beside me today.'

Chaos was breaking out beside the river. Everyone was shouting at once as men and horses scrambled onto the hundreds of rivercraft moored on the western bank. Horses slipped on wet planks, men cursed, orders were yelled above the cacophony, and amidst all this pandemonium, he saw his uncle Mago wildly rushing around, pointing, exhorting, cursing.

Varying in size from sturdy trading vessels with oars and sails to flimsy log rafts, hastily bound together with hemp, Sphax realised that most of the craft were so overcrowded they would never make it across. He saw rafts awash with water, crammed with Iberian swordsmen already cold and soaked to the skin, floundering with crude paddles they'd hewn from logs. He and Maharbal sat their horses and watched as Hasdrubal and Astegal struggled to get their men and horses on to the larger craft. He guessed that the Rhodanus was well over a mile wide at this point, but he could clearly see large numbers of Volcae gathering on the far bank.

For the first time the magnitude of what they were about to attempt dawned on him. A ramshackle fleet carrying a few lightly armed men were about to cross a great river. A river where the currents were so strong that even the local riverfolk feared them, and this morning the surface of its waters was being scoured by a cold wind howling down from the north that would drive every craft off course. Many would never make it, and the ones that did would immediately be set upon and overwhelmed by warriors wielding those deadly Gallic blades. Four thousand of them was the latest estimate. He'd been warned about those blades. Wrought from the finest iron, they were almost twice the length of his puny Roman weapon and all Gauls were skilled in their use. They had twelve eshrins and two thousand Iberian *caetrati* waiting to cross. An eshrin numbered thirty Numidians, but with losses and injuries, few could muster this number. To make things worse, they would not arrive as a powerful armada, but in dribs and drabs. Everything depended on Hanno. He held the key. Otherwise, he thought, this could easily be a disaster, a slaughter.

Past the thousands of cheering men awaiting their turn to cross, Sphax followed Maharbal down the bank to where their boats had been assembled. He was relieved to see that at least they would have riverfolk to row them across. Sphax was anxious about Dido. Never before had she swum such a broad river. In the event she bravely battled the currents and swam gamely, panting, ears pricked nervously forward, swimming swiftly beside Maharbal's Egyptian mare. Sphax was jammed into the stern with Maharbal's servant, both of them gripping the horses' lead ropes for dear life whilst Maharbal crouched in the bow, sword in hand, ready to spring from the boat when it touched the distant bank. At one point a swirling eddy shook the boat so violently that the bow careered downstream until the cursing oarsmen brought it back under control.

Upstream of them he saw an abandoned log raft slam into a rowing boat, splintering its sides and casting its occupants overboard into the swirling waters. Midstream, the river was choked with the wreckage of logs, paddles and abandoned rafts. Horses thrashed wildly around amidst the corpses of drowned men, some still clutching swords and spears, all swept away by the wind and that treacherous current. Casting anxious glances over his shoulder he could see that even with the valiant efforts of the rowers, all the boats around them were veering downstream, but at least that meant they would reach sections of the bank that were less thronged with warriors waiting to kill them.

Then the eastern bank was only a hundred strides away. They had almost made it. Sphax could hear the sounds of battle raging upstream. 'What will Hanno do, Sir?' he shouted above the racket.

'If he's any sense he'll wait until we've drawn all the savages away from their camp, then attack. I would start by burning their camp to the ground. But we shall see.'

As the boat ground to a halt in the mud, Maharbal leapt to the shore in search of prey. By the time Sphax was astride a dripping Dido a Volcae warrior already lay dying at Maharbal's feet. Anxiously looking around, Sphax could see that this section of the bank was lightly defended. They were surrounded by a thinly held ring of Volcae who should have charged immediately, but instead had hesitated and then started backing away, uncertain. This was their undoing, for by now ten Numidians were looking for targets for their javelins.

Maharbal, now astride his mare, bawled 'WAIT!' When twenty horsemen had formed up he pointed his sword at the enemy and yelled 'Forward!'

There wasn't enough ground for their mares to reach a headlong gallop, so javelins were hurled at the canter, four strides from the enemy. But the effect was almost the same. Fearsome iron spikes sailed through flesh and like knives through goat's cheese. Fifteen warriors were already down, some screaming in pain as Maharbal ploughed his mare into the survivors, hacking down any man yet standing. Sphax followed a stride behind, thrusting his sword into the gaping mouth of a warrior caught as he was about to turn and run. The sword went clean through the nape of the man's neck, making the blade difficult to retrieve, and Sphax was almost dragged from Dido as the man sank to his knees and his eyes glazed over. Finally he managed to jerk it free in time to face another warrior, shield thrust forward, spear raised, but before he'd taken another step javelins started to find their mark and his battlecry was cut short.

Sphax felt an arm on his shoulder and turned to see Maharbal beside him. 'The dying try to take the weapon that slew them into the underworld. Twist it lad, before you withdraw the blade.'

Horsemen were now milling above the fallen Volcae warriors, wrenching javelins from the dead and cutting short the agonised cries of the wounded. The survivors had fled to the cover of a stand of willows some eighty paces away, where a large group of Volcae were preparing to charge and drive them into the river.

With his sword raised aloft, Maharbal began signalling to an eshrin galloping towards them. At first he made a circling gesture before pointing at the willows ahead of them. As a body the horsemen veered off to the east and began circling around them. Looking around, Sphax guessed they now had more than thirty horsemen with them.

Then all sound was drowned by a fearful din that broke out amongst the trees ahead of them. It was a sound the like of which he'd never heard before. A sound like a shriek of pain or a wounded animal crying out in distress. Startled, he saw that several Volcae had raised thin-tubed bronze trumpets above their heads, some taller than the men themselves and decorated with boar's heads. Soon the cacophony was swelled by the rhythmic clashing of swords against shields and men yelling themselves into a state of frenzied rage.

Without a word from Maharbal the men began forming themselves into a ragged line as they had done yesterday in the face of Roman cavalry, leaving wide gaps between horsemen to allow them to turn freely without impeding the horses either side of them. Numidians always turned their mares to the left. This much he'd learnt. Maharbal threw him a spare javelin. Thankfully he caught it this time. They sat their horses and waited. Soon the racket under the trees reached a frenzied crescendo and a hundred screaming Volcae warriors emerged from the trees, charging straight for them.

Maharbal simply shouted, 'Now!' They moved forward as one, allowing their horses to pick up their natural pace without forcing them into a headlong rush to the gallop. There was a terrible calm and control about every movement he and Dido made, yet the hairs on the back of his head were standing on end and the knuckles gripping his javelin were white. As Dido stretched and flew he felt a soaring exhilaration, a thrill that was beyond all sensations of fear. It coursed and surged through his body like the richest wine, the exultation of flying with the gods. He knew at that moment his enemies were experiencing the same thrill. But they were going to die. Of this he was certain.

Three strides later he chose a target. Directly ahead of him a warrior was sprinting towards him with his shield carelessly held in his left forearm, exposing a bare chest and torso. Dido was now thundering forward. He aimed and let the javelin fly. Sphax never knew whether

it found its mark or not, for in that horrifying instant
he realised he'd made a terrible mistake. He'd left it
too late to turn Dido around. Numidians had trained
their mares to turn full circle in three strides, but like
a fool, he'd never practiced this manoeuvre with Dido,
thinking it would be easy!

He was almost on top of the leading Volcae now, and
in that heart-stopping moment all he saw was snarling
faces and those deadly Gallic blades. There was nothing
for it. Sliding forward on to her withers he clung to
Dido's neck and urged the mare to even greater speed.
Instinctively she made for gaps between the astounded
warriors. One was immediately struck and bowled aside
by the sheer momentum of her charge, but ahead of
them a small group had just enough time to crouch
and raise their shields in a protective wall. Without
a flicker of hesitation Dido leapt, soaring high through
the air several hands above the iron-rimmed shields and
landed sure-footed in the soft ground to their rear. In
the space of two breaths he'd broken clean through the
ranks of Volcae. Sphax hadn't even drawn his sword.
He slid backwards, releasing his hold on the mare's
neck, and with soothing words, let her ease her stride.

Ahead of him, in front of the willows where the
Volcae had begun their charge, horsemen were now
gathering. To his intense relief he saw they were
Numidians and guessed they were the eshrin Maharbal
had earlier signalled off to the flank. Dido was panting,
spent for the moment, so he approached slowly at a walk.

For some baffling reason the Numidians seemed to be cheering him and waving javelins in the air. A horseman broke away from the group and rode towards him. Sphax could see there was a great grin set on his handsome face. 'I've never seen the like of that before! What horsemanship,' he said, staring at him in astonishment.

Sphax was now totally bemused and could feel the colour rising to his cheeks. Lamely he said 'I got it all wrong, Sir. Do I have your permission to join this eshrin? I seem to have lost mine.'

It was as if he'd just told the best joke the officer had ever heard. He burst into great guffaws of laughter, doubling up over his mare. In between the guffaws he managed to blurt out, 'You must be Sphax, I've heard all about you! I'm Merbal. Let's go and finish off these bastards.' Still chortling, Merbal turned his mount and rode back to the line of Numidians that were forming-up behind him. Sphax joined the end of the line and the man next to him held out a javelin for him.

Once again, the eshrin began with that easy walk before picking up the pace naturally in perfect harmony with the gait of their mares. Sphax was not going to make the same mistake twice. This time he kept a steady eye on the horseman to his left, matching him stride for stride and watching closely what he did with his javelin. Ahead of them he could see that the Volcae charge had been halted by Maharbal's men; the warriors were still stalking forward, but were now wary and watchful. The ground was littered with their dead and dying. Maharbal's men had inflicted such a terrible toll on their numbers that all eyes were fixed to their front, awaiting the next charge. When they did look behind them it was too late.

The volley of javelins caught them completely off guard. Sphax's javelin missed by an arm's length, but as he turned Dido and retreated, his was one of few javelins not buried deep in the flesh of a warrior. Merbal halted them after fifty strides and they turned around to witness the effects of their charge. It was obvious that the Volcae had lost well over half the men that had charged so confidently from the trees. Now it was their turn to be surrounded and outnumbered. Sphax could see they were half-heartedly trying to rally, forming a circle around their chieftain. They looked beaten. The horseman to his left handed him the last of his spare javelins but Sphax refused it.

'It would be wasted on me,' he said bitterly. 'I don't think I could hit an elephant's arse if it stopped and offered it.'

'I'm Jugurtha,' laughed the Numidian, 'you're Sphax, aren't you?' He nodded. 'I fought alongside your father Navaras when I was your age. I saw you leap over those savages! I'm telling you lad, he would be proud of you today.'

Sphax was astonished! There was so much he wanted to ask this old veteran, but in the middle of a battle with screaming warriors was not the time to start asking questions.

Cheering started to break out somewhere to the north of them. At first it was just a few voices, but then it seemed to gather in force and volume as more men joined in the general jubilation. This was nothing like the frenzied screaming of Volcae warriors. Sphax was sure it was their men. What had they to cheer about? The Numidians were looking at one another, puzzled. Merbal signalled to his men to hold their position, then nudged his mare into the copse of willows. Sphax's curiosity got the better of him and he followed Merbal. Emerging from the trees they halted and stared north.

Suddenly all became clear. On rising ground, perhaps a mile north of them, the Volcae camp was in flames. Fanned by the fierce northerly wind the fires were spreading rapidly, throwing up great billows of smoke and ash that were covering the battlefield like a storm cloud. Beneath that storm cloud he could see phalanx after phalanx of Libyan pikes descending inexorably on the Volcae, now trapped beside the great river, their fate sealed.

'It's Hanno!' Sphax cried excitedly, 'he's started his attack. Maharbal said he would fire the Volcae camp.' Surprised, Merbal stared at him.

'I wasn't at Maharbal's meeting this morning. I had to see to the boats, so knew nothing of this. They certainly kept it dark. When did you hear about it, lad?'

'Only this morning, Sir. I was with my uncle when we saw Hanno's signal.'

Merbal returned his gaze to the Libyans. 'Praise ba 'al hamūn,' he said, and pointing his javelin at the

Volcae by the river, 'I'm beginning to feel sorry for the wretches,' he said, without a trace of pity in his voice.

When they returned through the trees, Sphax took up his position on the right of the line whilst Merbal rode out in front of his men. 'It's all over,' he grinned, 'two thousand Libyan pikes are skewering their arses and driving them into the river. Their camp's burnt to the ground. This lad tells me that Hanno crossed the river north of here three days ago. Now they've returned with a vengeance. He ought to know,' smiling in Sphax's direction, 'the young pup's uncle is, after all, our very own Hannibal.' Now there was general mirth along the line. 'Let's finish off this rabble, then we'll ride north and see how many savages they've left for us.'

Merbal waved his eshrin forward again and they slipped into that easy gait. Sphax drew his sword this time. Before they'd taken twenty strides the Volcae suddenly took to their heels and ran for their lives. It was easy to see why. Maharbal's men had also chosen that moment to charge what was left of them. Caught between two fires, the warriors had chosen the only option left to them besides certain death. Sphax was amazed how quickly they threw away anything that might impede headlong flight: shields were the first to go, followed by spears and helmets. Merbal ordered men forward to chase them and exact a toll for ruining their sport.

Sphax dismounted and walked over to where one of those infernal trumpets had been cast aside in flight. He was taken aback by how heavy it felt in his hands; its circular bronze tube reached to the height of his chest and was ribbed at intervals along its length with iron rings, each section wrought with intricately patterned gold and silver inlays. It was both exquisite and ugly at the same time. Instead of a trumpet's conical bell, the sound on this instrument emerged from the hideous gaping mouth of a dragon, its clawed wings and fearsome spiked tail modelled in pure gold. He carried the instrument over to Jugurtha.

'What is this?' he asked. The old Numidian eyed it warily.

'Fearful things those; the Gauls in Iberia call them carnyx. They summon their war goddess, Morrígu, who decides whether they live or die. Better throw it away, lad. No good will come of it.' Sphax decided to keep it, if only for the dragon.

He looked over to where Merbal was in conversation with Maharbal. Merbal seemed to be laughing and gesturing in his direction whilst Maharbal sat stiffly, unmoved. He knew he was in trouble again, and nudged Dido forward to join them.

'You're beginning to be more trouble than you're worth,' Maharbal said sternly, but seeing his miserable expression he relented a little and reached out to ruffle Sphax's thick curls. With all their eshrins now combined, the Numidians cantered north, beyond the stands of willows and on to the broad plain beside the river. Once through the trees the whole battlefield came into view.

Caught between Iberian swordsmen who'd landed on the eastern bank and the Libyan wall of pikes approaching in their rear, the Volcae had been thrown into a state of utter confusion. Some were racing back to the smouldering ruins of their camp, whilst others turned fretfully to face Hanno's pikes. But it was obvious to Sphax that the majority were looking for a way out of the rat-trap. The river was still being criss-crossed by vessels ferrying men and horses, soon they would have numbers on their side.

'Well, lad! What would you do?' Maharbal asked innocently, as if undecided whether to serve a guest fruit or cheese. Sphax was shocked by the question and it took him some time to answer.

'They look beaten to me, Sir. The only door open to them lies south, in our direction. I would spread out our men and try and bar the door.'

Maharbal glanced over his shoulder. Horsemen were constantly swelling their ranks from the ferries, but even so, Sphax guessed they had no more than eighty horsemen with them. Maharbal answered coolly, as if totting up a bill, 'Three eshrins against four thousand savages. I don't care for those odds. We could charge, lose half our number and slow their advance a little, but we could never stop them. Tell me, where does our duty lie?' Now Sphax was at a total loss.

'Sir, I'm a trainer of horses, not a general of war,' he bleated. Maharbal exploded.

'You are the son of Navaras! Born to command. Not some shitfaced stable boy! Sooner or later you will be faced with these dilemmas.' Maharbal glared at him severely. 'Our duty lies with the Iberians who have gained but a foothold on the eastern bank, not in some glorious charge! They are hard pressed and may be thrown back into the river.' His voice softened a little, but only a little. 'When faced with a choice between glory and duty, always choose duty. Duty sometimes brings glory, but there is no glory to be had in neglecting one's duty.' Raising his javelin he pointed towards the river and waved his Numidians forward.

This was now perfect horse country, rich grassland, a flat sweep of water meadow broken only by occasional stands of willow. Chariots could race here, twenty abreast. Horsemen either side of him began to fan out, leaving those now familiar gaps in their ranks to manoeuvre their mares. Dido and the other jennets, along with sleek African mares, cantered with effortless grace, barely raising their hooves as they floated over the sward in their easy lope. Soon, eighty Numidians were singling out prey for their javelins.

That first charge had a devastating effect, but Maharbal was right. The fiercest fighting was at the riverbank. His earlier look at the phalanxes bearing down on the rear of the Volcae had been enough to convince him that nothing would be able to stand in their path. But the fight at the riverbank was another matter. The only arms these Iberians carried were short falcata swords, javelins and small round shields. Few even had helmets. They wore no armour, just a simple white tunic edged in crimson. Speed and skill were their defence. Light on their feet, fast and nimble, in close combat where men fought shoulder to shoulder and movement was restricted, the falcata was more than a match for any slashing sword, which needed room for it to be wielded effectively.

If the Volcae had any discipline or organization they would have driven the Iberians into the river with a single determined charge. But they were neither organized nor disciplined, and the burning of their camp and the appearance of the pikemen in their rear had ripped the heart out of them.

As a mark of reckless bravery, many Volcae scorned armour and fought half naked. Bare chests and torsos were as much a badge of courage as their lime-slaked hair, spiked and combed back high above their heads represented a horse's mane, tossed back in frenzied anger. Brandishing their huge oval shields, blades raised aloft, they would goad one another into an ecstasy of violence before the carnyx awoke the gods who were to decide their fate. Then they would rush forward, screaming a torrent of curses at anyone who had the courage and temerity to stand against them.

But for the Iberian *caetrati*, temerity and courage were never in question. For them it was just a simple matter of discipline and long-practiced skill. Every charge was met by a hornet's nest of swordsmen, darting amongst them like fiends in a deadly dance, parrying blows with their bucklers, thrusting and probing, working their lightning-fast swordcraft. Screams and curses do not have the power to pierce flesh and bone. The Volcae warriors fought bravely that morning, but they died all too easily.

By now most of Maharbal's Numidians had dismounted and were stalking their prey on foot. Many were armed with deadly saunions, those long barbed javelins cast from good Iberian iron. Saunions pierced willow shields as effortlessly as a knife sails through cheese. If the Volcae rushed them they would beat a hasty retreat, whistle for their mares and ride out of harm's way. The Volcae soon learned that to break ranks and chase these shadows meant certain death. Once out in the open they were just fresh meat, easily picked off. Sphax rode in silence beside Maharbal, some distance behind the fight. Maharbal issued few orders, trusting his men to do what was required of them to drive back the Volcae and relieve the pressure on the swordsmen. The fight had been going on for some time when another great cheer arose amongst the Iberians. Soon it was echoed and taken up like some great wave that carried it from rank to rank along the entire riverbank.

'Hannibal is with us,' said Maharbal, pointing his javelin at a group of men and horses that had taken up a position on rising ground two hundred paces north of them. Sphax recognized the Carthaginian crescent standard, raised beside his uncle. But that's not what took his breath away. His uncle sat astride Arion, who'd been arrayed in a most elaborate saddle cloth dripping with gold and around his neck hung the complete head and mane of a lion. The stallion looked truly magnificent, a horse fit for an emperor. Inwardly, Sphax swelled with pride. Then, without any warning, the strangest thing happened.

The Volcae took to their heels and ran! It was as if they just melted away as a wave recedes from the shoreline. In the space of a single breath, four thousand Volcae warriors ceased to be deadly enemies and became fugitives, fleeing for their lives.

Mago and Astegal's eshrins soon joined them, swelling their ranks to over two hundred. The officers gathered around Maharbal, waiting for his command for the chase to begin. With a wicked grin and a glance in Sphax's direction, the general said, 'Follow the boy. He's the son of Navaras and your general for a day. I need to see Hannibal.' Before anyone could question or challenge this astonishing order he'd turned his mare and sped northwards.

All the officers were grinning, knowing full well that in the present circumstances orders were completely unnecessary. Sphax brazenly matched their grins and playing along with Maharbal's joke said, 'Well, you heard the man. Let the chase begin!'

Mago burst out laughing: 'An excellent order, general. Where you command, we will obey,' and after an over-elaborate bow to Sphax, waved his javelin forward.

From that moment it ceased to be a battle and became butchery. After a mile or so Dido was having to pick her way through a carpet of Volcae corpses. Once the Numidians had caught up with the rear of the fleeing warriors the fugitives had to turn and face javelins every fifty paces, or risk a javelin in the back. For Gauls, such a death was the mark of a true coward and the spirits of warriors who fell in this manner would be cursed by Morrigu through all eternity. Each stand did buy precious time for the survivors to continue their flight, but it was impossible to outrun Numidians. Of all the breeds of horses none could outrun a jennet. Stallions like Arion were undoubtedly swifter over shorter distances, but they tired easily. Jennets possessed exceptional stamina and could canter effortlessly all day long. Nothing could outrun them. This sealed the fate of the Volcae.

Small islands of warriors and pockets of resistance began to emerge, but they were rapidly surrounded by seas of horseman, and with each successive wave of hoof beats the islands were soon awash with horsemen dismounting to retrieve javelins, look for trophies and put the wounded out of their misery. For the Numidians this was a day of sport, a red day, a field day, when gold and silver were there for the taking. By midday every horseman was bedecked in precious amber and jewels, sporting arms thick with golden torques and Gallic swords strapped to their waists.

Sphax soon grew heartily sick of it. As the morning wore on and the butchery continued, the killing began to turn his stomach. These people were not Romans. The Volcae had foolishly allied themselves with Massilia and then Rome, but he had no quarrel with the Volcae, or any Gauls for that matter. His war was with Rome.

Around midday they encountered a particularly resistant island of warriors. A chieftain stood amongst twenty or so of his followers, all helmeted, well-armed and clad in mail. Behind them stood an equal number of more lightly armed warriors wielding spears. All were smartly clad in chequered tunics and braccae leggings. For the past mile or so Sphax had been riding in the company of Merbal's eshrin; now they halted and faced these last Volcae survivors. Mago quickly joined them, leading his eshrin in a wide sweep to the rear of the little island, completing the encirclement. Rather than skulking behind his warriors, the chief stood brazenly in the front rank, shield at the ready. Sphax could see the Numidians all around him eyeing the craftsmanship of his mail coat that was topped by a cape made of the same expensive material. He pitied the man. That mail coat would be sold to the highest bidder around a Numidian campfire this evening.

Merbal's eshrin charged, but they were in for a surprise. When they were within six strides from releasing their javelins the Volcae suddenly locked their shields, and with a great battle-roar charged forward.

When it seemed the two opposing lines were about to crash into one another the men behind the wall of shields released their spears into the startled line of horsemen. Merbal's charge was thoroughly disrupted as horsemen frantically struggled to turn their mares and retreat. At a more measured pace the Volcae continued their advance, shields still locked until the second rank were able to retrieve their spears, then they retreated in perfect order to where they'd begun their charge. By some miracle no hurt had been suffered by Merbal's eshrin, except of course to their pride! Sphax couldn't help smiling to himself. A sheepish looking Merbal rode over to him.

'What do you make of that?'

'This chieftain isn't some bare-chested savage,' Sphax replied thoughtfully. 'He's clever and his men fight with discipline.' In truth, Sphax was beginning to admire the man. As he and Merbal watched on, Mago's men charged them from the rear. In another demonstration of perfect drill, the shield wall and spearmen reversed positions. Having seen what had befallen Merbal's charge, Sphax guessed that Mago's men would be prepared to throw their javelins much earlier. But again, the Numidians were taken by complete surprise. This time the Volcae began their own charge much sooner, and if anything increased their pace as they sprinted towards the eshrin cantering forwards. In the confusion to turn their mares three horsemen did get tangled up with the shield wall and were lucky to escape with their lives. The Volcae didn't halt their charge this time, and now it was the turn of Mago's men to back away and beat a hasty retreat.

It had been obvious to Sphax that if Merbal had chosen to lead his men forward when the Volcae were charging Mago's eshrin, this little battle would be over by now and one of his men would have made a small fortune from the sale of that mail coat. But Merbal had grown wary, and it wasn't Sphax's place to issue *real* orders.

Sphax prodded Dido forward to within fifty strides of where the Volcae had organised their latest stand. Merbal's men followed warily behind. The Volcae had again reversed ranks, so he found himself gazing directly into the eyes of their chieftain. With his hands resting on top of a crimson shield that reached to his waist, the Gaul met his gaze and stared defiantly back at him. He couldn't be certain, because the cheek guards of the chief's helmet obscured some of his face, but Sphax was convinced the Gaul was brazenly smiling at him. That decided it. He would put a stop to this senseless butchery.

'You seem to be in some difficulty, *general*. With your permission my eshrin will happily resolve it for you.' Sphax had been so lost in his own thoughts that he hadn't noticed Astegal's approach. Astegal was one of Maharbal's senior officers; he didn't need Sphax's permission. This was his idea of a joke. For a moment Sphax was tempted to let his eshrin charge, knowing it would fail. It might even teach this arrogant captain a lesson. But he thought better of it. What had Maharbal said about duty?

Sliding off Dido he said 'That won't be necessary,' and strode briskly towards the wall of shields.

'By the gods! What are you doing? Stop, boy!' Astegal yelled behind him. Sphax ignored him and quickened his pace. As he got closer he could see the spearmen in the second rank raising their weapons ready to throw but their chief raised his arm, shouted a command, and the spears were lowered. Sphax halted ten paces short of the shield wall and began his address in Punic. Nothing. Just blank faces. The chief lowered his shield to the ground and walked to within a sword's length of Sphax.

'Do you have any Greek, horseman?' he said in that language, and began removing his helmet. He looked about the same age as Sphax and his voice was refined and confident. 'My Punic is a little rusty.' Sphax switched to that language and repeated his address.

'I am Sphax, son of Navaras. My uncle is Hannibal Barca, leader of the Carthaginians that have routed your army and scattered your warriors. I wish for no further senseless bloodshed. If you would lay down your weapons and become my prisoners, I guarantee you and your men your lives and safe conduct. My uncle will confirm this. I swear this before you. Enough blood has been spilt today.'

'Well Sphax, as you see,' and the chief half turned, gesturing theatrically towards the ranks of shields that had so far held firm, 'my little army remains undefeated, and my warriors have not been scattered to the winds.' The chief was half a head taller than him, with pale blue eyes and a fair complexion that reminded him of Fionn. 'Why should I trust your words? Especially when you have broken the alliance my father made with your uncle.'

Sphax flushed. 'That is a lie, Volcae! Hannibal made no such agreement with your people.' To Sphax's astonishment, the chief coolly smiled at him.

'But I am not Volcae, horseman. Though, like all Gauls, they are my cousins. I am Idwal, son of Cenno, Lord of the Cavari. Three weeks ago my father made an agreement with Hannibal to allow your army safe passage through our lands. I seem to remember your uncle paying my father generously in silver.' In a flash Idwal's smile disappeared. 'Tell me, horseman, why should I now trust the word of any Carthaginian?'

For some moments Sphax had been so taken aback and confused by these revelations that he just stared. But he quickly regained his wits. 'By the same token, Gaul, you have also broken this agreement by fighting alongside the Volcae. You can hardly blame us for our inability to distinguish a Volcae blade from a Cavari spear. As for trusting my word: in the past I too have regretted Carthaginian promises, but I am not a Carthaginian, I'm a Numidian. And as you will see if you lay down your weapons, Numidians are to be trusted. We keep our word.' Sphax had an amusing thought. 'There is of course a simple solution to our present dilemma. If you repay me the silver my uncle paid you, we can then kill you with a clear conscience!'

Thankfully Idwal laughed at this suggestion and grinned back at him. 'Numidians, it appears, have a humour that your uncle sadly lacks from what I remember of his sour expression.' Idwal paused and turned slightly to gaze at his men still rigidly holding their shields. He seemed to be making up his mind. Finally he turned and solemnly locked eyes on Sphax. 'I will trust you, Numidian. I care little for myself, but if any of my men suffer hurt from your horsemen, the Cavari will bring down the wrath of the gods on all Numidians. This I swear before you.'

Sphax had also come to a decision. 'You may keep your weapons. My men will simply escort you back to our camp and you can discuss these matters with Hannibal himself.' Idwal seemed satisfied with this and nodded agreement.

Astegal was furious and flew into a rage when Sphax informed him of the agreement he'd made with Idwal. But when Sphax invited him to kill the son of the Cavari chief Hannibal had just bribed with silver, he soon calmed down and thought better of it. After Astegal led his eshrin off to chase the last of the Volcae fugitives, Merbal told him he'd made a wise decision to negotiate and his men were grateful for it. They managed to find spare horses for Idwal and some of his followers and escorted by Mebal's eshrin, the little Cavari army made its way back to the river.

Sphax rode alongside Idwal. He was curious to find out why he'd ended up fighting for the Volcae after his father had allied the Cavari to Hannibal. Idwal told him that he was returning from Massilia to collect their horses stabled at Avenio. 'All Gauls are cousins in arms. It would have been dishonourable not to have come to their aid. Fortunately, by the time we arrived on the field it was already too late: our Volcae cousins had already fled.' Shaking his head he'd smiled politely at Sphax. 'I don't think we killed any of your people today, though we came close during that last charge.' Sphax returned the smile as he described Merbal's consternation at meeting with such tactics. Where had he learned the art of war, he'd asked? At length, Idwal described his mother's enlightened outlook on education and learning, how he'd been sent away at the age of seven to study with Greek scholars in Massilia, and of his studies of Xenophon and Zeno.

Affecting Elpis' scholarly high-flown Greek, Sphax quoted "You are well aware that it is not numbers or strength that bring the victories in war. No, it is when one side goes against the enemy with the gods' gift of a stronger morale that their adversaries, as a rule, cannot withstand them."

Idwal frowned, 'I too had to learn Xenophon by rote, but alas, I always found his thought pedestrian. I was much more interested in the teachings of Zeno and Solon. But tell me. How did a Numidian from the deserts of Africa learn to quote Xenophon?' Then it was Sphax's turn to describe how he too had been sent away at the age of seven, but in rather different circumstances. Idwal listened to Sphax's story with the deepest interest and sympathy, occasionally frowning or shaking his head in consternation. When the tale was told he smiled sadly at Sphax and said, 'I'm only a year older than you, but you remind me that little has happened in my life so far. How does it feel to be a free man again and your birth-right recognized by all around you?'

'Life is indeed sweet at the moment. My only disappointment is that my uncle has not yet appointed me general of cavalry and put me in charge of his campaign.' Idwal started chuckling again. Half a mile ahead he caught sight of Maharbal approaching with two eshrins in tow. 'Trouble does lie ahead, at least for me,' he told Idwal, briefly describing his relationship with the current general of Hannibal's cavalry. Merbal galloped off to meet him and Sphax watched as the captain began briefing him on the events of the morning, the general occasionally nodding. As the two of them halted before the Cavari, Merbal grinned at Sphax and winked slyly. This did little to alleviate the sinking feeling in Sphax's belly.

'My dear Idwal,' said Maharbal formally in perfect Greek, 'I'm pleased our little misunderstanding was resolved so swiftly. I had the honour of meeting your father, Lord Cenno, when Hannibal and I began negotiations at Nages. A fine and intelligent man.'

'It is kind of you to say so, Sir,' Idwal replied in an equally formal manner. 'The confusion was indeed quickly resolved thanks to the timely intervention of Sphax. I cannot commend his actions more highly, Sir.' So far Maharbal hadn't even acknowledged his presence.

'Unfortunately I will have to forgo the pleasure of your company for a while. I have to gather together my cavalry, which is rather scattered at present. But my excellent officer Merbal will escort you and your men to Hannibal. I'm sure our general will be delighted to see you and extend every courtesy to you and your men. But for now I must bid you farewell.' Maharbal waved his javelin in the air and signalled his eshrins to follow. As he sidled his mare past Sphax he growled, 'At least you've done something right today, boy.' And then he was off, with sixty Numidians struggling to keep up.

'I see what you mean,' Idwal said with sympathy. 'Somewhat difficult to please, I would say.'

'You might say that! Or, that he's just a miserable old bastard with the disposition of a bear with bellyache. But I mustn't be too disrespectful. He's already saved my life on at least two occasions so far.'

As they approached the river they saw Hannibal and his brother organising parties of engineers laying out a new camp to the south of the smouldering ashes of the old Volcae camp. Again, Merbal rode ahead of them to inform Hannibal of the events of the day and notify him of the approach of Idwal and his Cavari followers. The ferries were still busily criss-crossing the river, but now their cargoes were of food, tents and women and children. Some tents had already been erected and children were playing games on the blood-soaked grass where only a few hours earlier a battle had taken place. Sphax looked out for Fionn, but there was no sign of her.

Hannibal greeted Idwal warmly. Servants quickly brought tables and laid out bread, meat and wine for the Cavari. Sphax wasn't quite sure whether he'd been invited to this feast or not, but he was so famished he didn't care. Sitting in a quiet corner, hoping to go unnoticed, he demolished anything that was placed in front of him. At one point he overheard his uncle say to Idwal that his *visit* was timely. Sphax almost choked on the word. Visit! Had Astegal had his way, thought Sphax, Idwal's *visit* would have been on top of a bier.

After everyone had eaten their fill, Hannibal rose from the table with a cup of wine in his hand and gestured for silence. 'Honoured guests,' he began, 'tomorrow, on this very spot, we will hold a great council of war. It would not be an exaggeration if I were to tell you that at this meeting the fate of Carthage and the nations of Gaul will be decided. Guests and representatives from the Insubres and the Boii, your cousins from across the Alps, have been invited and will certainly attend. The policy and strategy of our forthcoming campaign will be decided at this historic council. So it is indeed timely and fitting that Idwal, in the absence of his esteemed father, will have the opportunity to represent the views of the Cavari people.' Hannibal paused theatrically, and gazed at the circle of faces seated all around him. Raising his cup he cried 'I salute and welcome you all.' Sphax managed to devour a bunch of grapes, a bowl full of olives and the last of the cheese during his uncle's speech.

Merbal swung himself onto the bench next to Sphax and in a hushed tone whispered, 'Your uncle wishes to have a private word with you later. When you've finished, just stand behind his chair and he'll join you.' Sphax nodded then asked, 'There's something else, Sir. I've been meaning to ask you all day.'

'Go on lad, what is it? You sound a bit solemn.'

'There are men in your eshrin who fought alongside my father. I know so little of him and cherish the few memories I have. But they are so few! It is my dearest wish to hear any stories of him or my mother. Would you and your men come to my tent this evening and I will gladly feast you all? Do say you will come, Sir, it would mean so much to me.'

Sphax could see that Merbal was deeply touched. 'My dear boy, your tent will not be big enough. Light a campfire and set benches around. I promise you a night to remember. There will be so many stories, such tales, such merriment!' Merbal stood. 'Remember to attend your uncle.'

After Merbal left Sphax casually walked around to where his uncle was engrossed in deep conversation with his brother Mago. Hannibal rose almost immediately and joined him. His uncle had eyes in the back of his head, thought Sphax.

'Shall we walk together?' It wasn't a question and Sphax had difficulty keeping up with him; his uncle seemed to do everything in a hurry. 'You did well today. Very well. I will not forget it.' For a few paces his uncle seemed to be gathering his thoughts. 'The Cavari chief's son Idwal speaks most highly of you. Both of you are of an age, are you not?' Sphax nodded. 'War is as much about alliances as battles and campaigns. Cavari territory lies at the heart of our supply route back to my brother Hasdrubal in New Carthage. If we are to receive reinforcements ... horses, weapons, supplies ... all will have to pass through their lands. The Cavari are vital to my plans and we must nurture their friendship. Whilst Idwal is our guest, you will be his host. Feast him this evening and cultivate his friendship. I shall send you servants and retainers to attend to their comforts. Spare nothing. Do you understand what is required of you, nephew?'

'Perfectly, Sir.'

'Then go and prepare.' Sphax was about to turn away when his uncle caught his eye again. 'One more thing. If all goes well I may have a further mission for you in a day or so. It will be in the nature of an embassy. I will speak of this later.'

As he went in search of Fionn he felt as if he was walking on air. Everyone had warned him that his uncle praised grudgingly, but now he was being entrusted with a mission, an embassy! His mind raced at the possibilities. After walking around the camp in circles for over an hour he finally caught sight of her outside a pair of grand pavilions that had been erected adjacent to one another. She looked lovely. Sphax had a terrible urge to disappear into the tent and take her there and then. But there were so many people milling around, most of whom he'd never seen before. His desire would have to wait.

'What's going on?'

'Your uncle. That's what is going on!' She sounded harassed.

'But this isn't our tent.' Around them servants were weaving in and out of the entrance carrying everything from couches to wine cups, and there was such a din going on around them that it was difficult for them to hear one another. The Iberian *caetrati* were camped nearby and Hannibal had sent them wooden casks of mead as reward for their services today. By now most of them were as drunk as Scythians and had either taken to song or brawling.

'Hannibal sent everything. Come and look. It is rather grand.' Sphax couldn't believe it. The floor was lush with carpets and set with couches. One end was taken up with a long banqueting table that would seat at least ten guests and their sleeping couch been screened off by a magnificent linen curtain dyed in saffron. A file of servants arrived, each one carrying a heavy oak chair, supervised by a bald-headed elderly man wearing a toga in the Greek style. 'That's Bostar,' said Fionn, rolling her eyes in irritation, 'our steward and now the head of our household servants.' Bostar overheard them, stepped between the chair setters and bowed low before Sphax. Speaking in cultivated Greek, he said 'I am here for you to command, Sir.'

'I don't have any commands,' Sphax replied, as bemused as Fionn was by all of this. Bostar frowned at him and began clucking like a mother hen with its feathers ruffled.

'Sir, it is your uncle's wish that Idwal and the Cavari are shown every possible courtesy and hospitality,' he clucked. 'It is for this reason that he's commanded me personally to supervise and ensure that every comfort is extended to both households.' The clucking continued as Bostar began to list and enumerate the comforts and conveniences to be extended. By now Sphax had stopped listening and was eyeing Fionn lustfully. Fionn knew him only too well, and a smile slowly played about her lips. Sphax tore his eyes away and smiling innocently at Bostar, cut him off mid-cluck.

'That's excellent, Bostar, but leave us now and attend to Idwal and the Cavari. With all this talk of hospitality that we need to extend, I have something urgently pressing that I need to extend to my lady.'

FIVE

I t was a strange sight. Even now, looking around him at the animated faces reflected in the firelight, Sphax found it hard to believe the laughter and toasting that was going on between Numidian and Cavari. A few hours ago they had tried their best to kill one another. It was a further mystery how they were managing to communicate with one another. Around him Sphax could hear snatches from every language bordering the Mediterranean.

When Sphax had suggested that afternoon they light campfires and place benches and tables outside, Bostar had been outraged and begun clucking in his high falsetto. It was only when he'd mentioned the additional thirty guests expected that evening that the steward reluctantly conceded; a reluctance eased by the placing of a silver didrachm in his palm. So the banqueting table they'd struggled with all afternoon was once more removed and reassembled out of doors. Benches and additional tables were found and the file of chair-bearers summoned to place them in strict precedence, according to protocol and custom.

As the honoured guest, Idwal was seated beside Sphax, who had chosen this occasion to wear his Roman toga, and as an insult to his ex-master had sought out Bostar's advice on how to fold it in the Greek manner. Then, as a final masterstroke, he'd remembered those beautiful red sandals that had once graced rat-face's feet. He searched them out and was flaunting them this evening. To his right sat Fionn, proudly wearing around her neck the solid gold torque he'd given her earlier that evening. Sphax hadn't told her the grisly details of how he'd acquired it. Beyond Fionn sat Merbal, who was much taken with her, and he'd been flirting courteously with her in his broken Latin. The Cavari had arrived first and were already seated when Merbal approached uncertainly with his Numidians, wearing the clothes they had fought in that day. At first the two peoples sat amongst one another in polite stiffness, but as the wine and ale began to flow, tongues were loosened and stories and jests began to be exchanged.

Then the food arrived hot and steaming from the kitchens and the Numidians ate as if they had never before tasted food from a plate. Be they Cavari or Numidian, everyone praised the feast that evening. To whet the appetite, guests had arrived to the aroma of great wafts of succulent meat from the ox that had been roasting all afternoon over a fire-pit. Salmon, trout and crayfish from the river were plentiful in these parts and

Bostar had also sought out lobster and oysters from the coast. There were delicacies of snails in cumin and hedgehogs boiled in sweet honeyed wine, all served on delicate earthenware plates. Each dish was served with its own sauce that varied from fiery garum to those delicately flavoured with saffron or fruit and seasoned with basil, rosemary and fennel. Soon, fat was running from the corners of mouths and lobster claws were being tossed from table to table. Amphorae of blood-red Campanian wines and casks of sweet Malacca were being drained with every course as a pleasurable silence descended on the guests.

Although Idwal was the honoured guest, it was an evening for Numidians. Sphax had distant memories of such nights in the house of his childhood. If a caravan arrived from across the great desert his mother and father would entertain and feast the travellers by firelight in their courtyard. Stories would be told, fantastical tales of serpents as long as a cypress is tall, of birds with feathers of flame that could carry off a gazelle, and of kings adorned with so much gold they had to be carried from place to place on mighty thrones.

Desert people are renowned storytellers. After the stories he would be sent to bed, protesting, yet already yawning and half asleep. He had a distant memory of falling asleep to the sound of laughter and merriment caught on the balmy air drifting in through the open shutters of his nursery. Was it a memory, or just a dream? It was all so long ago now.

As the night sky darkened and the stars began their journey through the heavens, an elderly Numidian rose from his table and stood before Sphax. Raising his cup to the assembled company he proclaimed, 'I salute you, son of Navaras, Prince among Numidians.' Sphax recognized him as Jugurtha, the veteran from Merbal's eshrin he'd fought alongside for most of the morning. He spoke in Tasusiyt, the ancient tongue of the peoples of the mountains in western Numidia. It was the dialect Sphax had learned from birth.

Jugurtha continued, 'I thank you and your beautiful lady for the splendour and generosity of the feast laid out before us this evening, especially for the rivers of wine that have sealed friendship between Numidian and Gaul.' This brought cheers and the raising of cups around the tables. When the exuberance died down he continued, 'Tonight I will tell the tale of Navaras, Prince of Numidia, and how he won the hand of the most beautiful and unattainable woman in Carthage.

'But I also speak of the darkest chapter in the history of my people, when Carthage refused to pay its mercenary armies returning from Sicily and abandoned them to roam the countryside like beggars. Great wrong was done on both sides and civil strife and mutiny spread across the land like a pestilence. Choosing what he thought was the lesser evil, our Prince allied himself to Spendios the Greek, the only man who could control the rebels and put an end to the discord that was laying waste to our lands. It was an alliance we soon came to regret, for Spendios was a serpent, a ravenous jackal bent only on filling his own purse. He cared as much for peace and justice as a viper feels for the mouse beneath its flickering tongue.'

Like all gifted storytellers, Jugurtha's words, however stirring and well chosen, merely painted a picture, a backdrop. It was his expressions, gestures and mimes that conveyed the real drama that held his audience spellbound. By turns heroic, pitiable or exultant, he strode amongst the tables like an actor on a stage. Throughout the course of Jugurtha's telling, Sphax heard whispered translations into Greek, but for most of the time, the expressions on his face and the gestures of his hands had his audience spellbound.

Jugurtha told of how the Numidians had come to trap the Carthaginian army of Hamilcar Barca in a steep-sided valley. Hopeless though Hamilcar's situation was, every morning he rode out to challenge the Numidians to battle; 'Fifty horsemen against two thousand! And every morning our Prince restrained us, thinking it dishonourable to massacre such a noble and courageous band.' Jugurtha spoke of their Prince's despair as the tyranny of Spendios spread like a plague. Broken and forlorn, Jugurtha described how on the sixth day Navaras assembled their entire company and begged them to return to their homes and families. "Through no fault of your own I have led you into a war that has become unjust, a stain on our honour. I have failed you."

Using all the wiles of the storyteller's art, Jugurtha then brought the story to a thrilling climax. Even Sphax was astonished at what his father had done next. Jugurtha described how Navaras rode alone into the Carthaginian camp, surrounded by thousands of jeering soldiers baying for his blood; how he'd dismounted in front of Hamilcar's pavilion and nobly placed his javelin at the feet of the Carthaginian and sworn his allegiance so the tyranny of Spendios could be justly ended. Jugurtha then told of how Hamilcar and Navaras rode out together to address them all.

"Valiant Numidians!" spoke Hamilcar. "Every warrior in the land fears your javelins and your skill on horseback. Rightly so, for few who meet you in battle live to tell the tale! Your noble Prince has offered me his service. By acting alone in good conscience, but without your consent, he fears he has forfeited the right to your love and allegiance. Furthermore, he insists that he no longer has the power to command you. Any decision must be yours and yours alone.

"Because of his courage and audacity this day, I have offered him high command in my army, and as a token of my esteem for him and to seal our alliance, I have also offered him my own daughter in marriage. From what I have already seen of his spirit and character, I know that I will come to love your Prince as a son.

"Will you help me end the tyranny of Spendios and this needless bloodletting? What say you? Will you

follow me? Will you follow your Prince once more?"
Instantly, two thousand javelins were raised in jubilant
affirmation.

'With our support and Hamilcar's wise leadership
the war against the mercenaries was swiftly won. When
peace was restored we all returned to Carthage to
celebrate the wedding of our Prince. I must tell you that
the Numidian people came to love Princess Similce as
much as Hamilcar came to love his new son.' Jugurtha
paused, looked around once more at the faces reflected in
the firelight, then gazed at Sphax with a curious mixture
of pride and sadness. 'And that is the tale,' he said finally,
'of how your father, Prince Navaras of Numidia, came
to win the hand of the fairest woman in Carthage.' He
raised a cup in toast and cried 'To the memory of our
long lost Prince, and the beautiful Similce.'

After cups were drained there was silence and
reflection for some moments as Jugurtha slowly returned
to his bench. For Fionn's benefit, Merbal had translated
Jugurtha's words into Latin, and now she reached out
for Sphax's hand. There were tears in her eyes as she
whispered, 'When I begged you to take me with you,
little did I know that I was running away with a prince.
I'm just an orphan of miserable Gauls.'

'Not any more,' replied Sphax with a teasing smile,
'you're now the *Princess* Fionn!' She spluttered a hollow
laugh. 'Besides,' he continued, 'I'm a prince without lands
or title, without even a country. I'm prince of nowhere …
Prince Pisspot!'

The stories continued well into the night. One after another, Numidians would stand and take the stage. They were consummate storytellers who could hold their audience in the palms of their hands, playing with them and causing them to weep or cheer, laugh or jeer. Most of the tales were comic, and seemed to involve his father getting his men into the most hair-raising scrapes, where it seemed they would barely escape with their lives but for his cunning and irrepressible charm. Patterns and traits he was all too familiar with. Perhaps he should not be blamed for the reckless impulsiveness of his own character, for it was abundantly clear that the same blood flowed in his father's veins.

Sphax suddenly felt the full force of a sandal scuff on his shins. Fionn, turning discreetly towards him, whispered earnestly 'You're neglecting Idwal and his followers, my love. Say something? Make a speech!'

Somehow he got to his feet, a hot flush of embarrassment rising to his cheeks. He'd never made a speech in his life, and felt childishly tongue-tied. 'Today,' he began awkwardly in Greek for the benefit of the Cavari, 'our general Maharbal placed his trust in my leadership and put me in charge of our Numidians.' Sphax paused, smiling to himself, for in that moment he knew exactly what he was going to say. 'Not before time, I may add! For having fought alongside my fellow Numidians for but two days, my skills with a javelin are already legendary and celebrated throughout our camp!' He was forced to pause as great guffaws of laughter had broken out amongst Merbal's men, and after the joke was passed on about his inability to hit an elephant's arse, the Cavari joined in. 'And my strategy worked so perfectly that I found it completely unnecessary to issue orders or commands of any kind. My veteran officers, such as the fearless Merbal seated beside me, read my intentions so completely that the merest hint of instruction on my part would have been deeply offensive to them.

'But then we did meet with a setback. A company had formed against us, small in number, but resolute and defiant. Merbal's veterans leapt forward, but at the last moment, instead of awaiting certain death from our javelins, the company had the audacity to charge forward and cast their spears at us. By all the gods! What effrontery! Warriors on foot are not *allowed* to charge cavalry. Why, it is against all the ancient rules of war!

'The excellent Mago next tried his luck, and sweeping his eshrin around he attacked from the rear. But quick as a bolt, the company faced about, and without even waiting for our mares to reach a trot, charged. Yes! Charged them!

'Behind me I heard men muttering, "who are these devils? They look like Gauls, but they fight like Hercules. What are we to do?"

'Every great general faces a crisis at some point in their career. It was just my bad luck this happened on my first day in the job. I had to do something. I was convinced that if I could but talk to the leader of these Herculeans, I could get them to see sense and abide by the rules of war. All who are present this evening witnessed our meeting on the battlefield, but none of you heard what was said between us. I will now give you a true and faithful account of that conversation.

'Keeping my introduction brief I said, "I am Sphax, son of Navaras, Prince of Numidia, nephew of Hannibal Barca and sixth cousin of Hanno the Diminutive."

"Have you come to surrender?" asked the Herculean. "I'm Idwal, by the way."

"I'm not sure. Do you think we should? Surrender I mean? It may be the only remedy," said I scratching my head, "for we are in a tight spot and only have two thousand with us."

"Then indeed, you are short on numbers. You have charged twice and failed on both

counts." Beside him, Idwal was shaking his head vigorously, but was by now so helpless with laughter he was hardly in a state to refute Sphax's comic invention.

"No! No! Hercules," said I, "you misunderstand. These were not *charges* as such! The first was merely a scouting mission to ascertain the speed at which your warriors run." Sphax had to pause again.

"And the second?" asked the mighty Idwal.

"To ascertain the distance and trajectory of your spear throwing! You must understand, Hercules, we Numidians study the art and science of war. We must gather such knowledge before risking life and limb against Volcae."

"But I am not Volcae," said Idwal.

"I thought not! Let me guess," said I, "then you must be descendants of Alexander, or the Spartan, Leonidas?"

"No. We are Cavari," answered Idwal proudly. And that is how the great misunderstanding between Numidian and Cavari was resolved this morning. I give you a toast to peace and friendship. To Lord Idwal and the noble Cavari.' Sphax raised his cup and saluted Idwal to the cheers of everyone gathered around the tables. Out of the corner of his eye Sphax caught sight of Maharbal standing beside Jugurtha. His pretty servant girl was wrapped around his waist and they were joking with a group of Numidians. How long had he been there, he wondered? It seemed his general missed nothing.

* * *

'Wake up, lad.' Sphax realised he was being shaken vigorously and there was no alternative but to open his eyes. He found himself staring at a Numidian with long plaited hair bound with golden rings. He was particularly ugly.

'What now?' moaned Sphax, his head throbbing and mouth as dry as a desert.

'Javelin practice. I'm Dubal. Maharbal told me to start you this morning so get up, you lazy bastard.'

'But I've only just got to bed.' This was not far from the truth. He and Fionn had been the last to take to their bed in the early hours of the morning after all the other guests had either staggered off or been carried from where they'd collapsed in a drunken heap. Beside him Fionn was snoring her head off. After emptying a jug of water and stuffing some stale bread in his mouth he followed Dubal to where the horses were tethered at the edge of the camp. It was barely light outside, but sentries were patrolling the perimeter; a camp never sleeps.

At least Dido was pleased to see him as he led her away to a flat grassy meadow within sight of the river. Jubal planted a shield fixed to a pole in the grass and then started counting steps away from it. Handing Sphax a javelin he said curtly, 'Aim for the shield'. He put everything into the throw but it still fell short. Counting as he paced, Jubal retrieved the javelin. 'Eighteen strides,' he said with a pitying smile. 'My young daughter throws further. But at least it's a start,' and handed Sphax the javelin. 'Try again.'

Before he'd even raised it above his shoulder Jubal yelled 'Stop!' and clipped him around the ear. 'You're holding the javelin like a whore tickles your prick! Find the point of balance, then grip.' Jubal demonstrated with his own weapon. 'I want to see all your knuckles lined up. Squeeze the life out of the bastard, then throw.' Sphax tried it and managed twenty paces. A dozen throws later he did hit the shield, but the barb glanced off the target and by now his right arm felt like lead.

Jubal sat down on the grass and reached for a leather pouch. 'Rest your arm and watch carefully.'

From the pouch he removed a thin strip of leather that was gathered in a loop at one end. After finding the point of balance on his javelin he started coiling one end of the leather around the shaft about a hand's length behind the grip. The coiling was precise; three turns around the shaft then two in the opposite direction, leaving a short length of leather ending in the loop. Jubal placed two fingers through the loop, kept the leather taut and raised the javelin. Sphax noticed he was holding the javelin differently. Jubal demonstrated the new grip. 'Now you try.'

It took Sphax some time to coil the leather to Jubal's satisfaction, but he eventually got it right. 'Now try it at the target.' He still missed, but was amazed that it sailed at least ten paces beyond the shield.

'How can that be? My arm's aching, yet I threw much further.' Sphax stared at the length of leather that had uncoiled itself from his javelin but was still looped around his fingers. 'That's impossible!'

Jubal just shrugged. 'The thong lengthens the arm, allowing us to throw further. It does something else though, something just as useful. As it uncoils from the shaft it makes the javelin spin, and a spinning javelin is much more likely to find its mark. Some men swear by the gods that one finger through the loop is best. I've always found two fingers to be more powerful and just as accurate. Bring me your javelin and I'll show you something.'

Placing both javelins on the ground in front of him he suddenly grinned at Sphax. 'Watch,' he said.

In a flash he had a javelin in his right hand and was rapidly coiling the thong. He let fly and the javelin buried itself into the shield, almost dead centre. As the tip sunk into the target Jubal already had the other javelin in his hand and was coiling in one skilful movement. The second javelin sank into the shield a finger's width from the first. Two deadly hits in the space of two breaths. Sphax stared at him. 'It's just practice lad ... just practice. Now I want you to try it from your mare.'

The sun was climbing in a clear blue sky when they set off back to camp. By that time Dido was tiring from an endless succession of headlong gallops and Sphax's right arm was throbbing from his fingertips to his shoulder. He could never have imagined that throwing a javelin at the gallop, whilst at the same time preparing Dido to slow to a standstill and turn around, could be so fiendishly complicated. But one thing was certain, when he used Dido's speed in combination with the throwing thong, the javelin became a deadly weapon with a surprising range. With one extremely lucky throw he'd sent the javelin point clean through the shield and watched as Jubal struggled to pull the entire shaft through to retrieve it. For the past two days he'd witnessed at first-hand how effective Numidian cavalry were; now he was beginning to understand why they were so deadly.

Back in camp he could hear the sound of querns grinding out the daily ration of barley that would be roasted over a thousand campfires. The faintly sweet aroma of roasted barley was to become a familiar smell every morning at first light. This morning it simply reminded him of his own hunger. Bostar met him at the entrance to his tent and clucked around him until servants arrived with more than enough food and drink to satisfy his needs. He could still hear Fionn snoring away and next door the Cavari were beginning to stir.

Picking up his javelin and the leather thong that Jubal had given him, he headed off for the riverbank. For the next few weeks the javelin was to become his constant companion. At meals it would rest on a bench beside him or sit across his lap. Soon he no longer had to search for the point of balance, his fingers could sense the grain of the wood where they needed to grip. As for folding the leather thong, after a few days he could tie it rapidly with his eyes closed. As Jubal had said, "it's just practice."

This morning he'd decided it was time for him to renew an acquaintance with a four-legged beast he'd not laid eyes on since childhood. They had been a common sight in his city, but here in Gaul they were as rare as dragons' eggs.

Even at this hour the riverbank was a hive of activity. Boats and rafts of every description were threading their way laden with supplies from the western bank. He soon found what he was looking for; an elderly gentleman wrapped in a filthy brown tunic with a hood that ended in a rumpled peak. His plaited raven-black hair was studded with gold and silver and in his right hand he carried a short wooden pole tipped with an iron spike. It was this that marked him out. He was a mahout. Arguing heatedly with a group of riverfolk gathered around several rowing boats it was difficult to make out what he was saying beyond a string of sibilants, for the poor old man seemed to possess only three serviceable teeth.

'Can I be of assistance, Sir?' Sphax asked politely in his mother tongue. The old Numidian gave him a near toothless grin. 'Thank ba 'al hamūn. A human at last! Can you tell these savages we need them on the other side of the river? They're as much use on this bank as a eunuch in a whorehouse.' He suddenly paused and squinted. 'By the gods … you're Sphax, aren't you?'

'The one and only.' He was beginning to find this irritating; everyone seemed to know who he was, yet he knew so few in this army of Hannibal. 'Are you bringing the elephants across today, Sir?'

'Yes. If we can get these lazy bastards to do some work,' pointing to the western bank with his spiked pole. 'I've thirty-seven elephants fed and watered on the other side, lined up with the experienced cows in the lead. The piers are built and the rafts are ready. All we need to do now is lead our old ladies on to the rafts and the rest will meekly follow. That is,' he broke off and glared at the Gauls, 'if we can get these savages to row the rafts across. Can you speak to them? They don't seem to understand a word I'm saying.'

Hardly surprising, thought Sphax. He tried Greek. Comprehension instantly dawned on several faces and it didn't take long to clear up the misunderstanding. Soon handshakes and backslapping were being exchanged as the old mahout was bundled into a boat and the crew prepared to cast off. 'Come and see this for yourself, Sphax,' the old man yelled as the craft drifted into the current. 'It will be a truly memorable sight ... a sight you'll never forget!'

He intended to. But he'd also promised to show these fabled beasts to his friend Idwal.

* * *

'Watch elephants! I forbid it, Sphax! You *have* to attend the Grand Council. It is your duty. Your uncle demands it. You are to sit beside Lord Idwal. All has been arranged.' Bostar was twitching, wringing his hands and shaking his head in despair. 'It would be unthinkable to disobey your uncle! And we're already late ... we must go. NOW!'

Sphax was incandescent with frustration. The last thing he wanted to do this morning was sit still and listen to speeches by old men. He'd risked everything to escape slavery only to find himself ordered from pillar to post, shackled by duties, training, obligations, and worst of all, grand councils of old men! He could still hear Fionn snoring like a pig. Picking up a bowl of olives he flung it in the direction of the noise. The only response was a stifled grunt, but the act seemed to release some of his frustration as he turned on his heels and followed Bostar.

The Grand Council of Gauls and leaders of Hannibal's armies was already in session. Guided by Bostar, Sphax slumped dejectedly into the chair provided for him beside Idwal. 'You're late,' his friend whispered as his uncle shot him a dark look, burning with disapproval.

Reluctantly, Sphax had to admit it was a splendid sight, and his spirits revived a little. Chairs and benches had been arranged in a huge oval, leaving a grassy sward in the centre for orators and their interpreters. Seated around this concourse were chieftains and delegates from every Gallic tribe from the Adria to the Tyrrhenian Sea. Gauls from the great plains bordering the river Padus sat beside tribesmen from the mountains in the far north, the land the Romans called Aemilia. Their dress and warlike attire presented a cacophony of colour and weaponry, at once resplendent and bewildering; Insubres, red cloaks clasped beneath golden torques and trousered in chequered braca interwoven with crimson and ochre squares; Ligurians clad in indigo cloaks and silvered conical helmets; moustachioed Vocontii in chequered green tunics; then there were the Taurini, the Cenomani, the Ingauni and the Boii, whilst he himself was seated amongst yet another tribe, the Cavari. It was like some grand re-union of an orphaned family whose members had been scattered to the four winds.

In hushed whispers, Idwal was listing them all and naming their chieftains, but there were too many for him to take in, let alone remember. For the first time he saw how vast and widespread the Gallic nation had become. But then he realised that Gaul was not a nation, at least not like Carthage, and certainly not like Rome. The Gauls were just a collection of peoples who spoke versions of a common tongue. His teacher Elpis had referred to them as the Celtoi, the savages, the tall ones from the north.

He guessed that each tribe would fiercely guard its own traditions and differences and would happily slaughter each other as kill Romans. How could his uncle possibly unite such a disparate people in his war with Rome? Was their hatred and fear of Rome greater than their rivalries and feuds with each other? His uncle also commanded fear and respect. But would that be enough to convince these proud, fractious people to follow his cause?

'Who is speaking?' he whispered to Idwal.

'The Boii chieftain, Magol.'

'What's he saying?'

'Be patient, Sphax, you'll hear a translation soon enough.' Sure enough, a silver-haired elderly man dressed in a Greek-style toga arose unsteadily from his chair to address the council in Punic. He had the air of a scholar and Idwal whispered that he was one of Hannibal's personal tutors. Frailty notwithstanding, the Greek's voice was firm and steady, and his powers of oratory exceptional.

'These are the words of Magol who speaks for the Boii. He warmly greets his brother Gauls and extends the peace and friendship of his people. To Hannibal and his illustrious army, he also extends the friendship of his people, in this, their greatest hour of need.

'Long have we suffered at the hands of Rome. They are as leeches, sucking the very life-blood of our people, driving us like sheep from our ancestral lands and settlements. First, their merchants inebriate and dull our young-folk with their wine, then they trespass and enslave. Legions trample our sacred ritual grounds, Roman settlements and outposts spring up on our farmlands, Praetors proscribe our trade and levy taxes on us. The only gods the Romans worship are those of conquest and theft. These are the words of Magol.

'But the Boii are not to be driven like sheep! On many occasions in the past we have risen up and fought our oppressors. With the aid of our brothers in arms, the Insubres and the Ligures, we have driven the Romans from our land. They are not invincible. On the field of battle we have defeated them and slaughtered their legions. But always they return, with more soldiers, more merchants, more tax collectors, farmers and settlers ... They are like an unstoppable floodtide, a ravenous beast that feeds on the carcasses of the oppressed and vanquished.

'Today the Boii are fighting to turn back this tide; we have marched on their outposts of Placentia and Cremona. We will burn them to the ground, but Rome has sent forth legions under Praetor Lucius Manlius.' Sphax's ears pricked up at this. He'd heard of these settlements in the north, and by reputation alone the name of Lucius Manlius would send shivers down any spine. The Greek continued, 'More legions will come and the Boii are few. If we do not receive succour now, by next spring my people will be driven from our lands and Rome will have triumphed. The Veneti have betrayed us and sided with the enemy. The Taurini are cautious and undecided. This is not a time for caution! This is a time for action. We appeal to all our friends and allies. Now is the time for deeds and courage. These are the words of Magol.

'For the last few days as I've walked amongst this noble army and spoken to its commanders, I have heard of only one dread, one fear, one terror. What could this be, you ask? Is it the might of Rome? Or its legions? Certainly not! For the victors that breached the walls of Saguntum, crossed the great Rhodanus and put the Volcae to flight, Rome's legions hold no terrors for them. Then what could it be?

'I will tell you. This brave and noble army is terrified of mountains. Mountains! The Boii would laugh in your faces and say, "Do they not know there are safe passes through these mountains? Even our women and children are familiar with these places and ofttimes journey over them. So what have brave warriors to fear from the Alps?" These are the words of Magol.

'As final proof, I myself, and all my followers travelled over the highest pass in these mountains two weeks ago. Our only misfortune was that my servant got a bout of the shits and was unable to pour my wine. Look around you. Many seated beside you, such as the Insubres and the Ligures have also crossed through these passes. If they had not undertaken such a journey they would not be here today. Do they look as if they are cowering in fear like little children at the prospect of returning home through these very passes? No! The idea is preposterous.

'I say to the Carthaginians and Libyans amongst you that there is nothing to fear from the Alps. The season grows late, but not too late to impede our progress, and if the legions of Gauis Scipio are foolish enough to follow us, nature and the lie of the land would offer ample opportunity to lure them into ambush and destroy them. But we must act now, and we must act swiftly. These are the words of Magol.

'Today the Boii and Insubres are holding back this Roman tide. But I promise you, your turn will come. It may be next spring or three winters hence, but one thing is certain, your turn will come. Sooner or later.

'I implore you. Let it be sooner! Let it be now, whilst we are strong and of one mind. With the wealth and power of Carthage behind us we surely cannot fail. Let us march with Hannibal on Rome. Let us crush the Romans and drive them from the face of the earth. These are the words of Magol.'

As one, every soldier in Hannibal's army rose to his feet and began cheering. Some even walked over to where the chieftain was seated and began slapping him on the back. Not so some of his fellow Gauls, who looked sullen and downcast. It took some time for order to be restored and the council to resume.

That's when the purgatory began for Sphax. An endless succession of speakers droned on and on, relentlessly. As the morning grew hot and the sun climbed in the sky, drowsiness took its toll. All too often he found his chin jerking upwards from his chest and realised he'd nodded off. After one such occasion he recalled he'd been dreaming of elephants. Later he felt a sharp prod to his side and Idwal whispered 'Wake up, Sphax. Hannibal is about to speak.' He stiffened and opened his eyes in time to see his uncle striding to the centre of the concourse. He spoke in Punic, but paused frequently to translate what he'd said into Gallic.

'I am decided. Carthage will honour our alliance with the Boii and Insubres. With the guides you have generously provided, my army will cross the Alps and meet with you on the plains beside the Padus, where together, united against our common foe, we will drive the enemy from your lands once and for all time. It pains me to think that we leave two Roman legions unmolested in our rear. Nevertheless, my army will strike camp tomorrow and march north.

'I say to those chieftains and delegates amongst you who still waver or are undecided, what Magol warned will come to pass.' A steely urgency now crept into his voice as he paused and gazed intensely at the sea of faces hanging on his every word. 'Carthage marches on Rome. We have sworn sacred oaths and sacrificed to Melqart. I say again, Carthage marches on Rome. Make no mistake in this. Gauls who join us will be welcomed as comrades, brothers in arms. Wealth and gifts will be showered on them, lands restored and given in reward. The wealth of Rome will be returned to the people they stole it from. All this will be given to those who willingly join our great cause.

'But to the doubters and naysayers I say this; if you are not with us, then you are against us.' Hannibal allowed his last sentence to hang in the hushed silence that followed. Slowly he returned to his seat at the head of the concourse. The spell was only broken by Bostar, who rose to his feet and clapped his hands, releasing a swarm of servants that weaved amongst the delegates, bearing food and wine.

It's now or never, thought Sphax, snatching a chicken leg and a chunk of bread from a passing servant. 'If you want to see elephants, Idwal, we must go now!' His friend frowned and a pained expression descended from his brow to his chin. Sphax was beginning to recognise this expression ... 'but I have duties and responsibilities,' it pleaded. Sphax was having none of it this morning. 'Dog's twat, Idwal, the meeting's over. After they've stuffed their bellies they might come back and drone on all afternoon, but Hannibal's already told them what they must do. There's nothing more to be said!'

'I don't know, Sphax…'

'You will never again see such a sight, I promise you. Let's *go!*' With bread and a chicken leg in one hand, and his javelin in the other, he rose and forced his way through the crowds behind him. By the time Idwal caught up with him Sphax was running at a swift pace towards the river. When they reached the riverbank both were panting and at the same time trying to stuff food in their mouths, with the result that crumbs and chicken skin were being spluttered in all directions.

Sphax was jubilant! The elephants had not crossed the river. He guessed something must have gone wrong, for it was hours since the old mahout had told him they were about to bring them across. Looking around for riverfolk, he saw a group upstream unloading cargo from a large craft with oars and a sail. That will do, he thought. Sphax had already learned that silver buys you anything in this world, and after some haggling, they were soon installed in the prow, watching the rowers ploughing the treacherous waters.

As they approached the eastern bank, Sphax marvelled at the Carthaginian engineers who'd constructed the twin piers that boldly jutted out into the great river. He guessed they were at least forty paces long and five wide. These must be for the elephants, he thought. At regular intervals enormous logs had been driven into the riverbed, acting as buttresses for longer lengths that had been laid horizontally to shutter the sides. Above this, what looked like a platform of planks had been laid and earth piled on top. Nearing the bank, Sphax signalled to the master to take them closer to one of the piers. It was only then that he noticed that the last section of each jetty was floating freely and was in fact a raft of sorts, lashed to the ends of each jetty, providing the means by which the animals would be ferried across. It was an ingenious solution. Mahouts could never have coaxed elephants to step down into a boat. Again, Sphax marvelled at the planning and labour involved; it must have been a colossal undertaking. He was puzzled by the earth piled on top of the platforms. It had been built up to the same height as the river bank, creating a continuous pathway from the bank to the rafts at the end of each jetty. Perhaps it was to fool the elephants into thinking they were still on dry land.

Several boats were tied up alongside the piers, their crews passing the time of day, but otherwise the eastern bank was deserted. There was no sign of the elephants or their mahouts. He and Idwal strode out in the direction of the abandoned Carthaginian camp. It was then that they saw them: two straggling columns of the great beasts, marching ponderously across the grasslands. Sphax smiled in wonder. They looked so out of place in this lush green landscape dotted with willow and birch groves. His memories were of parched desert soils and the creatures seeking shade under tamarisk and acacia. As a child, they were a common sight in his city. In his mind's eye, Sphax had imagined gigantic monsters with tusks the size of tree trunks. Childhood memories can play tricks with reality. Nevertheless, if not quite the monsters from his childhood, these creatures were still huge and fearsome. When driven to a state of wild frenzy by their mahouts, he would certainly not like to meet them in battle.

He counted thirty-six of them. Only the leading elephants were being ridden by their mahouts, the rest plodded on foot beside their charges. Sphax recognised the old mahout he'd spoken to earlier that morning, riding one of the larger cows leading out one of the columns. He had a face like thunder. Sphax wondered what calamity had befallen the herd. As he grew nearer he hailed him. 'You're late, Sir! Are you in need of my services again, Master of Ifil?' Sphax had spoken in Tasusiyt and used the ancient Numidian name for elephant, but all he got in return for his trouble was a stream of abuse.

'Mind your manners, young pup! I ought to give you a good thrashing. If this was the market place at Zag'ra, I would have hauled you by the ears to your father's house and watched him give you that thrashing, may ba 'al hamūn shelter his soul. He was a good man.'

'I beg your pardon, Sir, I meant no offence. But perhaps I would be more courteous if I knew your name. You seem to know mine, not to mention that of my father, and probably my mother also.'

'That is so, Master Sphax, and I've long mourned their passing. I was once Master of Ifil to your father, Navaras, and earlier this morning it truly filled me with joy to look upon the face of his son once more, as if returned from the dead. If I remember rightly, even as a child you showed some promise as a horseman. Your father had hopes for you. Have you fulfilled that promise?'

'I try, Sir. Every day I try ...' Sphax suddenly felt a lump in his throat. Grief had long since been beaten out of him at the hands of Romans, but like a thief in the night, at moments like this it still caught him unawares. It took only a memory, a fleeting image of recollection to open up that wound of pain and emptiness. The master of elephants caught something of this from his downcast expression and hurried on.

'When you and your family did not return, I offered my services to the Barcas, and now I serve your uncle. My name is Hiempsal.' Sphax had been walking abreast of Hiempsal's elephant, all the while stroking her flanks and patting her behind the ears when he suddenly remembered Idwal. Looking around, he saw him rooted to the spot, a safe twenty paces distant, cowed by the sight of these monsters.

'I am delighted to meet you, Hiempsal, and what's the name of this great lady?' he asked, patting the beast's flanks.

'Why, this is a true queen, and her name is Dido.'

'Come and meet another Dido, Idwal,' he shouted across to his friend. 'She's a bit bigger than my Dido, but just as friendly when you get to know her.' Idwal didn't move a muscle. 'Come on, Idwal, she won't bite you.' By now some of the mahouts were grinning at Idwal and waving him over to take a closer look. Reluctantly, Idwal screwed up the courage to walk alongside Sphax, making sure he stayed as far away from the beast's tusks as courtesy would permit. Sphax grinned up at Hiempsal and winked. 'Do you have such a thing as an apple for your queen, Master of Ifil?'

An apple was tossed down from on high. Sphax caught it and handed it over to Idwal. 'Now stretch out your arm and place the apple on your palm.' Bemused, Idwal did as he was told. In a flash a trunk appeared out of nowhere and the apple disappeared, as if by magic. Idwal recoiled with a stifled cry, and was left staring in disbelief at his empty palm as great guffaws of laughter broke out all around him.

'You see ... she likes you already! I think you've made a friend for life,' declared Sphax, struggling to keep a straight face. As they made steady progress towards the river, Hiempsal described the calamity that had befallen them earlier that morning. One of his mahouts hadn't noticed one of the younger cows was about to come into season for the first time. When their largest bull elephant, called Surus — which Sphax took to mean the Syrian — caught a whiff of her scent it sent him into an amorous frenzy, trumpeting his masculinity and chasing the little cow around the fields. The elderly matrons, including Dido tried to protect the young cow from his unwanted attentions, but by then all was in chaos and confusion. Hiempsal told him that when driven mad with such desires, bull elephants were very dangerous and almost impossible to control. They had lit torches and threatened the rampaging bull with fire, finally cornering the beast in an olive grove, miles away to the west. In the meantime they had managed to separate the young cow and keep her isolated from the rest of the herd. She was now the sole responsibility of the disgraced mahout, who would bring her across the river tomorrow.

The earthen piers were now a hundred paces distant. 'Is the soil there to make them think they're still on dry land?' Sphax asked. 'Yes,' nodded Hiempsal, 'we would never have persuaded our elephants to walk out into the river on wooden planks. Even so, I'm praying to ba 'al hamūn it will work.' He raised his hand as a signal for everyone to halt, and for a man of his years, dismounted with remarkable agility. 'Your friend may be of use to me. I have to explain to these savages what they must do when we have three elephants loaded securely on each raft. We think it safe to take three at a time. The towing ropes must be secure and taut, and when I give the signal, they must row as if their lives depended on it!'

Idwal was only too happy to put some distance between himself and Dido's tusks. The three of them walked the length of the piers and standing on the raft, beckoned the riverfolk to row over and hear his instruction. Hiempsal mimed every action his mahouts would undertake to place three elephants securely on the rafts. Then he demonstrated the signal he would make when the raft's ropes had been cast off. He did this several times, each with more exaggerated gestures. Finally, with bulging eyes and puffed out cheeks, he made rapid rowing motions with his arms that would have sent any boat shooting out of the water if the oarsmen had followed his demonstration.

By now most of the Gauls were grinning at this unexpected entertainment. With some interjections from Sphax, Idwal had translated everything, but he was not sure how much his friend had embellished Hiempsal's actions for the amusement of his fellow Gauls. Sphax gazed down at the current. It was so swift! A leaf could disappear downstream and be out of sight in the time it took a man to draw breath.

After checking that the ropes were securely tied to both the rafts and the twin pairs of rowing boats, Hiempsal seemed satisfied. At the last moment the Master of Ifil decided it wouldn't do for the elephants to be able to see for themselves what was happening, so the columns were led back to a scrubby area of willow that screened all sight of the river. Dido herself was saved to lead across two of the more skittish youngsters. Hiempsal selected the mahouts and two of the most experienced older cows to lead out the first elephants that would cross the great Rhodanus.

The first test would be the jetties themselves. Would the beasts step on to the earthen roadways that led out into the river? Sphax found his heart pounding as he walked beside the lead cow as it approached the right-hand jetty. To everyone's utter relief she didn't hesitate or falter, but padded onwards towards the waiting raft, leading out two elephants that followed meekly behind. So far so good, he thought. Idwal took up station on the riverbank. Nothing would have persuaded him to share a raft with an elephant! Hiempsal followed in the rear, ready to untie the ropes and give the signal for the rowers to haul away.

Once safely on the raft, Sphax stood beside the cow, gently stroking her flanks to keep her calm whilst Hiempsal worked feverishly at the ropes that would free the raft from the jetty. It was such a novel situation that he and the mahouts found themselves grinning at one another; here they were, men and beasts, standing on a raft in the middle of a mighty river. However, the grins were soon to be wiped from their faces.

It happened with shocking suddenness. As the raft drew free and the rowers hauled on the oars, the craft swayed and then lurched sickeningly in the current. The two younger cows squealed in terror, raising their trunks and backing away from the edge of the raft that had dipped into the swirling waters. Only the experienced older cow stood firm. In the next moment two mahouts had fallen from their mounts and slid into the river. Sphax looked on in horror as they were swept away downstream. Next it was the turn of one of the younger cows. Thrashing around in blind panic, she started sliding towards the edge of the raft tilting into the river. With one last desperate sweep of her tusks in an effort to stay on her feet, she dealt Sphax a powerful blow to his hip that sent him sprawling over the side. Man and elephant hit the water at the same moment, but by the grace of the gods, on either side of the careering raft. As his mouth filled with foul-tasting river water his last vision was of a watery world of swaying grasses and reeds. He'd never learned to swim.

What had almost certainly swept the two mahouts to a watery grave now saved his life. The current was so powerful that it slammed his head against the side of the raft. For one heart-stopping moment he thought he would be dragged under the craft and swept away. Frantically his hands sought out a purchase on the rough-hewn logs lashed together at the base of the raft. With his feet still being sucked underneath, he managed to haul himself coughing and spluttering to the surface.

He gasped air into his lungs, but instantly started choking and spewing river water. For some moments he just clung there, coughing and retching, whist the current dragged at his lower legs. He was suddenly aware of voices yelling and shouting nearby, but at that moment it was enough for him to cling on to the hemp lashings and gather his wits.

He checked his leather pouch strung around his neck was safe, then seeing lashings just above his head, he reached out for them and dragged himself further out of the water. Now only his ankles could feel the tug of the current and he felt safe enough to swivel his head around and get his bearings.

The chorus of voices had come from oarsmen in one of the boats yelling encouragement. Above him, he could just make out the huge wrinkled foot of the old cow elephant. Despite the oarsmen pointing and waving, Sphax guessed that the mahout mounted on her would not be able to see him clinging to the side and would have assumed he'd been swept away, along with his own comrades.

He looked up again at that monstrous wrinkled foot. What would happen if a hand suddenly appeared out of nowhere beside it? The poor creature was already enduring one of the most stressful events of her life. Sphax imagined the power of that stamping foot, crushing and splintering every bone from his knuckles to his fingernails. Even if he could work his way around the raft and away from those feet, the sudden appearance of a dripping body emerging from the river might equally spook an already jittery animal. It just wasn't worth risking. But the alternative was equally grim.

Sphax stared out at the eastern bank then glanced in the opposite direction. He judged they were roughly midstream by now. The far bank looked an eternity away. Pain and cold were beginning to seep into every bone in his body, his head throbbed and his hip ached from the blow he'd received from the young cow's tusk. But there was nothing for it. He would have to cling on for dear life and endure it.

There was a look of utter astonishment on the mahout's face as he staggered up the riverbank like a half-drowned rat. Sphax was beyond speech, let alone explanation. He just sat down in the mud with his head between his knees, shivering and shaking from the ordeal. The next moment he heard voices all around him. It was the oarsmen, patting him on the back and draping a dry cloak around his shoulders. Someone offered him a wineskin and he drank gratefully, coughing and spluttering between gulps.

Only the older cow and its mahout had made it across. Sphax hadn't seen the other young cow plunge into the river. But it was worse. He could see the other raft being rowed back to its starting point at the end of the pier. It was empty.

The mahout came and sat beside him, and they both stared out at the empty river in silence. Finally, the mahout said in a voice beyond sadness, 'I didn't see you clinging to the raft. I thought you had been swept away like Fuabal and Mintho. I'm sorry ...' he stammered, tears running down his cheeks.

Sphax put his arm around the lad's shoulder. 'You could not have seen me, mounted as you were. Besides, I was luckier than your friends.'

'What's that?' The mahout suddenly stiffened and stared into the middle distance. Sphax followed his gaze. There was something; a disturbance in the current; a shifting shape near the surface.

They both shot to their feet at the same moment, wide-eyed, mouths gaping. This could not be, thought

Sphax! How was this possible? But there was no mistake now. The swirling current was being disturbed by elephants' trunks, and the fleeting shapes they'd glimpsed were the ears and rumps of the beasts. It was a sight that Sphax would remember to the end of his days. Slowly, ponderously, the outline of five elephants gradually emerged from the waters of the river, like shades passing through the veil of the underworld into the land of the living. Flapping ears and trunks like dogs shaking water from their fur, they marched up the bank to be greeted by the old cow and a jubilant mahout, dancing and splashing around in the mud. Nothing could bring back Fuabal and Mintho, but at least they hadn't died in vain. Their elephants, and those on the other raft, were the first to make it across the great river.

Sphax imagined them pounding along the riverbed, in that underwater world of flowing grasses he'd glimpsed himself for an awful moment, trunks raised high out of water to fill their lungs with life-giving air, untroubled by the racing currents swirling above their heads. They were truly remarkable creatures. Nevertheless, it was nothing short of miraculous that they had made it across.

The mahout, whose name he discovered was Mathos, was now rounding up the six elephants and leading them to a holding area well supplied with low growing trees and shrubs for the animals to browse upon. 'I'll need your help, Sphax,' he said. 'You're now a mahout. Would you mount that older cow over there? She's sweet-natured and very placid.'

She didn't look it, thought Sphax, and her rump was at least a head taller than him. How would he mount her? Mathos stood in front of the creature, stared into those mournful brown eyes and muttered something which Sphax didn't quite catch. Immediately the creature bowed her tusks and bent her forelegs, and all he had to do was slide on to her back. He was a mahout. By the time they took up station by the riverbank, he'd not only learned a few commands, but was also beginning to enjoy the slow rhythmic rolling of an elephant's gait.

'There they are,' cried Mathos, pointing to midstream. Sphax could just make out the rafts and their precious cargoes. He counted four elephants. Had they already lost two to the river? As the rowing boats drew the rafts closer he could see that the mahouts were no longer mounted, but standing behind their charges. He and Mathos anxiously scanned the waters for the sight of raised trunks, but could see none, which meant that the elephants had been wisely restricted to two for each raft. Hiempsal was learning, and learning quickly.

As the afternoon wore on, a sight that should have been miraculous became commonplace, as raft after raft bearing a pair of elephants crossed the great river. Sadly, not without further mishap; another young mahout lost his life to the river, and three more elephants fell overboard, ploughing their way to the other side along the riverbed. But none of these calamities were due to lack of thought by Hiempsal or the skill of the rowers. By their very nature, elephants are jittery and unpredictable creatures. As the sun was beginning to set, Hiempsal himself came safely over with the large bull they called the Syrian. He came over alone, not wanting to risk any more lives with this dangerous animal. Still mounted on his elephant, Sphax greeted him at the riverbank.

'You have returned from the dead once more, master Sphax. Until the rowers brought back the news that you had clung to the side of the raft I had given you up for lost. You seem to have acquired the habit of cheating death itself. You must teach me this secret.'

'I was just very lucky, Sir, unlike Fuabal and Mintho.' They were joined by Idwal, who had crossed the river in the last rowing boat. 'Am I glad to see you!' he said, grinning up at Sphax.

Proudly he rode his elephant back through camp to the area that had been set aside for them. Of the thirty-seven elephants that had set out that morning to cross the great river, all but one had made it safely across, and he was sure the young cow in season would be brought across safely tomorrow morning. As he slid off his elephant, the sight of his bare feet reminded him of the one thing that aggrieved him that afternoon. His prized red sandals, with their lovely silver ornament were now at the bottom of the Rhodanus, where they would probably remain for all eternity. Then and there, he vowed he would acquire the most expensive pair of sandals money could buy for his triumphal entry into Rome.

SIX

'You're in trouble!' Fionn was glaring at him, seated imperiously on her sleeping couch, surrounded by Bostar's lackeys, every lamp in the pavilion glowing brightly. 'Maharbal's sent messengers every hour for you to attend him. Twice has your uncle summoned you. Where have you been?' she cried, exasperated at his seeming indifference.

'I went for a swim,' he answered, far too weary from the day's ordeal to say more.

'Swim!' She flung the word back at him. 'But you can't swim.' At that moment Bostar entered with a face like thunder. Before he had time to open his mouth, Sphax rounded on him, raising his hand in warning. 'SILENCE,' he boomed. 'I will not answer one single request, duty or summons until I have filled my belly. Bring food and drink. Do you understand?'

As he spoke, he'd strode menacingly towards Bostar, who'd retreated backwards in the direction of the awning and then the exit. Sphax gave Fionn a withering look and sat down at the banqueting table that had once more been brought indoors and re-assembled. Food arrived in double-quick time, so he ate and drank contentedly in blissful silence. At least to begin with, before the visitor and then the messenger arrived.

Merbal arrived first. He bowed to Fionn then joined him at table, helping himself to wine and cheese. 'Before you ask,' said Sphax, 'Hiempsal and I brought thirty-six elephants across the river this afternoon. Six mahouts were drowned. I nearly became the seventh.'

'I didn't know you were a mahout, lad?'

'Neither did I until today. So, whatever you think, I haven't been sitting on my arse all afternoon. Is Maharbal angry with me?' Merbal speared a chunk of cheese and poured himself more wine.

'No more than usual,' he shrugged. 'The problem is,' he continued, 'you should have been sitting on your arse all afternoon. At that council meeting!' Sphax rolled his eyes and put down his cup.

'I would have died of boredom, Sir. I would rather take my chances swimming the great river than listen to toothless old men bleating on about the perils to come. I'm looking forward to the perils to come.' Now warming to his subject he raised his cup in toast. 'That's why I'm here, to fight Romans, not talk about them!' He noticed that Merbal was smiling at him.

'You are so like your father.' Then the smile disappeared. 'This is what Maharbal fears.' Merbal paused and fixed his eyes on him. 'No one loved your father more than Maharbal. He would have laid down his life for him, almost did, on two occasions. But there is no doubting the fact that your father was one of the most reckless and foolhardy men that ever lived.' Merbal paused again, but still held his gaze.

'We face the might of Rome, lad, not just a few perils to come. It will take all our skill, discipline and intelligence to defeat her and overthrow the Republic. Recklessness will not be enough. It could never be enough. Maharbal rejoices in the knowledge that you are your father's son, but he also thinks you can be so much more! You're still a boy really, yet you speak four languages, can read and write and from what I've been told, are something of a scholar. Maharbal sees all this in you, and more. He wants to mould you into something greater than your father. Don't you see that, Sphax?'

Sphax lowered his eyes and stared at his empty plate. For the last ten years he'd been treated as the lowest of the low, lower even than a menial door-slave. Even Elpis said he'd a head as empty as a virgin's fanny. Without meeting Merbal's eyes he said, 'Then I will only disappoint him, Sir. I will never amount to much.' He was spared further anguish by the arrival of a uniformed Libyan who delivered a curt message. Hannibal awaited him.

Merbal rose from the table. 'Put on your toga, shave and smarten yourself up.' As he reached the awning he turned around. 'Think carefully on what I've said.' Then he was gone.

He could hardly keep pace with the Libyan, who bore a flaming torch aloft to light the way, but Hannibal's grand pavilion was only a short distance away. Guards posted at the entrance moved aside at their approach and as they entered the pavilion the Libyan announced his name. As his eyes adjusted to the brightness of the oil lamps, he began to take in the sumptuous richness of the furnishings. The last time he'd entered this tent he'd left in something of a hurry.

At the head of the room three divans had been placed in a semi-circular arrangement, so their occupants could recline and converse easily with one another. His uncle sat bolt upright on the central couch, whilst to his right Sphax recognized the venerable Greek who had translated at the grand council. To his uncle's left, another Greek, judging from his style of his toga, reclined on his elbow with a cup in his hand. Servants were busily removing plates and the leftovers of a supper. Sphax was not offered refreshment. He stood patiently before his uncle, who seemed in no hurry to begin the audience.

'I hear you have been extremely lucky this afternoon.'

'Six young mahouts were not so fortunate, Sir.'

'Mahouts can be replaced,' Hannibal said coldly. 'You, however, are of use to me. Refrain from such recklessness in future, unless you have ambitions to become a Master of Elephants.'

'You already have the finest Numidian in that position, Sir. Otherwise, my father would never have appointed him in the first place.' Momentarily, his uncle's dark eyes flashed up at him, perfectly aware of the subtle barb to his authority in his nephew's words. His uncle's jaw softened. There was no more than a slight lengthening and wrinkling of the lips, but it was sufficient to register what some might call a smile.

'Quite so, nephew. Quite so.' His uncle leant back on the divan and closed his eyes. 'Our alliance with the Gauls in Liguria hangs by a thread. I fear if we delay, all will be lost. Against my better judgement, tomorrow we break camp and march north to the Island, where the Tricastini will furnish us with food and clothing to sustain us over the mountains. We will either find a way, or make one.

'Two days hence, centurions will be poking around in the ashes of our campfires, but by then my army will be long gone. At least we will keep the initiative.' So far his uncle had spoken in Punic, but he suddenly switched to Greek and glanced to his right. 'The art of war is, in the last result, the art of keeping one's— '

'—freedom of action', Sphax interrupted in Greek, completing the quotation from Xenophon.

'You know something of Xenophon?' asked the silver-haired Greek.

'Yes. I have read and studied him,' Sphax replied in Greek.

'Can you read?'

'Of course, Sir. In Greek and Latin.' For the first time the reclining figure to his uncle's left seemed to take an interest in the proceedings. Wagging his finger at Sphax he sneered, 'You mean to tell me that the Romans are now educating their slaves in Greek and Latin! This is preposterous, boy.'

Sphax flushed and felt a rush of anger. With a great effort he took a deep breath and switched to Latin. If this was to be a battle of languages, Latin would undoubtedly give him the upper hand, so he spoke as rapidly as intonation would allow. 'In the household of Gaius Lucilus, a Greek scholar, Elpis of Corinth was employed as tutor to Gaius's son, Marcellus. Elpis and his wife Airla were the only people to show me kindness in Rome. In secret, Elpis taught me mathematics, logic and philosophy, whilst Airla taught me to read and write. I might add, Sir, at great risk to themselves.'

'I've never heard of this Elpis of ...,' the Greek retorted dismissively.

'Then you are the poorer, Sir. His Geographica Africanus and treatise on polygons are widely respected and much studied.' To his knowledge, Elpis had never written a treatise in his life! But the Greek was not to know that, and Sphax was enjoying the growing discomfort on the man's face. To Sphax's astonishment, his uncle appeared to be laughing.

'My dear Silenos, it appears I've found the perfect scholar to fill those lamentable gaps in your knowledge of geography and geometry.' His uncle's mirth only added to the Greek's discomfort. However, in an instant his uncle's expression changed to that familiar brooding seriousness. 'I have a task for you, nephew. That is why I have been so open about my plans.' His uncle closed his eyes once more and leant back on the divan. 'Idwal returns to Nages tomorrow with his followers. You are to accompany him. Alone. Your woman will join us on our march north. Be assured, Maharbal will see to her comfort and well-being.

'Your mission is twofold; to persuade Idwal's father to release his son and as many of his followers who can be persuaded to join our cause, and secondly, to ensure that the Cavari protect and keep open our supply lines to Iberia. The road west to the Pyrenees lies in the shadow of the great oppidum of Nages. Whoever holds Nages, holds the keys to the west. Without its protection we will not be able to bring reinforcements from our heartlands in Iberia. Rome controls the seas, so we must keep our overland routes open.

'You will find Idwal's father a different proposition from his son. Whereas your friend is content to pore over a Greek text, Lord Cenno is more suited to carousing with his warriors in the feasting hall. Idwal's mother was highborn, and Greek. It was she who insisted her son was to be educated in Massilia. I understand she died in childbirth some ten years ago. But do not underestimate Lord Cenno. He is no fool.

'Before you and Idwal became … unaccountably absent from the grand council this morning, you would have heard the address given by Magol, chief of the Boii. You will recall that he spoke of holding back the Roman tide. Roman ambitions are boundless. Carthage has always recognised this. The Gauls are only now waking to this threat. Either by conquest or treachery, they will be masters of all the lands surrounding the Mediterranean. In our last treaty Carthage foolishly gave them Sicily, and in return they stole Corsica from us. Rome has an insatiable appetite for war, conquest and taxes.

'These are the fears that will play best in Lord Cenno's mind. Plant them well, nephew. Nurture them, feed them, whisper them in his ears both day and night, so that Rome becomes for him a waking nightmare.

'As for Idwal: friendship and fellowship amongst men is the greatest pleasure the gods have bestowed on us. Make use of it.' Hannibal opened his eyes and gazed up at him. For the first time Sphax noticed that his uncle's eyes differed in hue; the left a penetrating steel-grey, whilst the right had a milky cast to it. He wondered if it caused pain and was the reason for him frequently closing them for relief. 'We will await you at the Island in the Rhodanus. Return in two weeks. Do you understand what is required of you?'

'Yes, Sir. Perfectly.'

'Then leave us and prepare for your journey tomorrow.'

After Sphax had left their presence, the venerable Sosylos turned to his pupil. 'That young man is full of surprises. Will he succeed or fail in this task?'

Hannibal shrugged. 'I've never enjoyed surprises. As to success or failure, we may never see him again, or he may return with Idwal and fifty men. Unfortunately, his father's blood courses through his veins, not my sister's, therefore he is as unpredictable as a throw of dice.'

'You have acknowledged him then,' enquired Silenos, slightly surprised. 'I mean as a blood relative, your nephew.'

'Every report I've received of him has confirmed that he's as wild and untamed as his father. There can be no doubt. He is the son of Navaras. Only ... looking into those clear emerald eyes brings back such sadness for me. They are the very colour of my dear sister's eyes.'

SEVEN

They set off early next morning after Sphax had completed a gruelling hour of javelin practice with Dubal. Maharbal grudgingly supplied sixty-two horses so that Idwal's followers would not have to march on foot, but grumbled about it all morning before surprising him with a gift of one of his prized saunions to encourage his javelin practice. Sphax took with him the carnyx he'd looted from the Volcae. Idwal had admired the exquisite metalwork on the trumpet, so Sphax decided it would make a perfect gift for his father, Lord Cenno.

Night was falling as the column of horsemen arrived below the gaunt battlements of Nages, but for Sphax, the time had flown swiftly. It had been a perfect day. The sun had shone from a cloudless sky and the windless air became rich with birdsong and the humming of insects gathering nectar before the first onset of autumn's chill. Villagers were gathering their harvests of golden grain and ripened fruit. Every village and settlement along the way offered them every manner of drink and refreshment. He and Idwal rode side by side, by turns wrapped in deep conversation or riotous laughter, but more often lending a sympathetic ear to one another's childhood memories. They talked of everything from stonemasons' tools to elephants' tusks, Roman roads and honeyed mead, stoic philosophers and Sphax's hero Themistocles, who'd saved Athens from the Persians. Girls, wine and cured meats were discussed at great length, along with Gallic metalwork and the failings of the Roman senate.

The roadway to what Idwal called the briga dūnan was very steep and wound its way through several defensive ditches before Sphax began to make out the outline of walls and towers in the gathering darkness. Idwal explained that a briga dūnan was the same as a Greek city wall. 'I suppose the Latin word for it would be an oppidum.'

'In Latin it would mean a walled town.' As the towering walls loomed ahead, Sphax shook his head. 'This is more like a citadel, Idwal,' impressed by the stone towers flanking the solid wooden gates.

'What do you think?' Idwal asked eagerly.

'This is all your work, is it? Very impressive!'

'As I was telling you earlier, most of the walls are still wooden, perfectly serviceable of course, but no match for the stone walls we're beginning to construct. I had to bring masons from Massilia, search for good stone in the area and begin quarrying. The Cavari have exceptional skills in metalwork, but we have never built in stone before. Look around you: my household have had to learn many new skills and master tools that are new to us. Now we have surveyors, tile-makers and plasterers amongst our party. Three years ago not one of us knew how to dress stone; now we have several craftsmen skilled in the art. I'm building a villa. Philipos, my master in Massilia, drew up the plans himself. Some of it is already completed, but there is still much to be done. You'll see it for yourself in a little while.'

Once inside the walls, Sphax was frankly disappointed. There were no public squares, paved streets or grand buildings, just a tightly packed ramshackle of round timbered houses with conical roofs thatched in reed, much the same as the villages they'd passed through that day, albeit on a grander scale. In the dimming twilight, above every roof smoke hung in the air like a fog, giving the impression the town had been put to the torch and was smouldering and burning.

'My father is expecting us. Tonight there will be a feast in your honour. Let us go and greet him.'

* * *

With his careworn face and furrowed brow, Sphax's first impression of Lord Cenno was of a man aged before his time, an old man of some forty years with grey hair and luxuriant mustachios in the Gallic fashion. He was somewhat stout and beginning to bulge around the middle, but there was no mistaking the keenness and intelligence of those eyes. They were of a striking blue, the same winter-blue as his son's, with the peculiar penetrating quality he'd come to recognise in his friend.

Lord Cenno greeted him politely in passable Greek. As they began to discuss the present situation of the Carthaginian army and his uncle's plans, Sphax detected a certain reticence and indifference in his replies and questioning, as if the fate of Rome or Carthage was of little consequence to the Cavari. The weight of responsibility his uncle had placed on him was making him tongue-tied and nervous. He managed to avoid broaching anything that might reveal the true purpose of his visit, but he got the distinct impression that the wily old chieftain had already guessed it. "Do not underestimate Lord Cenno. He is no fool," his uncle had warned him. He was beginning to see why.

'You must both be tired after your journey. Please allow my son to escort you to his ... villa. Rooms and refreshments have been prepared for you. Tonight we feast,' and with that the audience was over.

Servants brought torches to light their path as Idwal guided him to a flat open area some distance from the great hall. There was something about how Lord Cenno had spoken the word villa. 'Tell me, Idwal,' he asked, 'does your father approve of you building a villa?'

'Was it that obvious?'

'Well ... no, not obvious, I just—'

'He hates it,' Idwal groaned. 'As do most of the elders and older warriors. Like all things Greek, they see it as soft and unmanly, fit only for young girls and scholars. My people can be so backward and uncivilised at times. Sometimes I despair of their barbarian ways!' As his friend continued, Sphax sensed a new bitterness in his voice.

'But your own household followers have acquired many new skills. Surely this augurs well for the future?'

'Yes, because they have lived and worked amongst Greeks! All can read and write and speak good Greek ... I've ensured this. But as for the rest of my people, tradition is all, tradition is everything, they live in the past. Tradition is killing them!' Sphax was alarmed. He'd never suspected his friend was so out of step with his own people, let alone his own father.

They'd stopped in front of a fine portico giving entrance to an extensive single storey building. Inside, the darkness gave way to bright Grecian lamps, so that Sphax could see for himself how much Idwal had accomplished and what remained to be completed.

In some rooms, tiles had not been laid and walls awaited the last fine coat of stucco, but to Sphax's eyes, everything looked charming in the understated Greek style. But then, Sphax was a better judge of a well-appointed stable than a grand interior. His room was well lit and the sleeping couch looked soft and inviting. That's all he required.

Two hours later he found himself in a building that could not have been more different. A building where right angles had been banished and stucco replaced by solid oak. Sphax entered Cenno's circular great hall with Idwal and several from his household. All guests gathered and beginning to seat themselves were arrayed in full armour, at least for those who could afford to show off such expensive equipment: a fine mail shirt took skilled craftsmen weeks to make and that was why they were so coveted and expensive. Scores were on conspicuous display that evening, as were ornate Etruscan helmets wrought from the finest metals. Evidently a Cavari warrior felt undressed unless he had a long Gallic blade dangling from a chain around his waist. Unarmed and dressed in his simple toga, Sphax felt like a sheep among wolves.

Benches and long tables had been arranged in a square around a central area smoking with braziers, firedogs and ornate bronze cauldrons, the centrepiece of which was a whole pig, being slowly turned and roasted over the embers of a charcoal fire. Sphax's first impression was that of the acrid smell of wood smoke and roasting meat; it filled his nostrils and overwhelmed his senses. Looking upwards he saw the smoke coalescing as an impenetrable fog, blotting out any view of the roof-timbers or the thatch above, so he could only guess as to how such a roof had been constructed to cover this vast space. One side of the square, opposite the entrance, consisted of a raised platform, two hands in height above the earthen floor. On this platform had been placed a long oaken table and chairs, on the grandest of which sat Lord Cenno, resplendent in helmet and full armour with three hounds licking his heels, tongues eagerly awaiting scraps from the table.

As they slowly made their way through the throng to the high table, Idwal and his party were stopped and greeted warmly with raised cups, much back-slapping and high-spirited banter. Covered by its plain cloth, Sphax was carrying the carnyx he intended to present to Lord Cenno, making his progress through the crowds awkward. After bowing low to Lord Cenno, he was greeted cordially enough, but again, he recognised that reserve he'd sensed earlier.

Idwal gestured to the chair at his father's left, but there was suddenly a sharp exchange between them in Gallic. 'This chair is normally reserved for the warrior, Vertros,' Idwal explained to him in Greek, 'but as he's away hunting, I'm sure he won't mind you borrowing it for the evening.' Cenno was still glaring at his son and slowly shaking his head. 'This way, father, Sphax will not have to lean across me to converse with you. It will be convenient, not to say polite to our guest of honour.' Cenno gave Sphax a dismissive look, enough to say, 'I don't want to speak to this mouthpiece of Hannibal.'

He decided this was the moment to pour a little oil on the situation by presenting Lord Cenno with the carnyx. 'I have a humble gift for you, Lord

Cenno. I give it as a token of friendship on behalf of my people, the Numidians.' Without further ado he removed the cloth and pressed it into the hands of the chief. For some moments Cenno just stared at it, then he began to turn it this way and that, holding it up to a flaming torch behind him so that he might examine its intricate metalwork in closer detail. Silence had fallen on the benches around the high table as all eyes stared in admiration at the trumpet. Idwal was nodding and grinning at him. 'Perfect timing, my friend,' he said softly in Latin so that no one would understand.

At last Lord Cenno placed the carnyx carefully behind his chair and turned to Sphax. 'It is a magnificent gift and I will treasure it,' he said in his stumbling Greek. 'I know of Carthage, but little of Numidia. You must tell me about your people,' the earlier awkwardness now forgotten. 'How did you acquire this trumpet?'

'As part of the spoils of war, Sir. I'm afraid the warrior who blew its last fanfare was summoned by Morrígu.'

'Was this during the fight with the Volcae?' Sphax could see that Lord Cenno was now genuinely interested. 'I heard the Volcae had sworn to defend the river. How did the Carthaginians cross the Rhodanus and overcome them?' In a few brief sentences, Sphax described the course of the battle leading up to the flight of the Volcae. He spoke in a matter-of-fact way, keeping his tone modest and the descriptions factual.

'You mean to say they ran!' Cenno cried, aghast at the cowardice of his fellow Gauls.

'Yes, father,' Idwal interrupted, 'they turned tail and fled like rabbits.' Sphax was eager to paint his friend in a good light and not tar the Cavari with the same brush as the Volcae.

'All except for your son and his followers, Sir, who stood firm and repulsed all our charges.' Too late, Sphax realised the blunder he'd just made, remembering that the Cavari were not supposed to be there at all, let alone fighting on the side of the Volcae! To his consternation, this only sparked another heated exchange between father and son.

Desperate to make amends for his stupidity, Sphax racked his brain for a convincing explanation. As the argument between father and son relented and both sank into a temporary truce, he seized the moment.

'It was entirely our fault, Lord. In our ignorance and the heat of battle, we were unable to distinguish between Cavari and Volcae. The blame for this lies entirely with us, not your son, who was merely defending himself and his company. Our error was inexcusable and may have damaged the friendship between our peoples my uncle values so highly. Please accept my apologies for the entire incident.'

'It has already been forgotten,' Cenno replied graciously. 'But tell me, master Sphax, what part did you play in this fight?'

'I was leading part of our Numidian cavalry, Sir,' he answered, bending the truth somewhat.

'And how do Numidians fight; with spear or sword? And what armour do they wear?'

'Neither spear nor sword, Sir: with javelin. As for armour, we wear none, save for a small round shield I believe you would call a buckler.'

'So armed ... and yet you defeated Gauls.' Cenno was staring incredulously.

Sphax was about to say 'no Gaul is a match for a Numidian,' but managed to bite his tongue. Luckily, he was spared a reply by the timely arrival of servants with food and drink. Never before had he eaten food from silver plates; the wealth they represented would rival anything in Rome, let alone his uncle's finest tableware. He was handed an enormous silver cup that contained enough liquid to wash his face in. Gingerly he sipped, surprised to find it warm, sweet and quite delicious. He could see that Idwal was watching him with amusement. 'What do you think of our mead, Sphax?'

'So this is what the Greeks call nectar! It's quite wonderful, but I never expected it to be warm,' he said with enthusiasm. 'Does the sweetness come from honey?'

Lord Cenno answered, turning out to be something of an authority on its production and history. 'Honey brings to it sweetness, but we also add a few hops and I believe, six other herbs to give the drink its body and depth of taste. The custom of warming the liquid came from the peoples in the east, beyond the great forests, in the time of my great-grandfather.'

'Well, Sir, it is one of the finest things I've ever tasted,' he said truthfully. Cenno beamed. Sphax paused to spear a slice of roast pork and reach for a chunk of bread before gazing up at the impenetrable fog above their heads. 'You must excuse me, for I'm ignorant of Cavari ways and customs, but surely,' he continued, glancing briefly upwards again, 'if you were to make a hole in the thatch, all the smoke would quickly escape?' Father and son burst into laughter. Finally, Lord Cenno gestured to his son to explain.

'It is not an unreasonable question, Sphax,' said Idwal, still chuckling. 'But if you were to do that the smoke would be drawn upwards so swiftly and fiercely that it would begin to stir the embers of every fire in the room. Soon, sparks would be flying towards the roof faster than a flight of arrows, and before long—'

'We would all be crying fire!' interjected Lord Cenno, 'and beseeching every man to piss as high as he could.' Lord Cenno dissolved into laughter at his own joke.

As the golden nectar flowed and his belly felt warm and replete from the vast amounts of roasted pork he'd eaten, Sphax began to enjoy himself. Lord Cenno was an entertaining host with a salacious, down-to-earth humour. He was full of stories, most of which would have been completely unsuitable in mixed company, but here there was not a woman in sight. As the hours passed, the levels of laughter and boisterousness amongst the warriors on the benches grew at the same rate as the barrels emptied. Wagers were being offered and answered, possessions and silver changed hands, and occasionally a wrestling match would break out. But these seemed to be good natured affairs, usually ending in much back-slapping and toasting. Some of the younger men, already overcome by drink, were soundly asleep, heads slumped over tables, snoring like pigs. Older men, who'd learned to hold their drink, wandered from table to table or unashamedly relieved themselves in the huge wooden pails placed around the sides of the hall. Sphax had noted with disgust that these contained as much vomit as urine.

Lord Cenno had been questioning Sphax about his homeland. He was particularly interested in his tales of elephants, mentioning that he'd seen these curious creatures when the Carthaginian army passed through Nages on its way to the Rhodanus. Sphax was describing how the mahouts trapped and captured the creatures in the forests bordering the great desert, when everything around him suddenly froze in hushed silence. Something made him turn around. Glaring down at him was a mountain of a man.

The man-mountain was clad from head to foot in mail, so that he took on the appearance of a sculpture cast in iron. Hands gripped Sphax's shoulders and raised him bodily from his chair then held him out at arm's length for all the warriors to see. It was as if he weighed no more than a babe-in-arms and presented less trouble. The mountain let out a resounding fart, then started bellowing something in Gallic that had the entire hall erupting into fits of laughter. Sphax was too shocked and stunned to struggle. It would have been futile anyway. Nothing would have broken that iron-like grip on his shoulders.

With a few bounding strides the giant carried him away from the high table to the back of the hall and carefully lowered him into one of the piss-pails. Sphax was jammed inside, bent double with his chin almost touching his knees whilst the stinking liquid soaked and oozed through his toga.

There was now uproar. Warriors were either still helpless with laughter or arguing furiously with one another. Out of the corner of his eye he noticed a red-faced Idwal confronting the giant on the platform whilst Cenno remained seated, head buried in his hands. Everyone seemed to have forgotten him.

In a sleepless episode later that night, Sphax reflected in hindsight that he had been presented with a choice. He'd taken a decision and set a fateful course, but there had indeed been a way out for him. An alternative. Keeping to the shadows he could have left the hall unnoticed and slunk off into the night, and next morning everything might have been quietly forgotten as drunken foolery.

But this didn't happen. The gods had something else in mind.

Sphax struggled out of the pail, grabbed the handles and strengthened by the sheer power of rage managed to carry it slopping and spilling towards the high table. He seemed to have acquired a cloak of invisibility, for the great throng of warriors now gathered below the platform were so intent on argument with each other that they hardly noticed the figure in the dripping toga slithering past. As he stepped on to the high table, Idwal suddenly caught sight of him and froze. Sphax was staring at the back and shoulders of the man-mountain.

Everyone saw what was about to happen. The deathly silence was finally broken by the great roar Sphax made straining every muscle and sinew in his body to raise the pail and slam it over the giant's head. As the liquid deluge released its weight from the pail he grabbed the iron handles and thrust down with all his remaining strength. The giant staggered and then began to struggle wildly, but as the pail was jammed over his head, shoulders and upper arms, there wasn't much he could do about it. Maintaining his grip on the handle he twisted it viciously, swivelling his captive around so that he was now facing bucket-head. Sphax buried his knee deep into the giant's groin. He heard a satisfying groan from inside the bucket and watched as the man-mountain sank to his knees.

In that moment the spell was lifted. Everyone started shouting at once. Warriors rushed towards him whilst others fended them off. Idwal was trying to manhandle him off the platform. Sphax tore himself away and screamed 'SILENCE!'

To his astonishment everyone obeyed. Pointing to the figure still groaning inside the piss-pail he yelled, 'Tomorrow morning this man will meet me in single combat. He will fight in the custom of Numidians, on horseback. And tomorrow he will die! For I will be avenged for this insult.' For a moment Sphax glared at the sea of faces around him before striding from the hall.

* * *

Idwal woke him at dawn, fussing like a mother hen. 'I am to blame for this. I should have listened to my father last night. Our ancient customs of precedence ... I hate them! This is all my fault, Sphax. Anyway, thank the gods it's not too late to call it off. If you apologise he will laugh it off; you were drunk ... you didn't know anything of our customs ... He will understand. There's no shame in this, he's a warrior, and you're just a boy really, like me. There's not much honour in it for him. Killing a boy, I mean.'

Smarting at this last remark, Sphax threw off his furs and sat up on the sleeping couch. Except for that episode of doubt in the middle of the night, for a man seemingly condemned to die he'd slept remarkably well. 'Any chance of some breakfast? I'm starving.' As Idwal walked him over to the kitchens beside the great hall he continued bleating in his ear.

'This is madness, Sphax! He's killed more than twenty warriors in single combat. He's skilled with sword, axe and spear. He's the most feared warrior of all the Cavari. Please don't do this, I beg you, you will die. Let me speak to my father, he has the power to stop this. You are our guest, you must be honoured ...'

They sat at a bench by a huge iron brazier in the kitchens, grateful for its warmth in the early morning chill. As always, Sphax had his javelins on his lap and his fingers were continuously searching out balance points or playing with the leather thong. Even at this hour the place was bustling with women preparing food, whining hounds begging for scraps or servants carrying great platters of bread, meat and ale to various parts of the household. Hanging from the high beamed ceiling were hams and meats being dried and cured from the last slaughter, and the smell of wood smoke and freshly baked bread hung in the air. Idwal spoke to a slave boy who returned with a large jug and wooden bowls full of oats and what looked like dried blueberries and chopped apple. Before he could stop him, Idwal poured from the jug a white liquid into Sphax's bowl and then his own. 'Is that cow's milk?' he asked, wrinkling up the corners of his mouth.

'Try it. We sweeten it with honey. It's delicious.' Struggling to overcome his natural revulsion to drinking the milk of any creature, be it human or animal, he eventually dug his fingers into the bowl and tasted the result. He was pleasantly surprised, and quickly finished the rest of the bowl before meat and bread were brought to the table along with cups of honeyed ale. He could see his friend was about to launch into another sermon to dissuade him from his folly. Raising his hand in protest he asked, 'Tell me one thing, Idwal. Can Vertros ride well?'

'Well enough, I suppose, but he doesn't need a horse to kill you, Sphax.'

'Oh yes he does,' he said emphatically. 'If he can't ride a horse as well as I can, then he's dead meat. Few people ride as well as me. It's as simple as that.' This seemed to put an end to all conversation between them, so after he'd eaten his fill, Sphax wandered out to the stables to greet Dido. He was feeding her an apple when Lord Cenno entered with his guard. 'Are you determined to go ahead with this combat? My son has implored me to put a stop to it. He calls it madness. You are a guest of my people and I do not wish to return your corpse to your uncle.' Sphax could see that this would be slightly embarrassing, especially after Lord Cenno had accepted his uncle's silver. But it wasn't his problem.

'I understand your dilemma, Sir, but I have been insulted beyond measure. For this I will have redress, and there is nothing that you, your son, or even my uncle could say that would make me change my mind. It is the custom of my people to fight on horseback; in war our feet rarely touch the ground, so this is how the combat will be decided. But tell me Lord Cenno, what will you do if I should kill the Cavari's greatest warrior?'

'That is unlikely,' Lord Cenno answered coldly, avoiding his guest's eyes. Without further words, Cenno left the stables trailing his retinue. Sphax held each of his javelins in turn, choosing to use Dubal's first. It was light but true, with a barb of good Spanish iron the length of a finger. He would save Maharbal's deadly iron saunion for the kill. Gathering his leather shield he walked out of the stables, whistling Dido to follow. He decided not to use the shield; he was not skilled in its use and it would just get in the way. Discarding it in the face of Vertros might prove to be another useful act of bravado that might inflame him. He desperately needed every act of bravado he could conjure. In a straight fight, Sphax knew he would be dead before he'd even raised his sword, but if Vertros was angry and out of control, there might be a chance. Besides, bravado was the easiest way to conceal the sheer terror he was feeling at that moment.

Idwal was waiting for him outside the great hall. Together they walked through the ramshackle cluster of roundhouses enclosed by the walls of the briga dūnan. It seemed they were being followed by the entire town, everyone from excited young children to bent old men leaning on sticks, and all of them intent on avoiding his eyes. It seemed the arena was to be a field beside the river at the base of the hill. Crowds had already gathered for the entertainment, forming a tight circle in the centre of the field. This was not what he had in mind. He needed space. Pointing to the crowds already gathered, he said, 'Those people will get themselves trampled to death, Idwal. Could you clear a large area suitable for horses? I don't want to kill any more of your people than I have to this morning.' As the words left his mouth he realised this was the most ridiculous boast he'd ever uttered.

'I will see it done. But tell me honestly, Sphax, how do you intend to kill a warrior as skilled as Vertros? I know you Numidians are horsemen, but a fight such as this can only be decided by iron, face to face, either on foot or from the back of a horse; either way it makes no difference. He will kill you.'

'Soon enough you will see how Numidians fight, and you will not like what you see.'

'I have faced Numidians, remember, and lived to tell the tale.'

'But you have intelligence and the presence of mind to change tactics. I don't think Vertros has these gifts.' He handed Idwal his saunion. 'This will kill him.' His friend weighed it in the palm of his hand, then in some alarm said, 'But it's light, Sphax. Too light!'

Sphax just laughed. 'You wouldn't like to face such a weapon hurled from a galloping horse.' He didn't mention that in the fight at the Rhodanus, he'd seen one go clean through a chieftain's shield and bury itself in the man's chest.

When they reached the centre of the field Idwal began marshalling the crowds so they stood in a straggling line under the trees by the banks of the river. In places they were already four deep and complaining raucously that they couldn't see anything. He wanted Dido to be hot blooded when the fight began, so he let her trot around the field to her heart's content. Lord Cenno arrived on horseback trailing his warriors, all mounted and dressed in their finest polished armour. This was obviously quite an occasion for the Cavari. Idwal had told him that most fights were settled in the feasting hall.

Behind all came Vertros leading a big chestnut warhorse by the rein. Sphax thought he looked haggard and heavy limbed from the drinking and feasting last night. Or was this just wishful thinking? He'd certainly taken the trouble to look the part, dressed as he was in a thigh-length mail-shirt, trousers and glistening gold torque at his neck. But what caught everyone's eye was the resplendent bronze helmet, affixed with bull's horns that had been embossed in gold and silver. To his enemies, Vertros would appear as a raging bull, and that was exactly what Sphax wanted. Bulls were slow and dull witted.

With Idwal he walked over to the party of warriors gathered around Vertros. Out of the corner of his eye he caught a glimpse of a silver-haired man clad in hooded white cloak; one of the druidi perhaps? Those wise priests Idwal had talked about. There was something about him that reminded him of Elpis, and he wondered what Elpis would say to him right now?

As the thought occurred he could hear his teacher's voice in his head; "Well, my hot-headed wolf-cub, what a fine mess you've got yourself into this time. Have I not taught you that the man who is not in control of his emotions is a man no longer in control of his destiny? Such a man is at the mercy of every storm and tempest that life will surely throw at him." If only he'd swallowed his dignity and slunk out of the great hall into the darkness last night ... but it was too late for regrets now. As a stoic, Elpis had also taught him Zeno's wisdom: in a crisis be still, find the calm centre, unmoved by the raging of storms and tempests. All he had to do now was prick and goad the bull, conjure the storms and tempests, and stay calm himself.

As the two of them approached each other, the warriors stood aside, leaving Sphax to face his opponent, towering a good head and shoulders above him. He'd been told that Vertros understood Latin perfectly well. So he kept it simple.

'You look like a steaming turd this morning, Vertros. Have you not washed away the bath of vomit I gave you last night?' Sphax smiled at his stallion. 'I see you've brought an ox to ride.' It was only with the greatest of effort that the warriors around Vertros managed to restrain him from killing Sphax there on the spot. 'What's the name of the poor creature?' he continued calmly, 'he looks more used to a plough than a warrior.'

'Brega,' Vertros growled, still being restrained by several arms. Sphax whistled in that shrill way of his and called out, 'Brega.' The horse's ears immediately pricked up and its keen eyes gazed at him. That might be useful, he thought.

Making as much show as possible, Sphax handed his shield to Idwal, removed his belted sword then stripped off his tunic and sandals before handing them to his friend. Standing barefooted, naked except for a loincloth, he spoke as loudly as possible so that all would hear.

'You will fight on horseback, as my people have always settled such matters. Give me your spear and prepare to meet your raven goddess.' Vertros was leering pityingly as Sphax wrenched the spear from his grasp and walked away.

The crowds on the riverbank had been hushed and silent until he'd spoken, but now they broke into fits of laughter and jeering as he began counting the hundred paces from where he'd stood beside Vertros. He thrust the spear firmly into the ground so it stood perfectly upright, then walked on, counting steps until he'd reached fifty. Sphax paused again and turned to Idwal.

'My good friend, will you signal the start of this contest from here, the midway point. Raise your sword, then lower it quickly – that will be the signal.' Idwal just nodded acquiescence, not trusting himself to speak. Sphax smiled, 'Goodbye, my friend,' then turned and continued counting steps.

When he reached fifty he planted both his javelins in the ground, whistled for Dido, and measured the last one hundred paces. By now the crowds were growing restless, jeering and shouting insults at him; they'd come for a sword fight, not a horse race. As a slave he'd spent many a day in the Circus in Rome preparing Lucillus' chariot horses amidst crowds baying or cheering for their favourites. He was used to such noise. Be still, he told himself, find that calm. Mounting Dido he raised his hand to Idwal as a signal that he was ready, then held his precious leather pouch to his lips. Beyond him he could see that Vertros was being helped into his saddle. At last Idwal's sword fell.

Out of nervousness he must have nudged Dido too firmly, for within a few strides she flew into a full gallop, hurtling towards his javelins. He had them both firmly in his grasp a dozen strides before Vertros had even reached his spear. Then the sheer thrill and elation of speed and rushing wind took over his senses and he abandoned himself completely to instinct and nature. Dido was part of him and he was one with Dido. That's where the still centre lay, at that mysterious threshold where human became animal. In the midst of exhilarating movement there was always stillness. He stopped thinking. He'd already rehearsed each manoeuvre a dozen times in his head that morning.

He could see Vertros reining back Brega, fearing the horses would violently collide with one another. Sphax had no such fears. At the very last instant, without losing any speed, he gently nudged Dido and she veered off to the right, and at the same time clutching her neck with his left hand he twisted his upper body below her shoulder so as to offer no target to his adversary. 'Yoo, Dido... yoo, yoo.' In a few strides she'd slowed to a canter and he slid off her back to the ground, making it easier for her to turn around without his weight. He leapt back on to her as she gained speed. Vertros was desperately trying to rein in his big horse and turn him around, but Dido was too quick and was gaining on him with every stride.

When he was a few strides behind Brega, he gripped Dido's neck between his thighs, rose up and raised the javelin above his shoulder and let the leather thong fly. It struck Vertros on the side of his helmet, dislodging one of the horns, but glanced off and sailed harmlessly past him. He noted with satisfaction the expression of astonishment on Vertros's face. But this was no time to gloat. His enemy was unharmed and he didn't want to use his saunion just yet, so he had to recover that javelin. He and Dido thundered past Vertros in a wide circle, and rounding on the javelin he reached down and picked it from the ground at full gallop.

Giving his enemy a wide berth, he slowed Dido to a canter, held the javelin aloft and circled the now stationary warrior, frequently feinting a charge to his right or left to keep him guessing and off balance. All the while he glared at his enemy, looking him straight in the eye. It was evident that Vertros could barely ride a horse, let alone fight from one. He was unnerved, yanking the reins this way or that, shifting the position of his shield or spear, unsure and rattled. Vertros had never faced anything like this before and he was growing desperate. 'What's the matter with you, arsehole?' Sphax screamed at him, 'lost your appetite for a fight?'

This fanned the flames perfectly. Now the bull was beyond rage itself and Vertros yanked savagely down on the reins to get Brega moving in any direction. He let Dido follow until both horses reached a trot, then urged her to greater speed so he could circle his foe as leopards stalk their prey. He had one more trick that would finish off the bastard, but for that he needed more speed.

Keeping Dido three strides ahead, he encouraging Vertros to chase him, all the while gaining speed. When they reached a canter he sat back on Dido's croup, swung his left leg over her back, balanced, set himself again, then vaulted his right leg over her hip so that he was facing backwards on the mare. He caught the look of astonishment on Vertros's face. Sphax reached for his saunion and in one fluid movement had tied the thong, raised and levelled the weapon.

This time his aim was true. The javelin struck the mail shirt just below the shoulder and buried itself in flesh. He saw Vertros double in his saddle and wince in pain, but the warrior did not cry out, merely ripped the shaft from his flesh and cast it aside. The mail shirt must have softened the shock of the impact. Vertros was proving hard to kill.

Reversing his manoeuvre on Dido's back so that he was facing forwards once again, he began a series of furious charges at his enemy, always pulling out at the last moment. Sphax didn't bother retrieving his saunion. He still had Dubal's javelin and could see that Brega was tiring fast, unable to respond. Vertros was in pain, barely able to hold the shield in his left arm. He knew that sooner or later he would make a mistake. It came sooner than he'd expected.

After one such violent charge Vertros tried to follow, yanking Brega's bit so violently that the stallion's legs splayed then doubled under him, sending Vertros crashing heavily to the ground, followed by his horse. Brega eventually struggled to his feet, but his rider did not. Sphax brought Dido to a halt and began his shrill whistling, stopping occasionally to call out, 'Brega. Come Brega!' Eventually the stallion trotted happily over to him and stood beside Dido. For the first time since the fight had begun he noticed the crowds had fallen silent. Even as Vertros staggered to his feet and gathered his shield and spear, everyone was looking on in stunned silence.

One more trick, thought Sphax, he would give them just one more trick. Dismounting, he stroked Brega's neck and whispered to the stallion that he was free. With a gentle pat on his rump he trotted off to the far end of the field whilst Sphax recovered his saunion and re-mounted Dido. Vertros was now crouching on one knee, protected by his shield, spear angled upwards.

Sphax took his time. He would need speed for this, which meant space. He knew that at a flat-out gallop, if his aim was true his javelin would go clean through a shield and pierce any mail shirt. But he wasn't going to do that, he had something else in mind, something far more humiliating for Vertros. Something that would finish his reputation for good.

Dido was already gaining speed now. As she approached the crouching figure on the ground he steadied her slightly, placing his palms either side of her neck. For Dido such a touch meant one thing and one thing only. As the animal prepared to leap, all Sphax had to do was shift his weight forward and get his timing right. In that heart-stopping moment Dido's front legs soared over the shield, but also in that same moment he knew that he'd got it badly wrong. In mid-air he felt Dido shudder and her hoof strike something solid before horse and rider landed heavily beyond the warrior lying prone beside his shield. By a miracle he'd managed to stay on her back as they landed. He let her canter on for a few more strides before bringing her to a halt.

Leaping off immediately he spotted the ugly gash just above the hock joint of her rear left leg where the spear must have caught her. Dido's right hoof seemed to be unhurt, even though it had delivered an almighty blow to something. The moment he saw that gash to his beloved Dido the calm left him. He was now in a state of blind fury. Vertros was about to die.

The warrior lay face down, sprawled on the grass. With his bare foot he rolled Vertros on to his back and realised he was still breathing but out cold, with a bloody scar running down the length of his face through his shattered nose. Sphax wrenched the spear from his grasp and straddling the body, raised it high in the air above the warrior's chest. He heard the crowd gasp and sensed they were closing in all around him. In the breath it took before plunging the spear down with all his strength, something stayed his hand.

In that instant all his fury left him, and with it the full realisation of his own stupidity finally dawned on him. It was as if the sky had just fallen in. He wanted to cry out in despair. He alone was to blame for this calamity, not Vertros or Dido. He had risked the life of his horse for a showman's trick, an act of bravado calculated to humiliate his enemy and please the crowd. He'd become as a child again, showing off to his mother. Vertros had fought bravely, honourably. He had fought arrogantly, blinded by hubris, and now he would pay for it.

He buried the spear in the grass beside the warrior and oblivious to the sudden eruption of voices, walked through the crowds gathering around him to where he'd left Dido. Idwal was there, anxiously examining his face. Without a word, he recovered his tunic, ripped a length of cloth from the hem, and gently began staunching the blood from Dido's wound. It looked bad.

EIGHT

Cynbel, master of Lord Cenno's stables, prepared a stall with fresh straw for Dido. So as to take the pressure off the wound and help staunch the bleeding, Sphax got her to lie down. After closer examination, he decided the wound was too deep to heal of its own accord. It would have to be closed, which meant stitching it. He called for clean thread and a fine needle and Idwal brought oil lamps from his villa so that Sphax had good light to work in.

The trust between man and horse was so complete that although Dido flinched every time the needle punctured her skin, she lay still and did not kick out at him. Sphax felt her pain with every stitch. At last it was done, and all he could do now was wait and hope. He'd seen wounds like this before; in a matter of hours they could become diseased and putrid and then there was nothing to be done but to put the poor creature out of its misery.

For the rest of the day and through the long night he never left Dido's side, sitting on the straw beside her, gently stroking her mane and soothing her with soft words. Every few hours he would carefully bathe the wound in beer and apply a fresh coating of sticky honey to speed the healing. Idwal himself brought food, wine and gossip. 'You're the talk of Nages,' he told him. 'It was an extraordinary display, Sphax. I've certainly never seen anything like it in my life. How did you learn to ride like that?'

'Numidians learn to ride as soon as they can walk. At five I could pick up a pebble from the ground at the gallop. I've lived and worked with horses all my life. But it seems that only my people truly understand them. Every Numidian knows that it is the horse that has all the skill and intelligence. All we have to do is stay on their backs and not give them any trouble. This I have failed to do, and I'm ashamed of it.'

Idwal didn't really understand this. 'You're not to blame for Dido's injury, Sphax. It was an accident. Besides, you defeated the greatest warrior amongst the Cavari!'

'Dido killed Vertros for me, I could only wound him. And it was no accident. It was my misjudgement and arrogance that brought this about.' Now Idwal was truly baffled.

'Vertros is not dead, by the way. He sleeps and cannot be woken up. They've tried everything, even the holy man has seen him. The most ignorant slackheads in the town are claiming sorcery; they say that you and Dido are in league with Epona, and put Vertros under a spell.'

'Who is Epona?' he asked indifferently.

'Our goddess of horses.'

'Then I shall pray to her myself.'

* * *

He awoke to a joyous sight. Dido was standing firmly
on four legs directly above him. As he stretched out
his arms to shake off sleep she began nickering with
pleasure and bent down to lick his cheek. Praise the
gods, he thought, praise be to every god of horses,
whoever they are, even Epona.

Although still early, it was broad daylight outside as
the sun climbed through a cloudless blue sky. Yet in the
meadows and river valleys below the hilltop, a ghostly
grey mist shrouded the land, giving the appearance that
he was standing alone on an island. Nothing stirred in
the great hall or kitchens opposite save for a solitary
hound, sniffing around on the dew-laden grass. When
the sun burned away the autumnal mists, he knew they
were in for a beautiful day, warm and memorable.

Lord Cenno came to see him later that morning.
Sphax was surprised that he came alone, without
guards or attendants. After bowing low Sphax gestured
towards the stool, hardly suitable for the Lord of the
Cavari, but other than a bucket, it happened to be the
only thing to sit on in the stall. Cenno was content
to stand. 'I see your mare is recovering well,' he said,
glancing at the fresh dressing on Dido's hock.

'It is most kind of you to ask, Sir. And yes, she
seems to be making a good recovery, though I will not

be able to ride her until the wound has fully recovered and the stitches removed.' He knew he would have to enquire after Vertros, but dreaded raising the subject. Tentatively, he asked 'Is there any change in Vertros, Sir? I mean, is he likely to recover?'

'That is a matter for the gods now,' he said gravely. 'Unlike your mare, Vertros seems to be beyond the power of medicine.'

'Then I'm sorry for him,' Sphax said genuinely, 'he fought bravely and honourably.'

Cenno shot him a quizzical look. 'But did you fight honourably, Master Sphax?' Taken completely off guard, he flushed. This cut deep into a wound that was still fresh and raw in his conscience. It took him a few moments to recover and answer truthfully, without it sounding like self-justification. Lord Cenno was watching him closely.

'No,' he sighed, 'not entirely. I did not have to humiliate him. For this I am now ashamed. Even amongst Numidians, few ride as well as I, but most, if not all, are more skilled with the javelin. I practise every day and I'm improving, but any Numidian would have killed Vertros at the first pass.'

'No!' Lord Cenno exclaimed, disbelieving. 'This is not possible! Vertros is a great warrior, fearless and skilled in battle.' Sphax always had his javelins close to hand. He handed his saunion for Lord Cenno to examine and took his leather thong from its pouch. 'Unskilled as I am, from the back of a galloping horse and with the aid of this piece of leather, I can throw this weapon forty paces. During the fight against the Volcae I saw such javelins go clean through shields and pierce all manner of mail.'

'But this is a cowardly way to fight,' Cenno sneered. 'Where is the honour? Where's the glory in this?' Now it was Sphax's turn to be shocked.

'Numidians do not take the same pleasure in war as Gauls do. We fight when we must, if there is no other way, so that we can return home and live in peace. For us there is no glory in killing, only duty. As to honour? The only honour to be found in war is doing one's duty.'

'Tell me boy, how much courage does it take to throw this forty paces?' With that Lord Cenno tossed the saunion to the ground. With a supreme effort, Sphax managed to retain his composure.

'You are right, Lord, it takes little courage. What it calls for is skill, discipline and intelligence. The Volcae fought for honour and glory. That is why we were able to slaughter them like sheep, and when we were not butchering them they were running away like rabbits! Even Gauls fighting on foot were no match for our Iberian *caetrati*. Your blades are too long in a fight at close quarters, and your shields are heavy and clumsy. What use is courage or honour if you have no discipline and your weapons are useless?'

Lord Cenno could bear no more. Without a word he strode from the stall, leaving Sphax cursing himself for letting his tongue run away with him. Again! When would he ever learn to keep his mouth shut? His uncle would be furious with him. Insulting the Gauls could hardly be described as nurturing Cenno's fears about Roman conquest. He'd virtually called into question the very honour of the Gauls, as well as questioning their intelligence and skill. Not only was his mission now at an end, he may even have jeopardized the safety of the Carthaginians' supply route back to Iberia. That he might have made an enemy of the Lord of the Cavari was just too horrifying to contemplate.

After brooding alone throughout the day and early evening he decided to confide in Idwal and share his sorrows. His friend was sitting in the inner courtyard he called his peristyle. Torches and Grecian lamps illuminated the flowers and shrubs he and his gardeners had been planting out all day. The fragrant night air was still warm from the heat of the day and as Sphax sank back into the chair that was offered he gazed up at a night sky studded with stars. It was such a delightful setting that some of his anxieties began to recede a little. Servants brought bread and cheese and poured wine for them both. He took a deep draught and smiled at Idwal.

'You look as if you needed that. Has something happened?' In some alarm he asked, 'Has Dido taken a turn for the worse?'

'No,' said Sphax quickly, 'Dido is well. This time it's me ... and my big mouth.' He helped himself to another generous cup of wine and painfully recounted his conversation with Lord Cenno. Idwal listened in silence, at intervals either nodding or slowly shaking his head. When Sphax fell silent he said nothing for a while, staring at his newly planted myrtle tree, its leaves glistening in the flickering torchlight.

With a deep sigh, Idwal finally gazed at his friend and said, 'You have only told him the truth, Sphax. But for us, it is a bitter truth to swallow, for I believe the Cavari would have fared no better than the Volcae. We would have suffered the same fate. I also believe that somewhere, locked away in my father's soul, is the understanding that everything you said to him is true. But since my mother's death he has refused to face it. That's what drives him to anger and despair. He clings to the old ways, to the traditions of his forefathers; he lives in the past, not in hope for our future.'

'You spoke of this on our journey to Nages. Nevertheless, Idwal, I have insulted him and need to make amends. At this moment I would gladly kneel before him and beg his forgiveness—'

'You will do no such thing!' Idwal said sharply. 'He has also insulted you. It took courage to face Vertros in single combat. He knows this only too well. That you made a laughing stock of Vertros by your superior skills has only rubbed salt into my father's wounds.'

'But I didn't have to make a laughing stock of Vertros,' Sphax cried. 'To my shame I behaved arrogantly. I was fixed upon his humiliation and with pleasing the crowds, blind to all decency and honour. I did not act honourably. Don't you see that—'

'So that's what's been bothering you!' To Sphax's consternation Idwal was grinning at him. 'I've been wondering what it could be. At first I thought it was just your concern for Dido. Now everything is clear.' Idwal's grin was replaced by a grimace. 'Feel no guilt or shame over the downfall of Vertros. He has killed without pity or mercy for the last twenty years. His warband have murdered our neighbours and stolen their cattle, driving many into slavery. His great wealth comes from the slave markets of Massilia. Now the Cavari no longer live in peace and friendship with the Gabati or Vetavi. Instead we build walls and fear to trade with them. But there's worse! Since the death of my mother some ten years ago, Vertros has poisoned the mind of my father. I'm glad you humiliated him. I hope he rots in Hades for all eternity.'

'That still does not excuse my behaviour,' Sphax sighed, 'and neither will it mend bridges between me and your father, Idwal. So what am I to do? Let things fester?'

'Yes Sphax, let him fester! Either way he will ponder what you have said. I know my father; what you said to him will trouble him deeply. When a few Iberian *caetrati* and some horsemen armed only with javelins can slaughter some of the finest warriors in Gaul, he will see for himself that things must change. If your uncle and Carthage are defeated, Rome will turn its eyes on Gaul. This is certain. And what is also certain is that we are totally unprepared for such an onslaught.'

'Then you agree with what the Boii chieftain, Magol, said at the grand council.'

'Of course I do, Sphax. I didn't need Magol to tell me what I already knew. My Greek tutors have despaired for years and warned of Roman expansion. First Sicily, then Corsica, and now the Boii and Insubres face new Roman settlements in the north every year. Massilia is nothing better than a puppet, a vassal of Rome. She cannot wage war or sign a treaty without Rome's permission. She is like a dog feeding from scraps at the Roman table. Rome is on the march, and will crush anything that stands in her way.'

'Then join us, my friend. Let us march together on Rome and destroy its power once and for all time.' Sphax stared at Idwal, and held his breath.

'I was beginning to despair you would never ask! Of course I'll join you. There is nothing me and my men would rather do. But one thing stands in our way.'

'What's that?' asked Sphax, though he'd already guessed.

'My father.'

* * *

Next morning Sphax tried twice to gain an audience with Lord Cenno, but each time he was turned away by stewards at the great hall. As the day dragged on he decided to join Idwal at the main gate of the briga dūnan to watch the building work in progress. Soon he became lost in a world of measuring rods, lead lines and the huge machines that had been constructed to lift great blocks of stone to their final resting place on top of wall. Following Idwal up a rickety ladder they stood on a wooden platform built into the sides of the wall and watched masons laying stone on beds of lime and clay. It was from this vantage point that they both saw the approach of Cenno and his entourage. Retracing their steps they waited at the foot of the wall to greet the Lord of the Cavari.

'Show me your progress, Idwal. To my eyes it looks well.'

'All is well, father,' Idwal replied, 'but I will guide you over the works and you can judge for yourself.' With that Idwal gestured towards the length of the wall under construction that adjoined the towers. Not once did Cenno glance in Sphax's direction or acknowledge his presence. It was as if he was invisible. Then, just as he was about to turn and follow his son, Cenno said to him, 'I will expect you at *cena*, Master Sphax.'

Before he could reply, the Lord of the Cavari had turned to stride after his son, leaving him alone and bewildered. At last, it seemed, he had his audience. But why had he used the Roman word for dinner? Was it code, or something more troubling?

Sphax's most pressing concern about the evening ahead was what to wear. One of Idwal's servants had done her best to clean his toga, but it still stank of urine, and after he'd ripped strips from it to bind Dido's wound, his own tunic was in tatters and hardly suitable for a lord's table. Idwal came to his rescue, offering him one of his Greek-style togas that would not have looked out of place at a fashionable symposium in Athens. Along with the toga came a torrent of advice and instruction on what he should say, and what, under any circumstances he must not say.

It had the same effect on him as one of Elpis's more enthusiastic lessons on logic. It left him cold, with the same conclusions he'd drawn as a young boy; in the heat of argument, men are persuaded as much by passion and conviction as they are by cold reason.

The great hall looked very different that evening. Gone were the great cauldrons of steaming meat and the circle of blazing rush lights that had illuminated the feasting so brilliantly. Instead, a humble table stood on the high platform where Lord Cenno sat with three of his stewards eating from plain wooden plates. He was served fish.

Lord Cenno greeted him politely enough and gestured to a chair to his left where he found himself sitting opposite the stone-faced stewards. He felt as if the three fates were sitting in judgement of him. Cenno introduced them in turn and told him they spoke better Greek than he did. Lord Cenno's accent being what it was he caught only the first name, that of Judoc; the other two Sphax secretly named Lachesis and Clotho after the bleakest of the fates. Cenno began by asking him the strangest of questions.

'My son tells me that you have spent the last ten years of your life as a wretched slave in Rome. In which case you, more than most, are in a position to judge the character of Rome. What is the Roman character?'

'Rome has many faces, Sir. There is the Rome of slaves and the poor, the Rome of its citizens, and then there is the Rome of its ruling patricians.' Cenno seemed irritated by such a complicated answer.

'Then tell me plain, what is the character of these rulers, these patricians?'

'All patricians are driven by an insatiable ambition for high office and power. This is their only aim in life.'

'If this is the case,' stated Lord Cenno, 'we have little to fear from invasion or subjugation. There is no such high office to be sought in Gaul.' Sphax smiled at Cenno's innocence and ignorance of Rome.

'Now that the Boii and Insubres have risen against Rome, any ruthless praetor such as Flaminius Nepos will see this as a golden opportunity to make a name for himself. Crushing the rising will add to his lustre and open the way to higher office. The nations of Gaul mean nothing to him, whereas winning the consulship means everything. This is the true character of Rome, Lord Cenno.'

'What does it matter to us that there is a new Consul in Rome?'

'It should, my lord! They are worse than a pack of wolves, for they are driven not by hunger, but by insatiable ambition. When they have devoured every sheep in the valley, blind ambition will drive them on to the next. There will be no end to it.'

Lord Cenno remained silent. It was the steward Sphax had named Clotho who eventually asked, 'Then is it not more likely they will devour themselves by their own ambitions? From your description it would appear they are as much at war with each other as the world beyond Rome.'

'The laws of the republic allow them only to sip from the cup of power. But for many, this will never satisfy their unquenchable thirst. So I believe they can be driven to this, Sir, but only in extremis. This is also the conviction of my uncle, and many in his army. But this will only be achieved when Rome has been defeated, humiliated and stripped of her wealth and provinces. Then, we truly believe the pack will turn and Rome will devour itself.'

'It is your uncle,' Lord Cenno spoke at last, 'who has brought about this crisis. Without the sacking of Saguntum and his war on Rome the Boii and Insubres would not have been emboldened. Why could he not let sleeping dogs lie?'

'Only a fool would sleep beside a pack of wolves,' Sphax replied vehemently. 'My uncle is no such fool. He knows that Rome will not suffer rivals. Carthage became a rival, so Carthage had to be defeated. Now it is the turn of the Gauls of Liguria. Next it will be Hiero of Syracuse, then Massilia and Iberia. Perhaps they will look eastwards to Philip of Macedon, Corinth, or even Athens itself. Who will be next?' He paused, just as he'd seen his uncle do to such effect, and slowly examined the faces staring at him across the table. 'One thing is certain,' he continued, remembering Magol's words, 'your turn will come. Sooner or later the Cavari will have to face the tide of Rome.'

'You may think me a fool, Master Sphax, but I'm not such a fool as to think that your uncle's army could face the legions of Rome. They are a mongrel rabble, without loyalty; their only allegiance is to Carthaginian silver, and when that runs dry they will melt away as leaves fall in the first gusts of Samhain.'

Sphax felt the heat rising to his cheeks and his temper about to flare. Whatever it took, he knew he *had* to win this battle with his emotions. Everything now depended on it. It took a supreme effort to swallow these insults, but keeping his mouth firmly shut he forced himself to pick at the morsels of mullet still left on his plate. Slowly he regained enough composure to speak in a measured way.

'I think you will find, Lord Cenno, that we are united by something far more powerful than silver could ever buy. That which binds us is our common hatred of Rome, and because we are drawn from all the lands of the Mediterranean that have suffered persecution at her hands, every contingent has good reason for this hatred. I myself will not rest until Rome is burned to the ground so that I may walk amongst its ashes.'

'You above all have good reason to hate Rome.' For the first time that evening Sphax sensed a note of sympathy in Lord Cenno's tone. 'But I cannot be blinded by such hatred. I have my people to consider. The Cavari have never suffered hurt or injury at the hands of Romans. For as long as memory serves we have traded and lived in peace with them. Why should I forsake peace and risk their wrath?'

'When we descend from the Alps and begin our march on Rome, Liguria will rise and join us. The Boii and Insubres are already pledged, and I believe the Cenomani and Ligures will flock to our cause. If I should return with three hundred of your finest warriors sworn to Hannibal, you would not only be held in the highest regard by my uncle, but the whole of Gaul would surely look to your example and leadership. The Cavari would be joined by the Veltavi, the Helvii, and many others. Such a force would be irresistible! Rome could never withstand such an onslaught.'

At this the stony faces of the three fates sprang to life in heated discussion amongst themselves and their Lord. Sphax watched in total ignorance, for it was conducted in Gallic. Finally Lord Cenno turned to him and said in Greek, 'I will think on what you have said. We will talk again.'

Sphax realised he was being dismissed. Rising from his chair he bowed to Cenno, nodded at each of the stewards in turn and with a solemn 'good evening, my

Lord,' left the great hall as the four of them resumed their discussion.

Idwal was waiting for him. Servants lit lamps and brought chairs to the peristyle where they sat under the stars as they had on the previous evening. Sphax was grateful for the warmth of the toga, for there was an autumn chill in the air that evening. By the time he'd given Idwal a detailed account of what had been said at *cena* he was halfway through his second cup of wine. His friend had listened in rapt attention. Idwal finally broke his silence. 'Well my friend,' smiling thoughtfully across at Sphax, 'you have let your javelin fly. Let's hope it finds its mark.'

'Swiftly, I hope, for in nine days' time I must return back to my uncle.' Mention of his uncle reminded him of his fears concerning their supply routes back to New Carthage. He decided to take Idwal into his confidence and explain everything Hannibal had asked him to negotiate with Lord Cenno. When he'd finished he grinned at Idwal, 'So you see, he thinks more highly of you than he does of his wayward nephew,' adding more seriously, 'I think he sees in you a future leader of the Gauls.'

'I'm flattered,' said Idwal, returning the grin. 'But what a strange fellow your uncle is. Why did he not ask me to talk to my father?'

Sphax laughed. 'Because the mission was to test my mettle, and to use our friendship to get what he wants from your father. He must have guessed that sooner or later I would confide in you. In that way he ensured we work together to get what *he* wants. I'm beginning to realise that nothing is ever straightforward where my uncle is concerned. He has made conspiracy into an art.'

It was Idwal's turn to laugh. 'Does he ever think about anything other than grand strategy, devious plots and conspiracies? Only your uncle would bring along a famous historian and his Greek tutor on campaign with him. I suppose that says something about him.'

'Indeed it does! I would have thought it would appeal to you.' Sphax became serious for a moment. 'Truly Idwal, everyone I question about my uncle speaks of him in terms of the utmost respect, with awe almost. They say he has genius.' He gazed up at the waxing moon and shivered. 'I must attend to Dido,' he said, and folding the toga tightly around his shoulders asked, 'may I keep the toga until the morning?'

'But of course, it's yours now,' and with a secretive smile added, 'I have another gift for you tomorrow, but that will remain a surprise.'

'I love surprises,' said Sphax, as he rose and headed for the stables.

* * *

The surprise Idwal had in mind turned out to be a visit to the smithy. Here he was introduced to a great bear of a man called Aodhán. Idwal and Aodhán embraced each other like long lost brothers, and after much back-slapping and laughter the smith turned to him and in perfect Greek said, 'I watched you fight that dung-heap Vertros the other day. I've never seen anything like it! How did you manage to face about on a galloping horse?'

'It's just a trick, Sir,' said Sphax, grinning up into a face almost obscured by a haystack of red hair and beard. Idwal had told him earlier that the name Aodhán meant fire in Gaulish and that his full name was Aodhán the Red. Sphax had imagined someone forged by the fires of Hephaestus. He was not disappointed. Aodhán evidently despised the Keltoi obsession with shaving and seemed to have taken on the appearance of a fiery spindle in all its glorious autumn colour. Sphax found out later that the smith had been a Greek slave in Massilia, freed by Idwal so he could establish his own smithy in Nages.

'Well, you did us all a favour, lad. May his soul rot in Hades.' Rumour that morning was that Vertros was still sleeping like a babe and the gods were still undecided. Turning to Idwal he rested one of his great paws on his shoulder. 'This young good-for-nothing was once my most gifted and promising student, Sphax. Now he has a mind only for stone. He dreams of walls and towers and villas. Baah! I could have made him into a man of iron. Now he's turned himself to stone.' Aodhán thought this extremely amusing and roared with laughter.

'And where would I be without your nails, braces or chisels?' laughed Idwal, 'my walls would come crashing down.' Turning to Sphax he said, 'Aodhán is a true man of iron, Sphax, skilled in all forms of metalwork, and his swords are legendary, the best in Gaul. I've asked him to make one for you. It will be something for you to treasure, a thing of real beauty with a spirit and soul of its own. But first you must give Aodhán that useless Roman blade you carry.'

Aodhán did a strange thing with it. Balancing the sword horizontally on top of his bushy head, he carefully gripped the hilt and tip with each hand and pulled hard downwards towards his shoulders. Reluctantly, the sword began to bend, but at a crucial moment Aodhán stopped exerting pressure. 'The iron's telling me that if I took it a fingernail further, you would hear it cry out in shame and shatter. It's Roman iron. Believe me I've seen worse, but this is only good for my scrap pile.'

Idwal unsheathed his own sword and did exactly the same. The blade bent to a degree that Sphax had not thought possible. When the tip and hilt were almost touching his shoulders Idwal released it, sending it whistling high into the roof of the smithy. Keeping a keen eye on it, he caught it perfectly by the hilt on its descent to the ground and then handed it to Sphax, who was astonished. It had perfectly resumed its shape and was as straight and true as a die. 'Now that's a real sword, Sphax. It's Aodhán's finest, and will only be bettered by the blade he makes for you. But we have a problem, my friend. Because you fight on horseback, you will require a blade that is even longer, and master Aodhán doubts that Hephaestus will allow this. So you must sacrifice your Roman blade as a libation to the god and solemnly cast it into the river from the field where you overcame Vertros. Are you willing to do this?' Without a second thought Sphax nodded.

Later that morning, Sphax performed this ritual with due solemnity, and over the course of the next six days became a frequent visitor to the smithy, earning from Aodhán the name *little flea*, because of his pestering questions and generally getting in the way. Sphax became spellbound by everything that took place in the smithy; from the sounds of hammers working the iron amidst showers of golden sparks, to the sudden hiss as metal was plunged into barrels of cold water, something Aodhán explained as quenching the iron to give it strength. Then there was the steady breath of the bellows that could drive the fire to a white heat in moments, along with the all-pervasive smell of sweat and acrid charcoal smoke. Even the molten iron itself had a faint aroma that reminded him of mushrooms, or something more mysterious, garnered from the bowels of the underworld.

For someone with a pair of hands the size of bear's paws, Aodhán wielded his hammer and tongs with surprising delicacy and precision, stopping only occasionally to wipe the sweat on his leather apron or pass on a word of instruction to his apprentice, Bleda. Two curly-haired boys from the town, whom Aodhán affectionately called his little rats, worked the bellows and served the fire.

On the evening of the third day Aodhán proudly showed him the fruits of his labours so far. Placed side by side on the polished hammering stone were three separate strips of iron the length of a man's arm from shoulder to fingertip. It didn't look much to Sphax, politely reminding him that he only needed one sword, not three. Aodhán let out his great roaring laugh and patiently explained that it was now his task to meld the three into one. The outer strips, he told him, were made from the finest Noricum iron and would give the sword its cutting edges, whilst the central strip had been tempered from softer metal, to give the blade its overall strength and flexibility.

'A blade made entirely from Noricum iron will slice through anything, but will eventually shatter. Just as swords require the elements of earth, air, fire and water in equal measure, they also need the union of man and woman. A blade is a marriage of hardness and softness, the brittle and the supple; without the qualities of both, it will not endure.'

After the fifth day he was forbidden to enter the smithy. Aodhán had sent the scabbard to the silversmith and was now hard at work polishing and sharpening. 'Besides,' Aodhán told him, 'they say it brings bad luck for a swordsman to see his face reflected in a blade that has not been sharpened.'

* * *

The next three days passed pleasantly enough. Sphax helped the stonemasons at the wall or worked with Idwal in his peristyle, planting shrubs and fruit trees. Being able to allow Dido to follow him to the walls or down to the fields by the river only added to his pleasure. He'd vowed not to ride her until they'd reached the Island and removed the stitches. Javelin practice was not the same as thundering along astride Dido, but he made the best of it.

Evenings were spent in the peristyle drinking wine and picking at food amidst endless conversation. Sphax had come to love Idwal's courtyard garden. The flowers had been chosen as much for their scent as their colour, and although it was late in the season, in the heat of the day the air still felt heavy with perfume.

He and Idwal were examining the drawings and plans drawn up for the villa when Lord Cenno's steward Judoc arrived to inform them that Lord Cenno expected them both to attend dinner that evening in the great hall. When Judoc had left, Sphax asked, 'What do you think? Has your father come to a decision?'

'I hope so,' Idwal shrugged. 'You've given him time enough to chew on it. Perhaps he's come to his senses at last.'

'If he has decided, at least that will give us five days to prepare.'

'Four,' Idwal corrected, 'if we can't find enough horses for my men and have to march on foot. And we really do need to take pack animals to carry supplies, clothing and our tents. We will need furs for warmth. I fear those mountains. It's now so late in the season. We must expect the first snows within the month.'

'That's a little premature, my friend. If your father has been counselled by fear and caution, I will be facing those mountains alone. It will be with a heavy heart, but in five days' time I will have to say farewell and depart alone.'

'Whatever my father has decided, that is by no means the end of it, my friend,' Idwal said with a half-smile, as if there was something he was keeping from him.

It was as if Lord Cenno and his stewards had been turned to statues. He was seated at the same table, with the three fates sitting in exactly the same positions Sphax had left them four evenings ago. As they stepped on to the high platform Cenno arose from his seat to greet and embrace his son. All Sphax received was a cursory nod and a gesture towards a chair at the opposite end of the table. Lord Cenno looked particularly careworn that evening; the penetrating quality of those brilliant blue eyes seemed to have dimmed. As servants poured wine and brought plates of bread and meat the evening began with an uneasy silence. Without any preamble, Lord Cenno launched into a summary of the decision he'd already taken.

'The Cavari will not join Carthage in her war with Rome. To do so would be madness, for not only would we provoke the wrath of Rome, we would also make enemies of our neighbours, the Massiliots. But this is only the first of many arguments that have persuaded me. I doubt that Hannibal's army will ever get across the mountains. It is a frozen, forbidding place, inhabited only by wild beasts and savages. The snows will fall and they will freeze to death in their camps. Even if by some gift of the gods they were to cross into Liguria, Rome's legions will be waiting for them. What hope have Hannibal's mercenaries against the legions of Rome? They will be slaughtered and scattered to the winds. The enterprise is folly, it is a madness doomed to failure. I will not risk a single warrior in such a foolish war.'

So, thought Sphax, the die is cast. He would return to his uncle with his tail between his legs, a failure. Whilst Cenno had spoken he'd examined Idwal's expression carefully for signs of disagreement or disapproval, but Idwal was giving nothing away; his eyes had remained lowered, fixed on his plate. When his father had finished speaking, Idwal looked over at Sphax with raised eyebrows, as if inviting him to respond first. With a weary sigh Sphax began, 'It grieves me that you feel as you do, Lord Cenno. For I fear it is short-sighted. Surely it's in the best interests of the Cavari to throw in their lot with Hannibal and the rest of Gaul.'

'The rest of Gaul!' sneered Cenno. 'The Boii and the Insubres will not lift a finger to aid your uncle. At the first sight of a Roman legion they will slink away, back to their pigsties and dung heaps. They are no better than farmers!'

'You seem to think less of your fellow Gauls than you do of my uncle's army, Sir. But I see your mind is set, and that nothing I say will change it. But my uncle also seeks assurance that our communications with Iberia are secure, and that our convoys and supplies will not be molested. Can I give him that assurance?'

'And when Rome claims victory and Carthage is destroyed, do you think Rome will reward me for giving such an assurance, Master Sphax?' The negotiations had now taken an ugly twist.

'We ask only to be left alone, Sir. This implies neither assistance nor support. Simply that you do nothing ... something the Cavari seem to be rather good at. Do I at least have your assurance on that score, Lord Cenno?' The Cavari chief stared at him coldly, without answering.

Sphax wondered if the moment had arrived to use his last resort. Hannibal had told him Cenno might be open to bribery. If he offered him an annual tribute to be paid in silver and sealed this with an alliance between the Cavari and his brother Hasdrubal in Iberia, he might be sorely tempted. It would provide the two things that Cenno desired most in this uncertain world; wealth and security. But with Cenno already decided, it was too late for silver to work its magic. Besides, it seemed he feared Rome more than Carthage. It might be time to turn the tables. Sphax had an idea. But it was not without risk. An alliance refused could easily be turned into a warning. What had Hannibal himself said? 'If you are not with us, then you are against us.' He would turn his uncle's last resort on its head, and offer instead a veiled threat. It would be his last throw of the dice.

'Then if your mind is set, Lord,' he began, gazing coldly into the faces of the three fates, 'I must seek your permission to return to the Island, where my uncle's army is encamped. Of course,' he continued as airily as he could manage, 'these negotiations will have to be continued by my uncle Hasdrubal in Iberia. He has an army of sixty thousand Iberians poised on your borders to the west. Our communications with Iberia are vital, and must be kept open at all costs. I'm sure he will wish to pay you a visit …'

Sphax saw that Idwal was grinning at him. But this was not the case with Lord Cenno and the three stewards, who were glaring at him red-faced, barely able to conceal their anger.

'Are you threatening me?' He was relieved to hear a note of uncertainty in Lord Cenno's tone.

'Of course not!' replied Sphax, playing the offended innocent. 'I was simply reminding you of the forces available to Carthage west of your borders, should you ever need their assistance. Remember, Lord, you have already been paid generously for pledges made to my uncle to keep the passages to Iberia open.'

'I don't need a little runt like you to remind me of my duty, boy.' Sphax was getting better at swallowing insults. Even so, he flushed and had to bite his tongue.

'Then may I remind you of your duty, father,' Idwal spoke at last, 'which is to the Cavari people, and their right to hold their heads proudly amongst the peoples of Gaul. You did not attend Hannibal's grand council of Gauls, nor did you bother to send representatives. If you had been there you would have heard for yourself that there *is* support for Hannibal and this war with Rome. The Boii have already risen, and many more are pledged to follow. If you had spoken at that meeting in the terms you have espoused this evening, I would have felt only one thing; shame! I would have felt ashamed for my people, ashamed to be counted as Cavari.'

Idwal was now glaring contemptuously at his father. 'Much of what you say is foolish nonsense. Far too long have you been counselled by fear and timidity. You speak of Massilia as a friend and ally, when in reality she is nothing more than a puppet of Rome. Rome's fleets sail the Rhodanus with impunity, as if it was their river and not ours. Rome already has puppets and vassals west of us in Iberia. From the Ebro to the Rhodanus, Cavari lands are already surrounded, father. By Rome!'

'You are as headstrong as your mother, Idwal. This is not a time for impetuous decisions or reckless action. This is a time to watch the winds and the tides—'

'So you will do nothing!' Sphax had never witnessed his friend's anger before, and it was a chilling sight. 'You would have our friends and allies fight our battles for us, whilst we feast and sit content in our halls? This is the way of the coward, father. It is not the way of the Cavari. And it is certainly not my way! We need to show strength and leadership at this time, not slink away like jackals.' By now Idwal had risen to his feet, but despite his anger, there was also a measure of self-control in his voice that lent power and conviction to his words.

'Sit down and restrain yourself,' Lord Cenno commanded. 'What do you know of the world and its ways? What do you know of war? You're just a boy, softened by too much learning and education. Why could I not have had a warrior for a son—'

'Like Vertros, you mean?' Idwal said this with such chilling effect that it sent shivers down Sphax's spine. For a few moments it seemed as if Lord Cenno and the three fates had in fact been turned into stone. Idwal walked quietly from the hall.

Sphax also got to his feet. 'You have insulted your son beyond all sufferance. I take my leave of you, Sir— '

'You will not be so impertinent as to leave my table without my permission, boy!' Cenno sneered.

'I am a Prince of Numidia, a noble of Carthage. I don't need your permission!'

'So! You whore's son, you would challenge me … like Vertros?'

Sphax flushed. The three stewards leapt to their feet and stood nervously between Sphax and their lord. There was a deathly silence.

'I don't kill old men,' was all he said as he stormed out.

NINE

Sphax decided to leave Idwal alone for the rest of the evening. He could offer little comfort and there seemed no point in going over matters that had become so painful for both of them, especially for poor Idwal. He slept in the stall beside Dido, but so fitfully that when the first fingers of dawn's light crept into the stables he gave up on sleep, reached for his javelins and whistled Dido to follow. After javelin practice in the fields beside the river he put Dido through her paces, carefully watching her every stride for signs of stiffness or weakness. He saw none, which put him in a better frame of mind to face the new day.

As he was leading his mare back to the stables he noticed that groups of young men seemed to be making their way towards Idwal's villa. Once Dido was safely back in her stall he decided it was high time he went to console his friend.

He found Idwal in the centre of the courtyard garden, addressing a huge crowd of young men in Gallic from atop a bench. There must have been sixty men crammed into the courtyard, and judging from the animated faces and shouts of agreement, whatever his friend was saying was being greeted with unanimous approval. He recognised many of the faces from that night of feasting with Merbal's Numidians. To Sphax, that evening now seemed like a lifetime ago. So these were Idwal's household warriors, his faithful band. But what was he saying to them? What was going on?

As Idwal finished speaking a rousing cry of approval broke out amongst the entire gathering. When this eventually subsided, individuals began raising their hands and each in turn addressed the assembly. Some briefly, some at length, but all were allowed a fair hearing. When silence again fell on the gathering and everyone seemed satisfied, Idwal climbed back on the bench and gave a brief concluding speech. This was not met with a rousing ovation as before, but seemed to stir up a buzz of conversations around the courtyard. Small knots of men gathered together and began urgent discussions amongst themselves. All now became a scene of animated gesticulation, pointing and the nodding or shaking of heads.

By now Sphax was totally confused and desperate to find out what was going on, but Idwal was still surrounded by a dozen men babbling away in Gallic. Eventually the discussion seemed to reach some sort of resolution and men scurried away in ones and twos. Silence suddenly descended on an empty courtyard, and they found themselves grinning at one another.

This was not the Idwal he'd expected to encounter this morning. 'Have you breakfasted?' Idwal asked jauntily in a language he could understood at last. Sphax shook his head. 'Then let's go and get something to eat. I have news for you.' Later, in between mouthfuls of honeyed milk and oats, Idwal said, 'I'm going to war with you.' Sphax's jaw dropped.

'But you can't, Idwal,' he said in disbelief, 'you would be defying your father, going against everything he said to us last night. You can't do this!' Idwal simply carried on eating, seemingly oblivious to everything Sphax had just said.

'And why not?' he said at last, smiling.

'Because he is your father, Idwal. You owe him your obedience and loyalty. He is to be honoured and respected, not disobeyed!'

'I'm not disobeying him. The Cavari are not going to war, only Idwal of the Cavari and his followers are going to war. That's a subtle, yet significant difference, don't you think? My father has chosen for the Cavari, which means that I'm at liberty to choose for my household.'

'So that's what it was about. The meeting I mean.' Idwal nodded. 'I take it they have all agreed to follow you?'

'Of course! But from now on we haven't a moment to lose. We need more warriors, supplies, horses, carts, tents, warm clothing, especially furs, everything an army needs on campaign ... and we only have four, perhaps five days. Cáel is riding to the villages in the north to gather more men and anything he can lay his hands on – we have many friends in the north. Ioduc rides south to Uchad then east to collect food and clothing. Drust has kin and many friends in the west at Aubai. That's good horse country, and where you come in. I've allotted you to his party. You should only be away for two days, three at the most. You don't mind, do you?'

Sphax burst out laughing. 'Shall I bring back a few elephants whilst I'm there?'

'This is serious, Sphax.' His friend's familiar frown had returned. 'Not a laughing matter. Not one amongst the Cavari knows horses like you do. Will you help Drust?'

'Gladly. I would do anything to put a few miles between myself and your father when he finds out what you're up to,' Sphax answered truthfully.

*　*　*

Next morning, when he collected Dido from the stables he'd noticed another horse had been left in one of the stalls. It was Brega, Vertros's stallion. 'Come boy,' Sphax spoke gently to him, 'come with me. You deserve a better life than this.'

Leaving Dido in the care of Idwal he'd ridden Brega, and it did take three days, not two. There was always another village to visit, another elder to speak with or a stud at a farmstead some miles distant. Idwal was right, the rolling wooded countryside around Aubai was perfect horse country, and the chestnut stallions bred in these parts were renowned for their size and stamina. Drust was an entertaining companion with a mischievous sense of humour, so the time flew pleasantly by. As the hilltop battlements of Nages came into view on the afternoon of the third day, he and Drust led eighty warriors and a string of over three hundred horses up through the warren of ditches to the gate between the twin towers.

But Nages had changed. This was not the town they left three days ago. It was evident from the cheerless stares and indifference of the townsfolk gathered in doorways to watch their passing that something was wrong. An atmosphere of fear and dread hung over the place like a funeral pall. As he was soon to discover from Idwal, Nages was divided. Nages was a place at war with itself; fathers against sons, brothers at loggerheads with one another. Are you for Lord Cenno or for Idwal? If you are not with us, then you're against us, he reminded himself. Why was there never a middle way, thought Sphax? Did it always have to be like this?

The fields around Idwal's villa had become an armed camp. Tents had been erected and lines of horses had been tethered in orderly lines. Guards had even been posted to protect the dozens of wagons piled high with supplies. Idwal greeted them joyously, amazed at the number of men and horses they'd managed to muster. It took some time to find a quiet corner in the villa where they could talk in peace, for every room was full of the laughter and conversation of animated young men, seated on chairs, benches or anything they could find.

Idwal told them that the trouble had begun the day after they left. By then the whole town knew that the rumours were true. His father had stormed down from the great hall, surrounded by his household warriors and demanded Idwal disband *his* household warriors and send them back to their villages. When he'd refused, there had been a stand-off. By then Idwal had been able to muster over a hundred men. Lord Cenno had realised he was outnumbered and that his son was never going to back down. The stalemate had only been broken by the news that Ioduc was arriving at the western gate with twenty wagons and fifty warriors. Ioduc had more than tipped the scales and his father had retreated back to the great hall, posting dozens of guards outside to defend it.

But that wasn't the worst of it, Idwal told him. Ever since Vertros's downfall his followers had been spoiling for a fight to prove themselves and stake their claim to his mantle, so the next day they'd gathered outside the villa, hurling insults and taunting his men. Idwal had posted guards and given strict instructions that no one was to leave their post or be tempted into single combat. Sadly, two hot-headed young lads had been unable to weather the taunting and had chanced their luck. Both had been slain by Loic, chief pretender to Vertros's crown.

Under cover of twilight Idwal himself had gathered twenty men at the back of the villa and circled around Loic's men so they could charge them from the rear. This surprise attack was decisive; six of Loic's band had been badly wounded and the rest had fled, amongst them Loic. But this skirmish had only made the situation worse. Now there were scores to settle and bad blood on both sides.

Sphax was in despair. This is not what his uncle Hannibal had intended! The last thing Sphax wanted was to drive a wedge between Idwal and his father. But that was precisely what he'd done. And it was all his fault. Instead of recruiting an ally, he'd started a war.

'Now we are alike,' Idwal had said bitterly, 'both our mothers and our fathers are lost to us in this life.'

* * *

As dusk fell and night began to draw in, something quite unexpected began to unfold outside the gates of the villa. At first in dribs and drabs, then in large groups, young men from the town begged to be given admittance so they could pledge themselves to Idwal's cause. They were carpenters, potters, ploughboys and stable lads. Few were warriors, but they were all big-boned lusty lads, who could easily be trained to hold a shield and wield a spear. Idwal questioned them all in turn, but they seemed to be of one mind, one resolve: they would go to war to restore Cavari pride amongst the Gauls. By midnight Idwal's ranks had swollen by over three hundred men, some even from his father's household. Sphax was under no illusions. Nages and the Cavari were still as divided as ever, but it was heartening that so many young men had chosen to join them. Perhaps the tide had turned.

Idwal was waiting for him next morning when he returned from javelin practice. Without saying a word, he took Sphax's arm and guided him along the corridor that led to the courtyard garden. In the centre of the peristyle, where he and Idwal had spent so many nights in pleasant conversation under the stars, stood Aodhán the smith. Placed on a table in front of him lay something wrapped in scarlet cloth. As Sphax approached, the smith gestured towards the cloth with his great bear's paw. Sphax had by now guessed what lay hidden beneath the folds of the cloth, but nothing could have prepared him for that first sight of the scabbard and the blade it held within. Crafted in bronze with a gold tip, a silver inlay ran down the length of the scabbard depicting a dragon, its wings furled and tongue breathing forth flames. It was astonishing, and perfect.

'Turn it over,' Idwal said excitedly. He did, and then gasped. A similar inlay decorated this side, but this time the scene depicted was of a line of elephants approaching a river. The detail was extraordinary; even the mahouts had been meticulously sculptured and the water etched and engraved to produce the effect of eddies and currents. By now tears were streaming down

Sphax's cheeks. Never before had he held an object so beautiful, precious and perfect. Wherever he looked his eyes lighted on something new and extraordinary. The craftsmanship was exquisite; the sword's hilt had been made from two pieces of ivory, clasped and reinforced with bands of gold, whilst the guard and pommel had been formed in the shape of elephant's tusks and were made from pure silver.

'I think it's time to draw your sword, Sphax,' said Aodhán solemnly. Sphax drew the sword from the scabbard in one movement and raised the blade in the air. 'But it's so light!' he cried in astonishment, eyes wide and mouth gaping. Aodhán roared with laughter and even Idwal joined in. Sphax walked a safe distance away and started swishing the blade through the air. He loved the metallic sound it made as it hissed and slashed; it was as if he had become a child again, slaying dragons with his wooden sword. Finally, he held the sword by its tip and hilt and raised it so he could see his face reflected in the polished metal of the blade.

'This is a gift worthy of a king,' he said, deeply moved, 'not a Numidian horseman.' Running his finger along the sword's razor sharp edge he deliberately nicked his finger and smeared the blood along the flat of the blade. Addressing Aodhán, he said 'With my blood, I swear to the maker of this wondrous sword that I will never dishonour it,' and to Idwal he said, 'To the giver of this sword, I swear by my blood that as long as I have breath, I will defend him with it.' There was a grave silence as Sphax swore his oaths, then Sphax embraced each of them in turn before sliding the sword back into its scabbard.

Cáel arrived shortly before midday with over two hundred warriors, all mounted on horseback and leading strings of mules laden with everything from sacks of barley to furs and wooden shields. Idwal now mustered an army worthy of any contingent Carthage could field.

For the next two hours harnesses, ropes and leather fastenings were checked on every pack-mule, axles packed with fresh fat, and everything that might be of use or value removed from the villa and loaded onto wagons. There was a great deal of argument and discussion about the route they should take through Nages to reach the western gate.

Drust thought it presented an excellent opportunity for a final show of strength to intimidate Lord Cenno and the townsfolk into joining them, so he favoured marching directly past the great hall and through the centre of the town. Idwal and many of his lieutenants thought this too risky; the ramshackle streets and alleyways offered too many opportunities for ambush or injury, especially for those with scores to settle or who wanted to punish the lads from town that had sworn to Idwal.

Prudence won out, and it was decided that the column would skirt the town by following the wooden wall until it reached the new stone wall beside the western gate. An hour later, Sphax was astride Brega at the head of the column when Idwal raised his arm and yelled 'Forward.' With Dido running freely beside him they reached the western gate without incident or interference.

After they passed through the wooden gate between the twin stone towers, Sphax looked up to see Lord Cenno on top of the battlements with his arms raised to the heavens, as if beseeching the gods themselves. 'Did you see him?' he asked Idwal, riding beside him.

'Yes,' answered Idwal wearily, 'I saw him.'

'He had his arms raised. I think he was offering you his blessing.'

'No, Sphax. He was cursing me.'

PART THREE

THE WALLS OF ROME

TEN

R iding into the Carthaginian camp at the head of Idwal's column was the proudest moment of his life. As he and Idwal rode through the cheering ranks gathered to welcome them his heart swelled with pride. He felt like Agamemnon riding triumphantly into Troy. With good reason.

Idwal had mustered over eight hundred men for Carthage, many of them seasoned warriors. Besides men, Idwal had brought over eighty spare horses, more than enough to replace the sixty-two lent by Maharbal. But what would be equally important for their journey over the snowbound mountains were the strings of pack-mules laden with furs and warm clothing, shoes, woollen cloaks and hemp-woven tents, sacks of oats and barley and flagons of mead, everything an army would need to sustain it on the epic journey they were about to undertake.

Their column had stretched back for almost two miles, so the entire camp had been given plenty of warning of their coming. By the time they reached

Hannibal's magnificent pavilion in the centre of the encampment, every general and captain of significance had gathered to welcome their new allies.

Idwal did a noble and splendid thing. Leaping from his horse he drew his sword and kneeling before Hannibal, placed it at his feet. 'The Cavari have come to swear their solemn allegiance to Lord Hannibal and Carthage. Death to Rome!' he cried.

Sphax noticed his uncle's Greek tutors exchange significant looks. He imagined them recording Idwal's speech for the histories they would undoubtedly write after Rome had fallen. He smiled at the thought that even he might get a mention on this page of history. On reflection, he decided it would be the merest of footnotes.

As usual, he was ignored by his uncles and all the generals gathered for the welcoming. Sphax didn't give a fig! He'd spotted Fionn in the crowds, smiling and waving at him. At that moment all he wanted was to sweep her off her feet and hold her in his arms. So that's what he did. Nobody seemed to notice, or take the slightest interest in this little scene of joy, so when Fionn's feet were firmly back on the ground he whistled Brega and Dido to follow and walked arm in arm with Fionn back to their place in this grand encampment. Invisibility had its advantages sometimes.

He was delighted to see their old tent had been restored to them. In his absence Fionn had acquired two large pinewood chests, chairs and a simple table, but Sphax had only eyes for their comfortable sleeping couch. He had lots to tell her, but it could wait.

At dawn next morning he was awoken by the most unpleasant sight imaginable; Dubal's ugly face peering down at him. 'Wake up, arsehole! Maharbal reckons that after your little holiday with the Gauls you will have forgotten how to hold one of these,' he said, brandishing a couple of javelins in his fist. Rubbing the sleep from his eyes, Sphax swung his legs off the couch, covered the sleeping Fionn with his toga and dressed quickly. Javelins indeed! Would he have a surprise for his ugly tutor.

He was amazed to see so few guards had been posted around the camp, guessing the Island offered a safe and secure refuge for any army. It was well named, positioned as it was between the Rhodanus and a broad tributary that entered its waters from the north east, forming a narrow neck of land protected on three sides by water. Describing Dido's injury along the way, he followed Dubal to a flat area of ground beyond the camp. Grudgingly, Dubal had to admit that he'd improved a little. But he still found fault. Sphax's wrist was bent, elbow too straight, arm too high or shoulder too low. Whatever he did was wrong. He got the feeling that whatever he did it would always be wrong. There was just no pleasing Dubal.

He spent the rest of the morning in pleasant idleness. After Fionn's servants Cesti and Lulin made them breakfast he showed her the fur cloak he'd brought back from Nages. 'I hope you like it? It's fox fur, and there's a pretty silver clasp. I've got one made of beaver. Idwal says we'll need them in the mountains.' She did like it. So much so that she wore it for the rest of the day, even though it was swelteringly hot. Maharbal's woman Ayzabel came to visit Fionn in the afternoon. In Sphax's absence they'd become as thick as thieves. After Fionn had twirled around in her new cloak for her friend to admire, Ayzabel jauntily said to him, 'You're the talk of the camp. They say you killed a chief of the Gauls in single combat.'

'Dog's twat!' Sphax exclaimed angrily. 'Of course I didn't kill Lord Cenno, he's Idwal's father! Who's spreading these lies?'

Ayzabel shrugged. 'Well, that's what the servants told me this morning. It's all round the camp.' Sphax looked sharply at Cesti and Lulin sitting quietly at the back of the tent.

'Have you two heard anything?' he asked. They looked sheepishly at one another, then nodded.

'I better put a stop to these lies right now,' Sphax muttered, reaching for the leggings and smock that Idwal had given him. They were woven of fine cloth in the traditional Cavari chequered patterns and Sphax had taken to wearing them recently. He noticed that Fionn and Ayzabel had their hands over their mouths, trying to stop themselves giggling. 'What's wrong now?' he said in exasperation.

'You, my darling,' said Fionn, no longer able to hold back her laughter, 'look like a Gaul that's been dipped in a bucket of tar.'

He stomped off to look for Idwal. But he didn't get very far. Maharbal caught sight of him and beckoned him over to his pavilion. The general looked at his most severe that afternoon. Sphax got that sinking feeling whenever his mentor had that look about him. Chairs were found and the general called for wine.

'You have a habit of disappearing. You were missed. Your uncles, and I for that matter, wanted to question you. But instead, you slunk away. I've learned more from Dubal this morning than I have from you.' This wasn't going at all well, thought Sphax.

'I thought I would leave it all to Idwal, Sir;' adding unconvincingly, 'he's much better at explaining things than me.'

'Indeed. I think I will be the judge of that. I want to hear it from your own mouth. Start at the beginning … the very beginning.'

'A lot happened, Sir. It's a long story.'

'I have all the time in the world, young man. Begin.'

It *was* a long story, and except for the occasional sip of wine to collect his thoughts, Sphax talked continuously for the best part of the afternoon. Maharbal listened intently, interrupting rarely and only at the mention of a name he was unfamiliar with. When Sphax had finished the general gazed into space for a moment, then asked to see Sphax's sword, his gift from Idwal. Maharbal examined it closely, turning it over in his hands before getting to his feet to draw the blade from its scabbard. After cutting the air around him with a few passes he carefully sheathed the blade and handed it back to him. 'That is a fine blade, lad. Pity it's wasted on you.'

'Idwal says he'll teach me, Sir.'

'Good. Someone needs to.' Maharbal began pacing slowly around the tent. 'Tell me, why did you not offer Lord Cenno the bribe your uncle had instructed you to offer him?'

'Because he would have taken it and still done nothing for our cause.'

'But instead, you threatened him with another of your uncles, Hasdrubal in Iberia. Why, Sphax? What could possibly be gained by this?'

'Lord Cenno is ruled by wealth and fear. His wealth comes from trade with Massilia and Rome. This is why he fears Rome more than Carthage, I just turned those fears on its head and bought them closer to home, that's all. Anyway, it didn't work. Nothing would have persuaded him.'

'What makes you say that? Are you so certain?' Maharbal asked, stopping mid-stride and staring at him.

'Absolutely, Sir. Besides, Cenno is a broken man. His own son has turned his back on him along with most of his people. Any Cavari worthy of the name is now in our camp. I believe many more will follow Idwal's example. Lord Cenno is finished.'

'Are our supply lines back to Iberia secure? Will Lord Cenno molest our trains? I ask you now because this will be the first question your uncle will ask you.'

'Yes! Perfectly secure, Sir. Who would follow him? He no longer commands warriors. I killed the worst of the troublemakers.'

'According to you, he's just sleeping. The way you fight he probably fell asleep out of sheer boredom.' Sphax had to smile at this image. Maharbal sat back in his chair and picked up his cup. 'Well,' he said finally, 'it's done now. May ba 'al hamūn prove you right.'

Maharbal was wrong. Later, when they were both ushered into Hannibal's pavilion it wasn't the first question his uncle asked, but the second. His uncle was seated on his divan, flanked by the Greeks Silenos and Sosylos, just as they had been on his last visit, two weeks ago. The only difference this evening was that his uncle Mago had drawn up a chair beside his brother.

It seemed Hannibal couldn't bear to look at him. 'When I commission an officer to perform a duty, I expect that officer to wait upon me on his return, so he can make a full and complete report. Only by this means am I able to determine whether his duty has been performed to my satisfaction, or that he has failed in the fulfilment of those tasks. Reports are not given at the whim or discretion of my officers, they are given when I demand them. Reporting to me is more than a mere duty, it is a solemn obligation. Do I make myself perfectly clear? You have failed in your duties. What are your excuses?'

Sphax knew this had better be good. 'With respect, Sir, I have not failed in a single duty. For I have never been told what my duties or obligations are. Your officers are trained and schooled in your service, they are aware of their duties and obligations to you. I have received no such instruction or training. The only guidance has been my own conscience and honour, and on both counts you will find me blameless. Might I remind you, Sir, that until I joined your great army less than three weeks ago, I received instruction from the whips of my Roman masters.'

'I may have recourse to those measures, boy, if you don't mend your ways!' Sphax couldn't help noticing that Mago was grinning slyly at him.

'I think the lad has a point, brother,' said Mago. 'Don't you?'

'This ... lad, doesn't seem to have *any* point or a purpose! That seems to be the crux of our problem with him.' This time his uncle gave him the benefit of a cold stare. It was not pleasant. 'Idwal assures me that our supply lines with Iberia and New Carthage are secure. What is your assessment?' Sphax got the impression that he'd ridden out the worst of the storm.

'Perfectly secure, Sir. The Cavari are divided and Lord Cenno's power and authority has been broken. He now fears Carthage more than Rome and would never risk the wrath of your brother in Iberia. Hasdrubal is only three days' march away. I did remind him of this fact, Sir.'

'So I'm given to understand! Though I gave you no such instruction to do so.' For a moment there was even a hint of a smile on his uncle's lips. In that moment Sphax realised that he would never be able to understand this man. His uncle seemed to inhabit some quicksilver world where right or wrong, day or night or even the power of life and death could be flipped as easily as a dice.

For the next hour his uncle questioned him on every aspect of his discussions with Idwal and Lord Cenno. In the manner a judge would interrogate a witness, or indeed, a criminal. He wanted an account of every conversation. When at last it was over, Sphax felt drained and exhausted.

'Leave us now, Nephew. You have given us much to think on.' Sphax bowed to his uncles and turned to leave. If he could have lingered unnoticed at the entrance to the pavilion, he would have heard the silver-haired Sosylos turn to his pupil and heard him say, 'We have all underestimated that young man.'

But by the time the Greek spoke these words, Sphax was gathering his cloak against the evening chill, and his only thought was of his sleeping couch and Fionn's warm body.

* * *

The weather broke on the morning they set out for the mountains. It rained steadily for the next two days, bringing a real autumn chill to the air and the misery of cold nights spent in sodden tents. They marched north, keeping to the eastern bank of the Rhodanus. For over a week the glittering ribbon of the great river became their constant companion. At night they would gather around fires and cook what food they had. When it wasn't raining they just spread rugs and blankets on the ground and slept under the stars, too exhausted to bother assembling tents, which in any case had to be collected from the baggage trains at the rear of the army. Sphax was riding his beloved Dido again, now as strong and swift as ever. He'd given Vertros's horse to Fionn. Unlike his previous owner, Brega turned out to have the gentlest and most placid character of any stallion he'd ever ridden. Perfect for Fionn.

Sphax rode alongside Maharbal. But this largely consisted of trying to keep up with the general as he galloped to the head of the column to organize scouting patrols, or to the rear to sort out the interminable delays that frequently beset the mule trains. Then there were daily meetings with the captains of each of his eshrins, meetings with generals of infantry, of cavalry, or even with Hannibal himself. Night watches and guards had to be posted, areas cleared in camp for the tethered lines of hemp that secured over twelve thousand horses every night.

Sphax had never had to think about fodder before, let alone *worry* about it. Now it occupied a great deal of his thoughts, as it did Maharbal's. The pack-mules at the rear of the column carried all the dry fodder the animals would need for the journey, including thirty-seven elephants with voracious appetites, but they also needed to graze along the way. By the time Hannibal's vast host had marched half a mile, the ground became no better than a ploughed-up sea of mud with not a blade of grass left standing. The rain hadn't helped. Animals eat grass. Mud is of little use, except to frogs.

Then there were the men. He'd never realised before how much his countrymen grumbled and bellyached! If it wasn't about the ripeness of the barley that was doled out for their grinding stones, it would be about the wine they drank around their campfires. Sphax had to admit that it tasted no better than vinegar. If it was neither of these, then it would be the weather. It was always the weather. Be it too hot, too cold, windy, wet, dry or cloudy, it was never right. Numidians, it seemed, could find fault with everything under the sun. He was reminded of Jubal and his javelin practice. When he pointed this out to Maharbal the general just laughed.

'It's good they grumble,' he told him, 'it takes their mind off their empty bellies!' In the rare moments when they rode side by side at the marching pace of the columns, Sphax questioned the general on every aspect of military life. He guessed that Maharbal had taken to heart what he'd said to his uncle about his ignorance of military duties, for the general answered all his questions with uncharacteristic patience and eloquence. But then another crisis would arise and they were off, at the gallop, dashing here or everywhere.

In the evenings, after cramming down every morsel of food he could lay his hands on, he would fall asleep exhausted, having ridden at least three times further than the nine miles his army had managed that day.

As the days wore on he was beginning to understand the Herculean challenges of keeping an army on the march. Hannibal had with him just over forty-two thousand infantry from eleven different races and nations. These ranged from the disciplined ranks of Libyan pikemen to Mallorcans, armed with little more than their slingshots and a dagger.

Of the nine thousand cavalry, the greater part was made up of heavily armed Iberians riding big stallions with saddles and bridles. His Numidians dismissed their horsemanship and called them *h'mar zobi*, an uncouth phrase referring to a donkey's penis; nevertheless, Sphax would not like to meet these fearsome warriors in battle.

Everything else Maharbal referred to as the army's baggage, which could mean anything from a skilled weapon-smith to a camp-following whore or muleteer. Three columns marched side by side and covered a distance five miles long and three miles wide. Camps covered as small an area as possible so they could be easily defended and require fewer sentries for the night watches.

Sphax learned that their progress was determined by the slowest creature in the army, which was not, as he'd first guessed, the plodding stride of a Libyan pikeman, but the gait of the herd of cattle that accompanied them to be slaughtered on the hoof. At every river ford or pathway through a forest, detachments had to be posted to guide the columns along the route just as milestones pointed the way along a Roman road.

For the moment the army was marching through the friendly territory of the Tricastini and had little to fear from attack or ambush. Even so, Maharbal constantly sent out scouting eshrin*s* that ranged far to the north and east looking for threats from these directions. Marching beside the Rhodanus meant that their left flank was always protected by the great river. As Maharbal was at pains to point out, a march conducted through enemy territory was always a perilous undertaking. The dispositions and arrangement of the columns had to be such that they could mutually support one another and cope with any contingency, from whatever direction. Get those dispositions wrong, and an army could be annihilated in an afternoon.

As they marched steadily north a general unease began to spread through the ranks. In every village they heard rumours that the Allobroges were massing to the northeast to defend their lands and passes through the mountains. Sphax was not worried. If they were anything like the Volcae he was certain they could be brushed aside. But Maharbal was not so sure; in a mountainous land of narrow passes and thickly wooded valleys it would be difficult to deploy their cavalry. Hannibal sent envoys and emissaries to meet with them, offering them silver and treaties of alliance. But all attempts at negotiation failed, and sometimes emissaries never returned.

At last they reached a broad swift-flowing river whose icy waters were fed from mountain streams and cascades, or so they were told by the people thereabouts, who called this river the Droma. Here they turned their backs on the Rhodanus and headed east, keeping to the southern bank of the river. At dawn next morning Sphax found himself gazing into the distance at the hazy outline of a range of mountains etched in blue and silver. He climbed a rocky outcrop at the edge of the camp to gain a better view. Standing on a wide ledge of rock, shielding the sun from his eyes, he was joined by his uncle and a small party of officers. 'What can you see, Nephew?'

'A wide arc of mountains, Sir. It must be the Alps.'

'And how far away?' Sphax did a quick calculation.

'Three days' march. No more than that, Sir.' His uncle examined the faces of his generals for confirmation. They were all nodding agreement. Then they were gone, leaving him alone, gazing at a horizon three days' march into the future, into the unknown. Inwardly, somehow he knew with disquieting certainty that their trials were about to begin.

* * *

That morning his uncle completely changed the dispositions of the marching columns and reduced them to two. Unlike the Rhodanus, the Droma offered little flank protection; its shallow waters could be forded in many places. Maharbal placed four eshrins of Numidians on either bank of the river, acting as a screen for the rest of the army marching beside its southern bank. Behind this screen of cavalry, Hannibal himself placed the Cavari at the head of the infantry columns. His uncle was well aware of the age-old enmity between the Cavari and the Allobroges, a hatred rekindled of late by Vertros's frequent raids into their territory for captives that made good money in the slave markets of Massilia. His uncle's reasoning was simple: it was easier to kill in hatred. But this worked both ways.

Sphax was worried. Idwal had already mustered his Cavari into a fighting line when he found him. They grinned at one another and embraced. Sphax had missed his friend's easy smile and lively conversation. 'How are you faring, my friend?' asked Idwal. 'I've seen so little of you since we began this adventure.'

'I know … Maharbal keeps me astride Dido from dawn to dusk. There are never enough hours in the day.' Sphax stopped smiling. 'You do realise that my uncle is using you. He knows of the hatred that exists between Cavari and Allobroges.'

'It had crossed my mind,' answered Idwal, still grinning.

'Then please be careful, my friend. Do not let hatred and enmity cloud your judgment today. We are here to clear a path, not settle old scores.'

'… those who look upon death as common to all, and unavoidable, and are only solicitous to die with honour, oftener arrive at old age and, while they live, live happier.'

Sphax groaned. 'Then Xenophon is wrong, Idwal. Honour may well prove to be the undoing of the Cavari today. Just make sure you and your men live to enjoy that old age.' He embraced his friend once more and left the Cavari to their fate.

He was riding beside Maharbal later that morning when he got his first look at the Allobroges. There were perhaps twenty of them scampering amongst the rocks in the riverbed half a mile ahead of them. Dressed in leggings and tunics woven in distinctive chequered patterns of red and green, to his eyes they looked exactly like every other Gaul he'd seen, but Maharbal pointed out the subtle differences in cloth pattern and shield design that marked them out as Allobroges. Of one thing there could be no doubting; they were dressed for battle. Some were bare-chested and all had lime-slaked their hair and combed it high above their foreheads like a horse's mane.

Merbal rode over. 'Shall I chase those fellows off, general? My eshrin needs the exercise this morning.'

'Very well. But you may flush out more of the wretches than you bargained for. Ask Mago to move forward with you to cover your flank.' Maharbal paused for a moment in thought then turned to Sphax. 'Cross the river, lad, and ask Adherbal to move forward on my signal and coordinate a charge with Merbal on this side of the river. Ask Fuabal to cover his flank. They must wait for my signal. Have you got that?'

'Yes, Sir.' Sphax hesitated, then asked sheepishly, 'May I join the charge, Sir?' For a moment Maharbal looked like thunder, but catching Sphax's pleading expression the general's scowl softened to a grin. 'Yes,' he said impatiently, 'now be gone!' Sphax was off before minds were changed. Behind him he heard the general say, 'Well at least he asked this time, Merbal. That's progress, I suppose.'

Sphax walked Dido carefully across the river, allowing her to find her own path through the treacherous pebbles and boulders. He soon found Adherbal, and sensing something was afoot, Fuabal himself rode over to join them. With these two old hands it didn't take him long to explain what the general required. Adherbal's eshrin had almost formed itself into line by the time Dido joined it nearest the river. All eyes were now on their general. Sphax had his saunion in his fist and was fingering the leather thong when Maharbal raised his javelin.

He nudged Dido into a walk and within ten strides the line began trotting in step together. Because the ground was so uneven and strewn with boulders, Sphax doubted Adherbal would risk a full-blown gallop. But he was wrong. As if as one, the entire line flew into a thunderous gallop. Though his heart was pounding faster than Dido's hooves, these were the moments he lived for. But it was over before it had begun. Within a few strides the eshrin's mares were brought to a stumbling halt.

An almost comic sight was taking place ahead of them. Dozens of Allobroges had turned tail and were splashing back down the river, many slipping head first into the water on the pebbles that lined the riverbed. Nowhere was the water deep enough to drown in, yet they all seemed to be making a brave attempt to do just that. Whilst this was taking place, as if by magic dozens more warriors appeared from behind rocks and boulders and made a headlong dash for the river. Instinctively they must have known that the only place horses would not be able to follow them was in the river. No horseman would risk breaking his mare's legs galloping over those slippery stones.

By now Adherbal's entire eshrin had broken into great guffaws of laughter that was echoed by the Numidians across the river. 'So these are the Allobroges,' spat the Numidian beside him. 'The fish must be shitting themselves.' Sphax laughed and watched the comedy for a moment before raising his javelin to Adherbal in farewell, and making his way slowly across the river to join the general.

This futile charge seemed to set the pattern for the rest of the day, except that the Allobroges grew warier, and would take to their heels at the slightest intimation the Numidians were about to charge. Ominously, their numbers seemed to be growing. Hannibal doubled the guards around the camp that night.

* * *

Maharbal grew gloomier with each passing day. Not because he'd failed to bring the Allobroges to battle, though he'd tried every cavalryman's trick to force their hand, but because of the mountains. The land of the Allobroges was not the gentle water meadows and broad grasslands of the Rhodanus. This was a rocky, mountainous country where cavalry were of little use. And the mountains were beginning to close in on them. The Allobroges knew this, and led them a merry dance from valley to valley, luring them on into ever more inhospitable country. They seemed to know every rock and tree, mountain stream and cliff top. By the third day Maharbal had given up chasing shadows.

They had been following a great loop of the Droma, first north, then east, before the river finally turned due south, heading for what looked like a narrow ravine in the forested hills. After passing through this rocky ravine without sighting a single Allobroges, Maharbal turned to him and shaking his head said, 'ba 'al hamūn! Give me fifty Libyans and I could have held that place for a week against all the legions of Rome. What game are they playing? What trap are they setting?'

Beyond the ravine they were gazing out at a lush green valley and for the moment at least, the mountains seemed to have retreated. It didn't last long. Soon the two flanking eshrins had to be reduced to one, and Hannibal reduced the march to a single column that straggled back some twenty miles. By midday they halted to rest and water their mares in the river. Nudging his Egyptian mare around, Maharbal stared at the column that was still being led by Idwal's Cavari. 'Why have they stopped?'

Half a mile back, where a mountain stream entered the Droma, Sphax could see Idwal in heated discussion with a group of Gauls. 'Come on lad,' said Maharbal. 'Let's see what's going on.'

It wasn't so much Idwal, but their guides who were engaged in the heated discussion. As the argument was being conducted in three Gaulish dialects, Maharbal appealed to Idwal for explanation.

'The Tricastini are arguing with the Boii and the Insubres about the direction we should take. Ronec from the Tricastini is convinced the shortest route to the high mountains lies due east of here along this stream. As you see, Sir, the others disagree. Vehemently!' As he spoke, Sphax could read the frustration on Idwal's face. By now all seven guides seemed to be pointing and gesticulating in different directions. Tempers were flaring and it was obvious a fight would break out soon if nothing was done.

'Silence!' yelled Maharbal in Greek. None of the guides knew what this meant, but it shut them up instantly. In a milder voice he asked Idwal, 'What is the opinion of the other Tricastini guide?'

'Ael has never travelled that way. He believes it may be quicker ... but he's not sure.' Whilst this was taking place, Drust, who'd been standing beside Idwal, caught Sphax's eye and walked over to where he and Maharbal sat astride their mares. In broken Latin he spoke quietly so the guides would not hear or understand. The drift of what he said was that the guide Ronec was not to be trusted. Maharbal's Latin was not much better than Drust's, but it was evident from his expression that he'd also understood the message. Drust raised his eyebrows and gave Maharbal a meaningful look before returning to Idwal and appearing to take no further interest in the deliberations.

'We must seek advice on this, Idwal. Halt your men whilst I bring Hannibal to see what shall be done.' Turning to Sphax, he said 'Tell the men to rest their mares. Be on your guard,' and nodding towards Drust added, 'Why not take Idwal's young captain; an extra pair of eyes might be useful?' Maharbal's message couldn't have been clearer.

Sphax slid off Dido and walked back with Drust to where the Numidians were watering their horses. Once out of earshot he asked Drust about his suspicions. 'You remember that after we arrived at the Island we were told the story of how your uncle had to arbitrate in the quarrel between Brancus and his younger brother Lito?' Sphax nodded. 'Following the advice of the Tricastini council of elders, Hannibal decided in favour of Brancus. He was restored as chieftain and Lito was banished for life. Well, a few nights ago some of my men were drinking with the Tricastini and Veltavi Gauls when Ronec started shouting his mouth off that Lito was twice the man Brancus was and should have been made chief. Ronec was very drunk by then, but my men reported that he started bragging that Lito would have his revenge. He would have the last laugh.' Drust paused for a moment and gave Sphax a significant look. 'He also claimed that Lito had found new allies.'

'And who might they be?' asked Sphax.

'My men were convinced he meant the Allobroges. I trust my men, Sphax. If they're right, and Ronec is Lito's man and Lito is in league with the Allobroges, then we can't trust him. He may be trying to deliver us into the arms of the Allobroges.' Drust stopped and pointed in the same direction that Ronec had indicated. 'He's setting a trap for us. Somewhere out there.' All Sphax could see was an impenetrable barrier of mountains. Everything looked like a trap to him.

'We must heed this warning. Will you wait with me until Maharbal returns?' Drust nodded. 'Does Idwal know of this?' he added.

'Yes, he does. But Idwal is eager to come to battle with the Allobroges, whatever the price.'

'This is what I feared, my friend ...' Curse the obligations of honour, thought Sphax, curse them and cast them into Hades.

The column was now so strung out that it seemed like an age before Maharbal returned with Hannibal. Even so, judging from the sweat on Arion's flanks, the two of them had ridden back at speed. In the presence of Hannibal the argument between the guides resumed, but now in a more sober manner, without raised voices or tempers flaring. Maharbal rode over to where Sphax was watching with Drust. 'Tell the general what you've just told me, Drust.'

Maharbal listened in grave silence. When Drust had finished his story he turned to Sphax. 'I must warn your uncle. I believe your friend may be right about this. We had to drive out Lito and his followers like wolves from a kill. I've never seen such rage and bitterness on a man's face. It was only my Numidians and Hanno's Libyans that decided it.'

'Believe me, general, Lito left many of his followers behind to stir up trouble,' said Drust. 'Some have even joined this army. I wouldn't swear to their loyalty if they saw Lito's standard raised alongside the Allobroges.'

Sphax and Drust watched as Maharbal rode over to the guides and beckoned Hannibal aside. Moments later he returned, looking agitated. 'We are to follow the guide Ronec, who, if he's to be believed, will save us three precious days. Three days are worth a little trouble, according to our leader. By the gods, we've been marching for three months ... what are three days! Let's hope he's right.' Maharbal paused and gave them both a weary smile.

'I have a task for you two when we camp this evening. I want you to seek out this Ronec and question him carefully. And it wouldn't hurt to let him know what will happen to him if he betrays us. I for one will require his tongue and both ears... that's before I rip out the bastard's heart.' Maharbal gazed over at his men lounging in the water meadows beside the river. 'I'm going to wake those lazy sons-of-whores and get them on their mares. We have work to do today,' and with that he was off.

For an hour they followed Ronec's river, for that's what the Numidians named it after the rumours did the rounds. And within the hour they were all cursing it and longing for the wide banks of the Droma. It was nothing more than a mountain stream, tumbling down through rock pools and shallow waterfalls, its banks thick with pine trees and rocky outcrops which became almost impenetrable at times. It was impossible to see further ahead than a man could throw a javelin. This was no place for cavalry, and the men knew it. Sphax was again riding beside Maharbal, but for much of the time the path became so narrow that they could only proceed in single file. All around him voices echoed through the shallow valley as men called to one another to seek directions or locate their eshrin.

By now Maharbal was desperate. 'If we're ambushed here we will be slaughtered like rats in a trap. I'm calling a stop to this. Try and locate all our captains and tell them to halt and gather their men around them. It's time the Cavari put their necks on the block and faced their sworn enemies. This is no place for our mares.'

Sphax didn't find this easy. He'd managed to locate Merbal, whose eshrin was furthest forward, when Idwal suddenly appeared through the trees with several of his warriors. His friend was grinning from ear to ear. 'Maharbal has ordered the Cavari to lead the march,' he said with evident delight. 'I'm to spread out my men in a long line either side of the stream. All Numidians have been ordered to dismount and lead their horses behind my men.'

'You mean we are to dismount? Fight like infantry?' cried Merbal, outraged.

'I'm afraid so, Sir. I simply repeat the words of your own general. You are to dismount.'

Sphax could see the sense in this. Cavalry were a liability here. They could neither scout nor fight in this labyrinth of rocks and trees. Frowning at Idwal he said, 'Our men won't like this, Idwal, not one little bit.' And they didn't like it. When Merbal passed the order to the rest of his eshrin there was a chorus of curses and oaths. The old storyteller, Jugurtha, refused to get off his mare. Merbal turned a blind eye to this minor disobedience.

But it did get better. Within a mile or so the stream emerged into a more open country bordered by water meadows and copses of willow and rowan. Sphax was once again riding beside Maharbal, whose eshrins had been restored to their rightful position in the van.

All day they had felt the presence of invisible eyes upon them, watching, waiting. No one had seen so much as a glint of metal from an Allobroges blade, but everyone knew they were out there somewhere, biding their time. An ominous silence began to spread through the ranks like a plague, festering away at their nerves, making everyone edgy and anxious. Scares and false alarms were frequent.

An hour later all eyes were transfixed by a sight some two miles away, where the stream cut through a rock cleft in the mountains that looked as if it narrowed to the width of a Roman road. To the south of this ravine a conical mountain barred their way, its slopes clothed in dense forests of pine. But it was the north side of the ravine to which all eyes were drawn. Here the mountains soared upwards to meet towering walls of vertical rock that looked like the battlements of a great city. Once through that narrow cleft there could be no escape. And what awaited them in the valley beyond lay completely hidden.

Maharbal was convinced the Allobroges were massed in the hidden valley and would rush out and defend the ravine as they approached. Scorning Hannibal's silver and a treaty of safe passage, they had sworn to defend their homeland, and the armies of Carthage were now deep within their mountain home. This portal of rock beside the stream offered the perfect natural defence.

Scouts were sent out to get a closer look but reported seeing nothing. Maharbal didn't believe this for a moment. For the first time, Sphax could see indecision etched on every line of the general's face. He called a council of his captains, but they offered little in the way of advice, just sat their horses in grim silence and stared at the ravine. 'Your men scouted the passage, Astegal, how wide is it at the mouth of the cleft?'

'Two horsemen could ride abreast beside the stream, but no more than that. The ground is soft, but good enough for our mares.'

'Did they ride through the cleft into the valley beyond?' Astegal hesitated and looked sheepish.

'I don't think so...'

'Then they offer me little more than I can see for myself,' Maharbal said sharply. 'Must I do everything myself?'

'I shall go myself, Sir,' bleated Astegal, 'and report back ...'

'It's too late for that! The sun is beginning to set. If we do not act promptly we will lose the light. However, the half-light of dusk also offers opportunities for those who are bold enough to use it. We will prepare a column of sixty, rush through the passage and gain the valley beyond. At whatever cost! Once through, the sixty horsemen will turn and attack whatever force has dared to oppose the passage of Numidians. If we are engaged, you, Astegal, will lead the rest of our forces – every man we have – on a similar charge. We will strike the Allobroges from the front and rear.'

Now everyone was desperate to lead the charge and be the first through the jaws of Hades and on to glory. Or death, thought Sphax, for he too was of the opinion that Maharbal was right and the valley beyond would be thronged with a host of screaming Allobroges, beating blades against shields amidst the cacophony of carnyx.

Maharbal raised his hand to stay the arguments that were flaring around him. 'Silence,' he yelled. 'I will not risk the life of my officers on this charge. I will lead it. There will be no more argument. Ask your eshrins for volunteers. There will be many, so choose only the fleetest horsemen.' Sphax braced himself and put on his best pleading expression. 'Sir,' he began.

'Yes, Sphax.' To his infernal irritation, Maharbal was actually grinning at him.

'May I be permitted to join your charge?' He could see that it was hopeless. Maharbal had turned away and seemed more interested in watching the sinking sun. 'I have arguments,' pleaded Sphax. 'Are you at least prepared to listen to them, Sir?'

'No,' said the general distractedly. Sphax's heart sank. It was as he foresaw. Maharbal finally turned to face him, but the grin had been replaced by a scowl. 'As you will be riding beside me, there is little to argue about. However, I will gladly listen to any arguments that you should *not* take part in this charge. That would be more sensible. Direct your intelligence to getting *out* of this, not joining it.' Sphax was dumbstruck.

'Thank you, Sir. Thank you—'

'For what?' interrupted Maharbal irritably. 'I'm not taking you for your fighting skills. I hear you can leap that mare of yours over a man's head. You may have recourse to this trick soon enough. Make no mistake, this is a desperate measure, perhaps even a foolish thing to try.'

When everyone was mustered the general rode out to the front and addressed them. They would form up in pairs in a long column, approaching the narrowest section of the ravine at the gallop. Once through the passage it would be every man for himself. Not for a moment were they to stand and fight. If they were confronted by an enemy host they were to weave their way through or skirt around it, at the gallop. They were to gain open ground at least half a mile beyond the enemy. Maharbal assured them that once they had re-assembled they would take revenge for any Numidian who'd fallen. Sphax noted the grunt of satisfaction at this.

No further commands or instruction was given. The men simply chose a partner to ride with and found a place within the column. Sphax took his place at the head of the column and waited.

Maharbal took his time. Sphax realised he was waiting for the sun to sink a little and create the perfect conditions: light enough to be able to ride with safety at speed, but gloomy enough to create that shadowy twilight haze that might give them a slender advantage. At last he seemed satisfied and took up his position beside Sphax at the head of the column. He even managed a smile. 'You better draw that fancy sword of yours, lad. There won't be time to aim javelins.' Without a spoken command he simply nudged his mare into a walk.

Dido and Maharbal's Egyptian mare were perfectly matched. Both were not much more than twelve hands high and of a similar build and stature. Within six paces Maharbal again nudged his mare, this time to the trot. The horses were now matching each other stride for stride. They were riding so close that occasionally Sphax felt the touch of Maharbal's sandals on his own; it was if they were seated on a pair of chariot horses yoked together, working as a team. Sphax's throat felt parched, yet he could feel the exhilaration rising like flames through his chest.

This time Maharbal raised his right arm before nudging his mare to the canter. The thunder of sixty hooves now drowned out all sound from the stream beside them. Rocks and trees flashed by. It was vital he let Dido choose her own path and not interfere, becoming one with her movement, a willing passenger.

Now they were rapidly approaching the jaws of the cleft. It was impossible to make out anything on the other side of the stream where the forest rose steeply from the water's edge. They could now see the cleft itself, little more than a mossy sward flanked by a great buttress of rock that soared upwards like some giant sentinel. There was nothing for it now. Maharbal nudged his mare to the gallop and Sphax responded. Hemmed in by rock and water, Sphax felt he was plunging into the narrowest of alleyways in Rome. For a few rasping breaths he had the fleeting impression of rock walls, glittering water and trunks of pines. Then they were through.

To everyone's utter astonishment they emerged into a lush green meadow, as flat as a table and broader than the Rhodanus. It was empty.

The only thing confronting the sixty Numidians was a herd of nervous goats. As the men brought their mares to a halt and gathered in the pasture, Sphax sensed a palpable sigh of relief amongst them, a relief that soon turned to comic amusement at the sight of the goats. Maharbal was shaking his head and looking around in bewilderment. 'Go and tell Astegal the good news, Sphax.' For the first time that day he laughed, 'Tell him there will be goat for supper.'

ELEVEN

'Well, Ronec, where does this stream take us?' The Tricastini guide looked terrified. With good reason. He'd stopped struggling only because Drust had his arms pinned behind his back and a knife at his throat. Ronec was dribbling, copiously.

'I've told you,' he whimpered, 'it leads to a village.' For Sphax's benefit Drust was translating the wretch's words into Greek.

'How many miles before we reach that village?' Sphax asked coldly.

'I don't understand your miles,' Ronec replied defiantly. Drust's blade pressed closer. 'A day and a half ... maybe two. No more than that.'

Sphax made a show of slowly drawing his sword from its scabbard and resting the blade on Ronec's left ear. 'Maharbal wants both these ears... and then I'm to rip out your tongue.' By now the guide was shaking so much Sphax had to raise the blade a little to stop him losing the ear by accident. 'If you are lying to me,

Ronec, I swear I will bear these parts of your miserable body to his pavilion this evening. Tell me about those two days before we reach this village. How wide is the valley the stream flows through?'

Ronec hesitated. Sphax lowered the blade again. 'Narrow!' Ronec cried as the blade nicked his earlobe, 'very narrow … in places.'

'Then it's more like a ravine or a gorge,' Sphax yelled at him. Drust translated. Ronec nodded.

No wonder the Allobroges had not defended the entry to the valley in which the army was now camped, thought Sphax. For almost two days the army would be strung out in a narrow ravine. Women with their children, elephants, a cumbersome baggage train, men and horses, all trapped in the narrow confines of a ravine. The Allobroges would be able to ambush or attack at will. They could even seal off the entrance and exit. 'Are there ways out of the ravine?' he asked.

'You can climb out … in places,' answered Ronec. Sphax raised his sword then lowered it so the point was touching the guide's ribs.

'When will the Allobroges attack – tomorrow, or the day after?' Ronec's eyes shifted wildly.

'I know nothing of this.' In that moment Sphax knew the wretch was lying. He might not know *when*, but he had a good idea *where* it would take place! His task had been to deliver them. Sphax was certain of this now. Ronec was Lito's man, and Lito was in league with the Allobroges. They were walking into a carefully arranged trap.

'Let him go, Drust.' Before he could slink away Sphax gripped his arm viciously and pulled him face to face. 'At dawn tomorrow I will dress you in the uniform of a Numidian. You will be the first to enter that ravine, Ronec. You will be the first to draw an enemy spear and the first to die. This I swear to you,' and with that he let the wretch go.

Sphax and Drust walked back slowly through the encampment to Maharbal's pavilion. They had questioned Ronec away from prying eyes in the forest on the far side of the stream. They walked back in silence. There seemed little further to say.

Maharbal was seated beside Ayzabel on his sleeping divan. Fionn sat curled up on a couch beside a low table piled high with food and wine. Servants entered to serve them as Sphax made himself comfortable on the general's luxurious Seleucid carpet and leaned back against Fionn's couch. She reached out and ran her fingers through his thick curls.

Earlier that evening, he and their servants Cesti and Lulin had helped her erect their tent and make it comfortable for the evening they planned to spend together, alone at last. For too many nights he'd slept wherever he could, usually on hard ground wrapped in his beaver-skin cloak. This would be their first night together for over a week. Then, to his intense irritation, he'd remembered the task Maharbal had entrusted him with. He'd asked Fionn to wait for him in Maharbal's pavilion, then called on Drust and together they had gone in search of Ronec.

Between mouthfuls of bread and pork, Drust gave the general a word by word account of Ronec's interrogation. When Drust had finished and he'd turned his attention to a large bunch of grapes, Maharbal stood and walked to the entrance. 'Stay and eat your fill. You've both earned it. I will return shortly after I've informed Hannibal that we are walking into a trap.'

The general returned within the hour, mercifully for Drust, who'd been teased wickedly by Ayzabel and Fionn on everything from the size of his appetite to being shy and tongue-tied in the company of women. Sphax had come to his defence, but had not got off lightly himself. Together, the two women were a force to be reckoned with. Maharbal's grave expression brought the good-natured teasing to an end. 'I have orders for you both. Hannibal wants you to scout deep into that ravine and discover the Allobroges positions. Merbal and a few from his eshrin will accompany you. Drust is to bind his hands and drag that creature Ronec by a rope around his miserable neck. You're to set out at dawn. Is that clear?' Sphax and Drust had already got to their feet.

'Thank you for your generous hospitality, Sir.' After the general nodded, Drust bowed in turn to Ayzabel and Fionn who promptly burst out laughing, hastening the Cavari's retreat. Sphax and Fionn left with their arms wrapped around one another. They had until dawn together.

* * *

Merbal greeted him with a slap on the back. He looked cheerful and rested after a good night's sleep, which was more than could be said of Sphax, who was still rubbing the sleep from his eyes. He'd selected eight Numidians from his eshrin, including the old storyteller, Jugurtha. Sphax could see from the thunderous expression on Drust's face that something was wrong. 'No sign of that treacherous bastard Ronec, Sphax. The other guides told me he didn't return last night. He must have taken off into the woods after we got the truth out of him.'

'I look forward to meeting him in Hades,' Sphax said, resignedly. In truth, he never wanted the wretch with them; even bound, he was sure Ronec would have found some way of betraying them.

'What's all this about?' asked Merbal.

'One of the Tricastini guides has betrayed us,' answered Drust, 'and has been leading us into the arms of the Allobroges.' Shocked, Merbal stared at him for a moment and then spat, but before he had time to comment on this unpleasant turn of events all eyes turned to see Hannibal himself striding towards them, trailing a score of generals in his wake.

'Dog's twat!' hissed Jugurtha. 'What a send-off! It must be serious to wake that lot before breakfast.'

Hannibal stood gravely before them. Merbal spoke for them all. 'It is an honour, Sir, that you have troubled yourself to see us off.'

'Thank you Merbal, but I also come with further instruction.' His uncle spoke in that manner of his that seemed to engage personally with everyone present. It was as if he were speaking to each one of them in private conversation. Sphax never discovered how he did this. Was it those darting eyes, shifting from face to face? Whatever the trick was, he came to value its effectiveness. Whenever Hannibal commanded, men did their duty. 'It is imperative this morning that you all stay out of sight and unseen by the enemy. If you can achieve this we will gain the upper hand and keep the initiative.' Again those shifting eyes darted amongst them. 'Stay unseen and hidden.' They all nodded solemnly. 'Then I wish you good hunting. May Melqart be with you.'

The stars began to fade in the first flush of dawn as they set out. It promised to be a fine day, clear and cloudless, but the cold was intense in these regions. Even though Sphax was wearing the chequered woollen leggings Idwal had given him, he was praying for the sun to rise and put some warmth into his bones. For the first few miles the valley was flat and broad enough for the column to ride beside one another in groups of four. Sphax guessed this valley would make perfect grazing or pasture, but that morning they didn't see so much as a solitary goat. It was an empty land, still and silent. Even the birds, it seemed, had refused to welcome the rising of the sun that morning.

They stayed to the north of the stream. On the other side of its shallow waters dense forests of pine and cedar rose steeply to a ridge of hills that marked the southern boundary of the valley. And it was to the south that all eyes were drawn. Virtually impenetrable for horses, forests could hide armies of warriors on foot. Merbal had asked them all to ride in silence and raise an arm if anyone spotted something. For hours they rode on in an eerie silence, broken only by the cries of eagles and the bark of ravens. Sphax judged it to be around mid-morning when the nature of the valley changed suddenly and dramatically. It came as a shock to them all.

Within half a mile the valley narrowed alarmingly. To the south of the stream, the forested hills gave way to towering cliffs of rock dotted with pine and rowan wherever they could gain a foothold. To the north it was even worse. Here they would be hemmed in by soaring walls of white rock, flecked in places by bands of yellow and pink stone. Even the most tenacious of trees had difficulty finding a foothold here. This was no ravine. They were entering a narrow gorge, created by the stream cleaving its way through solid rock.

Merbal halted them. 'Now our work begins in earnest,' he said, almost in a whisper. 'Jugurtha will scout well ahead of us. Where we can ride it will be in single file, otherwise we dismount and lead our horses. There is to be no talking and we move quietly.' Merbal hesitated and stared at Sphax. He seemed to be coming to a decision. 'Sphax, you will accompany Jugurtha. You will learn much this morning.'

Sphax had mixed feelings as he nudged Dido to a walk behind the old Numidian. He was proud to be entrusted with the task, but he didn't like this place. It was like entering a stone tomb, open to the skies but otherwise encased in rock, and he feared to be a target for an Allobroges spear. In this place he wouldn't see it coming. At least there was good cover. The ground either side of the stream was scattered with dense thickets of willow and hazel or stands of taller pines. Great boulders, sometimes taller than a man on horseback, were strewn around on the floor of the gorge. There was perhaps twenty paces either side of the stream before the floor met towering walls of solid rock. From time to time the cliffs were broken by ravines and gullies where it might be possible for a man to scramble out of the gorge, but this would be impossible on horseback.

Jugurtha stopped frequently, sat his mare and listened. The first time he did this he pointed to Sphax's ears and flapped at his own. It was rather comical, but his message was clear. Sometimes he stopped and signalled him to scan the tops of the cliffs for activity or any movement. Sphax soon understood Jugurtha's simple sign language, and after a while his heart stopped pounding and he even began to appreciate the savage beauty of the place. Pointing them out as they passed, Jugurtha missed nothing, be it a tuft of sheep's wool caught on a thorn or an old hoof-print. Sphax could see the significance of these tiny details. Taken as a whole they added up to human activity and habitation. People lived here. But where were they?

They were steadily approaching a narrow section where there was little cover from boulders or trees. Jugurtha signalled him to halt, then dismounted and led his mare to the centre of a stand of pines where he would have a clear view of this section of the gorge. He then did an astonishing thing, or rather his mare did. Sphax saw him make a peculiar gesture with his hands at which his mare promptly laid down on the ground at his feet. Jugurtha then lay on her flank. Sphax had never seen anything like it. Man and horse looked perfectly comfortable, yet so low above the ground that they would only be seen at close range, and in the dappled light amongst the trees, even then they might well have gone unnoticed. He was impressed and couldn't wait to teach Dido this trick.

Jugurtha seemed satisfied, returned his mare to her feet and signalled that the way was clear. They approached the narrow section on foot. Sphax guessed there would be just enough room for an elephant to squeeze through without getting its feet wet in the stream. It was yet another perfect ambush position, but the Allobroges had not availed themselves of it.

Sphax knew this couldn't go on for much longer. The armies of Carthage had been lured into taking this path for one reason only – so they could be destroyed on ground carefully chosen by their enemies. Ground their enemies knew well, ground where the sheer weight of Carthaginian numbers would make little difference in this hostile place. It would be so easy to trap and surround the baggage train and loot its wealth, especially Hannibal's fabled chests of silver. This alone represented untold riches for these simple mountain Gauls. Yet mile after mile, they saw nothing.

The gorge itself was full of surprises. At one point the cliffs retreated and opened out into a broad flat meadow that had been cleared of trees and thickets. All around they saw signs of grazing, but no animals. Beyond this they entered another narrow section where there was no alternative but to wade through the stream itself, leading their mares.

When they did hear human voices it came as a perfect shock. They both froze, brought their mares to a stop and listened intently. Men's voices, scores of them, laughing and bantering, but not in any language he or Jugurtha would ever understand. The most pressing questions were how far away were they? And were they heading their way? Sound had a peculiar character here, echoing endlessly across the chasms of stone, making it difficult to pinpoint where it was coming from.

Jugurtha was frantically looking around for cover. He pointed to a dense thicket of hazels some way ahead. Dismounting, they led their mares into its tangle of branches so they would remain hidden. Jugurtha then signalled he unstrap his sword and leave it behind, along with his iron saunion. Sphax could see the sense in this. It would be easy for metal to scrape against stone, and the sound would carry in this place.

Crouching, they crept forward using whatever cover they could find. The voices were growing louder. Sphax could now distinguish individual voices. Worryingly, there seemed to be many. They were getting close now. Jugurtha lay down and began to crawl from bush to bush, Sphax following his example.

Jugurtha suddenly signalled for him to stay absolutely still. From the shady depths of a clump of willows they finally saw their enemy. Sphax had been looking in the wrong direction. The Allobroges were not on the floor of the gorge, but on top of a massive cliff no more than four hundred paces in front of him. And there were more than a few. Sphax stopped counting when he reached two hundred.

At this point the gorge played another of its tricks, opening out into something like an amphitheatre of rock before closing its jaws once again at the entrance to another narrow section. On the northern bank of the stream, guarding the entrance like some impregnable white citadel, stood the cliff where the Allobroges had massed to defend their homeland. Although Sphax saw the occasional glint of a Gallic blade, the warriors were mostly armed with spears.

He saw many more of these weapons had been neatly stacked on the clifftop. Anyone trying to enter that narrow section of the gorge would face a deluge of spears for their trouble. Thrown accurately from such a height, every barb that found its mark would be lethal. Sphax guessed the Allobroges were skilled with the spear, that this was their weapon of choice. In which case the gorge was impassable. It would be madness to try and force it.

The Allobroges had lit fires to ward off the chill, and were doing what all soldiers do in the interminable wait for a battle to begin: jesting with each other and indulging in idle banter. For all Sphax knew they had been up there for days, waiting for their enemy to arrive. With a series of elaborate hand gestures Jugurtha explained that he was going back to get Merbal. Sphax was to stay put, and watch.

Straining his neck upwards soon became painful. He discovered that the most comfortable position was to lie on his back, cradling his head in his hands. The only problem then was to find a suitable gap in the foliage. After he'd wriggled himself into such a position there was nothing more to do but lie there and watch. Sphax had never been good at sitting still and doing nothing. As a child it had always got him into trouble, and as a slave often earned him a whipping.

To stave off fidgeting and utter boredom he set himself a problem. It would be a problem in the true philosophical tradition and in his most hated of all subjects: formal logic and deductive reasoning. Sphax first considered how his teacher Elpis would approach it. With Elpis' voice clearly ringing in his head he thought: firstly, state the problem.

In a flash all became clear and obvious. The Allobroges are up there and we are down here. They have the advantage. To fight them on equal terms we must find a way to scale the cliffs. Sphax recalled the numerous ravines and gullies he'd passed that morning. But this was where the fight must take place, on the clifftops, and not as they had all imagined, in the depths of the gorge itself. He was feeling pleased with himself.

Carefully re-examining the amphitheatre of rock that formed the Allobroges' cliff he could see possibilities. There were a couple of boulder-strewn gullies that might be climbed. But to attempt this in broad daylight would be to invite the same disaster as forcing the entrance to the gorge. No, this wouldn't work. They would have to find a gully somewhere further back, out of sight of the Allobroges. Sphax carried on examining the problem, but he must have fallen asleep. Thinking often had this effect. He was woken by a gentle slap on his cheek and the sight of Merbal grinning down at him.

Sphax indicated where Merbal should lie to get a good view of the Allobroges. It was getting somewhat overcrowded in their makeshift hideout, but Merbal managed to wriggle into position and after staring upwards for a while seemed satisfied. He then indicated that Sphax should follow him back to their men. Once they had crept out of sight of the cliff they both relaxed and walked swiftly. The Numidians were watering their horses and he was pleased to see Dido amongst them. Jugurtha must have collected his sword and saunion, and then led both horses. Drust joined them.

'Is it safe to speak here?' he whispered.

'Yes,' replied Sphax quietly, but not in a whisper. 'But sound does carry great distances in the gorge. So we must be careful.'

'Jugurtha said the Allobroges position is unassailable. Is this so?'

'I'm afraid so, Drust,' answered Merbal resignedly, 'a mountain goat couldn't climb that precipice. We will have to find a different path to the high mountains. This one is barred shut.'

'There may be an alternative,' ventured Sphax, tentatively. 'But not today. I counted two hundred warriors. There may be hundreds more up there, so we need to strike them with a considerable force.' Merbal was smiling in disbelief.

'What have you in mind, young Alexander, that we scale it with ladders and ropes? Have you lost your senses? It's unassailable!' Sphax continued patiently.

'This is true, Sir. So we must find somewhere that is not.' Sphax pointed to the top of the gorge. 'All we have to do is find a way up there. All day I've noticed gullies and ravines that could be climbed. Once we are up there in numbers we can meet them on our terms.'

Merbal's smile widened. 'Dog's twat, young pup, you are indeed the heir to Alexander,' handing him his sword and saunion.

'This is not a task for horsemen,' said Drust thoughtfully.

'This will be for Hannibal to decide,' said Merbal. 'We must return and report back to him immediately.' Turning to Sphax he added, 'You must stay here with Jugurtha and keep an eye on that cliff. I'll send men to relieve you when I get back to camp.'

Back in their cramped hideaway the hours passed slowly and tediously. They took it in turns to sleep, but for some reason Sphax now felt wide awake and all attempts at sleep evaded him. It began to annoy him that Jugurtha could simply close his eyes and immediately drift off into a deep sleep.

As dusk gathered and the sun began to set Sphax noticed a change in the behaviour of the warriors. There was less banter and they seemed to be gathering things together, as if preparing for something. What that could be was anyone's guess. Then it occurred to him the Allobroges might be preparing for a scouting mission down into the gorge. He woke Jugurtha.

They watched together until it grew dark. And what they saw was utterly inexplicable, but certain. The enemy had left. The clifftop had been abandoned. Fires were still burning and the neat stacks of spears left in place, but otherwise, the clifftop was utterly silent and deserted. They hadn't even bothered to leave sentries on watch.

'They may have a camp somewhere, away from the cliff,' whispered Sphax, finding it strange to hear his own voice after the hours of enforced silence.

'No, Sphax. We would be able to see the glow from their campfires.'

'Well … there's only one way to find out,' and he began to crawl out of the thicket. The full moon had risen in the south, and this combined with the dying fires on the clifftop provided enough light to see well enough. The two of them stared up at the cliff in disbelief. 'It seems the Allobroges don't fight at night.'

'You're right. Do the slackheads think that war ceases at sunset? I think we'll teach the fools otherwise.' Jugurtha was right of course, but he could see some sense in the Allobroges' thinking: no army would attempt a passage through the gorge at night. But why they hadn't left sentries was a mystery. To leave the walls of a city unguarded at night was to invite their capture.

They had been whispering, but now Jugurtha spoke quietly. 'We must return to camp and report this. Your uncle will be delighted.'

'First I must climb that cliff and make absolutely certain of our information.'

'In the dark, Sphax! Are you mad?'

'I've been staring at that wretched cliff all afternoon. I know there is a gulley to the left, and I think it can be climbed. I need to be certain before we report back.'

Even by moonlight they found the gulley quite easily and Sphax began to climb from boulder to boulder. At one point he was confronted by a vertical wall of rock that seemed impossible to scale, but then he noticed a crevice from which a tree had anchored its roots, and using this for handholds he managed to scramble to the top. Stopping to catch his breath he noticed an easier way around this obstacle. He would use it on the way down. After this the going was much easier, just a series of rock ledges and easy scrambles. He arrived at the top breathing heavily but otherwise unscathed.

Looking around in the moonlight he saw that he was on top of a vast table of solid rock, bereft of trees or features of any kind. In daylight he realised it would take on the same appearance as those escarpments of white rock near the Rhodanus, where he and Fionn had watched the progress of the Roman cavalry. Gazing north, he saw that beyond the rock shelf he was standing on the mountains rose to a pine clothed ridge. Then he noticed it. Fires and lights, far to the east.

In the moonlight it was almost impossible to judge the distance. The Allobroges camp? A village? Then he remembered what Ronec had said. Beyond the gorge lay a village. He was sure that's what he was looking at, and to where the warriors had returned, never imagining for one moment that anyone would attempt to storm their eyrie in the dark.

'If I can climb it in the dark, anyone can,' he said to Jugurtha on his return.

'I'll stay here and keep watch, lad. You better get back to camp and report this to your uncle straight away. It looks as if the savages have just made our lives a lot easier.'

His journey back to camp was a nightmare. Sphax rode as often as he dared. But in the depths of the gorge the darkness was sometimes profound when he lost sight of the moon to clouds or trees. During those moments he dismounted and walked, navigating by starlight and hoping for the best, for he couldn't risk Dido breaking a leg. It came as a welcome relief when he left the gorge behind and entered the broad pastures of the valley. Ahead, the glow of campfires now beckoned.

* * *

Hannibal's pavilion was crowded that evening. Every officer of note seemed to have gathered for a grand council of war. As Sphax politely pushed his way through the press to where his uncle was seated beside Maharbal and Hanno, an expectant hush fell on the company. His uncle listened with increasing astonishment as Sphax described the events that had taken place at dusk.

'It seems our enemies shun the rigours of war and at night return for their suppers and the comfort of their wives and cots! How *civilised*,' said Hannibal dryly, to the general mirth of all around him. 'We must teach them that the gods of war do not sleep. It will be a lesson they will come to regret.' Smiling benevolently at Sphax he said, 'You have done well, nephew. Now sleep and rest, for tomorrow night you will be my guide to that clifftop, and behind us will be a thousand men.'

Sphax enjoyed the luxury of a leisurely start next morning. He and Fionn had been invited to breakfast with Maharbal, and the two of them gorged themselves on freshly caught trout, cold meats and fruit. It made a welcome change from their usual meagre fare and he was hoping to hear something of the plan Hannibal had devised. He wasn't disappointed.

'From your journey into the gorge yesterday, do you recall entering a wide meadow that the savages use for grazing? Merbal tells me there is such a place?' inquired Maharbal.

'I remember it well, Sir,' said Sphax, eager to hear more. 'It's about two miles short of the clifftop the Allobroges have occupied.'

'Then it will serve our purpose.' The general broke off and smiling indulgently, gazed over to where Ayzabel and Fionn were merrily gossiping on a couch in the corner. Sphax's keen hearing picked up the name Drust frequently. Poor Drust. The gods alone knew what these two harpies had in store for him. Maharbal raised his eyebrows to the heavens and continued. 'We will make camp there this afternoon and make a great show of it, lighting extra fires and making a deal of noise.' Maharbal nodded in the direction of the women. 'We may even ask these two to sing and dance for us. When the savages believe we are bedded down and at our ease for the night, you will guide your uncle and a thousand men to the top of that cliff, praying all the while that they have not left sentries. You and I will then spend a comfortable night on our couches whilst your uncle and his men sit shivering on their frozen arses. When the savages return at dawn the choice will be theirs; they can either fight and be slaughtered, or flee and be chased back to their village. Either way, that village will burn.'

Maharbal sipped from his cup and offered Sphax a chunk of the delicious goat's cheese he was particularly fond of. 'Your uncle will have some of Hanno's Libyans with him. Your friend Idwal has also persuaded him to allow his men to join this enterprise. I understand the Cavari have no love of the Allobroges.'

'The Cavari's love of the Allobroges is less than my love of Rome.' The general grinned and shook his head.

'Your uncle is clever. He makes use of whatever weapon is available to him, and hatred is an excellent tool, do you not think?'

'I am fond of my friend, Sir, and wish to keep him alive. In the grip of this hatred he can be reckless and take unnecessary risks.' Maharbal laughed loudly, cocking an eyebrow.

'By the gods … I never thought to hear the son of Navaras talk of *unnecessary risks*! We are making progress at last;' adding more seriously, 'we are all at risk, Sphax, that is the nature of war.'

Sphax asked soberly, 'And what of our Numidians, Sir, whilst this slaughter is taking place above our heads?'

'We stroll through the gorge at our leisure and meet Hannibal on the other side,' the general answered confidently. Sphax doubted it would be that simple.

Something was nagging away at him. He understood the Allobroges to be a simple mountain folk and knew they would return to their clifftop citadel at dawn, but what will happen when they found it occupied, by what they would consider as shameful trickery? What then, when all their carefully laid plans had been foiled? Would they simply take flight and return to their village like dogs with their tails between their legs? Somehow he doubted it, but he kept his fears to himself.

The rest of that day did indeed become a leisurely stroll. The pasture lay only a few miles into the gorge and even the baggage train had reached it by late afternoon. For much of the day Sphax was able to ride alongside Fionn on her stallion Brega. Campfires were lit early, far earlier than was necessary, and by dusk the whole pasture was aglow with light. Sphax didn't see any dancing, but the wine flowed generously that evening and there was plenty of music and singing. As darkness fell, every Allobroges within ten miles of the place would know that Hannibal had arrived with his great host.

Hannibal had chosen midnight as the hour of departure, the dead of night, when all the world slept and the shades of the dead roamed freely in the dark places of this world. At midnight Sphax found the cold so intense that it seemed to penetrate every bone beneath his beaver-skin cloak. But they were in luck, the skies remained clear and the moon seemed to be at its zenith as they set out. Sphax walked beside

Merbal and his uncle at the head of the column. They had known hours ago that the Allobroges had returned to their village and had not left sentries, but as a precaution, Hannibal insisted everyone remain silent. But it was impossible to disguise the sound of a thousand marching boots. Merbal had placed men every thirty paces to act as way-markers and guides. In the darkness of the gorge it was all too easy to lose the way.

In the moonlight Sphax found the gulley easily and pointed the way to the top. His uncle gestured for him to lead the way. He climbed slowly and deliberately, allowing plenty of time for those following to see the way he'd selected. Faced with the unscalable wall of rock he remembered to traverse to the left and tackle a series of boulders that eventually led to the rocky ledges. Hardly out of breath this evening, he arrived at the top. The dying embers of the Allobroges fires offered a faint glow of light. Sphax pointed to the flickering lights of the village and his uncle nodded. 'Do be careful at the edge of the cliff, Sir,' he said quietly, 'there is a fearful drop.' Again, his uncle nodded. Men were now gathering all around them, some trying to warm their hands at what was left of the fires whilst others began examining the stands of spears. His uncle took him aside.

'I have ordered that you be given the honour of leading out our army tomorrow. Return now, Nephew, and at dawn lead them to safety. With the grace of the gods I will welcome you at the village over yonder,' Hannibal gazed once more at the lights in the distance, 'then we will begin our ascent of the high mountains.'

Sphax bowed. 'May Melqart be with you, Sir.' He must have been waiting for well over an hour before the last of Hannibal's one thousand made it to the top of the cliff. He was overjoyed to see that one of the last to ascend was Idwal. When his friend had caught his breath they embraced one another warmly.

'Good luck to you, my friend,' Sphax said solemnly. 'Try and stay alive!'

Merbal was waiting beside his men at the willow thicket. 'All is well,' Sphax said, in answer to the officer's anxious looks. Together they walked back to camp to snatch whatever sleep they could before dawn. Sphax slept fitfully, and the little sleep he managed was troubled by dreams of his father fighting armies of scorpions and writhing snakes.

TWELVE

Sphax was near the head of the Carthaginian cavalcade that set out at dawn, but there was no question of him leading it. This had been a rhetorical gesture on the part of his uncle to make him feel rewarded. Maharbal was firmly in command, with Merbal's eshrin given the honour of the van. Behind Merbal rode the rest of the Numidians. Mago had been given charge of the rear and the vital baggage trains. He had eight thousand Iberian heavy cavalry and most of Hanno's Libyans with him, but because of the confined nature of the gorge, they would not be able to set out until late morning. Sphax realised that over sixty thousand men would be squeezed into an area that at times was no more than eight paces wide. This is what worried him.

The first shock that day was that there were no sounds of battle above the amphitheatre of rock where the Allobroges cliff soared to bar their path. A deadly struggle should be raging somewhere above their heads. They would surely hear the clash of iron on shield and the fearful cries of men in battle. Ears strained in every direction, but met with a deafening silence.

It was ominous, unnerving. Where was Hannibal? Or Idwal? Was he in pursuit of the Allobroges fleeing back to their village? Had the Libyans been defeated or scattered? These were the unspoken questions that lingered on the lips of everyone astride their mares as they approached the cliff.

Sphax was beside Maharbal. 'Should I climb the cliff again, Sir? I might be able to see what has befallen Hannibal and the Cavari.'

'No, lad. It would take an hour, and we haven't an hour to waste. We must press on with all speed. Forward Numidians!' he yelled. Sphax knew it would take him less than half that time to climb the gulley and report back what he'd seen, but the general was not to be argued with that morning. He was in a hurry to get this over with. So much for the leisurely stroll.

The Allobroges had chosen well. To enter the gorge beside their cliff they had to wade through the streambed, whose banks now became walls of rock towering above them. There was room for an elephant, but not much more. In less than a quarter of a mile it did open out a little into terrain that Sphax had become more familiar with; dense thickets of willow and hazel, taller stands of pines and great boulders strewn across their path. They used both sides of the stream, depending on which bank offered the more open path. Progress was painfully slow.

And so it went on, mile after mile, hour by hour. Around mid-morning they halted in one of the wider sections of the gorge to listen again for sounds of battle. Looking around, Sphax could see the strain and anxiety on the men's faces as they craned their necks to search the clifftops for Hannibal and his thousand men. Once more they heard nothing. No one dared to mention the ominous sight of circling vultures, soaring high above their heads.

At mid-day they halted again and stopped to listen. Nothing. Just silence. It sent him into a cold sweat to think that only now would the baggage train be reaching that first narrow section below the Allobroges cliff. Fionn would be riding beside Ayzabel, surrounded by wagons and carts, women, children and camp-followers. From where he stood, there was now a fragile thread of humanity stretching back through all those terrible miles to the pleasant pasture where they had camped last night.

They seemed to have lost touch with Astegal's eshrin, who should have been directly behind them. Maharbal, growing increasingly impatient and anxious, decided to ride back and see what was holding them up. Sphax was ordered to stay with Merbal. It was obvious from the men's faces that none of them wanted to linger in this place. Everyone felt the need to keep moving, to get through it, whatever fate had in store for them.

He was riding beside Merbal when it happened. Out of nowhere a score of bare-chested warriors leapt out of hiding and charged. Spears flew and men began to die.

All he could hear now were screams and war cries and the stomach-churning wail of carnyx. His instinct was to cover his ears and flee, but instead he clutched his javelin, knotted the thong and swung back his arm ready to throw. In front of him a mare reared on its hind legs and screamed, skewered by a spear thrust, its rider thrown to the ground. The warrior received Sphax's first javelin full in the chest. 'Fall back,' Merbal yelled. 'Retreat!'

Sphax was fingering his saunion, already knotted, as he nudged Dido backwards. Something to his right caught his eye and he had just enough time to register a painted shield and a raised blade before he let fly. The barb sailed above the shield and stopped whoever was behind it in their tracks. He was still urging Dido backwards when three more Allobroges let out frenzied screams and leapt at them. Javelins gone, Sphax was defenceless. The Numidian who'd been thrown by his dying mare accounted for one of them, but he paid for it with a spear through his guts. Javelins launched from somewhere behind him slew the other two, but more warriors were now screaming forward.

Then a rage such as he'd never experienced before surged through his veins like white-hot molten iron. It was a madness, a frenzy, an irresistible urge to kill, to mete out death and destruction. He drew his blade and dug both knees so savagely into Dido's flanks that she leapt forward and crashed into their foe as he frenziedly slashed away at anything that moved or stood before him. Curses poured from his mouth that he barely understood, and for the first time his dragon sword tasted blood. Then there was no one left to kill. In his reckless slashing and scything it was a miracle that he'd not decapitated poor Dido.

After it was over Sphax felt a hand grip his shoulder. His entire body was quivering with rage, but the hand was calming, reassuring. Slowly he came to his senses. Merbal was beside him, gripping his shoulders. Sphax looked around at the carnage he'd wrought, at the severed heads, arms and still writhing torsos that littered the ground. His face and tunic was splattered with warm blood.

'Are you wounded?' asked Merbal. Sphax shook his head, unable to speak. 'Sometimes in battle we become possessed by the gods. In Tashynt there is a saying. *Tannith pene ba 'al hamūn*, our flaming goddess with the face of Baal. As often as not, lad, it's the moment you face your own death. Don't try that again.'

'I don't intend to, Sir. I don't know what happened to me,' he said, wiping his bloodied sword on his tunic and sheathing it. Behind him the gorge had now come alive with the sound of battle. It echoed and reverberated from cliff to cliff, raging throughout the gorge. Silence had at last been banished. Sphax guessed the Allobroges who had attacked them had been sent to block the gorge. They had paid for it with their lives. Even so, four Numidians had also fallen and many more had minor wounds. The eshrin's survivors had dismounted and were rooting around the bodies for their javelins. Jugurtha handed him his saunion and a spare javelin. When everyone was mounted again, Merbal spoke to them. 'Astegal's eshrin is behind us; we must ride to his aid. Follow me.'

They never reached Astegal. As they came abreast a steeply wooded gulley that cleaved into the gorge they were assailed by dozens more Allobroges who had been waiting there in ambush. Sphax looked swiftly around him and saw a clearing on the other side of the stream. 'Cross the stream, Numidians,' he yelled. Merbal, who was beside him, glanced across at the southern bank and instantly came to the same conclusion.

'Follow Sphax, men,' he bellowed. 'Cross the stream.' Sphax was already backing Dido away and others were doing their best to follow. Most horses are not trained in this skill, but eventually, most of the eshrin caught up in the crush managed to turn their mares and ride for the stream unopposed. From the middle of the stream Sphax watched as Merbal led the remainder of his men forward to attack. A Numidian charge requires enough ground for the mares to reach a canter. Here, hemmed in by rock and tree, they barely managed a trot. But it was enough, and it bought the rest of them some time. Twelve javelins flew and most met their mark. Merbal returned across the stream a man down, but the more enthusiastic amongst the Allobroges were now moving more warily.

Sphax had been wrong about one thing. It was hardly a clearing, just that the pines were more widely spaced on this bank. Still, skilful horsemen could easily weave between them and a few had tried it by the time Merbal crossed the stream with the rest of his men. 'Sir, if we start at the cliff edge over yonder we can manage eighteen strides before we meet the stream,' said one of them.

'Then it's enough,' cried Merbal defiantly, 'we will fight like Numidians! Jugurtha, go and keep an eye on those bastards whilst we form our line.'

'I know the stream isn't much of a barrier,' said Sphax, 'but it will slow down a headlong charge.' The men nodded in agreement.

'Sphax is right,' said Merbal. 'We must use this to our advantage and strike as they're stumbling across. Three javelins, men, the first at speed and the rest after we turn.'

Jugurtha returned. 'They will be upon us shortly,' he said calmly.

'How many, Jugurtha?' asked Merbal? The old Numidian shrugged.

'Eighty.'

'The usual odds then.' Jugurtha just grinned. With their backs to the cliff wall the horsemen spaced themselves out in a line. Twenty-seven Numidians against eighty screaming Allobroges. Looking down the ranks at the men's faces, Sphax saw only grim determination. Odds meant nothing to these men who lived only for war.

Sphax had a good view across the stream. They were gathering in the trees beyond. He didn't need to see them. By now they were making a fearful racket, screaming curses and beating blades against shields. He knew that when this reached a crescendo the carnyx would trumpet their sickening calls and the warriors would emerge from the trees in a headlong rush.

As the carnyx blared and the first Allobroges came into view, Merbal yelled 'Forward Numidians!' and as one they nudged their mares into a walk. They were trotting as they began weaving through the pines and had reached a canter when they emerged onto the open ground beside the stream. Merbal's timing had been perfect. Their first flight of javelins caught the startled Allobroges stumbling through the stream. As they turned and then halted their mares, the second and third flights brought about their destruction. Soon the stream became choked with dead and dying. Sphax saw his own javelin bury itself harmlessly into a warrior's shield before he checked Dido's stride and slithered from her rump so she could turn around unimpeded by his weight. For the two breaths it took for Dido to return, Allobroges and Numidian stood and faced one another. Contemptuously, the warrior snapped off the javelin lodged in his shield, raised his sword and arrogantly swaggered towards him. Sphax didn't remount Dido, but taking a step towards his enemy he screamed, 'I am the Morrígu. I am death!' and with all his strength hurled his saunion. This time he made no mistake. The iron barb tore into the warrior's throat with such force that he staggered backwards, spewing blood and sprawling into the stream.

For the first time since he'd nudged Dido to the walk and the charge had begun, Sphax began to notice his surroundings again. It was a peculiar sensation, and he'd experienced it before. It was as if his world had shrunk to the size of a point of light, and as he hurtled towards it his mind excluded all other sensation beyond this single vision.

Few of the Allobroges had survived. Stumbling across the stream, many had lowered their shields believing it impossible that they themselves would be charged. Like many Gauls, some had fought naked above their chequered leggings. Bare chests are not the best defence against javelins hurled at speed. He saw a handful of them casting away their weapons, fleeing for their lives to the safety of the trees. Merbal had dismounted and was standing beside the stream, watching their flight. Sphax joined him.

'You must teach my men that trick of yours. If we could slide off our mares as you do we could ride closer to the enemy.' Sphax nodded. Merbal stared at the warrior Sphax had slain. 'What did you shout at him? It wasn't in our language.'

'No,' replied Sphax gravely. 'It was a powerful curse Idwal taught me. These things are useful at times. It seemed to work,' he added, looking closely for the first time at the man he'd killed. He was no ordinary warrior. His conical helmet was iron, with riveted silver cheek pieces and gold inlays. His full mail coat was one of the finest he'd ever seen, with a separate shoulder cape for added protection. Sphax noted with some satisfaction that it hadn't served him well. There was no protection around the neck, a man's most vulnerable area in battle.

'This one is not an Allobroges,' Merbal noted as he reached down to remove the man's helmet. 'He must be a chieftain.' Merbal stared at the lifeless blue eyes and the drooping blond moustache. 'By the gods! This is Lito, brother of Brancus, chief of the Tricastini. Lito was banished from the Island by none other than your uncle.'

'Then he is a traitor, and deserves his fate,' said Sphax with some feeling. Drust had been certain that the guide Ronec had been in the service of this man. They had been brought to this terrible place by the deceitful scheming of the man lying at his feet and his treacherous creature, Ronec. There was some justice in this world after all, thought Sphax.

After wrenching out his saunion and washing it in the stream he carefully removed the mail coat and picked up the helmet. He gave Lito's sword to Merbal, who was delighted with the gift. 'My friend Drust deserves the helmet and coat,' he said. 'If we had all listened to him in the first place we wouldn't be in this mess.'

Suddenly the noise of battle swelled from somewhere back down the gorge. The men were retrieving javelins and looking for trophies. 'We better get them back on their mares,' said Merbal. 'It sounds as if we've more work to do this afternoon.'

As they crossed the bloodied waters of the stream, he remembered the stories Elpis had told him of ancient battles, where it was said that rivers had run red with blood. Sphax had scoffed, never believing that such a thing was possible. He was wiser now.

They warily re-traced their steps to the edge of the gulley where they'd been ambushed, the sounds of battle growing ever closer. The gulley was steep, choked with rocks, boulders and pine trees. Impassable on horseback; but on foot it offered the perfect descent into the gorge. Peering upwards, Sphax could see a few Allobroges making good their escape from the fight at the stream. But how many more were up there, he wondered, awaiting their moment to strike. He was about to find out.

As the last of their eshrin cleared the entrance to the gulley, Sphax once again heard those terrible screams and battle-cries behind him. He and Merbal turned to see swarms of warriors once more pouring down the gulley to the foot of the gorge. This time there were hundreds of them, and this time there could be no escape across the stream. There was only one thing for it. They would have to ride with all speed to where the battle was raging, somewhere back down the gorge.

After no more than a mile they came upon a sight everyone had been dreading. The fight that had been raging ahead of them was taking place in one of the narrowest sections of the gorge. Sphax recalled the place: it was a death trap. Here, the sheer walls of the gorge formed the stream's banks, and the only way through was to wade in its waters. But now blocking the entrance were hundreds of warriors.

They were now caught between two fires. Trapped like wild beasts, with no way out.

Sphax couldn't see who were opposing the Allobroges, but they were at a considerable disadvantage. Scores of warriors had climbed the cliffs above and were hurling down spears. It must be butchery in that narrow space, he thought. But so far at least, they hadn't been spotted.

Merbal looked around at the grim faces of his men. All hope now gone. 'There's nothing for it, lads,' he said desperately. 'If we go forward at least we'll surprise the savages. Let's add our blood to the stream.' Sphax drew his sword. Javelins would be useless in such a confined space. Merbal must have had the same thought, for he drew the sword Sphax had just given him, pointed it at the enemy, and yelled 'Charge!'

Their mares had taken no more than four strides when every horseman halted and gaped in astonishment. The great host of warriors suddenly parted, and into the gap blundered five elephants with the giant Syrian leading the way. The beasts were enraged, bellowing forth an ear-piercing chorus of trumpeting as they stomped forward. Sphax had a fleeting vision of the elephant master Hiempsal astride the Syrian, before the screaming began.

It was the Allobroges who were screaming, but this time in abject terror as they fled for their lives. It was one of the most magnificent sights any of them had ever beheld.

'Quick, men,' yelled Merbal. 'When their blood is up they can't distinguish friend from foe. Get out of their path!' Crossing the stream they pressed their mares flat against the walls of the gorge and prayed they wouldn't be trampled to death. Sphax counted eighteen elephants as they charged past him. He was amazed at the swiftness of their gait as they thundered by. No man could ever outrun those terrible tusks and crunching feet.

In their terror and haste to escape, many of the Allobroges who'd climbed the cliffs now fell to their deaths. Most fled to the forests above, but the few who made it down into the gorge received a javelin for their trouble, joining the scores of warriors already wounded or felled by the elephants. Merbal's Numidians hunted them down remorselessly.

When Sphax and Merbal entered the narrow section they met a sickening sight. The stream was choked with broken and bloodied bodies. Those of their men that had survived an Allobroges spear had been trampled to death by their own elephants. The fighting here must have been desperate. Sphax recognised the Gallic tunics of Iberians from the north and caetrati from the south, alongside Lusitanians and many Numidians. The eshrin dismounted, leading their mares gingerly over bodies and the debris of war, looking for anyone who still lived. They found none.

As they emerged from the narrow cleft into a broader area of pasture, he and Merbal were greeted with the most reassuring sight they'd seen all day. Phalanx upon phalanx of Libyan pikemen had been drawn up and were arrayed across the breadth of the gorge. To Sphax's eyes they looked as solid and immovable as the walls of the gorge itself. In front of the ranks of pikemen, Maharbal sat astride his Egyptian mare, grinning with delight at the two of them.

'Ba 'al hamūn! May the gods be blessed. I had given you both up for dead.'

'It has been close, Sir,' said Merbal soberly, 'but thanks to this young man and the courage of my men, we have endured.'

'I am grateful for it. What are your losses?'

'Four, Sir, but many have wounds.'

'It's a miracle that any of you live!' Maharbal turned to Sphax. 'What of our charge by our Master of Elephants, was it effective?' Despite the trials of the day, Sphax couldn't help smiling.

'It was devastating. The most magnificent sight—'

'Never mind that, lad,' Maharbal interrupted impatiently. 'Did it drive the savages off?'

'More than that, Sir. They are routed and flee for their lives.'

'Good,' Maharbal grunted. He fell silent for a moment and seemed lost in thought. 'What now though?' he said in exasperation. 'Give me a wide flat plain and a thousand Numidians and I will give you victory. But in this shit-hole! I would rather be in Hades. What do we do next?' He was appealing to Merbal, but Merbal just stared at Sphax.

'If Hiempsal and his beasts have not done our work for us, Sir, I believe we must do it in short strides,' answered Sphax. 'One mile ahead of us there is a gulley that must be blocked. Beyond this, Merbal and I have learned the passage. We know something of its twists and turns. If we could have the assurance of these Libyans behind us, we would be able to flee from ambush and take refuge amongst their ranks. In this way we could proceed through the gorge in short bounds, blocking off those gullies and ravines as we progressed, so that those who followed would be safe from ambush.' Maharbal turned to Merbal.

'What do you think, Merbal? Is the lad making any sense?' Scowling, he added, 'For as sure as money is the sinew of war, those savages will re-group and return. They have eyes only for our silver and the bounty that lies in our baggage. They *will* be back.'

'Sphax is making perfect sense, general,' said Merbal. 'Our first objective should be that gulley. Then he is right, we can do it in short strides. With a phalanx of spearmen behind us we would feel secure enough if we had to beat a hasty retreat. But what of Astegal, Sir, and the rest of our eshrins?'

'Astegal lives, but his eshrin is cut to pieces,' answered the general, grimly. 'The same is true of Mago and Adherbal. My eshrins have suffered in this terrible place. This is not a fit place for our mares. We should never have come this way.'

'We were lured to this place, Sir, by the treachery of that creature Ronec, and his master Lito,' said Sphax. 'None of us could have foreseen this. My uncle undoubtedly drove the enemy from the clifftops, but they must have withdrawn and regrouped. The Allobroges know this place like the back of their hands. They must have known we would be strung out and vulnerable.' The lure of those treasure chests had proved too much for the Allobroges and they had decided to risk everything by attacking down the gullies and ravines.

'I know you're right, lad. But it brings me little comfort,' said Maharbal. Sphax felt a twinge of guilt at this. He had played a part in all of this, and it had failed. The general eyed them both gravely. 'We will gather what eshrins remain and follow our master of elephants. You and I, Merbal, will lead them through this rat trap with the Libyans directly behind us in support. You, Sphax, will ride back to our baggage train and report to your uncle Mago. After you've informed him of the situation you will act as his guide for the trains. Mago has Hanno with him, half our elephants and the rest of our Libyans, but we must prepare for any eventuality.'

Progress back though the gorge was slow. It seemed that every officer in the army wanted to know what they faced around the next corner and where the Allobroges were gathering. By the time he reached his uncle Mago at the head of the trains, Sphax had spoken to Garamatians, Gaetuli, Adyrmachids and virtually every race and tribe from Numidia to Libya.

Sphax liked the younger of his uncles. Away from the shadow of his older brother, Mago had an easy smile and ready wit, but after hearing of the disasters that had befallen the columns ahead of them, that familiar Barca gloom had descended like a black cloud. 'What of my brother? Has he not joined you by now?'

'There has been no sign or sighting of him all day,' said Sphax. 'I suspect he has his hands full dealing with the Allobroges arrayed on the cliffs above our heads. But we have no way of knowing this for certain, Sir.' The giant figure of Hanno strode over to where they sat astride their horses and Mago gave him a brief account of what had happened.

'Then if the gullies and ravines that enter the gorge are secure, it is our duty to press on with all speed. If your brother was needed down here in the gorge he would be here. It's unthinkable that he'd let us down.' Hanno's dark eyes burned into Sphax's, then glanced over his blood-spattered tunic, more red than white. 'We now have this excellent young man to act as our guide. What could go wrong?'

Plenty, thought Sphax, but it was clear who was really in charge of the baggage trains, so it was to Hanno that he said, 'I think I should mention, Sir, the Allobroges are terrified of our elephants. At the sight of them they shit themselves and take to their heels.' Hanno roared with laughter at this.

'Then I'm putting you in charge of the elephants, Master Sphax. Let them lead the way.'

'And some in the rear, Sir, in case we become surrounded.' Hanno looked puzzled, as if the word *surrounded* was not part of his vocabulary.

'If you like, lad. Yes. Certainly.' Sphax was relieved. That morning, he himself had learned the true meaning of this word.

And so for the second time that day, Sphax rode eastwards through the gorge. His friend Mathos from the crossing of the Rhodanus was in charge of the mahouts, leading out eleven elephants at the head of the column. Sphax had made sure he sent back eight beasts to guard the rear.

But everywhere he looked there was chaos. Whenever they entered a narrow section where the walls closed in around them, ox carts and wagons had to be dragged or manhandled along the bed of the stream, strings of reluctant mules coaxed through and worst of all, grumbling camp followers unwilling to get their feet wet. Amidst oaths and curses the teams hauled on ropes or pushed from behind, slithering on wet stones, sweating yet knee-deep in icy water.

Some vehicles lost a wheel or an axle but still had to be carried through so as not to block the way for those that followed. Once through, the cart had to be unloaded and room found elsewhere for whatever they carried, for there was no time for repairs. Some laden vehicles had to be abandoned altogether for want of space in other wagons. By sheer brute force they forged ahead, but it was exhausting work and taking an age.

As the afternoon wore on and the shadows lengthened, Sphax anxiously checked the position of the sun. The thought of spending a night in the depths of this gorge filled him with horror.

The mood of the column changed when the trains arrived at the narrow section where the elephants had charged. For half a mile the stream was choked with the dead, its waters stained a muddy crimson. What remained of their bodies and limbs had to be removed before any progress could be made. From that point onwards the path was strewn with the dead, and a pall of silence descended on the wagon masters and camp followers.

When they reached the gulley where he and Merbal's eshrin had been twice ambushed, Sphax was relieved to see that Maharbal had left three hundred heavily armoured Iberian Gauls guarding this gateway into the gorge. The Carthaginian officer left in charge told him that he had orders not to move until the last of the wagons had passed through.

Reassuring as this was, it was impossible to locate every single gulley and ravine that led from the cliffs down into the gorge. There had been no time for exploration or reconnaissance. They would simply have to trust to the luck of the gods. When they reached another narrow section, Sphax decided to ride back and find Fionn, trusting that the Allobroges would never attack elephants in such a confined space.

When he was not fighting for his life that day, his thoughts had increasingly turned to Fionn's safety. In this place, death was never far away. They were all being hunted down. Men and women.

He found her riding beside Ayzabel, surrounded by their servants. When she caught sight of him and his blood-soaked tunic he could see the tears begin to well up. 'I thought you were dead, my love.' Her face was ashen grey. Sphax leapt from Dido and ran over to her, lifting her out of the saddle; they clung to one another, her tears staining his tunic and the smell of her rosewater perfume filling his nostrils. Then he remembered Ayzabel.

'The general is safe and unharmed, Ayzabel. You are not to worry on his behalf.' If anything, poor Ayzabel looked even paler than Fionn. Sphax looked around at the armed men they had with them. They were thin on the ground. Just a rag-tag mixture of Iberian caetrati, slingers and horsemen on their big stallions. Sphax guessed they were all stragglers who'd fallen behind their main bodies. Six hundred paces ahead of them were three phalanxes of Libyan pikemen. He'd passed through their disciplined ranks only moments before.

Lifting Fionn back on to Brega's saddle he said, 'Listen to me carefully. Ride as fast as you can to the Libyans up yonder.' Sphax turned and pointed at their ranks. 'If either of you should hear battle-cries or screaming, hide behind them. You will be quite safe amongst their ranks and they can be relied upon to stand firm.' Sphax looked them both squarely in the eye.

'Do you understand?' They both nodded solemnly. 'Remember, Allobroges warriors scream as they charge into battle. Listen out for it and do as I say.' With that he whistled for Dido, leapt on to her back and rode to the head of the column.

He was greeted by a disgruntled Mathos. 'Trust the Master to get all the glory today.' He meant Hiempsal, the Master of Elephants who'd led the magnificent charge earlier that day. 'So far I haven't seen a single savage.' Sphax sighed.

'I wouldn't wish for glory too eagerly, my friend. It sometimes comes at a heavy price.' But Mathos was right. As Sphax silently counted down the miles, they neither saw nor heard an Allobroges, and they still had three hours of precious daylight left. Sphax was beginning to believe that Mathos was right, and by the grace of the gods there would be no more glory that day.

He first saw it when he looked back down the gorge to check on the progress of their columns; it was just a thin pall of smoke rising to the heavens in the late afternoon sunshine, easily missed or ignored. It was only later that its significance dawned on him. He was a slackhead, a dumb half-witted imbecile! It could mean only one thing. It was be a signal fire.

'Turn them around, Mathos!' he yelled. 'Turn them around and head back down the gorge.' Digging his knees into Dido he weaved his way through the elephants and raced back through the gorge, now certain, for the sound of men gathering for battle grew closer with every stride.

A growing rage began to seethe through his body like a quickening fire. If they dared harm a single hair on Fionn's head he would kill them, slay them to a man. Knuckle-white, his fingers tightened on his saunion.

Now the sounds of war grew near. He threaded his way through hordes of Libyans, all sprinting back in the same direction as him. Dido was now reduced to a trot, but somehow the pikemen made room for him and he pressed on, the noise growing to a shrill crescendo. Another twist of the gorge and he was there.

It was a terrible sight. Across the stream a great host of warriors had assembled. It looked as if the entire Allobroges nation were preparing for a last desperate attempt to destroy Hannibal's army and reap the spoils of war. But the gods were not on their side that afternoon. The Allobroges had chosen to attack in one of the broadest sections of the gorge, where numbers could be brought to bear, and numbers mattered. In that earlier slaughter where the gorge had narrowed to the width of the stream bed numbers had counted for nothing. It had been man against man, hacking away until one of them fell or gave way.

But here, every man in Mago's rear-guard was now making his way to swell the ranks of the forces already formed up for battle. And that was their second mistake. The Allobroges had chosen the wrong opponents. That sealed their fate.

In a wide arc covering the entire northern bank of the stream, five phalanxes of Libyans were already drawn up, each several ranks deep, shields and iron-tipped pikes at the ready. Sphax halted Dido and watched as two more phalanxes began to form up directly in front of him, their ranks swelling all the while as men joined them from the hundreds sprinting back to join their comrades. They formed up shoulder to shoulder in bristling ranks, officers barking commands as weapons were readied for battle.

Sphax stared at their pikes and shuddered. Since joining this army he'd been fascinated by the Libyans. Rome had nothing like these fighting men in their legions. All wore peaked Macedonian helmets of bronze, oval shields that were not so heavy and unwieldy as their Gallic opponents', and bronze greaves protecting their shins and lower legs. Officers were resplendent in gleaming cuirasses, polished like mirrors, and their helmets were adorned with flowing manes of horsehair dyed crimson or white to match their long cloaks. The pike itself was nothing short of an instrument of death, a killing weapon as lethal as his saunion, its sturdy shaft half-again the height of a man and tipped with a leaf-shaped spike of iron. At its other end the lizard-killer spike was just as deadly, but when thrust into the ground rested its weight for the Libyan bearing it.

Sphax nudged Dido into the narrow gap between two phalanxes. Then, for some inexplicable reason, he began to laugh. The truth of the matter was that astride Dido, defended by a thousand Libyan pikes he hadn't felt safer all day. The laughter had nothing to do with joy, just his palpable sense of relief from the terrors of the day.

Hundreds upon hundreds of Allobroges were still pouring down what looked like a sheer cliff-face. Only it wasn't sheer. At this point the southern walls of the gorge were no more of a barrier than a stone staircase. Yet from the northern bank it looked unscalable, and that's why they'd been fooled. To Sphax, the cliff took on the appearance of a human waterfall that was about to flood into the gorge and drown them all. Yet he was still smiling. All the men around him had faced such sights on countless occasions from Iberia to the Rhodanus, and every man knew that to charge their pikes was to die on them. On his side of the stream the leaf-spiked wall stood in deadly silence, immoveable, steadfast. Then, on the southern bank, the frenzy began.

It started with the din of blades beaten against shields, followed by war-cries and insults as warriors goaded one another into a state of raging madness.

Then the screaming began and the carnyx wailed. Sphax thought they would be better saving their breath, for on his side of the stream the racket fell on deaf ears. Captains walked calmly in front of their ranks, checking spacing, looking for gaps, hardly casting a glance in the direction of the screaming hordes who were about to charge them. Whether it was feigned or not, Sphax was full of admiration for their cool indifference in the face of such wild savagery.

'Pikes!' rang out the order all along the line.

As one, the front two ranks lowered their pikes to a horizontal position. From where he sat astride Dido there was now a bristling line of pikes stretching eighty paces in either direction, and it was growing all the time.

The screaming reached its crescendo and the Allobroges charged.

For all the ferocity of that first charge, the only result was a pile of dead and writhing wounded left gutted and strewn on the ground beneath Libyan pikes. With a recklessness bordering on madness the Allobroges had tried to cut and slash their way through that deadly forest with their blades or tried to thrust them aside with shields, but if the first rank of pikemen had failed to gut them, the rank behind made no mistake. Nowhere along the entire length of the Libyan line had a single savage managed to close with a Libyan.

When the warriors next came forward it was as a weasel approaches a thousand-spined hedgehog. In small groups they goaded one another forward to slash away at the outermost pikes whilst desperately trying to avoid their lethal thrusts. They were in for an unpleasant surprise.

'Forward,' came the cry, as the front ranks yanked their shafts backwards before striding forwards to viciously thrust them forward again. The result was as deadly as before.

Now the Allobroges were backing away, cowed and sullen. Some found the courage to stand out of range of the pikes and scream torrents of abuse on the Libyans, challenging them to single combat. Not that any Libyan understood a single word of these tirades. Others launched their spears, but half-heartedly, and most fell short or were parried by shields.

One particular warrior was beginning to annoy Sphax, and judging from the jeers and muttering from the ranks around him, he was having the same effect on the Libyans. He was no ordinary warrior: his long mail-coat and helmet marked him out as a chief. Yelling abuse, he'd already lowered his leggings and pissed on the pikes of the leading rank. Despite all the jabbing and poking he'd managed to retain his manhood. But the final insult came when he began launching spears at them, for he had a mighty arm that could cast a spear as far as any Numidian could throw a javelin. After a Libyan in the sixth rank was struck in the shoulder and another took a glancing blow to his helmet Sphax sensed that Libyan patience was growing thin. They wanted this pest gutted.

'Hold your ground, men,' an officer barked. But his men could clearly see the man's followers supplying him with yet more spears to pester them with.

He'd positioned Dido in the narrow corridor between two phalanxes. The offending warrior was no more than forty paces in front of him, ten strides for Dido, and he had a clear run. He tightened his grip on the saunion's thong and buried his knees into the mare's flanks. Dido leapt forward so swiftly that she covered the ground in eight strides. Two strides before Sphax launched his saunion the warrior caught sight of him and hurriedly cast his spear. Saunion and spear passed in mid-air, and whereas the spear narrowly missed its mark the saunion struck home to a great cheer from the Libyan ranks. The last Sphax saw of him was his followers carrying him from the field.

As he took up his position between the phalanxes men broke ranks to pat him on the back and ruffle Dido's mane. Cheering broke out again, but this time along the entire length of the Libyan line on the northern bank of the stream. It grew wilder, at times almost ecstatic. Those with keener eyes than his had recognized their leader, sword held aloft and flanked by his Adrymachid bodyguards, leaping from ledge to ledge down the cliff the Allobroges had descended. Hannibal had at last found his quarry and was hurling his thousand men at the Allobroges in the depths of the gorge. Sphax knew the Cavari would be amongst them, and that Idwal would at last face his enemies.

All around him officers were now yelling commands as each phalanx readied themselves. Young boys at the rear began beating drums in a relentless tattoo that was taken up along the length of the Libyan line. With pikes still levelled, two thousand feet pounded inexorably forward to their beat. The Libyans were on the move, and a slaughter was about to take place. Sphax had seen it all before at the Rhodanus, and it troubled him. He nudged Dido around and left them to it. He would find Fionn and make sure she was safe.

They camped that night beside the Allobroges village in a broad meadow beyond the gorge. It kept them warm on that bitterly cold night, for it was slowly burning to the ground.

THIRTEEN

For eight days their weary columns straggled through the rugged foothills towards the high mountains and the pass that would lead them to Rome. On the first day after leaving the smouldering ashes of the Allobroges village they caught their first glimpse of the towering snow-capped peaks, glittering in the distance, ice-bound and forbidding. Men shrank at the sight of them, averting their eyes, fearing they had been given a task beyond the endurance of soldiers. For the first time since the army left the warmth of an Iberian springtime, men talked openly of turning back, or waiting for the winter to pass and the snows to melt, or spoke of a different path that would take them around these accursed mountains. And every day those mountains loomed nearer. Every day the fear that gripped their souls grew tighter, strangling all hope and what remained of their courage. On the second day it began to snow. Not the winter drifts and blizzards that would arrive in a month or so, but enough to soak them through to the skin and add to their misery.

Overhead, great flocks of swifts and songbirds flew south in search of the caves in which they would over-winter and bears were already seeking out their forest dens to sleep out the season's cold. Soon, all that would be left to stalk these desolate mountains would be hungry wolves and sharp-eyed eagles.

The land was utterly deserted. They passed farms and villages empty and abandoned, their inhabitants flown, along with their livestock and everything that could be carried away. The Allobroges village they burned would have been seen for miles around and had acted as a terrible beacon to the people who lived in this wild region. And yet they had not come to burn and kill. Carthage had no enemies here. They only wanted safe passage through this land, and Hannibal was prepared to pay good Carthaginian silver for the privilege. But the mountain Gauls were a proud and stubborn people who preferred war to treaties.

Hannibal was everywhere during those dark days. Magnificent astride Arion, he tirelessly rode the length of the columns by day and at night strode amongst the campfires, slapping backs and jesting with his men, exuding confidence and vitality. He seemed to feed on adversity and hardship, making him stronger, bolder and more certain that Carthage would prevail. 'See those peaks,' he would cry at the top of a pass they'd just ascended, 'beyond them lies all the wealth of Rome. They have opened the doors of the temple of Janus and unleashed the dogs of war, yet they cower in fear and dread beyond those mountains, praying to their gods that our courage will fail us and we will turn back. Since when have Iberians, Libyans and all the races under Carthage been defeated by rock and stone? Soon you will be filling your bellies with Umbrian pork and drinking the finest wines that Etruria has to offer. We are so close. Have courage, men. Have courage!'

If he didn't bring hope, at least he instilled resolve. And where courage waned he brought tenacity. At times during those terrible days, Sphax believed that the only thing holding the army together was the iron will of its leader, his uncle. But would it be enough?

On the ninth day they came up against a great barrier. Not the towering peaks of the high mountains, for they still loomed in the distance, but a broad river that had become a raging torrent. The fickle snows of early autumn had soon melted, setting in motion every stream and brook to swell the river that now barred their path. Their Boii guides called this river the Druentia and told them it flowed into the Rhodanus, close to where they'd crossed that great river to defeat the Volcae some weeks before. They said it was a plague river that brought nothing but floods and misery to its lower reaches. All Sphax saw was an icy cold torrent of foaming water.

At first light Maharbal had ordered his eshrins to search for a crossing point. Some had gone upstream, but Merbal, thinking to find a wide shallow stretch where the current would not be so fierce, had followed its course downstream. Although he'd lost a Numidian in an attempt to swim his mare across, Merbal thought the river could be forded at that point with the aid of guide ropes stretched between its banks.

'Most of the time your mare is up to her flanks,' he was saying to the general, 'the danger is when she steps into a deep pool. Then she's lost. The current is too strong and she's swept away. If we can avoid those deeper pools, I think it can be done.'

'Let's take a look,' said Maharbal, gesturing to Merbal to lead the way. Sphax rode behind the two of them as they picked their way along the rocky northern bank of the river. For a couple of miles or so the Druentia's torrent filled their ears, making conversation difficult above its roar, but then the valley seemed to flatten out and here the river broadened its course, breaching its shallow banks and swamping the stands of willow that marked its course.

They arrived at the same time as Mathos' eshrin, who had been scouting the river further downstream. In answer to Maharbal's 'any luck?' Mathos just shook his head. Almost sixty Numidians now grimly sat their horses, fetlock deep in the floodwaters, staring out at the far bank sixty paces distant.

'Within half a mile of here,' Mathos said at last, 'it goes back to being a cascade. We either ford here, or not at all. My men have followed it for at least five miles downstream.' Maharbal said nothing but gazed up at the sullen grey sky, considering what they were all thinking. So far that morning it hadn't rained. But that sky promised rain or snow, Sphax could smell it in the air. It was now or never, and if it rained for a couple of days, it would be never, thought Sphax. He nudged Dido beyond the willows and into the river's current.

'Be careful, lad,' Merbal shouted after him, 'I've already lost Carthalo to this spate.' Sphax sensed the change in gradient as Dido trod warily down the river's submerged bank and into its streambed of pebbles and boulders. He also sensed her stiffen as she braced herself against the swift current. But at least here it was just a swift current and not a raging torrent. Soon the water was up to her flanks and racing past his calves, rapidly numbing in the icy water. He remembered what Merbal had said about stepping into hidden deep pools. That's how Carthalo had been swept away. He lent over Dido's neck to peer down into the water. It had taken on the colour of a dirty washtub, seeded with tiny particles of dirt and sand thrown up by the flood. He could barely see below the surface, let alone to the riverbed, making it impossible to gauge the depth of the water. He would be taking a foolish risk if he continued across, and he would never risk Dido. Very slowly, he coaxed Dido to turn about and return to the safety of the shallow water below the trees. Then an idea came to him.

'It's impossible to see the bottom, so there's no way of knowing where the deeper pools lie. But I have an idea, Sir.' Sphax paused and saw Maharbal raise a sceptical eyebrow.

'Go on, lad.'

'If I cut a long length of willow I could prod it down into the streambed to gauge its depth. In this way I could work my way slowly across the river, avoiding the deeper pools.'

Mathos burst out laughing. Even Merbal was grinning at this preposterous idea, but Maharbal was staring at him, lost in thought. 'A pike would be better ... or even a stout pole. But I don't think it can be done on horseback, Sphax. I doubt if you could reach forward enough beyond a mare's forelegs. Some poor bastard will have to wade into that river with a pole. Can you swim, lad?' Sphax gratefully shook his head.

Leaving strict instructions that no one from the two eshrins was to attempt to cross, Maharbal set out with Sphax to find Hannibal. It was almost midday when they did, but as the journey had been conducted in silence with the general in deep thought, Sphax guessed that Maharbal was about to present his uncle with a plan to get the army safely across the Druentia.

* * *

In the end it was two Iberians who waded across the river, cheered on by thousands watching from the western bank. They were brothers, shepherds from the mountainous south of the country who could swim like salmon and thought nothing of wading a mountain stream in search of a lamb. Naked except for a rag of loincloth and with hemp rope tied around their waists, they waded into the freezing waters grasping a Libyan pike in each hand. The water soon reached their ribs and midstream one of the brothers stumbled into a deep pool, lost his footing and begun swimming for his life. But the current was too swift and he was only saved from being swept away by the rope that had been paid out behind him. Nevertheless, soon two stout hemp ropes had been tied to stakes hammered into the ground on the eastern bank. The Druentia had been crossed.

It took three days for the rest of the army to get across and by then the ropes had been strengthened by additional stakes driven into the riverbed where the current was fiercest. Mercifully it didn't rain. Over those three days Sphax waded across the river many times, bringing Fionn and her servants as well as their tent and baggage safely to the eastern bank. Hiempsal, the old mahout and Master of Elephants had the easiest time of it. Astride the big Syrian bull, he led out the creatures as if they were paddling through a shallow brook in springtime.

There were mishaps of course; several wagons and their precious contents, and a few pack animals that panicked midstream were swept away. By the time Hannibal called for a complete day of rest after the crossing, some Gaul sitting on a muddy bank of the Rhodanus would receive the bounty of a wagon full of salted pork or boots made from fine Iberian leather. For some reason his uncle found this highly amusing. Sphax, who was desperately in need of new boots, did not. Now new pairs could not be purchased at any price in the camp!

They met the Tricorii on the morning they set out from their camp beside the Druentia. There were twelve of them, and they came on foot. Two young men garbed in filthy hide cloaks and waving olive branches led the column. Behind were six young children and four elderly men dressed in heavy furs.

Sphax's first instinct was to reach for his saunion, but Adherbal, whose eshrin he'd been accompanying all morning, placed a firm hand on his arm. 'They're waving olive branches, lad, which means they've come to talk, not fight. Not that this lot look as if they've got much fight in them.' He slid from his mare and walked towards the group with his palm raised in a gesture of peace. Sphax watched with the rest of the eshrin as the four old men shuffled forward to speak. After a few moments Adherbal shrugged and yelled back, 'I can't understand a word these savages are saying. You speak Greek and Latin, Sphax, come and try that on them.'

One of the quartet seemed to be their leader. He furled back the hood of his bearskin cloak to reveal a few wisps of silver hair on a bald head, and skin the colour of papyrus. He looked as if the three spinners might carry him off any moment. But he did speak some Latin, and Sphax soon discovered that he was the leader of the Tricorii council of elders, and that his name was Brice. They sought embassy with Hannibal. No one lesser would do!

He passed all this all on to a bemused Adherbal. 'Also, Sir,' Sphax added, 'he says that he brings great gifts for the lord of the Carthaginians as well as guides to take us safely over the mountain passes.' Adherbal raised a quizzical eyebrow at this, but at that moment they were astonished to see another party of Gauls herding cattle, sheep and pigs towards them.

'Well,' said Adherbal shaking his head, 'even if he's lying through those fangs of his, it looks as if we might feast well this evening. Take the old goat to meet your uncle.'

By the time they found Hannibal their little party had swollen to over fifty. It seemed that every officer in the army, including Hanno and even Maharbal was curious to know what these Gauls were doing here. Sphax walked beside Brice, questioning the old man about his tribe, their territory, and alliances with neighbouring tribes. He found out their city lay somewhere to the northwest, in the upper reaches of the valley of the Druentia, and that they were the chief tribe of the alpine Gauls, holding sway over all the lesser tribes. The other thing he'd discovered was that Brice's breath smelt worse than a dog-turd.

After staring for some moments at the strange collection of Gauls on their knees before him, Hannibal turned to Sphax. 'Well nephew, what new surprise have you brought before me this morning?'

Hannibal had spoken in Greek, and Sphax continued in that language so as to pass on information that would not be understood by the delegation. 'May I present Brice, Sir, leader of the Tricorii elders, who come in embassy. He says the Tricorii speak for the other tribes in the mountains. He offers truce, and brings gifts and tribute as a measure of good faith. He even offers guides to lead us over the mountains.'

'And the children. What is their purpose?'

'He says they are to be offered as hostages, as surety and guarantee for any treaty. He assures me they are the sons and daughters of chieftains, and are dear to them.'

'Is that all, Nephew?'

'No, uncle.' Sphax couldn't resist. 'His breath is unspeakable and his Latin execrable. You'll need a translator.'

'Thank you,' his uncle replied formally, without even a hint of a smile. Sphax bowed and left them to it. Not soon enough he was mounted and galloping as fast as Dido could be ridden back to Adherbal's Numidians.

* * *

That night, beside a Cavari campfire, he learned of the interminable negotiations that had taken place all afternoon. Bostar and his lackeys had even assembled Hannibal's pavilion so the Tricorii delegation could be honoured and waited upon within its splendour. His uncle never wasted an opportunity to impress guests with his power and wealth. Sosylos the Greek historian had translated, but some words were unfamiliar to him, so Idwal and the Boii guides had been summoned to ensure there could be no misunderstandings of the terms and conditions of the treaty.

For all the endless hours of empty talk that afternoon, Sphax realised that he himself had teased out of Brice everything the Tricorii were offering on their brief walk to find his uncle. When Idwal had finished his description, Cáel refilled their cups and handed him a platter of pork ribs. At least they were enjoying the fruits of the Gauls' tribute. The pork was delicious, the best thing he'd eaten for a week.

Drust was standing, cup in hand, warming his backside on the campfire. 'They're all weasels,' he spat. 'I wouldn't trust them any more than I would trust a drunken Scythian. I went to speak with the hostages this evening, Sphax. They are no more wellborn than my cook, just slaves that Brice rounded up this morning.'

Sphax turned to Idwal who was sitting beside him, staring into the firelight. 'Did you know about this?'

'Yes. I sent Drust to question them,' he said without shifting his gaze.

Sphax thought for a moment then mused, 'What I don't understand is what they hope to gain from this treaty. They are offering us safe passage, guides, hostages and gifts, whilst we give them nothing in return. Bread must be paid for in coin, not promises. This is not a fair exchange.'

'Ah, but that's where you're wrong, Sphax,' said Cáel, laughing. 'It's not so much about what we give them, but rather, what we *don't* give them! They saw the burning Allobroges village. They heard how Hannibal slaughtered the Volcae and how we massacred our enemies the Allobroges. I think they have everything to gain, if they value their miserable skins.'

Sphax felt a surge of irritation at this but managed to let it go. If memory served, it was Libyan spears and elephants that defeated the Allobroges. And for much of that terrible day it was the Allobroges doing the slaughtering, not the Cavari.

Drust sensed his irritation. 'We should also fear them. Those children, our *hostages*, are from three different tribes in the mountains. The Tricorii have allies, and if they should gather ...' Drust left the words hanging in the cold night air. 'We have been led astray before by the treachery of guides.'

Idwal seemed to awaken from his reverie and shifted on the bench. 'You know your uncle as well as anyone, Sphax. Surely he will not be deceived by the Tricorii?'

Sphax sighed deeply. 'My uncle is like a knock on the door. Only when you open it will you discover which guest is visiting today. And it could be one of many. But one thing is as certain as the gods. He is no fool.' He drained his cup and got to his feet.

Lamps were still burning in Maharbal's pavilion. On an impulse, Sphax strode over to the Numidian sentries guarding the entrance. 'Is he awake?' he asked Bartho, the general's standard bearer. Bartho nodded and pulled the flap aside.

Maharbal was seated at the far end in front of an iron brazier that was using up his precious allotment of charcoal. When he caught sight of Sphax he put a finger to his lips and pointed to the sleeping divan in the corner. Under a mountain of furs, Sphax could just make out the head and bare shoulder of Ayzabel, snoring fit to wake the gods. Silently he padded over to the general, who beckoned to a couch beside him. The general had a bearskin around his shoulders and was wearing his peaked Phoenician cap that marked him out as a *Shophet* of Carthage. Even so, both were grateful for the warmth of the brazier that night. 'I'm sorry, Sir,' Sphax whispered apologetically, 'I'll leave before I wake her.'

Maharbal started chortling, he was trying not to laugh out loud. 'Not even the hounds of Melqart would wake that girl when she starts bellowing like that! Speak quietly lad, and she will sleep like the dead.'

'Fionn snores like that. Do all women snore, Sir?'

'I hope you live long enough to conduct a thorough survey, lad. But I'm sure you haven't come at this late hour to discuss the habits of women.'

'Quite so, Sir. Do you remember Drust…'

'Of course. The Cavari. I like that young man.'

'Well, Sir, earlier this evening Idwal sent him to talk to those children Brice offered as hostages. Brice assured us they were wellborn, the sons and daughters of chieftains. They are not, Sir. They are slaves, of no value to anyone except their masters. What is even more puzzling, is that Drust found out that they are from three different tribes of mountain Gauls.' At this the general raised an eyebrow and folded his hands on his lap.

'We knew they were slaves, Sphax. Your uncle's Greek tutor also questioned them. But he didn't discover that they were from separate tribes.' Maharbal re-clasped his hands and stared into the glowing brazier. 'What might this tell us, I wonder?'

'At the very least, Sir, it tells us that three tribes are working in alliance. Of the six children, Drust found that there were two from each tribe. It seems likely that each tribe contributed two slaves. It also tells us that Brice lied. In the event of a truce being broken, a slave is of little consequence, is expendable. There's something else, Sir.' Sphax hesitated for a moment before continuing. 'It may be unimportant, but I couldn't help noticing that as I walked beside Brice to meet Hannibal, his eyes were darting everywhere; at our arms, our weapons, our equipment, horses. He was assessing, calculating, counting numbers, I'm sure of it. That old man missed nothing.'

'I'm sure you're right,' Maharbal said casually.

'Then surely, Sir, we're not going to trust this truce of theirs?'

'What alternative do we have?' The general was slowly shaking his head and grinning. Sphax was shocked.

'But they intend to break this truce, Sir!'

'Almost certainly.'

'And those guides will lead us straight into another ambush,' he cried in exasperation, 'just like that bastard Ronec did.'

'Keep your voice down, lad,' Maharbal hissed. Sphax glared down at the carpet as the general slowly got to his feet and stretched his arms and shoulders as if measuring his own weariness.

'Look at it this way. Today we gained a small advantage over our enemies. I grant you it is inconsequential, but nevertheless, it is an advantage. This afternoon your uncle treated the embassy with courtesy and respect, showing gratitude for the gifts, tributes and guides. He refused their surety of hostages, saying that it was unnecessary amongst peoples who trusted one another. They insisted, so he graciously accepted this measure of their good faith. He also acceded willingly to their demands that the lives and property of the Tricorii be respected during our passage through their lands. So the Tricorii now think they are dealing with fools, and believe they can lead us like cattle to their slaughter pens. This is the advantage we have gained today.' Maharbal abruptly resumed his stool by the brazier and glared at him.

'We are not fools, Sphax! This embassy was intended to keep us off our guard, lull us into sleep. But now we are awake! We will be prepared, alert, ready, and from the knowledge that Drust has gained, we now know that we'll be attacked by at least three tribes.' Sphax was beginning to understand.

'But what about those guides, Sir?'

Maharbal chuckled. 'Your uncle was at his most subtle and devious on that point. He begged their guides to describe in great detail the route we were about to undertake to the high passes, pleading his army had no such guides and was ill prepared for such a perilous journey. Whilst the guides blabbed, Silenos and Sosylos scribbled with their quills. After the embassy returned to their camp, we compared their description with what our guides had planned; the two are the same, they are identical. Bear in mind, Sphax, that we trust the Boii and Insubres with our lives. That the two routes are the same tells us something else.' The general paused, inviting Sphax to draw his own conclusions from this statement.

'That they have no need to lead us astray. The route offers ample opportunity for ambush anywhere along its path.'

'Quite so,' the general replied, evidently pleased with him. Sphax stood, about to take his leave when a question sprang into his mind that had haunted him ever since the grand council of Gauls. It was a question that remained unanswered and had been gnawing away at him for weeks. He turned to face Maharbal and blurted out, 'Why did we come this way, Sir? Surely the rout of the Volcae opened up easier paths to Liguria? Along the coast to Genua or through the foothills ... even by ship! Instead, we chose to struggle through these wretched mountains with winter almost upon us, risking rivers in spate and dogged every step of the way by savage Gauls who only have eyes for our silver. It was madness, Sir. Utter madness!'

Maharbal had angrily risen from his stool when Sphax had begun his outburst, but then abruptly checked himself and listened in shocked silence. When Sphax fell silent he sank back and buried his head in his hands. Eventually he spoke.

'You're right. We should never have come this way.' There was another painful silence before he continued. 'We begged your uncle, we pleaded with him, argued and debated our case, point by point, reason by reason. We were of one mind. All of us ... Hanno, Mago, Mathos, the Iberians, all of us! All we had to do when we'd crossed the river and routed the Volcae was to march south and crush Consul Scipio's two legions. It would've been easy. They were ripe for plucking! Our army had three times their number and we had the better ground. We would have slaughtered them. Any survivors fleeing back to their ships would have been run down by my Numidians. Then we would have captured their fleet anchored in the mouth of the Rhodanus. This would have removed the threat of a Roman army in our rear, an army sitting squarely on our supply lines back to Iberia. It would have changed everything. Everything!

'Rome would have tasted her first defeat, we would have secured our supply lines back to New Carthage and opened up an easy march into the heart of Liguria.

We could have burned Genua to the ground and threatened every seaport and town from there to Pisae, even to Ostia, at the very gates of Rome.' Maharbal paused and gazed up at him with eyes that seemed to mist over, unseeing. 'But it was not to be … not to be,' he repeated.

'Why did he not listen to you?' Sphax whispered, appalled by what he'd just heard. Maharbal gave a heart-felt sigh and shuffled awkwardly on his stool before composing himself sufficiently to reply.

'Magol of the Boii persuaded him. He told Hannibal that unless the Boii and Insubres received help this winter, they would be driven from their lands and their war with Rome would be over. They would be forced to sue for peace. He also told your uncle he'd brought sixty of his household over the high passes without mishap, and that only those passes led directly into Boii territory.' Maharbal gazed up at him, a thin smile on his lips. 'We almost persuaded him. He knew full well that it's against all the rules of war to leave a dangerous enemy in your rear, astride your supply lines. I suppose that's why he sent you on that fool's errand to win over the Cavari, and when that succeeded beyond his expectations, it encouraged him to think that all these savage Gauls could be won over or bribed.' The general's gaze returned to what was left of the embers in the brazier. 'At the time the bane of Melqart had descended upon him and he retired to his pavilion for two days.'

'The bane of what?' asked Sphax, now thoroughly confused.

'The bane of Melqart,' explained Maharbal, 'is how your uncle describes the black despair that descends on him from time to time. When in the grip of this stupor he shuns all company, lies on his divan and becomes dead to the world. When the bane descends he's incapable of any action, let alone of making a momentous decision.'

'How often does this happen, Sir?'

'Infrequently, praise ba 'al hamūn. But when the god takes him it can last for weeks. He swears it's because of the oath he made to his own father, your grandfather, Hamilcar Barca.'

'What oath?'

'When your uncle was a boy of nine he was taken by Hamilcar to the great temple of Baal in Carthage. On that sacred altar your grandfather sacrificed a lamb and then bade his son kneel and wash his hands in the blood of the animal. Then, in the presence of priests, he made him swear a solemn oath that to his dying day he would remain an enemy of Rome. This, your uncle claims, is the origin of his curse. The blessing, he has always told us, is that his life has a higher purpose rarely bestowed on mortals. He has been touched by fate and must follow the star of his destiny. But if he falters in this divine purpose through doubt or indecision, the wrath of Melqart will descend upon him as a punishment. This is his curse, Sphax, and because of it he is deserving of our pity and compassion. We are here in this bleak place at the will of Melqart, not your uncle. So be it. Our fate is ever in the hands of our gods.' The general finally smiled at him, indulgently. 'Now go and get some sleep, lad. You're going to need it for what's to come.'

Being careful not to wake Fionn, he quietly lay down on their sleeping couch and crept under the toga they always used as a blanket. Her breath was sweet and gentle. Something made him touch her cheek, and he tenderly ran his fingers down her face and removed a wisp of golden hair that had tumbled on to her forehead. Sleep didn't come easily that night.

* * *

His uncle had decided to change the entire disposition of the marching columns. So at daybreak all was chaos amidst a racket of orders and counter-orders, curses and argument. Now the Iberian cavalry were placed in the van, all six thousand of them, bristling with spears astride their dark-bay stallions. Behind these fearsome horsemen Hannibal and his officers were cajoling and struggling to get the heavy baggage-trains into place. Next came the bulk of the army, with the elephants and contingents from every race and nation around the Mediterranean, and after these the camp followers. Some, like Fionn and Ayzabel, were lucky to travel on horseback, but the vast majority toiled on foot. Behind these the Numidians were given charge of the strings of pack-trains and mule-trains, the army's lifeline, carrying everything from fodder and barley, to wine, tents and salted pork. Last of all, guarding the vulnerable rear came phalanx after phalanx of Libyan pikemen interspersed with Iberians from the north, hefting their great oval shields.

It was mid-morning before this great column was ready to slither forward like some mythical serpent born of Erebus, in a time before the gods. But Sphax saw nothing of this. By then he was seven miles ahead of the great serpent, in a wild place where the very air seemed thin and rare. And he felt strong, elated, the happiest of men. At last Maharbal had given him command and a mission. The command wasn't much, just a smallish half-eshrin of Numidians and the two Boii guides. But Maharbal himself had handpicked the men, including their best scouts Jugurtha and Hiram, and warriors of the calibre of his javelin teacher, Dubal.

For several miles they'd followed the broad valley of the Druentia north. At midday they halted to rest and quench their thirsts in another swift-flowing stream that flowed into the Druentia at a place where wide sandy flats were beginning to dry out after the recent floods. Their guides, Leuca and Uinda, told him they must follow this stream to its headwaters where they would find the pass over the mountains that would take them into Boii territory. This news filled him with joy, until further questioning revealed this final pass was still eight marches distant, perhaps even ten. Ten more days. Still, he thought, the end was at last in sight.

His orders were clear and unequivocal. He was to ride as swiftly as possible and scout as much of the path ahead as one day would allow, then return the following evening to make his report to his uncle. As well as a detailed description of the route, he had to find where the column would be at its most vulnerable to attack or ambush. If they encountered Tricorii warbands assembling, he was to send back the guides with a small escort, then stay hidden and shadow the enemy until he'd discovered their intentions. As this was a far more exciting prospect than a day's hard riding, Sphax had been praying for such an encounter, a sign from Artemis that the hunt was on. But so far he'd been disappointed.

The stream they'd been following now entered a narrow valley, the sides of which grew precipitously steeper with every step they took. Sphax's heart sank. This was familiar territory; a rocky ravine with towering cliff faces thickly wooded in pine and cedar. Jugurtha who was riding beside him scowled. 'This look familiar to you?'

'All too familiar. Perfect ambush country.' They rode more cautiously now, stopping every hundred strides or so to listen, then the guides began pointing to what looked like a shallow ford across the stream. Once across to the northern bank the track climbed steeply and soon left the cover of the trees behind and entered a bleak wilderness of boulders and rocky crags high above the ravine.

The mountainside was so steep here that one false step or stumble would result in a plunge into the ravine and certain death. They nudged their mares to a cautious walk and were forced into single file. Here the path was little better than a sheep track. Sphax judged it wide enough for elephants, bullock carts and wagons. But only just. Elephants were more surefooted than horses, so it wouldn't be a problem for them unless a particular animal had a fear of heights! Do elephants fear heights, he wondered? He smiled as the guides stopped and gingerly dismounted, preferring to lead their horses rather than risk a fall from them. His Numidians were scathing, and there was a great deal of laughter and banter.

'You're safer trusting four legs than your own two,' Sphax suggested. But the Boii were having none of it. They were poor horsemen at best, so he could understand their anxiety; the drop to their right sheered away so alarmingly it was virtually a precipice. Even skilled horsemen like Numidians would never have risked nudging their mares to a trot on this path.

Sphax trusted Dido so completely that he could leave her to it, freeing him to keep a sharp eye on his surroundings. High above them the ridge line was marked by a series of crags and cliffs that rose like battlements from the boulder-strewn hillside. He noticed the rock was a different colour from the gorge where they had fought the Allobroges. There it had been almost white in places, flecked with pink and pale green in bright sunlight. Here it was a uniform grey, the colour of a brooding sky before a winter storm. Looking across at the southern side of the valley, perhaps a mile distant, he could see that it was heavily forested and cleft with gullies and ravines that would make it impassable on horseback. Sphax guessed the riverbed was equally impassable, and that's why they had been guided onto this bleak mountainside.

All the while the path had been steadily climbing, but after three miles or so it shelved out on to a mossy knoll. Sphax halted them. From here the prospect was magnificent; a panoramic vista of mountains rising above a mosaic of valleys with glittering ribbons of rivers and streams. High above him, he watched as a peregrine plunged, drew in its wings and begun its dizzying stoop on the prey it had spied far below them.

What was absent from this vista were people, or any signs of their presence. 'Who has the sharpest eyes?' he asked.

'It used to be me,' answered Jugurtha, 'but now it's Hiram. He can tell you the colour of a lark's eye when it's soaring into the sky.' Hiram's boyish face lit up at this unexpected praise.

'Then look for smoke or flocks of sheep … anything! There's an army out there somewhere!' But Hiram saw nothing. At night it would be different, he suddenly realised. Campfires could not be hidden so

easily and men had to cook and stay warm in these
bitter nights. He would have to find a similar vantage
point after dark.

For the next few miles the sheep track gradually
descended until it came once more under the shelter of
the trees and they heard again the sound of gushing
water in the depths of the ravine. They crossed the
stream and followed its southern bank, stopping
frequently to listen and look for tracks in the sand
and mud. For the rest of the afternoon the only alarm
turned out to be a big stag they flushed in a birch
grove.

As the sun began to sink behind them Sphax
noticed the ravine was narrowing and closing in on
them. Trees grew so thickly here it was difficult to see
more than five strides ahead. Then the trees gave way
to a boulder-strewn clearing and ahead of them was an
extraordinary sight. It looked just like a giant doorway,
a doorway created by the gap between two towering
pillars of rock through which the stream gushed noisily
into the ravine. It strongly reminded Sphax of the
narrowest sections of the gorge where they had fought
the Allobroges, and he knew from bitter experience
that a small force could hold off an entire army if such
a natural feature was defended vigorously.

Once through that doorway it was as if they had
crossed the threshold into a different country. Here the
valley opened out into broad meadows and pastures
where farmers could sow crops and gather flocks. But

they saw neither farms nor flocks, and Sphax made a mental note that armies could also camp here.

They were beginning to lose the light and he was anxious to find some vantage point which could be scaled safely in the dark. He decided to take a chance and throw caution to the wind. He urged Dido into a canter and signalled his men to follow. Fast or slow, there was always the danger of blundering into a horde of warriors. At least they would be able to explore more of this valley, and that's what Maharbal had sent him out to do.

For three miles they made good progress up the valley, the guides keeping up as best they could. It was twilight when he halted and let their sweating mares rest and drink from the stream. He dismounted and began looking around, sensing that with every breath the air was growing colder as it lost the last warmth of the sun. He had stopped initially because he'd spotted a forested conical hill on the north side of the valley which would give him an excellent vantage point to look for campfires. There would be a half-moon tonight, enough light to climb the hill safely.

It was Dubal who found a place to camp, not two hundred paces from where they now stood. It was perfect. Hidden amongst pine trees he'd come upon the base of a sheer cliff that buttressed the north side of the valley. At its base a cave-like semi-circular shelf had been hollowed out of the cliff. A campfire in that hollow would not be seen from above or from anywhere higher up the valley, and the pine trees would shield it from the south. They had all brought thick woollen cloaks with them, but they were grateful for the fire and soon licking their lips and tossing lentils, onions and salted meat into a cauldron of steaming broth.

After filling his belly with some hot stew he tried to get some sleep. Hiram, who had volunteered for the first watch, had strict instructions to wake him when the moon had fully risen. He found sleep difficult, but must have nodded off because he awoke to being shaken by the lad.

Sphax looked up at the sky. There were scudding silvery clouds but he could still make out some stars and the pale moon had indeed risen. As his eyes adjusted to the darkness he found he could just make out the faint outline of hills to the south. Looking east up the valley he could also trace the course of the stream glittering in the moonlight. 'I'll relieve you when I get back and you can get some sleep. Stay awake!' he warned.

Sphax could see the top of the hill he was aiming for but there was no obvious path to follow. He would simply have to plunge into the forest and keep climbing. It was worse than he'd imagined. The pines were so dense and the moonlight so thin that he could barely see his hand before his face. The only faculty he could trust was his sense of direction. At least he knew where *up* was. So that's where he groped.

The climb was a nightmare, most of it spent dragging himself upwards from root to root on his hands and knees. It must have taken well over an hour and by the time he reached the treeless hilltop he was scratched, bleeding and cursing. For some moments he just lay there with his eyes closed, gasping for breath. Wearily he got to his feet and began to explore the boulder-strewn hilltop for a vantage point. He didn't need one. A blind man could have seen it. To the east, higher up the valley was a bright glow of golden light that could only be made by the fire from a thousand campfires. He'd found the Tricorii army: now the only problem was to determine how far away they were.

'You look terrible,' whispered Hiram when he caught sight of him. Sphax grimaced.

'Believe me, it feels even worse than it must look! Now go and get some sleep. At first light

we'll be shadowing savages.'

'You've found them!' Hiram exclaimed.

'Six miles higher up the valley. We need to send the guides back to report to Hannibal, but you and Jugurtha will stay with me. Now go and get some sleep.' Sphax was grateful to be left alone in the darkness. He had much to think about.

FOURTEEN

‘Nephew, you have returned at last!’ Hannibal was almost beaming. By the gods, thought Sphax, he'll be embracing me next! But in truth he was relieved to see his uncle still in that buoyant, cheerful mood he'd retained for some weeks; it meant his interrogation would not be so gruelling.

His uncle sat on his usual divan flanked by his Greek tutors. Maharbal and the Libyan general Hanno were also present. For the first time Hannibal seemed to notice the rents and tears in his cloak and tunic and the scratches on his face. ‘You look as if you've been dragged through a thorn bush,’ he remarked without sympathy.

‘I apologise for my appearance, Sir. Two nights ago I had to climb a mountain in the dark. But it was worth the inconvenience, for it was then that I discovered the enemy camp.’

‘Yesterday the Boii guides reported six thousand, drawn from three tribes besides the Tricorii. I suspect you have more news for me. Is this why you have returned?'

'Exactly so, Sir.' Sphax took a deep breath and gathered his thoughts. 'This morning Jugurtha discovered another warband with perhaps a thousand warriors.'

'Are they massing for battle, Nephew?'

'No, Sir, that's what's so puzzling, and why I decided to return. The Tricastini still remain massed as a single body, but the rest appear to be splitting up into warbands, each about five hundred strong. Jugurtha or Hiram have orders to return immediately and report any changes to these dispositions.' His uncle closed his eyes in that familiar gesture and sank back into the divan.

'So, we now face seven thousand Gauls who appear to be dividing their forces, yet still retaining a strong body of around five thousand warriors.' There was a slight pause before he continued. 'Have they broken camp?'

'I left at midday, Sir. There were no signs of it then.' His uncle's eyes flashed wide open and he stared intently.

'Describe our march tomorrow, Nephew. Spare nothing, even the most trivial of details.' Sphax begun his description, and except for the sound of his own voice, the only other noise in the room came from the crinkling of a parchment scroll Silenos appeared to be reading from. Sphax guessed this was the written description of the route the Greeks had compiled.

There was a long silence when he'd finished. He'd expected an exhausting session of questions, but there were none. Instead, his uncle asked abruptly, 'Where will they attack?' Sphax was taken aback by the directness of the question, so began hesitantly.

'There are any number of opportunities for ambush along the route, Sir. But if I were to choose a place and strategy, I would place a warband to block the entrance to that rocky doorway I described, hide my main body south of where we re-crossed the stream, wait until our van was engaged at the doorway then strike with my main body. We would be trapped, Sir, just as effectively as the Allobroges managed to trap us.' There was another moment of silence as everyone considered this.

'I see,' his uncle said at last. 'There, rather than the point where our army would be exposed on a bare mountainside, reduced to a walking pace and single file, on little more than a sheep track! It strikes me that it is precisely *there* that we would be at our most vulnerable.' Hannibal stared at him coldly, inviting contradiction. Frowning and shaking his head, his nephew duly obliged.

'It would be difficult to hide a host on that ridge, Sir, it is rocky and barren, and the mountainside is so steep that a charge down its slope would be almost impossible. They would stumble and fall into the ravine a mile below.' His uncle shrugged, still unconvinced.

'I would find a way, Nephew, if the gods offered me such a golden opportunity.'

'But you have genius, Sir. The best they have to offer is low cunning.' His uncle laughed at this outrageous piece of flattery.

'Remember, the enemy are dividing their forces. So we must expect several attacks. If they can coordinate them, and this may take some time. I need more information on these warbands. When will your scouts report?'

'Hiram will report to you tomorrow, Sir. No later.'

'Then it is my turn to flatter,' his uncle said with that peculiar half-smile of his. 'You have done well. Leave us now and rest.'

* * *

Sphax was relieved to find that Fionn and her servants had also erected their modest tent. Fionn took one look at him and insisted he hand over his tattered cloak and tunic for mending. It was bitingly cold in the tent. Sphax objected. She insisted. He only relented when his toga was found. Then she saw the extent of his cuts and bruises, so their servant Luli was sent to find ointment. He had to admit, lying back on their sleeping couch with Fionn's warm hands gently caressing the knitbone oil into every cut and bruise, that this pleasure almost made up for that terrible climb. Even the odour, though earthy and pungent, was not unpleasant.

He reported to Maharbal at first light, the camp already alive and bustling with activity as tents were being taken down and wagons stowed with everything from cooking pots to carpets, the air thick with the smell of oats being roasted over campfires. Maharbal was giving orders, surrounded by the chiefs of his Iberian cavalry. He noticed the Master of Elephants was present amongst the group. Strange, he thought, wondering what was going on. Hiempsal was the last to leave, ruffling Sphax's hair as he strode passed.

Maharbal caught sight of him and grinned. 'Not everyone is astute enough to recognize your uncle's genius. Bask in that sunshine!' The general took one look at Sphax's wincing embarrassment and burst into great guffaws of laughter. 'Don't worry, lad, it won't last. It never does.'

'What's that old rogue Hiempsal, doing here, Sir?' he asked, eager to change the subject.

'After your great lesson in strategy last night, your uncle thought it wise for our elephants to lead out our van and terrify the savages into submission. You see the influence you now have on our higher strategy!' There was always a wicked edge of sarcasm to Maharbal's teasing, but Sphax knew the general delighted in such harmless mischief. He made light of most things in this world, so it became impossible to take offence at his banter.

'Seriously, Sir, what are my duties today?'

'Seriously! Duties!' Maharbal mocked, 'what has happened to that reckless, carefree young man I met beside the Rhodanus?'

'He is older, Sir.'

'And perhaps wiser? We shall see.' In an instant the general's expression changed. 'Our Numidians are nursemaiding the pack-trains so there's not much to do. If the savages strike it will be either at the front or the rear, or both at the same time if they can co-ordinate such an attack. Which I doubt. Everything else is in the hands of ba 'al hamūn.' Maharbal glanced over at the Iberians who were beginning to mount their big stallions. 'Why don't you ride with that lovely lady of yours for a few days? I'm sure she will be glad of your company, and Merbal's eshrin will not be far behind if you're needed.'

Dawn had promised another grey day of rain and sleet. So it proved, but by mid-morning the threatening clouds retreated and the sun shone more brightly than it had for weeks. Sphax felt the cold more than Fionn. Whilst he was constantly wrapped in his beaver-skin cloak and Cavari leggings, she was quite content to ride in her pretty rose-pink cape over her stola. By the time they were splashing across the stream to its northern bank he was sweating. A novel experience latterly! He slid from Dido and filled all their canteens from the stream, and insisted they encourage the horses to drink. Once beyond the trees he knew it was a steep climb up the mountainside to the mossy knoll at the top, and then it would be a good few miles before they descended to re-join the stream once more.

Since mid-morning Ayzabel had run out of things to tease him about and had grown bored with flirting, so all morning she and Fionn had prattled away on their favourite topic; the eligible young men in Idwal's household. Although Idwal himself was rather aloof and not at all sociable, Drust and Cáel were frequent visitors to both their households. Fionn and Ayzabel were incorrigible matchmakers. And so they had prattled on happily all morning, leaving him free to ride ahead or laugh at some of their more improbable suggestions.

By now they had ridden out from beneath the trees on to the bare mountainside. From here it looked almost vertical, but Sphax knew this to be a trick of perspective. He noticed Fionn looking up in alarm. Ahead of them groups of women, some with babes in arms or clutching the hands of young children, had already formed themselves into a ragged, single-file column that was making its way up the mountainside. Higher up he saw two abandoned wagons that had lost wheels or axles and were now causing bottlenecks for the people waiting to climb around them. Sphax never imagined such chaos when he'd ridden this stretch three days ago, but he estimated that since dawn, twenty thousand feet and probably double that number of hooves had churned this track into a mud slick.

He halted his little group and slid from Dido. 'It's single file from here. I want all the servants to walk ahead and everyone must stay together. Ayzabel, Fionn and I will ride behind at a pace you set for us. It's a long way to the top so don't set off too quickly. If you wish to stop and rest, all you have to do is raise your hand and we'll all stop together.' He'd spoken calmly, forcing himself to smile with a confidence he wasn't feeling, knowing full well that a false step here would result in a fatal fall down the mountainside. 'Does everybody understand?' They all nodded.

Behind them a group of about forty men and women were trying to push their way past. Sphax strode over and pointed his saunion at the throat of a man wearing a grubby brown tunic. 'You will all wait here until I've spoken to my people.' With that the man took a hasty step backwards and the rest of them froze. They looked like a random collection of servants, cooks and tradespeople, some leading horses and donkeys. Sphax pointed at Dido with his saunion then raised it threateningly. 'If anyone tries to overtake my mare I'll stick this in their guts and feed their entrails to the crows. Is that clear?' They either nodded sheepishly or stared at the ground.

Ayzabel was an experienced horsewoman and didn't seem at all worried at the prospect of riding up a mountainside, but he could see Fionn biting back tears, and her face had turned ashen. 'It's really not as bad as it looks,' he said, gently taking Brega's reins from her hands. 'You won't need these. Brega is a gentle and placid creature. He will gladly carry you up this hill without you having to instruct him.' Placing her hands on the horns of the saddle, he said 'Just let him follow Ayzabel's mare. Do you see that knoll up there?'

She squinted upwards, nodding. 'Keep your eyes fixed on it. Don't look anywhere else and don't look down. Once we reach that knoll it's all downhill to the river. Be brave, my love.' Their servants were now a hundred paces up the track. 'Off you go Ayzabel, let's catch up with our footsloggers.'

To begin with he walked beside Brega, talking to Fionn about any nonsense that came into his head. But after half a mile or so he began to relax. He could see that she'd settled perfectly into Brega's easy rhythm and horse and rider were now swaying as one. Mounting Dido he kept pace close behind her. A little later she confidently turned around in the saddle and grinned at him proudly and he was relieved to see the colour had returned to her cheeks. Negotiating the abandoned wagons proved much easier than he'd feared. He made Fionn and Ayzabel dismount, then led their horses around the wagons for them.

They had almost made it to the top when a forest of hands begun to be raised and he realised the footsloggers would never make it to the knoll without a rest. Six hundred paces above him he saw the reassuring sight of sixty Iberian caetrati, basking in the unexpected sunshine. He handed a couple of canteens of water to the servants now stretched out on the turf above the path. And that's when the savages chose to attack.

There was no warning. No battle cries, no screaming, no din of wailing carnyx. Nothing. All that came later.

What came first were great boulders. A torrent of rock and stone rolling down the mountainside that tore into men, women and beasts with a sickening crump, then tossed them like rags into the abyss below. The screams of mothers, children, cooks and fletchers, carpenters, donkeys and mules echoed all around him. It took Sphax some moments to gather his wits, realize this was not a rock fall and cast his gaze upwards. Lining the top of the ridge he saw there were hundreds of Tricorii warriors hurling or dislodging the boulders that were raining down death on them.

Hannibal had been right all along. A sheep track on a mountainside! It was a golden opportunity too good to miss. So the savages had found a way.

'Run to the Iberians,' he screamed at their servants, pointing towards the knoll. 'Run for your lives. Go! Go! Go!' Fionn and Ayzabel were gaping at him, paralysed with fear astride their horses. A horse was such a big target. 'Get down,' he yelled at them, 'get off your horses.' He leapt to grab Fionn from the saddle. Ayzabel had already dismounted and was staring at him, frozen to the spot. Once Fionn was firmly on her feet he gave Ayzabel's mare an almighty slap on her rump and she leapt up the track. He did the same to Brega then turned to Dido. 'Flee, Dido ... flee!' She obeyed instantly. 'Now it's your turn, Ayzabel. Run to the soldiers up there. We'll follow you. Run, Ayzabel. Run!' She suddenly came to her senses, turned and stumbled up the track.

Spears were being thrown now but were mercifully falling short. Warriors must be coming down from the heights, he realised. He looked up just in time to see a boulder the size of a cauldron careering straight at them. Throwing Fionn to the ground he lay on top of her as it whistled miraculously over their heads. Sphax dragged her to her feet and they started up the track. He was holding his saunion and javelin in his right fist, which meant he only had his left free to drag Fionn along, but his sword had been strapped to Dido and he wasn't about to throw away his only weapons.

Looking up he saw that a few warriors were making their way down the mountainside, but it was steep, and their progress slow. The rest remained at the top, jeering at them whilst loosening yet more deadly boulders. Sphax thought they still had time to reach the safety of the knoll. But then, in absolute horror, he saw what was happening to the pack-trains on the track below. He realised they had only moments to get off the track. A stampede of pack animals was thundering towards them.

On the first night of the Cerealia Festival, Romans tie flaming firebrands to the tails of foxes and release them in the Circus. Driven into a wild frenzy of pain and terror, such a madness comes over them that they hurl themselves into crowds or at bystanders, howling into the night. Now he saw the same thing happening below him. Only these were not foxes, but pack horses and mules, heavier than men, hundreds of them, driven wild and crazy by the landslide of rocks thundering down on them. And their instinct was to stampede.

Down was too steep, he thought. They would have to climb upwards and take their chances with the savages. 'Climb,' he yelled, yanking her off the track. 'Lift up the skirts of your stola and climb!' he pleaded.

'Stop breaking the bones in my hand and I will!' she cried.

He let go of her hand. In that instant she was struck in the chest by a rock and bowled backwards.

He watched, frozen in a heartbeat of abject horror as her body was tossed down the mountainside like some bundle of rose-pink rags. Then she was gone.

He crouched there in dumb shock, staring after her. Then the agony raged through his breast like a tempest and he screamed. 'No! No! No!' He was on his knees now, wailing, in the grip of a pain so real and searing it was as if he'd been pierced by a blade.

And it was only because Sphax was on his knees, with his head buried in his hands, that he was saved from suffering the same fate as Fionn. For in that instant scores of frenzied horses driven mad with terror stampeded past him, their hoofs avoiding the prone body on the ground. If he'd been standing, he would have been bowled over and cast into the abyss. Until the animals were utterly spent and could run no more, hundreds suffered this fate that afternoon.

Then he was suddenly alone, surrounded by a deathly silence. Sphax knew the warriors must still be at the top of the ridge. Men would be fighting. Men would be killing and dying. War was all around him, but he didn't hear it or see it. And it was of no concern to him. Sphax had only one thought now. He must find her. The thought of just leaving her out there, alone and abandoned was unbearable. He would find Fionn and hold her. One last time.

He slid down the mountainside on his back, digging the points of his javelin and saunion into the turf to control his descent. He soon lost sight of the track above him and below he could now see the pines and cedars that cloaked the bottom of the ravine. All he remembered later was that the point of his saunion struck a rock and slid off, taking him with it. His head swam sickeningly as he was tossed over and over as his descent quickened. There was a sudden searing pain, then nothing.

FIFTEEN

As golden sunlight filtered through the Elysian green high above him, for a blessed instant he imagined he'd joined Artemis in the hunt that would last for all eternity. Then memory and pain flooded through his body like a torrent. Not the pain from the bruises on his thigh and leg, but a deeper, bitter anguish. He had let go of her hand, and now she was gone. Fionn was dead. And he must find her.

Sphax had no idea how long he'd lain there, senseless. The sun was a good deal lower, so he judged it to be the middle of the afternoon. He was jammed against the great ochre trunk of the pine tree that had arrested his fall, his javelin and saunion lying beside him. Painfully he got to his feet and limped forward. Amongst the trees the slope was not as fearsome as it was on the mountainside, but it was steep enough to warrant caution and he trod warily, holding on to roots or anything that would give him purchase. He'd gone no more than forty paces when he stopped dead. He was looking over a precipice into the void, the edge of a cliff that fell vertically to the floor of the ravine sixty paces below. There was nothing for it; he would have to follow its edge until he found some way down.

Above him there looked to be some sort of goat track that kept to the cliff's edge, so he followed it, his right leg and thigh throbbing with pain. That's when he started to come upon the bodies. Men, women and children, horses and mules, all smashed and broken by their fall. He came upon a horse that was still alive, wedged between two pines and had to put the poor creature out of its misery with his saunion. Gradually he noticed that the track was descending, and eventually it met a tree-lined gulley that sloped steeply to the floor of the ravine. Sphax fell again here, his right leg suddenly giving way, but all he suffered were a few fresh bruises.

When he got to his feet he heard the stream bubbling from somewhere behind him and realised his throat was so parched he could hardly swallow. The ice-cold water was refreshing and revived him a little. Now he retraced his steps westwards, following the base of the cliff. Bodies lay everywhere. He tried to avoid looking at them after a while, averting his eyes and gingerly stepping over them. He would know when he found her.

And there she was. Just a bundle of blue and rose-pink rags, beneath the branches of a young cedar tree, hard by the stream. When he caught sight of her face and blood-bathed hair he turned away, retching and spewing. For a time he knelt with his hands over his face, sobbing uncontrollably. Willing himself to his feet he covered her face with her cape and gently wrapped her stola around her like a winding sheet. Sphax knew now what he must do.

Fionn was a Gaul from the northern lands. Sphax had learned from Idwal and Drust many of their customs and beliefs. At death her body should be burned on a pyre that would release her immortal soul to the heavens. He had neither the means nor the time for this. Yet he could not bear to leave her to the mercy of wild beasts and vultures. Sphax had once done this. But he had not loved that man.

Idwal had once told him that some Gauls place the dead in rock passages, deep within a mound of earth. He could not give his love a mound of earth, but he would give her rock and stone. Collecting rocks from the streambed he began to surround her in stones, the largest he could carry. Before he began to rest stones on her body he removed the oval fibulae clasp set with carnelian stones she had bought in Arretium, the day he'd fallen in love with her. One last time he buried his cheek on her breast, then with tears in his eyes began solemnly covering her in stones.

Dusk was falling as he completed his labours. Fionn had her mound of stone. Until the end of all time no beast or bird of the air would desecrate her loveliness.

* * *

Sphax could never recall much of his journey from twilight into the gathering darkness. He remembered following the sound of bubbling water upstream. It was a clear night and the moon rose and the stars shone, but amongst the trees in the depths of the ravine he could see no further than a step ahead, so he limped and stumbled forward, ever eastwards. Silence seemed to have descended on the place, a silence as deep and impenetrable as Tartarus, for he heard neither the screech of owls nor the scurrying of night creatures. The last thing he remembered was being overcome by a weariness so profound that he simply stopped, curled himself up into a ball on a mossy bank and closed his eyes.

It was raining steadily when he opened them. Shrouds of mist swirled under the trees and above the streambed. By the time he cupped his hands to drink from the stream he was shivering and already soaked to the skin. His right leg felt stiff and throbbed with pain. Untying the draw-string of his leggings he examined it carefully. There was bruising from hip to ankle, but nothing seemed broken. He was lucky. He was alive. And that thought brought back another stab of pain.

The light seemed strange, unnatural, yet as far as the mist would allow he could see through the trees and across the ravine. Somewhere above the sun had surely risen, though there was no sign of it that morning. No bird sang or animal stirred. The only sounds were those of water, either gushing in the streambed or dripping from every leaf and branch as the rain fell incessantly.

As the morning wore on the mist slowly dispersed and he caught glimpses of a sullen grey sky above his head. But without a sight of the sun he couldn't even be sure it was morning. He had no idea how long he'd slept and by now he'd lost all sense of time. He was looking for the ford where the track came down from the mountainside and crossed the stream, but Sphax wasn't even sure he would recognise it coming from this direction. When he did eventually stumble upon it there could be no mistake. A river of oozing mud stretched upwards through the trees, churned by thousands of feet.

At least he knew where he was now. Sphax remembered riding a good few miles before the ravine narrowed to form that rock doorway he'd described to his uncle. Only the gods knew how long it would take him on foot.

Other than the dead, there had been no sight or sound of people. He began to wonder what had happened yesterday. Where was everyone? An army couldn't just disappear. Had the battle been lost? On such narrow tracks their columns must have straggled for over twenty miles from van to rear. But he'd been in the middle of this column, in the middle of the entire army. Behind him were the pack trains and his Numidians, not to mention the rear-guard phalanxes of Libyans and Iberians. All twenty thousand of them! Surely all of them could not have overtaken him when he'd gone in search of Fionn? Had they marched through the night? Was he the last straggler?

And what of Dido? His thoughts had been turning increasingly to the fate of his mare. Sphax prayed fervently to the goddess that Dido had been spared. Would those of his party that survived take care of her? Ayzabel would, he was certain of that. If she lived.

Then there was the enemy. Where were the Tricorii? Ready to ambush in some birch grove up ahead? Hiding? Skulking? They were no better than woman-killers, child-killers, lower than dogs with less scruple than wild beasts. The bastards would pay, and pay dearly! He would have his revenge! He swore it out loud to Artemis, a sacred oath that would be paid for in blood, and his words echoed around the ravine. He begged the goddess to show him their hiding places so he could slaughter them. He would sink his saunion into their rancid flesh, then tear them limb from limb. They would die. All of them! He realised the knuckles gripping his weapons had turned a bloodless white. For some reason Elpis's fatherly voice came into his head with soothing, calming reasonableness. 'This is *khŏesthai*, young man,' the voice told him. 'You are confusing anger with grief. Like Achilles, you must turn your rage into grief and recognise it for what it is. Passion unbridled invites the nemesis of the gods, not their sympathy and guidance.' Had his teacher ever said this to him? Sphax couldn't remember.

He was shivering from the cold, dripping wet and miserable when at last he saw the great stone doorway, half a mile ahead. He had seen only the dead for over a day, and they were neither friend nor foe, but now he could hear voices up ahead. Friend or foe? Sphax's spirits were at such a low ebb that he cared little about either outcome; if they were Tricorii he would kill them, if not he would beg food and shelter. It was as simple as that.

It was *friend*. Iberian caetrati in their distinctive white tunics. A score of them had drawn the short straw that day and been given sentry duty guarding the entrance to the ravine. They were more concerned with staying dry than their duties, but nevertheless they were alert enough to reach for their falcata as he approached. Despite his sopping beaver-skin cloak and Gallic leggings, one look at his jet-black curls and the colour of his skin would convince anyone that he was not a Gaul. Sphax couldn't understand a word they were saying, but he could recognize variations of the word Numidian in most languages, and that's what they were shouting at him. He nodded, and with capering gestures two men seemed to take it upon themselves to escort him to someone who would understand him.

They led him to a crude shelter of canvas stretched over wooden poles the height of a man. A gust of wind would have sent the flimsy contraption crashing to the ground, but today there was no wind, just the incessant rain, and underneath this canopy it was mercifully dry.

Sitting astride a bench under this shelter was another caetrati, but he was wearing a fancy bronze helmet and polished greaves and spoke perfect high-born Punic. 'A Numidian, eh?'

Sphax stood there nodding, a puddle of water collecting at his feet. 'The Numidians rode through here this morning. They said there had been a terrible fight on the mountain. Some of them had women and children on their horses! Women and children! My men had such a laugh! Carthalo told me yesterday that our caetrati had seen off all the savages by mid-day. By the look of you I don't suppose you saw much fighting yesterday. Left behind, were you?'

Sphax guessed this sneering young captain to be in his early twenties. He had an air of un-deserved arrogance about him. Obviously some Carthaginian noble that had been foisted on these poor Iberians by his uncle to curry favour with some family back in Carthage. Sphax disliked him, instinctively. He was delighted to hear that his Numidians had rescued women and children, but otherwise there was little in the captain's manner that delighted him. He sat down wearily astride the bench and glared.

'That's strange,' he said mildly, 'I came upon scores of caetrati yesterday, and they were certainly not fighting savages. But the dead can't, can they? Corpses can't even raise their own pricks, let alone a falcata!'

'Who are you?' the man asked, shifting awkwardly on the bench.

'I am Sphax, son of Navaras, Prince of Numidia and nephew of Hannibal Barca. And now, you arrogant shitload of horse-dung, I want you to tell me everything you know about yesterday and every scrap of rumour that's passed your way since then. Is that clear?' Miraculously, bread, cheese and wine soon appeared, which Sphax devoured whilst listening intently.

What Sphax heard made perfect sense, but left the most important question unanswered. The Tricorii and their allies had attacked in several places yesterday, at times completely severing the route of the march, cutting off and isolating some of its columns. Hardly surprising, thought Sphax, they had been stretched so thin yesterday. Hannibal himself had been cut off for a while and spent the night on some rock higher up the valley. All afternoon there had been a stiff fight nearby in the narrow entrance to the ravine, but their caetrati, or rather Cathalo's caetrati Sphax suspected, had driven them off with great slaughter. How many attacked, he'd asked? And received an answer that suggested two hundred, or at most three hundred savages. Just a warband, thought Sphax.

He cast his mind back to those terrible events on the mountainside yesterday. Everything had happened so quickly, but whenever he'd looked up at the ridge he'd seen scores, not hundreds of warriors, and certainly not thousands of them. It was a long ridge, but he doubted if more than three hundred of them could have been hiding amongst the crags at the top. They didn't need more than that to start those deadly avalanches. Three hundred could do the work of thousands! So again, they had probably been attacked by a single warband. The picture that was emerging was that the enemy had attacked with at least three separate warbands at different places along their march. That accounted for no more than nine hundred warriors. Where were the rest of them? Jugurtha had come up with an estimate of seven thousand. So where were they? Six thousand battle-crazed savages couldn't stay hidden for long.

Then he understood. They had not been attacked by the Tricorii yesterday, but by warbands from each of their allies, on ground they knew best. The Tricorii had attacked elsewhere, all six thousand of them! The only section of the army not accounted for was their rear-guard. Sphax had questioned the captain closely; he had neither seen the Libyans nor had any news of them. But that's where the Tricorii had unleashed their warriors yesterday. Sphax was certain of it now. Armies marched with their straggling baggage trains at the rear. That's where the plunder was. And that's where low cunning suggested they would strike. But they had been tricked!

He had to admire his uncle's cunning and foresight. Three days ago everyone had grumbled and argued about it, but Hannibal had insisted, and completely reorganised the marching columns so that the heavy baggage was directly behind his powerful vanguard of cavalry, including the elephants. Even the pack-trains were in the middle of the columns, protected by Numidians. And where had his uncle placed his most powerful and trusted forces? The man was either very lucky, or indeed a genius. Even so, Sphax prayed silently that their Libyan and Iberian pikemen of the rear-guard had seen the savages off.

It was far too late to do anything about it now. Reinforcements would not change the outcome of a battle that had been decided yesterday. They would discover the fate of Hanno, his uncle Mago and the rest of the rear-guard soon enough. Twenty thousand against six were hopeful odds.

'Do you know where the Numidians are camped, captain?' he asked.

'About three miles up the valley, where it next broadens out.'

'And what are your orders, if I may enquire?'

'Cathalo has told me to hold this place until our rear-guard arrives,' he answered irritably. 'The laggards should have arrived today. Only the gods know what's keeping the lazy bastards.' Quite, thought Sphax, offering up another silent prayer to the goddess that they'd prevailed.

'Since our little *unpleasantness*, captain, you have been most courteous and I thank you for it. But I have one last favour to ask.' Sphax mustered a smile from somewhere. 'May I borrow a horse? It will be returned to you tomorrow, you have my word.' To Sphax's relief, this most unpleasant of men nodded, wanting to be shot of him as soon as possible.

The only family left to him now were in that Numidian camp. As he slid into the saddle and nudged the creature eastwards, he realised that from now on, this was the closest he would ever get to the feeling of going home.

Fionn's servants Cesti and Lulin were waiting for him beside a campfire. To his great joy and relief, Dido stood beside them, nickering and affectionately nuzzling his neck in greeting. Even Brega had come through, but at the sight of him Sphax felt a new stab of pain. Ayzabel was safe, but many of their servants had fallen. When he told them of Fionn's death they began wailing. Nothing more was said that evening and the three of them slept huddled together beside the fire.

* * *

In the days that followed he ate, sometimes slept, took messages and obeyed orders, all in a desolate state of emptiness. It was as if the world had lost something of its substance, its reality, or that he himself was numb to it. He spoke only to relay a message or pass on an order, for the rest remaining silent, riding between the camps all day until his body ached with a weariness that would ensure some sleep. 'Listen to my silence,' the ancients had said, but Sphax's silence sprang from nothing more profound than dumb grief.

Hannibal had called a halt for a few days so the army could rest and be gathered together after its ordeal. Great numbers of stragglers, both men and horses, returned to the camps every day. The only thing he really noticed was the cold. It had snowed heavily every day, freezing at night so that men and horses slithered and stumbled on each day's fresh layer of ice, whilst the cold gnawed away at every bone in his body.

Everyone had been kind. Even Maharbal had tears in his eyes as he'd embraced him and thanked him for saving Ayzabel. Idwal spent most evenings sitting beside him around their campfire, telling him about the events of the day and trying to encourage his friend. Drust also did his best. The only person who seemed to be avoiding him was his uncle, who instead showered him with gifts. Sphax had lost everything that day. All his possessions, including most of rat-face's coins and silver lay smashed or scattered, somewhere at the bottom of that ravine. He cared not. But every day a couch or table, oil lamp or fine woollen cloak arrived from his uncle. In the end Cesti and Lulin didn't know what to do with it all so he began to give it away. What he truly ached for could never be returned to him.

And he was not alone. Widows and widowers stalked the camps bearing their grief. A shadow had fallen over the army that day. So many had been lost. Amongst the Numidians, his dearest friend Merbal had fallen, along with a score of officers and men he counted as friends. It was worse amongst the Libyans and Iberians. The rear-guard had faced the entire Tricorii nation that day, assailed and attacked on every side, trapped like hunted beasts beside the stream in a narrow, rock-walled section of the ravine. Grimly they had fought their way out, but at such a terrible cost that now their ranks were decimated. But the savages' hatred knew no bounds. They too had been slaughtered in their thousands and the survivors were now bent on revenge. Not a day passed without some marauding band of savages assaulting one of their camps.

And then there was Cesti and Lulin. He'd never really noticed them before, but now they took charge of him, fussing and clucking like mother hens. Both were some years older than him, plump and pretty with rosy cheeks, raven haired curls and skin not much paler than his. He'd never wanted servants, it was Fionn who had insisted on keeping them, but now he was grateful for their company.

Maharbal had given him Merbal's eshrin, but the command gave him little joy. Two weeks ago he would have been insufferable with pride and self-regard, but now it seemed meaningless, just another burden to shoulder. 'I'm not fit to be an officer,' he confessed bitterly to Idwal one night as they sat beside the brazier in his spacious new pavilion, another gift from his uncle. They had been back on the march for several uneventful days. 'I'll never be able to fill Merbal's shoes. His men worshipped him. By the gods, I loved him too!' he cried with feeling. 'He was like a father to me, always wise and forgiving. His first thought was always his men, he cared for them, looked after their welfare. Me ... I'm useless, just a burden to them. They look at me with pity in their eyes'.

'And so they should,' said his friend, gently. 'Fionn has been in her grave but a week. They know you are suffering. You must be patient. They will be patient also, and give you time to heal. Trust me, Sphax. Give it time.' Idwal stood and embraced him. 'I must go and check if my sentries are still awake,' he said as he turned to leave.

SIXTEEN

Sphax was woken before dawn by a howling wind so violent that it threatened to tear the pavilion from the ground. Untying the flaps securing the vestibule entrance he gingerly peered out. He could see no further than a hand before his face. It was snowing heavily and the blizzard seemed to be driving and swirling snowflakes in every direction at the same time. Putting on almost every stitch of clothing he possessed he braved the elements and went in search of his men.

He was soon flipped onto his backside. At least a hand's length of snow had fallen during the night, but under this soft layer his boots had met solid ice, sending him sliding arsewards. Only when there was a slight lull in the blizzard could he see anything in front of him, so mostly he blundered forwards, sliding and lurching through the blinding whirlwind, trusting to where he remembered his eshrin's camp was located.

What had taken him sixty strides last night became a fearful ordeal this morning. By the time he arrived at the little line of tents he was frozen to the bone and his teeth were chattering like door-slaves. The little he could see through the whirlwind was already a calamity. Two tents had disappeared, ripped from the ground by the blizzard, their frozen inhabitants huddling together around the four tents that still remained upright. And these were flapping so wildly they looked as if they might be torn from their moorings with the next icy blast.

He spotted Agbal crouching before one of the tents, swathed from head to foot in borrowed cloaks. 'Tell the men to join me in my pavilion,' he yelled over the howling gale. 'But first they must take down their tents, otherwise they'll lose them in this wind.' Moving down the line of tents he repeated the message to the men huddled outside. Soon everyone was hauling on ropes, storing poles or folding the coarse hemp fabric as best they could in the freezing squalls of snow. Gathering up their weapons and meagre possessions the first group followed him back to his pavilion. Cesti and Lulin screamed at the sight of six men barging through the vestibule entrance and dived beneath their mountains of furs. 'You two better get up,' he shouted above the ribald comments, 'we have visitors.'

With his head bowed low against the driving snow he re-traced his tracks and helped take down the last two tents. There was now a straggling column of frozen Numidians shuffling between their camp and his pavilion, carrying everything from grindstones to tent poles. As Sphax fastened the last of the ropes that secured the vestibule entrance he was met with the sight of twenty-four shivering Numidians huddled together in a pavilion designed for a high-born Libyan, his servants and a few evening guests. Cesti and Lulin, now respectably dressed, were handing out spare furs and cloaks to anyone in need. He noticed Jugurtha was swathed in his best toga, the one Idwal had given him, and the luxuriant Seleucid carpet – another gift from his uncle – was already sodden. The air smelt stale and damp, as if they were sheltering a flock of wet sheep rather than an eshrin of Numidians. But his pavilion had been made from finely woven linen and was far less likely to succumb to the blizzard than their crude tents, and Hannon had already organized a party to secure additional guide-ropes and pegs to make sure this didn't happen. The next problem was food, thought Sphax.

It turned out that his Numidians were old hands at *borrowing* and *scrounging*. Soon they had the brazier lit with a mixture of dry wood and charcoal. Only the gods knew how they'd got their hands on charcoal. For weeks in the camp it had fetched a higher price than gold! Soon barley was being roasted and ground to make the flat loaves which were the men's staple fare. Sphax himself scoured every pavilion thereabouts, haggling and begging for wine, cheese, pork, smoked fish, anything he could get hold of. None of them went hungry that day, or the next.

Sphax was concerned for their mares. He sent out parties every few hours to check they had fodder and water, and their tethered lines were secure. They returned with grim stories of frozen bodies, human and animal, covered by snowdrifts, of men and women huddled together behind anything that offered shelter from the howling blizzard.

No one noticed the sun rise or set that day, or the next. Beyond the skin of fine linen that sheltered them from the storm, the heavens had become a seething vortex of white, where day or night meant nothing any longer. It lasted for almost two days.

At twilight on the following evening the snowstorm abated just as swiftly as it had begun. Men gingerly poked their heads out of tents or wagons and carts, to look upon the catastrophe that had befallen them. Beneath the huge drifts of snow lay men and beasts, frozen solid in their icy tombs. Everything not secured by good hemp rope had been scattered to the winds, and everything that should have remained dry was soaked and sodden. His Numidians found one of their tents almost a mile away, stiff as iron, caught on the frozen branches of a thorn bush. Although many of the mules and pack animals had perished from want of care by their masters, those of the Iberians and Numidians who had found fodder and tended their horses had survived the ordeal. To their eternal credit, Hiempsal and his mahouts had not lost a single elephant.

* * *

When they set out next morning they looked more like
a ragged horde of survivors from some natural disaster
than an invading army, ready to take on the might of
Rome. Dirty and unshaven, hair wild and unkempt,
flea-ridden and half-starved, they resembled the wild
savages they had been fighting rather than the neat
uniformed ranks that had set out from the Rhodanus
two months ago. Back at the Island comrades had
laughed and scoffed at Sphax's Cavari leggings and
beaver-skin cloak, but now these Gallic braccae were
a commonplace sight on Libyan, Iberian or Numidian,
and a cloak of fur had become an essential item of
survival. Even his uncle sported a great bearskin cloak,
so it would not be unreasonable to say that his army
had been clothed by their enemies. The dead had little
need of clothing.

Sphax and Adherbal's eshrins now shared the van.
Maharbal's Iberians were suffering, many of their big
stallions having broken down or gone lame, struggling
with the relentless cold and rugged terrain. They were
proving no match for the thoroughbred jennets and
Egyptian mares of the Numidians, whose surefooted
gait would carry them from dawn to dusk, indifferent
to rain, snow or terrain.

Sphax had ridden all morning beside the Boii
guides Leuca and Uinda. In these desolate mountains
there was little danger of attack or ambush. No Gauls
lived in these high places and the only living creatures
they glimpsed were ibex and circling eagles. The only

misfortune they faced was the prospect of taking a wrong path, and the guides were there to make sure this didn't happen.

'Almost the last leg, Sphax,' said Uinda, and pointing ahead; 'when we round those rocks you will see the mountain and the pass over it.' When they reached that vantage point Sphax halted Dido and gaped upwards, frozen in horror, an expression shared by the score of Numidians all around him. It looked unscalable, a towering snow-bound peak that seemed to soar vertically in its efforts to join the clouds.

'But ...' he began, dumbfounded, 'we can't climb that!' Leuca laughed.

'Of course we're not going to climb it, you slackhead! Do you see that dip below the great buttress of rock leading to the summit? That's the pass, to the right of those pinnacles.' Sphax could make out the jagged fingers of rock, but he would hardly describe the space between those pinnacles and the towering peak as a *dip*!

'We'll never get our horses up there, Leuca. It's impossible!'

'You managed it, didn't you boy?' he taunted, stroking the neck of his stallion and grinning at the Numidians staring at him in disbelief. The guide was evidently enjoying their alarm, but to his Numidians, the suggestion that the Gaul's graceless stallion was in any way superior to their mares was deeply offensive. Nothing more was said on the subject, and they resumed the journey in pointed silence.

By late afternoon they reached a remarkable feature that became their camping ground that evening. Beneath the great stone buttress of the peak lay a broad flat plateau that stretched for a mile in every direction. They found fresh water in streams and standing pools, but what was even more remarkable lay under the snow.

Once they had cleared away the soft fresh snow from the surface and broken up the layers of ice below, they exposed rich patches of mountain turf, mosses and lichens. After the stale fodder their mares had survived on for the last week this turned out to be a banquet, so the horses were untethered and left to graze and feast. When the rest of their columns began to arrive the Numidians grabbed whatever tools they could lay their hands on and set to work with a will. Soon, large areas of this bleak plateau had been cleared of snow and men feasted their eyes, like their horses, on the pleasant sight of greenery. It was like a reminder of the spring to come, and it filled them with hope.

Sphax was looking out for Cesti and Lulin. Yesterday he'd managed to persuade both of them to mount Brega and trust to his steady gait. Seeing the two of them nervously huddled together on the back of the big stallion was a slightly comic sight, but nevertheless a welcome one. All around him he could now hear the familiar sounds of a camp being established, and on this day, of all days, it felt especially comforting, for his journey was almost at an end.

* * *

'Now is the time for you to eat your words, Master Sphax.' It was Uinda, the Boii guide, who was gloating.

Maharbal, Sphax and a dozen Numidian officers were staring up at a track that weaved its way up the seemingly sheer mountainside. Granted it was steep, thought Sphax, but despite the patches of snow and ice it was perfectly serviceable, and easily wide enough for their elephants. They would have to dismount from their mares and step carefully, but it was no worse than many such stretches they'd encountered before.

'If words would fill my belly with nourishment, Uinda, I would happily eat them,' he sighed. 'You are perfectly right of course, and I was wrong. But it gladdens my heart to think that by tomorrow we'll have seen the last of these wretched mountains and the only sight of them will be over our shoulder. I for one don't intend to look backwards when we reach the other side.'

'Nor me!' agreed Adherbal with feeling.

'You two sound like a pair of old cocksuckers! We still have to climb the damned thing. What are you waiting for? Organize your men.' Maharbal could always be relied upon to see situations with a directness few could match.

But Sphax couldn't believe their luck. They could not have chosen a more perfect day to climb the pass. Above their heads the sun shone out of a cloudless blue sky, there was not a murmur of wind and everyone was as eager as Maharbal to get this over with.

By mid-morning they had gained sufficient height to view the magnificent vista back down the valley they had journeyed for the past week. Men were pointing out their campsites, or where they'd been struck by the blizzard. Somehow the carefree banter of his men had returned and Sphax could sense their hope and faith had been restored. They were climbing in single file, every man leading his mare behind him. Adherbal's eshrin was ahead with the guides. The going was steep and tiring, made treacherous in parts by patches of snow and ice, so care was needed. Nevertheless, each man strode eagerly upwards, knowing this was the last leg, the last climb, on the last mountain.

Rounding a corner marked the difference between elation and despair.

Sphax knew instantly that something was wrong. He was leading his eshrin when he came upon Adherbal's men examining great slabs of rock that barred their path.

'What's wrong?' he shouted up to Adherbal, sitting gloomily on a boulder surrounded by his men. It was the guide Leuca who answered.

'There's been a rock fall.'

'How can that be? You and Uinda came down this track only weeks ago! Why didn't you warn us?'

'Because it's happened since then, Sphax,' Leuca answered, not unreasonably. 'They usually occur with the spring thaw, but this looks recent.' Sphax gazed up at the tangle of slabs and boulders strewn across the path, some twice the height of a man.

'Our path is blocked,' said Uinda with sickening finality. 'We will have to find another pass over the mountains, Sphax.' It was as if the guide had slapped him across the face.

'How far to the next pass?' he asked. Grim-faced, the guides were staring at each other, unable to meet his gaze. It was Leuca who finally answered.

'We're not sure … maybe forty miles … perhaps fifty. We never go that way.'

'But that could take weeks!' Sphax cried in despair, looking around at the downcast faces. 'Then we are lost,' he said finally as his shoulders and legs slumped and he crumpled to the ground. His men were beginning to arrive and gather around him. Sphax hadn't the heart to tell them himself, so he waved a lame arm in the direction of the barrier that had dashed all their hopes, and left it to the guides to give them the bad news.

It was much later when Hannibal found them. Most of Sphax's eshrin and some of Adherbal's men were still sitting dejectedly on slabs of rock below the rock fall. A pall of silence hung over the gathering and Sphax's face was buried in his hands. Hannibal strode over to his nephew and gripping him by the shoulders, raised him to his feet.

'Rise up! Despair is beneath you, Sphax, and I will not hear of it. This is a setback, not a calamity. The gods cast their thunderbolts to test our intelligence and ingenuity. This is a challenge, and we must rise to meet it, not cast ourselves into a pit of despair.' Hannibal released his grip on his nephew's shoulders and gazed stoically into the faces of the Numidians who had all risen to their feet in his presence.

'Did I not say to you all when we set out on our journey together that I will find a pass or make one. Now we must *make* one!'

None had the heart to cheer, but for some their dark mood lifted a little. Sphax was not one of these, but he did find his voice again. 'Come, men. Our leader says there is work to be done.' And collecting their mares along the way, he led his men back down the mountain to where they had set out so eagerly that morning.

* * *

Idwal found Sphax brooding alone in his pavilion that evening. He was sitting at the table Fionn had purchased during her stay at the Island, the only stick of furniture of hers to survive that tragic day on the mountainside. By the meagre light of a small oil lamp Sphax was examining items he'd carefully placed on its surface. Idwal recognized the lovely carnelian brooch Fionn always wore at her throat, but the other pieces were unknown to him, except perhaps the blackened leather pouch that he'd glimpsed occasionally around his friend's neck.

'It's gloomy in here, Sphax. Don't you have more lamps?

'Yes,' he answered distractedly, 'but no oil for them.'

'Where are Cesti and Lulin?'

'I sent them away to wait upon Ayzabel. I have no need of them now.' Sphax picked up the carnelian brooch and delicately turned it in the lamplight. Without looking at his friend he asked, 'Do you think that a man who is only driven by hatred and the desire for revenge is to be despised, Idwal? I mean, is there anything noble or just in these emotions? Do they possess qualities or attributes that could be said to be virtuous, or honourable? Worthy of a good man ... a righteous man? Or are they base instincts, unworthy and evil, to be cast out and shunned?'

Idwal had never before seen his friend in such a dark mood, and so was slow to answer, feeling his way. 'There are many questions, tied in many knots, in what you ask,' he said at last. 'But of one thing I am certain. Of themselves, hatred and revenge only harm the vessel that carries them. We both know the stoics teach us that these are unruly emotions, to be tamed by our rational minds. But if hatred and revenge can be transmuted from their baser elements, they may lead to justice and truth, which are noble and virtuous.'

'But are they evil, Idwal? Intrinsically, I mean. Are hatred and vengeance just base elements of pure evil?'

'Evil exists to be transmuted into virtue, my friend. That is its purpose, its fate. Remember what Chrysippus tells us: 'Evil cannot be removed, nor is it well that it should be removed.'

'So you believe my evil is redeemable, transmutable?'

'I've never seen this evil you speak of, Sphax, only virtue and nobility.' Sphax replaced Fionn's brooch on the table, reached for the leather pouch and removed two items. The first looked like a short section cut from a papyrus roll, no more than a hand's length and breadth; the second item was a ragged piece of saffron linen, neatly tied with a leather bow. Without a word Sphax handed Idwal the length of scroll.

Unrolling it Idwal could see that it contained a list of names, written in Latin in a fair hand. There were eight names in all, none of which he recognized except for the first on the list; that of Caius Flaminius Nepos, a great noise in Rome and viewed as a future consul. 'What is this?' Idwal asked, handing the scroll back to Sphax.

'A death list,' he said simply, meeting his friend's eyes for the first time. 'Romans who were directly responsible for the murder of my parents. A list I've researched and compiled since the time Airla taught me to write in Latin.' Idwal shuddered.

'And that?' Idwal asked, nodding towards the scrap of linen on the table. Sphax lowered his eyes and carefully untied the leather knot, spreading the faded fabric flat on the table.

'As I was being dragged up to the deck, I begged the soldiers to let me stay with my mother. I knew a little of death, but I thought if I kissed her and held her I might return her to life, just as she had often taken away my pain by kissing away the hurt. I was only seven. But they just mocked and taunted me. 'I'll make an Amazon of her and bring you her right tit, boy,' one had cried. To put a stop to my wailing one of the soldiers ripped a strip from the hem of my mother's tunic and stuffed it into my mouth.' Overcome, Sphax fell silent for a moment. 'That's all I have left of my mother.'

Finding it impossible to look upon his friend, Idwal rose to his feet and paced around in the gloom. After several agitated turns of the pavilion he stopped abruptly and turned to face his friend.

'I see these objects in a different light, Sphax, and not at all as you see them. One is a token of your grief for an unspeakable act of evil. The other is an instrument of justice to redress that evil. Both tokens have virtue.'

Sphax sighed. 'You are right of course, for there are always knots within knots. But there is a line between grief and hatred, vengeance and justice; it is a fine line, but nevertheless it exists. When the Boii guides told me this morning that we would have to find another pass, all I felt was despair and frustration, not for our great enterprise, or our just grievances with Rome, but for my own petty hatreds and quest for vengeance. I felt that vengeance was being denied me, that I might never look upon the Romans on that list as they died and answered for their crimes. There is nothing noble or virtuous about that, Idwal. Something you said earlier rings true; my unruly emotions are corroding the vessel that harbours them. I must rid myself of this hatred and desire for vengeance before they poison me.'

'Then put your tokens back in the pouch and throw it in a fire: the flames will purge you of this poison.' Sphax looked sharply at his friend, but made no reply. 'I came this evening to tell you the news. Your general slipped on the path near the rock fall this afternoon and is injured ...'

'Maharbal,' he cried in alarm, 'how is he hurt?'

'Don't worry, Sphax, it's not that serious, a sprained ankle ... though I believe he may have broken a bone in his shin.' Sphax got to his feet.

'I must go to him and ...'

'I wouldn't if I were you,' warned Idwal, vigorously shaking his head. 'The last time I saw him he was being carried around on a litter and the air around him was thick with curses. He's like a viper at the moment that will spit sympathy back in your face. Leave it until the morrow, he may have cooled by then.' Sphax was relieved that he'd sent Cesti and Lulin to wait on Ayzabel. They would have their hands full now.

'I also came to tell you the good news. A solution to the rock fall has been found through the genius of your uncle and his engineers. All hope is not lost!'

'I saw that rock fall with my own eyes, Idwal. There is no solution. It's not possible to go around it. So we have to go back and find another way.'

'Who said anything about going around it?'

'Then how?' cried Sphax in exasperation.

'We go *through* it.' Sphax shot him a look of utter incredulity. Unperturbed, Idwal continued, 'By the application of an age-old technique: we set a great fire in the rock and when it has reached a critical temperature we pour vinegar over it. By this means the rock cools so abruptly that it cracks and splits. The rest is easy, just a matter of wedges and chisels to break the rock into manageable portions that can be moved aside or cast down the mountainside.'

Sphax was dismissive. 'Where will we find this lake of vinegar?' he sneered.

'Have you tasted the Libyans' wine ration recently?'

'And wood? I haven't a stick to burn this evening, nor have my men!'

'Ah! That's where you come in, Sphax.'

* * *

'None of us is above despair, Sphax. It has been my companion since childhood, an evil shadow that I struggle with every day.' Hannibal had never spoken so intimately before, and Sphax was touched. He'd been looking for his uncle since dawn, eventually finding him examining the rock fall with his officers. Tactfully, he'd taken Sphax aside, so he was able to fully apologize for his behaviour yesterday.

'But this is not a moment to succumb to its evil,' Hannibal warned. 'Our enterprise lies on a knife-edge: falter for one moment and all will be lost. Our people need us and look to us for their strength and courage. We must not fail them. Your Numidians need you. I need you!'

'How may I serve, Sir?'

'To produce the heat required to burn the rock we'll need large quantities of wood. Forests of wood, Sphax. Besides wood to feed the fires, my engineers tell me we will also need logs and timber to re-make the roadway where the rock fall has carried away the edge of the path.'

'But the forests are miles away, Sir, back down the valley.'

'Yet another challenge for you to overcome, nephew,' his uncle responded, almost cheerfully. 'With Maharbal's injury a great deal now rests on your shoulders.' Hannibal turned to his officers, 'Gisgo, I have a task for you.' A burly middle-aged Carthaginian lumbered towards them. He had a bluff, cheerful expression enclosed by an unruly thatch of a beard.

'This is my Nephew, Sphax. His Numidians will transport all the timber you can fell to the start of the path down yonder. Summon all the foresters and woodsmen you need for the task. Take axes, saws and rope.' His uncle's eyes darted between the two of them. 'You have my authority to call on every eshrin, Sphax. Find carts and wagons, anything that has wheels and will move, every horse that is not lame and every man that stands idle. I suggest you do it in relays. You are in command of this task,' adding severely, 'but you will listen to Gisgo's advice at every step, young man. Is that clear?' Sphax nodded then bowed, despair and all the unruly emotions of life now forgotten.

For the next three days Sphax hardly ate or slept. Somehow he'd managed to gather together nine eshrins and all Adherbal's spare horses to transport the logs to the foot of the mountain, and he'd needed every man and mare of them. And of all the tasks, Sphax had been allotted the easiest. Poor Adherbal and the rest of the Numidians were risking their lives on the mountainside laying the roadway and shoring up the track, whilst the Libyans did the backbreaking work of splitting rock with wooden wedges and hammers.

But none of these labours compared with the drudgery of hauling the logs up the mountain track to feed the fires and make the roadway. Hannibal had charged his brother with this task and Mago had called upon the Iberians, the Cavari or anyone willing to lend a hand. The Iberians' stallions that were not lame or half-starved were of some use dragging the logs up the mountain, but they snagged on rocks so often it was simpler to manhandle them up to the rock fall.

Winter was almost upon them. If they were to stand any chance of breaking through the rock fall before the weather brought yet more blizzards and snow they had to move fast, so the engineers insisted that the fires had to be fed both day and night. At night the entire mountainside blazed in torchlight from its base to the great fires beneath the rock fall where the intense heat could turn stone to powder. When buckets of sour wine were sluiced over the glowing rocks they would instantly shatter and splinter, sometimes showering the arms and faces of the Libyans with shards of white-hot stone. For the more stubborn pieces, where ice-cold wine merely cracked the rock, the backbreaking task of hammering wedges and chisels into the cracks would begin to sunder the boulders into smaller pieces. Behind the engineers and Libyans, Adherbal's Numidians laboured to make the roadway, heaving stone or lashing timbers together to make a surface fit for the passage of an army. Men worked in teams, resting whilst others laboured, so the task could be maintained throughout all the hours of the day.

Gisgo found suitable stands of pines some eleven miles down the valley and almost immediately the air began to sing with the sound of axe and saw. Transporting the logs was a different matter. For the first few hours, Sphax and his Numidians experimented with every conceivable method of transporting logs over distance. The first thing they discovered was that the carts and wagons were useless; they were simply not designed to carry such weights or great lengths. In the end they used them to carry smaller branches and trimmings from each tree, wood still useful to stoke the flames.

To begin with Gisgo's woodsmen had expected them to drag entire trunks of trees, some of which were over thirty paces long and would have exhausted a score of mares after half a mile. Sphax insisted they be sawn into manageable lengths. Gisgo grumbled, pleading that sawing trunks into smaller lengths would create too much additional work for his men, but after a sharp argument, during which Sphax pointed out that they would have to be sawn anyway if they were to be manhandled up the mountainside, Gisgo agreed on a compromise. They settled on a length a little longer than a Libyan pike.

The next problem was how to attach ropes to mares unaccustomed to saddles and bridles. Their ladies were proud and haughty, and at first resented being asked to perform the task of a common cart horse. To begin with they used a simple hemp collar placed around a mares' neck that looped from her shoulders to her withers. Two longer ropes attached either side of the collar were then tied to the end of the log. After a few hours use it was found that the hemp collars were badly chafing their mares' necks.

Sphax and dozens of his Numidians rushed back to camp and seized every strap, belt or scrap of leather they could lay their hands on to fashion broader leather collars that didn't bite into the necks of their precious mares. After much trial and error, his Numidians found that two of their mares, working in tandem, could drag a log a couple of miles without exhausting them, one man walking ahead as guide, whilst the other walked beside the log to make sure it didn't snag. To begin with Sphax praised the goddess for providing them with such a soft blanket of snow on which to slither the logs, but by the second day the passage of each team had reduced the ground to a quagmire of mud and snow and the going got tougher.

Sphax remembered his uncle mentioning something about relays, and this turned out to be the key. He positioned teams of fifty Numidians every two miles, and working in pairs, teams dragged their logs to the next team in the chain until they reached Hanno's team on the last leg who dragged them to the plateau and the base of the mountain. Because the climb up to the plateau was steep and exhausting, Hanno had been given the last mile. Walking their unburdened mares the two miles back to the start lines gave them time to recover, but even so, Sphax continually reminded his men not to exhaust their ladies, otherwise the whole system would break down.

By the morning of the third day there was enough timber stockpiled below the mountain to call a halt, and three hundred famished Numidians staggered back into camp, found their tents and lay down to sleep, too exhausted even to fill their bellies. The day before, Sphax had made the remarkable discovery that it was possible to fall asleep on a moving horse.

One by one that night, the torches lighting the mountainside were doused and the great fire quenched. At last the moon rose over a mountain returned to darkness and the night. The task had been completed. Hannibal had *made* his pass.

* * *

The invasion of Rome began with the worst of all possible omens. At dawn as Sphax led Dido up the track, the top of the mountain was shrouded in a brooding mass of leaden cloud that threatened to bring down a tempest. But miraculously, as the columns climbed heavenwards, so did the clouds. It was as if the gods had lifted them like a blanket and wafted them away. So what began as an ill omen became an unmistakable sign that the gods approved of their enterprise, and were even willing to dissipate the heavens to speed them on their way.

Hiempsal's elephants were at the head of the column so as to test the width of the breach that had been made through the rock fall. And so it was Numidian elephants that were the first to reach the summit of the pass and cross into Italia.

Sphax and his men arrived at the snowbound summit in dazzling sunshine. Traversing the shallow plateau at the top they gathered at its southern edge to gaze out at the extraordinary panorama that lay before them. The cold Alpine air seemed to sharpen every detail and fold in the landscape, marking out rivers and valleys, forest and grassland plain. This was the land of the Boii, and beyond lay Rome itself.

'A fine sight for a Numidian.' Sphax grinned. He hadn't noticed that Idwal had joined them and was also gazing out at the vista. 'And for Gauls I suspect.'

'Come, Sphax. I think your uncle is about to speak to us all.' Sphax followed Idwal to where thousands were now gathering on the little plateau at the top of the pass. The two of them stood by a great bonfire that Hannibal described as his beacon to warn Rome that he had come. As the crowds parted to allow his uncle to stride to the centre of the gathering, a reverent silence descended on all those present. Then he began.

'Around me stand the strongest, the bravest, the most valiant of the host that set out with me from the Rhodanus. Only you have endured the trials and tribulations. Only you have had the strength and courage to survive this ordeal. You are the bravest of the brave! The strongest of the strong!

'The rest have fallen by the wayside or at the hands of our enemies. But their memory will remain forever sacred to us, they will never be forgotten, for their sacrifice has put you where you now stand. You are the noble survivors. You stand on top of this world, on the verge of history.

'Look yonder, for there lies Rome, in all her pomp and splendour, in all her riches and untold wealth. Yet we tower above her, we look down on her as an eagle looks down on its prey. We hold her in the palm of our hand. For the bravest of the brave, Rome now lies at your feet, to be trampled and crushed at our leisure. For not only have we scaled the mighty Alps, I believe we have climbed the very walls of Rome itself. So hear me oh Romans, in fear and dread, for I cry death to Rome!'

Sphax felt for the pouch at his breast, snapped the leather cord that secured it around his neck and raised it to his lips for the last time. He was aware that Idwal was staring at him. As he tossed it into the flames, thirty thousand men took up the chant that reverberated around the mountain at the top of the world. 'Death to Rome!'

Printed in Great Britain
by Amazon